Praise for
William Bernhardt and his
Ben Kincaid novels

PRIMARY JUSTICE

"Skillfully combines a cast of richly drawn characters, multiple plots, a damning portrait of a big law firm, and a climax that will take most readers by surprise."
—*Chicago Tribune*

BLIND JUSTICE

"Writers of popular fiction must have some gift of readability, but only a few have as unerring a narrative flair as Bernhardt. This is one of the best new series going."
—*Ellery Queen's Mystery Magazine*

DEADLY JUSTICE

"Compelling and fast-paced."
—*Tulsa World*

CRUEL JUSTICE

"An enthralling murder mystery...The ending is both surprising and explosive."
—*The Sunday Oklahoman*

NAKED JUSTICE

"In his sixth book featuring Ben Kincaid, Bernhardt again proves himself master of the courtroom drama. Buy two!"
—*Library Journal*

By William Bernhardt
Published by The Ballantine Publishing Group:

PRIMARY JUSTICE
BLIND JUSTICE
DEADLY JUSTICE
PERFECT JUSTICE
CRUEL JUSTICE
NAKED JUSTICE
EXTREME JUSTICE
DARK JUSTICE
SILENT JUSTICE
MURDER ONE
CRIMINAL INTENT

DOUBLE JEOPARDY
THE MIDNIGHT BEFORE CHRISTMAS
NATURAL SUSPECT
FINAL ROUND

PERFECT JUSTICE

William Bernhardt

BALLANTINE BOOKS • NEW YORK

A Ballantine Book
Published by The Ballantine Publishing Group
Copyright © 1993 by William Bernhardt
Excerpt from *Naked Justice* copyright © 1997 by William Bernhardt

www.ballantinebooks.com

Library of Congress Catalog Card Number: 93-22135

ISBN 0-345-39133-0

Manufactured in the United States of America

First Hardcover Edition: January 1994
First Mass Market Edition: March 1995

10
OPM

To Joe Blades,
for his extraordinary good taste,
and for making writing the joy it should be.

*Le coeur a ses raisons que la raison ne connaît
point.*

(The heart has its reasons, whereof reason knows
nothing.)

—Blaise Pascal (1623–1662), *Pensées*

After the fall of Saigon, over one million Vietnamese fled their homeland seeking political asylum. The largest share of these homeless men, women, and children came to the United States. Because Arkansas's Fort Chaffee was a major processing point for these immigrants, many of them settled in Arkansas and the surrounding states.

Almost immediately after their arrival, hate groups began to protest. The protests took the form of propaganda, political maneuvering, and terrorism. In 1992, thirty-eight different hate groups were identified in Arkansas alone.

* Prologue *

"Someone's going to die," the younger of the two men said as they walked together down a dark country road.

The older man shook his head. "We must prevent it. We must find another way."

"No other way!" The young man paused, searching for words. English did not come easily to him, and the Colonel insisted that he use it, even when they were alone. "Must . . . resist."

"We must survive, Tommy. We must protect our families."

"Like in Porto Cristo?" In the darkness, the young man's eyes seemed to burn with an inner fire. "I will not run again."

Colonel Khue Van Nguyen's forehead creased. He tried to summon words that would calm his companion's fury. Nguyen had no problem with the language; he had mastered English before he left Vietnam. But no words came to him. Perhaps, he mused, that was because no such words existed.

"A cold wind blows through the Ouachitas, Tommy." As if on cue, a harsh mountain breeze whipped their faces. Colonel Nguyen shuddered. "Bad times are coming. We must be careful. There is great evil here."

"Evil . . . everywhere. This no different!"

"We must make it different, Tommy." When they came to America, they adopted English first names and reversed the order of their names to conform with Anglo-Saxon tradition. Vuong Quang Thuy became *Tommy*.

"I plan nothing. . . ."

Colonel Nguyen placed his hand on Tommy's shoulder. How could he make him understand? He was so young, so full of anger. Uprooted from one country, dumped in another. "I am your friend. Your neighbor. There is no reason to keep secrets from me. I know you have been meeting with Dinh Pham and his group."

"And so?"

"Pham is . . . unwise. He wants to take extreme measures."

"We want to resist!" Tommy pushed himself away from Colonel Nguyen. "Tired of running. Hiding. Ready to fight!"

"Fight for what?"

"For our homes. For Coi Than Tien."

"Is that why you fought that barroom brawl? For Coi Than Tien?"

Tommy's eyes became hooded. "Was not my fault."

"Fault is for children. The incident did not help Coi Than Tien."

"They are killers! They hide beneath hoods . . . and slaughter us!"

"Still—" Before Nguyen could complete his thought, he heard a rustling sound off the side of the road.

He peered into the darkness, but didn't see anything. Probably an owl, or a rabbit. Perhaps he'd imagined it altogether. He realized how edgy he was. The consequence of spending one's entire life waiting for adversity to reappear.

He grasped both of Tommy's arms firmly. "Promise

that you and Pham will consult with me, or the elders, before you take matters into your own hands."

"I will . . . try."

"Thank you," Colonel Nguyen said, bowing slightly. "That is all I can ask."

The road brought them to the northern perimeter of the Coi Than Tien settlement. They embraced in their traditional manner, then parted. Vuong walked toward the south end; he had a shack there he shared with three other single men.

Nguyen trudged toward his home, wishing he could shake this overpowering sensation of dread. He drew his coat tighter around him. The elders had chosen this place because of its beauty, its isolation, its tranquillity. Now it was a powder keg. An explosion seemed imminent. And Coi Than Tien was certain to be caught in the flames.

A sudden noise riveted his attention. It was a whistling sound, like the call of the sparrow, only quicker, sharper. He heard it a second time. He peered down the road, into the darkness that had swallowed Vuong.

There was a sudden brightness visible through the trees to the immediate south. It was an eerie, flickering glow. Nguyen felt the hairs on the back of his neck rise.

He plunged into the dark forest, cursing himself. He should never have let Tommy walk home alone. Nguyen raced as fast as he could through the trees, then emerged on the south road.

He was instantly blinded by brilliant, white-hot light. He shielded his eyes, then slowly opened them. And gasped in horror.

The darkness was shattered by a burning wooden cross. And at the foot of the cross, Tommy's body lay twisted and motionless.

Covering his nose and mouth, Nguyen ran to his

young friend. Nguyen's eyes teared and he coughed on the acrid smoke billowing out from the cross. The heat was searing; he forced himself to ignore it.

There was a metal shaft in Tommy's chest, and another protruding from the side of his neck. Blood was gushing from his neck like steam from a geyser.

Nguyen clasped Tommy's hand, feeling for a pulse. The hand twitched; Nguyen jumped. To his astonishment, Tommy's eyelids lifted. His eyes lighted upon Nguyen's face.

Tommy's lips parted. His voice was barely more than a whisper. "Don't . . . let them. . . ." he managed. "Not again."

Tommy's eyelids closed and his head fell to one side. A harrowing rattle sounded in his throat. Nguyen had seen and heard this before, many times over. He didn't need a coroner to confirm that his friend was dead.

Choking and sputtering, Nguyen scrambled away from the burning cross. Just as he left, the top of the cross snapped and fell forward onto Tommy. Nguyen watched as Tommy's clothes caught fire and burned. The fire spread quickly, engulfing the corpse in flame. Tommy's skin began to blacken and peel away from his skull.

Nguyen clenched his eyes to shut out the horrific scene, but a fleeting image remained. He peered into the dark forested area on the other side of the road. There was something there—some*one*, actually. Nguyen could not get a clear view; the silhouetted figure was distorted by the shimmering heat waves.

Nguyen darted past the cross and into the forest. He searched all around, but he could find no trace of the fleeing figure. He paused a moment and listened for the shuffling of leaves or the crunching of twigs. Just like in the jungle. At Phu Cuong. He and the enemy. Waiting.

Nguyen forced himself back to the present. It was too late. Whoever had been there was gone.

On his way back to the road he almost tripped over a bundle of papers lying on the ground. He picked them up. Pamphlets, tracts, fliers. In the darkness he couldn't make out the details, but he knew what they were. Hate literature. He had seen enough of it during the last few years.

Suddenly the night was split apart by the piercing wail of a siren a few hundred yards down the road. The sheriff from Silver Springs, probably; he'd arrive in a few minutes.

Nguyen shoved the papers inside his coat, dove back into the forest, and followed a serpentine route to Coi Than Tien. Even as he ran he knew what he was doing was wrong and he hated himself for doing it. Just the same, he kept on running, all the way back to Coi Than Tien, with the certain knowledge that everything was about to change. For the worse.

The fuse on the powder keg had been lit.

PART ONE

* *

The Powder Keg

* 1 *

"Ben, stop splashing around so much. You're scaring the fish."

"I'm trying to get this stupid hook out of the water."

"Use the reel, Ben. That's what it's there for."

After fumbling a few more moments, Ben Kincaid tightened the drag and began drawing in his line. Why, he asked himself for the millionth time, had he ever allowed Christina to talk him into a camp-out? As a legal assistant, she was first rate; as a travel agent, she had serious drawbacks.

So far, this sojourn to the Ouachitas had succeeded only as a demonstration of his incompetence as an outdoorsman. Ben didn't know the first thing about camping. To make matters worse, Christina did.

Christina waded across the water and stood beside Ben. "I think I understand why you haven't caught any bass all morning."

"The fish don't appreciate my wit and charm?"

"No. You haven't got any bait on your hook. *Très pathétique.*"

Ben checked the end of his line. Sure enough. Sharp eyes on that woman. "I thought you promised no French on this alleged vacation."

"That was during the drive from Tulsa. Now that I'm out in the wild, I can't be restrained. *Joie de vivre!*"

Ben continued reeling in his line, but it caught in a snarl. "I hate baiting the hook. Worms are so squishy and disgusting."

"Worms?" Christina propped her rod against the bank. "I've got some more bad news for you, *mon ami*. We're fly-fishing."

"Fly-fishing, huh?" Ben decided to bluff his way through. "Does that mean I'm supposed to bait my hook with a dead fly?"

"Not exactly, no." She suppressed her laughter as she untangled his line.

It hardly seemed fair that she should make fun. After all, this whole escapade had been her idea. One minute she was talking about a pleasant drive to soak up some Arkansas scenery; before he could say "Get a reality check," he was standing in Fulton Lake, deep in the Ouachita Mountains, in green hip-high waders. "You must think I look pretty silly, huh?"

"Oh, I don't know," Christina replied, trying to avoid eye contact. "Relatively silly, I guess. Not as silly as last night when you were trying to pitch your tent."

"Well, excuse me. We didn't pitch tents when I was growing up in Nichols Hills."

"That much was clear." Christina whirled her line in the air and delivered it expertly to the middle of the lake. "Assuming anyone from Nichols Hills ever went camping, they probably had servants follow them in RVs stocked with fine china and an assortment of exotic wines."

"Now wait a minute—"

"I think you've had enough fishing for one day, Ben. Let's get some grub."

After a concerted effort and about half a can of lighter fluid, Ben managed to get the campfire started.

In fact, it blazed. Out of control. Christina had to throw dirt on the flames just to keep them inside the ring of stones that theoretically defined the campfire.

"Thanks for the assist," Ben said sheepishly, after the inferno was contained.

"No problem," Christina replied. "Stay away from the matches."

Christina had released all the fish she caught, and neither of them was particularly hungry for more canned beans, so they decided to settle for roasted marshmallows. Christina placed a white fluffy one on the end of her roasting stick and tossed the rest to Ben. *"Bon appétit."*

Ben sat beside the campfire and admired the scenery. The camp area was surrounded by tall, majestic loblolly pines. It had been a lovely summer day, and now the light of the setting sun trickled through the pine needles and cast a hazy glow over the lake and the hills. Even a confirmed city boy like Ben had to admit this was not bad.

After skillfully toasting a marshmallow to a deep golden brown, Christina removed her harmonica from its velvet case. "How about a sing-along? I can play 'Kum Bah Ya.' "

"Ugh," said Ben. "No thanks." Now that they were out of the water, he noticed how sharp Christina looked in her Banana Republic khaki shorts. If camping accomplished nothing else, it had at least distanced her from her usual dismal wardrobe.

"What's your problem? You love music."

"Music, yes. 'Kum Bah Ya,' no." Ben lowered his marshmallow over the flames of the campfire.

Christina brushed her long strawberry-blond hair behind her shoulders. "What would you like to hear, then? I can't do the Ring Cycle on my harmonica."

"More's the pity."

"Would you settle for some Burl Ives? I can play 'Glow Little Glowworm.' "

"Thanks, no. Don't you know any French songs?"

"Like 'Que Sera Sera'?"

"I don't think so. How about some Bobby Darin tunes?"

"Bobby Darin tunes? Ben, no one plays Bobby Darin anymore."

"Of course they do. He was a genius. *Ahk!*" Ben yanked his stick back just after the marshmallow caught fire. "Rats. I hate it when it burns."

"You held it too close to the fire."

"I was distracted."

Christina smiled. "Miss the office?"

"No. That's all that prevents me from complaining about being impressed into this vacation. I don't miss the office."

"Not even Jones? Or Loving? You're his hero, you know."

Ben placed another marshmallow on the end of his stick. "It's always been my dream to be worshiped by a barrel-chested, two-hundred-and-fifty-pound gumshoe who considers eyeball gouging a form of gentle persuasion."

"What about Jones?"

"Jones and his typing and filing skills are marginal at best. On the other hand, he's never dragged me on a fly-fishing expedition."

Christina burrowed in the ice chest. "Giselle, then. You must miss your cat."

"Why? Is that a requirement for sensitive-guy status? Mrs. Marmelstein is looking after Giselle. She'll be fine."

Christina passed Ben a carton of chocolate milk. "You seem a tad grumpy this afternoon."

"Yeah, well, I wanted to go to Silver Dollar City." Ben plucked the sticky marshmallow from the end of his stick. It was underdone, but that was better than charred.

"Camping will be good for you," Christina said. "You need to get out more. Relax, unwind. Get in touch with nature."

"Aha! So this purported vacation is actually thinly disguised therapy. Part of your long-range plan to make me warm and cuddly."

Christina shrugged. "What are friends for?"

Ben's response was interrupted by the sound of a car backfiring. Someone was ascending the narrow dirt lane linking the main road to the campground.

"Any idea who that is?" Ben asked.

"Maybe Smokey the Bear, dropping by to lecture you on the dangers of excessive lighter fluid."

"Somehow I doubt it." Ben dropped his marshmallow stick. "Guess there's one way to find out."

Ben and Christina walked toward the edge of the campground. A red pickup stopped in front of them, a top-of-the-line number with mudgrip tires and a smoked-glass Western panorama on the rear window.

A thinnish man in blue jeans and flannel shirt stepped out of the driver's side and extended his hand. "My name's Harlan Payne. Are you Ben Kincaid?"

How on earth . . . ? "That would be me. This is Christina McCall."

"You're an attorney?"

"Yes. Why do you ask?" Ben suddenly realized he was still wearing his green waders. He yanked them off. "There. Now maybe I look a little more professional."

"Don't matter to me what you look like," Payne said. "You're from Tulsa?"

"True."

"Long way from home."

"Well, I like to get away from time to time." He ignored Christina's smirk.

"I've been looking for you all over the lake."

Now Ben was definitely intrigued. "How did you know I was here?"

"Sammy Dean told me."

"Sammy Dean?"

"At the bait-and-tackle shop up the road a piece."

"Oh. Right." Christina had regaled the man at the bait-and-tackle with stories about Ben's courtroom prowess, most of them exaggerated vastly out of proportion to reality, while she selected lures and other fishing paraphernalia. "Why would Sammy Dean tell you about me?"

"Because I'm looking for a lawyer. To handle a case."

"Really?" Normally Ben would be less than thrilled to have someone offer him work in the middle of his vacation, but if it gave him an excuse to duck Christina's fly-casting tutelage for a few days . . .

"Civil or criminal?" Ben asked.

"Criminal. You'd be representing the defendant."

"Great." Ben grinned. "What's the charge—fishing over the limit?"

"Not exactly." Payne stepped closer and looked Ben straight in the eyes. "It's murder. Gruesome, premeditated murder. In the first degree."

* 2 *

"Murder?" Ben had to pause a moment to re-collect himself. "You committed a murder?"

"No, no. Of course not. I'm a lawyer, just like you. Well, not *just* like you." Payne fumbled for his wallet. "See? Here's my bar card."

Ben scrutinized the plastic card. Sure enough, Payne was a member in good standing of the Arkansas Bar. "Why don't you handle the case yourself?"

"I don't know diddly-squat about murder trials. I'm a probate lawyer. I draft wills for folks, take care of their estates—you know, pleasant, easygoing stuff. I was appointed to this case by the court because the defendant can't afford his own lawyer. And I don't know word one about criminal law."

"Ben does," Christina said, without missing a beat. "Ben's a murder-trial expert. He's handled dozens of big cases. He won one of the biggest, most controversial murder trials Tulsa has ever seen!"

Ben rolled his eyes. Good ol' Christina, his personal PR agent.

"That's what Sammy Dean was telling me," Payne said to Christina, as if Ben were a million miles away. "He must be a humdinger."

"If he weren't," Christina said, "I wouldn't be stand-

15

ing here. I'd be in a cell somewhere waiting for the Big Needle."

Payne's eyes glowed with admiration. "I've never been around one of you superstar litigators before."

"Now wait a minute," Ben said, edging Christina out of the way. "I'm no superstar. I've only been out of law school four years. I've handled a few criminal matters." He shot Christina a disapproving look. "Not dozens."

Payne appeared crestfallen. "Then you haven't handled murder trials?"

"Well, I have, but—"

Ben was interrupted by the impact of Christina's elbow in his ribs. "*Pardonnez-moi.* May I speak with you for a moment, Mr. Kincaid?"

Ben frowned. "Excuse me, Mr. Payne, while I confer with my legal assistant."

"A lady legal assistant. I reckon you *are* big-time. Sure, take as long as you need."

Christina and Ben strolled behind their two tents. "Okay," Ben said, "what's the big idea—"

"Listen up." She pressed her finger against his chest. "You may not care whether you make any money during the current fiscal year, but believe me, your staff does."

"I hardly think—"

"You are very lucky to have a loyal and dedicated staff—Jones, Loving, and best of all, me—who do not complain about the—how shall I say it?—erratic manner in which you pay us. I know getting a solo practice started is slow, hard work. But the fact remains, you haven't had a bona fide blue-ribbon case since you left the Apollo Consortium, and that's been many moons."

"Nonetheless—"

"Ben, be quiet. This case probably won't make us rich, but if the court is paying, at least we won't have to worry about collecting the fee. Plus, this is exactly the kind of exposure you need to attract big-time cases. So march over there and tell Mr. Payne you'll take the case."

It was clear to Ben that nothing other than blind obedience would be acceptable. "Yes, ma'am."

Payne was waiting patiently by his pickup. "After conferring with my staff," Ben said, "I've decided to consider taking the case."

"Great." Payne mopped his brow. "What a relief."

"I haven't agreed to represent him yet," Ben insisted, more for Christina's benefit than Payne's. "Where can I find the defendant?"

"At the city jail. I'll drive you into town."

"When can we do it?"

"The sooner the better. There's a pretrial conference set for half an hour from now."

"What?"

* 3 *

There wasn't enough room in the cab of Payne's pickup for three people and Payne's extensive rifle collection, so Christina had to ride in the back. Normally Ben would've insisted that she ride up front; under the current circumstances, however, he thought it was only fitting.

The truck handled the winding mountain roads considerably better than Ben's aging Honda Accord had the day before. Ben had another opportunity to admire the Ouachita scenery: dogwood trees surrounded by brilliant yellow coreopsis.

The road swerved up and down and in and out as it wound through the Arkansas hills. Ben began to feel nauseated. The back roads were bad enough, and Payne's foot was heavy on the pedal. Ben assumed Payne was worried about making the conference.

"Are you sure it's safe to drive this fast?" Ben asked.

"Oh, yeah. These mudgrip wheels can handle anything. They could take twice this speed. I just don't want your girlfriend to fall out."

"Very thoughtful. By the way, she's not my girlfriend. She's a good friend, and coworker. But that's it."

"And you two ... *coworkers* are camping out together?"

"Separate tents."

"Boy, you metropolitan types play by a different set of rules. My wife wouldn't let me anywhere near a campground with another woman. Even if I were glued to my sleeping bag."

They descended from the mountains and followed a dirt road into Silver Springs. Ben had seen the town only briefly when he and Christina arrived. Most of the residences on the outskirts of Silver Springs had a decided Victorian flavor—bright colors and prominent gables. As they passed into the downtown business district the buildings became predominantly gray limestone. Ben spotted the bingo parlor, the mercantile store, and the five-and-dime, all constructed in a turn-of-the-century style.

It appeared to be a two-street town; Main intersected with Maple, and both streets extended three blocks in either direction. Ben spotted a small grocery, a hardware store, and a drugstore that looked like a relic from the Roosevelt administration. The Teddy Roosevelt administration.

Ben heard the low wail of a train in the distance; otherwise the town was still. The streetfront stores were closed. A small group of teenage boys in bib overalls sat on the tailgate of a parked pickup, sharing a six-pack. Another group of kids pitched pennies against the side of a broken-down filling station. The only real signs of activity came from a pool hall and a few bars. One in particular, the Bluebell Bar, had a row of pickups outside that stretched all the way down the block.

"The Bluebell looks like the local hot spot," Ben observed.

Payne grinned. "That's for certain. We're right on the outer edge of Reeves County, which is just about the only wet county between Fort Smith and Hot Springs.

The good ol' boys get tanked up, then head home 'fore it gets too dark."

"After appointing a designated driver, I'm sure."

"Uh, right."

Ben noticed a restaurant offering OZARK BAR-B-Q. "We're a bit south of the Ozarks, aren't we?"

"Ozark barbecue describes a kind of cooking, not the place you get it. Like Mexican food. You don't have to be in Mexico to eat a burrito."

"Gotcha."

"See that auditorium over there?" Payne pointed at a flat limestone building at the crest of the next hill. "Bill Clinton once played with his high-school band in that very building. That was in 1963. They've got a plaque up there now."

"Do tell."

A few minutes later Payne parked in front of the county sheriff's office. They went inside, where Ben was introduced to the local lawman.

Sheriff George Collier was a wiry man with a brown-and-gray-flecked mustache. He was wearing a western shirt, Levi's, and silver-tipped cowboy boots.

"You're out of uniform, Sheriff," Payne said jokingly.

"One of the perks of being the boss," he replied.

"My friend Ben is here to see your prisoner," Payne explained.

"That a fact? You'll be the first. Other than Mr. Payne, of course. When's this case going to trial, anyway?"

"Next week," Payne answered.

Ben did a double take.

"Good," Collier said. "I'll be glad to get him out of my cell."

"Has he been troublesome?" Ben asked.

"Naw. It's just a hell of a lot of work, keeping a pris-

oner. Bringing him meals, cleaning the toilet. I got bigger fish to fry."

Ben tried to appear sympathetic. As they spoke a man
in a gray uniform entered from the back.

"Ben, this is Deputy Gustafson."

Ben extended his hand. "Nice to meet you."

"Ben is going to represent your prisoner," Payne explained. "Well, probably."

Gustafson withdrew his hand. "That so?"

"Well, I don't know," Ben said. "I haven't even met
the man yet. . . ."

"You'd best watch yourself," Gustafson said coolly.
He waved them toward the back door.

Payne steered Ben and Christina through a wooden
door to the iron-barred cells.

"What was that all about?" Ben asked.

"Oh, nothing. You know how law-enforcement boys
hate to see anyone get a fair trial. They think they ought
to be allowed to perform executions from their patrol
car."

The sole resident of the jailhouse was in the first of
three cells. He was a young man, probably in his early
twenties, with a muscular build. His hair was a sandy
red; he had a clean-cut, boy-next-door look about him.

Ben smiled, pleased. The accused would look great in
front of a jury.

"Ben," Payne said, "meet Donald Vick. Donald, this
is Ben Kincaid. I've asked him to be my co-counsel on
your case. Actually, I want him to take over. He's a
murder-trial expert."

Ben tried not to grimace. "Pleased to meet you."

Instead of taking Ben's outstretched hand, Vick
folded his arms across his chest and scrutinized Ben
through the iron bars. "Whose side are you on?"

"Whose . . . side?" Ben's brow furrowed. "Well, if I take the case, I'll be on your side."

"That's not what I mean."

"I guess I don't understand."

"Ben," Payne interceded, "why don't you ask Donald whatever you need to know to get through this pretrial? We've only got a few more minutes."

"What can you tell me about—"

"What's in it for you?" Vick interrupted.

"What?" This was turning into the strangest client interview Ben had ever conducted. "I suppose I'll be paid by the court, if I accept the case. There's probably a flat fee. Is that what you mean?"

"Hardly." Vick threw his shoulders back and walked to his cot.

Ben lowered his voice to a whisper. "What's bugging him?"

Payne smiled halfheartedly. "Oh, you know how it is. He's been in jail for weeks. He's scared, and he doesn't know how to deal with it. I'm sure a trial expert such as yourself has seen this before. So, will you take the case?"

"Don't rush me. Who's he accused of murdering?"

"A Vietnamese boy about his age. Name of Vuong. Friends called him Tommy. Lived in a communal settlement a few miles outside of town—about twenty or so families all running a chicken farm. You know, Fort Chaffee was a major intake point for Vietnamese hightailin' it out of their country. Since then, Arkansas has been drowning in 'em. Most of 'em are no trouble, but this Vuong kid was no damn good. He'd been in trouble with the law ever since he got here."

"Why do the police think Vick killed him?"

"Apparently he and Vuong got into a fight in a local bar the afternoon before Vuong was killed. I'm sure

Vuong picked the fight—like I said, he was no damn good. Anyway, Vuong got the better of Donald, and Donald got tossed out on his butt. There were several witnesses who say Donald threatened Vuong. And that night, Vuong was killed. Sheriff didn't have a good suspect, so he went for the obvious."

Ben had seen that happen before. He knew that when a high-profile crime occurs, the pressure is on the police to haul in a suspect. "If that's all they have on him, we should be able to get an acquittal. In fact, we should be able to get the charges dropped."

"That's great," Payne said. "Exactly what I wanted to hear. Does this mean you'll take the case?"

Christina interrupted. "You seem in an awful big hurry to enlist Ben's services."

"Well, like I said, the pretrial is only a few minutes away, and I don't have the slightest notion what to do."

"I don't want to be rude," Christina said, "but I have the feeling there's something you haven't told us."

Ben had learned to trust Christina's instincts. "Is that true? Are you withholding information?"

Payne glanced nervously at his watch. "Gosh, Ben, I'll be happy to tell you whatever you want to know after the pretrial, but we just don't have time—"

"We'll make time," Ben said firmly. "Tell me now, or you'll be on your own at the pretrial."

Payne sighed. "I suppose you might want to know . . . that Donald is a member of ASP."

"ASP? What's that?"

Another deep sigh. "It's a white supremacy group. The Anglo-Saxon Patrol. They have a paramilitary training camp not too far from here."

"You're kidding." Ben looked back at the innocent-looking youth eyeing them warily from his cot. *"Him?"*

" 'Fraid so."

"Is he a Silver Springs native?"

"Oh, no," Payne explained. "None of them are. They came over from Alabama and set up this camp a few months ago. Apparently some Silver Springers didn't appreciate having all those Vietnamese so nearby, especially when it looked like they were going to cut into the local chicken-farming profits. That's a big-bucks concern around here, you know."

"So they called for their friendly neighborhood racist terrorist group," Christina said. "That's revolting."

"I don't know who called for them," Payne explained, "but the town hasn't been the same since they arrived. They've been stirring up trouble—making threats, setting fires, bombing cars. No one can prove they're the culprits, but no one has much doubt, either. Then we got a bunch of lawyers in from some Montgomery organization called Hatewatch. They go around trying to shut down outfits like ASP by compiling evidence and filing civil suits. That made matters even worse. Everybody in town's tense, afraid of their own shadow. There's more hate going around than a small town like this can bear."

Ben nodded. The fog was finally clearing. "That's why you were appointed to represent him. No lawyer would voluntarily take this case."

"That's true," Payne grudgingly admitted.

"And you thought you could buffalo Ben into relieving you," Christina said. "Sorry, no luck." She gestured toward the door. "Come on, Ben. Let's get out of here."

"Just a minute." Ben fixed his gaze on Payne. "What else haven't you told us?"

"Only details," Payne said. "Nothing else bad. Honest."

Ben frowned. "And you've been unable to find anyone to represent him?"

"Honest Injun, Ben. I've called every lawyer in Reeves County."

"Ben, what is this?" Christina tugged at his sleeve. "Let's leave."

"I don't think I can," Ben said. "Apparently no one else will represent this kid. And every man has a right to competent counsel."

"Ben, what are you saying? You aren't seriously considering representing this racist pig, are you?"

"Personally, I find his politics reprehensible. But the Rules of Professional Conduct give attorneys a particular obligation to represent unpopular persons who have had difficulty obtaining counsel."

"You're going to take the case?"

"Someone has to do it."

"Ben, this man is *vile*!"

"All the more reason to take the case, under the Rules."

"He came to town with his squad of thugs looking for trouble. And he found it. End of story."

"Aren't you the one who was pushing me to take this case a few minutes ago?"

"Before I knew he was a fascist hatemonger, yes. Now I've changed my mind."

"According to you, I need high-profile cases to build a reputation."

"That's right, Ben. While we're at it, why don't we line up some child molesters and presidential assassins?" She grabbed his arm. "Ben, don't do this!"

"Sorry, Christina. You know I respect your opinion, but I've already made up my mind." He turned back toward Payne. "I'll take the case."

"Then you'll do it without me!" Christina pivoted on her heel and bolted toward the door at the end of the corridor.

·

"Christina!"

She slammed the door behind her.

Ben offered Payne a lopsided smile. "She's very temperamental," he said. "Redheads—you know how they are. I'm sure she'll come around."

"I'm just glad to have you on board," Payne said. "We should be getting to the pretrial now."

"Just a minute." Ben grabbed the bars of Vick's cell. "I'm willing to represent you, Donald, if that's what you want."

Vick didn't even look up. "Suit yourself."

"I guess that'll do. I'll consider myself retained. The pretrial is no great shakes. We'll just tell the judge he's not guilty and that we—"

"What?" Vick's head jerked up sharply. He pushed himself off the cot and approached the bars. "Who said anything about pleading not guilty?"

Ben felt a cold chill run down his spine. He didn't like having this kid so close to him. "Well, I just assumed. . . ."

"Don't assume anything, city boy."

"You must've pleaded not guilty at your arraignment."

"I've changed my mind."

"As your attorney, it's my duty to seek an acquittal if—"

"It's your duty to do what I tell you to do. I'm guilty, understand?"

Ben's jaw dropped. "You're—"

"You heard me," Vick said. "Guilty. And I want you to tell the judge I'm guilty. Guilty as charged."

* 4 *

Ben felt his heart drop into the pit of his stomach. When would he learn to trust Christina's instincts? "Are you saying you killed this man . . . Vuong?"

Vick looked away. "I'm saying I want you to plead me guilty. Got it?"

"That isn't what I asked. And look at me when I'm talking to you."

Vick obeyed, grudgingly.

"Did you kill him?" Ben asked.

"What do you care? I said I want you to plead me guilty. And that's all I'm saying."

"If you really killed Vuong and you want to plead guilty, that's your business. But if you're just saying this to be noble or because you're having a bad day, that's different."

Vick turned and faced the back wall of his cell.

"Wait a minute." Ben pressed his nose through the cell bars. "I have more questions to ask."

The only response was a faint rippling of Vick's shoulder blades.

"How can I represent you if you won't talk to me?"

No change. Ben glared at Payne. "I don't believe this. I want to know—"

"We can chat later." Payne pointed to his watch. "We're already five minutes late for the pretrial. Judge

Tyler will be madder'n a wet hen." Payne hustled Ben down the corridor.

"But—" Ben blinked uncomprehendingly as a closed door separated him from the cold shoulders of his new client. What had he gotten himself into?

Payne whisked Ben to the county courthouse on Main Street in less than five minutes. The courthouse looked like a sepia-toned image from a history book—an oversized white-and-red brick town center. It was easily the largest building in Silver Springs, and by far the most interesting architecturally. A cornerstone near the front door told Ben it had been constructed in 1892. Ben wondered how a town this size ever became the county seat. Must be a small county.

Two men were already in the judge's chambers when Ben and Payne arrived. Ben assumed the man sitting behind the desk was the judge. He had a distinguished, rugged face and a closely cropped head of gray hair. The other man was considerably younger, close to Ben's age. Ben would normally have assumed he was the district attorney. The only detail preventing that conclusion in this instance was that he was bouncing a baby on his knee.

"Watch this, Judge," said the man. He smiled at the child, who appeared to be perhaps a year and a half old. "Sweetheart, what do doggies say?"

"Foof-foof," came the reply.

"Exactly right," the man said, applauding. The little girl beamed. "Okay, honey, what do ducks say?"

"Wack-wack."

"Very good!" The man looked up. "She's two for two." He turned the girl around to face the judge. "Okay, here's the tough one. Tell Judge Tyler what judges say."

"Ovewooled." She giggled happily.

"Well, I'll be," Judge Tyler replied. He reached across his desk and patted her on the head. "Amber, I believe you must be the smartest little girl in all of Reeves County." The judge clapped enthusiastically. Amber turned red and hid her face in her hands.

Ben watched in amazement. What the heck kind of pretrial conference was this?

Payne stepped through the doorway and cleared his throat. "Excuse me, Judge. Are you ready for us now?"

"Of course we are, Mr. Payne. Come on in." Judge Tyler gave Payne a big friendly smile and clapped him on the shoulder. "Make yourself at home."

Ben and Payne took the two available chairs. The judge's chambers were, to put it kindly, intimate; to put it bluntly, minuscule—basically a closet tucked away behind the courtroom. There was enough room for a desk and four chairs and very little else. Ben and the man he assumed was the DA were shoulder to shoulder. The little girl began playing with the sleeve of Ben's shirt.

"Who's your friend, Mr. Payne?" the judge asked.

"This is Ben Kincaid, your honor. He practices law over in Tulsa County. I'm going to ask that he be admitted pro hac vice"—Ben winced at the pronunciation—"so he can assist me with this case."

"I see." Ben felt the judge give him the once-over. "Does Mr. Kincaid have experience with cases of this nature?"

"Oh, yes," Payne replied. "He's a murder-trial expert."

Ben pressed his fingers against his temples. He was really going to have to sit down with Christina and explain the principle of false advertising.

"A murder-trial expert. My word." The judge continued his silent appraisal. "Wouldn't find no one like that around here. 'Course, we haven't had a murder in twelve years. Why don't you tell us about yourself, Mr. Kincaid?"

"Well . . . I've been practicing law for several years now in Tulsa—"

"Several years? You look to be—what, twenty-seven, twenty-eight?"

"I'm . . . thirty-one, your honor."

"Huh. Guess you look young for your age."

"So I've been told."

"You practice with some big firm?"

"I did, sir. A few years back. We had a parting of the ways."

The judge arched an eyebrow. "Where are you now, some corporation?"

"Well, I've done that, too . . . but it didn't work out."

"For such a young fella, you seem to have trouble keeping a job."

"I've been maintaining a solo practice for some time now, your honor. I think I've found my niche."

Judge Tyler placed a finger across his lips. "I don't normally cotton to big-city lawyers strolling in to try our cases. They always seem to think they know more about how I should perform my job than I do. But given the gravity of the charges, and Mr. Payne's lack of experience with criminal matters, I'll allow it. You are hereby admitted to act as counsel for the defendant in the present case."

"Thank you, your honor." Ben made a mental note to avoid acting like a big-city lawyer, whatever that meant.

"Why don't we welcome Mr. Kincaid with a drink?" the judge said exuberantly.

"A drink?"

Judge Tyler opened his bottom desk drawer and removed a bottle of Scotch. "I'm afraid Mabel took all my glasses, gentlemen. We'll have to drink from the same bottle."

"Fine by me," Payne said.

The judge thrust the bottle under Ben's nose. What was this, some weird initiation rite? Well, when in Rome . . .

Ben raised the bottle and swallowed. The whisky seared his throat and made his eyes water. Tough drink for a guy whose staple was chocolate milk.

Ben passed the bottle back to Judge Tyler. "I apologize for my informal attire and unkempt appearance, your honor. Mr. Payne just contacted me about an hour ago and I haven't had a chance to dress appropriately."

The judge waved his concerns away. "Don't give it a second thought, son. I don't give a rat's ass what people wear outside the courtroom. You could show up in swimming trunks for all I care." He grinned. "Of course, little Amber might be somewhat shocked."

Ben did his best to play along. "Nice little girl," he said, nodding in her direction.

"That she is," the proud daddy replied. "She's our precious gift from heaven. Marjorie and I had been trying for years to have children. No luck. Then, just as we had given up hope, God sent us this perfect ray of sunshine." He rubbed noses with Amber. "That's what you are. You're a perfect ray of sunshine."

"You two haven't been properly introduced," the judge said, as he passed the bottle. "This here's Henry Swain. You can probably get away with calling him Hank. I've known Hank since he was a pup. His father and I used to go deer hunting together."

"I see." Ben began to be concerned about this tight-knit little legal community. "You must be the district attorney."

"That he is," the judge answered for him.

"Good." Ben rose to his feet. "Shall we go into the courtroom now?"

"No need for that," the judge said. "I think we can handle this right here."

"Here?"

"I don't see why not. We like to handle cases informally in Reeves County, whenever possible. Tell you the truth, there's not much I need to know. I've read the file."

Ben was stunned. "You've read the district attorney's file?"

"I like to know what's going on."

Ben thought it prudent not to comment. At least not yet. "Why has my client been denied bail?"

"That was my decision," Judge Tyler said firmly. "This is a capital crime, after all, and your client has no permanent ties to this community. Not to mention the fact that some folks might like to throw a rope around his neck and swing him from a cottonwood tree. No, I think he's best right where he is."

"When I visited him, I wasn't able to enter his cell."

"That's my order, too. We have good reason to believe he's a dangerous character. I'm not letting anyone in there unless a peace officer is present. And since I assume you want to talk to your client in private, you'll just have to do it from the other side of the iron bars."

Ben drummed his fingers on the chair. "When's the probable cause hearing, your honor?"

"I'm not much for those big dog-and-pony shows," the judge muttered.

"But, your honor—the probable cause hearing is my chance to learn about the state's case."

"Hell, son, they'll tell you whatever you want to know. There's plenty of evidence. Hank's got statements from half a dozen people who heard your boy threaten to kill that Vuong kid."

"The fact that he made a threat doesn't prove—"

"The boy practically confessed when the sheriff arrested him. And his motive is obvious. Do you know how Vuong died?"

Ben had to admit that he did not.

"He was killed by two crossbow bolts, one to the chest, and the other to his neck."

Ben checked Payne for confirmation. "A crossbow bolt?"

"Yes," the judge replied. "That's what you call them big-ass metal arrows crossbows shoot. Made a mess of that kid, let me tell you. The killer fired from close range. And then planted a great big ol' burning cross right over Vuong's head. Piece of the cross fell down and caught the body on fire. Good in a way—the flames cauterized the neck wound. Unfortunately they also burned his body to a crisp. Those ASP sumbitches just don't have no mercy in them."

"Your honor, I believe you're jumping to conclusions—"

"What other conclusion is there?"

Ben took a deep breath. There was no sense in alienating the judge. But he couldn't let him walk all over his client's rights, either. "I must insist that we have a formal in-court probable cause hearing. So I can cross-examine Mr. Swain's witnesses."

"He'll give you the names of all his witnesses. You can talk to them whenever you want."

Ben tried to remain composed. "Sir, I want a court reporter in here. So we can make a record for the appellate court to review."

The judge leaned across his desk. "Mr. Kincaid, I'm afraid you are beginning to get on my nerves. Are you suggesting that you're already planning to take me up on appeal?"

"I have to consider the possibility, Judge. This case just isn't being handled according to the proper procedures."

"Goddamn you big-city lawyers!" Tyler pounded his fist on his desk. "You've been in my chambers for less than ten minutes and you're already telling me how I should handle my cases!"

"I have to do my job—"

"Fine. Do your job. But stay the hell away from mine."

"My client has an absolute right to a probable cause hearing—"

"Not anymore."

Ben blinked. "What?"

"Mr. Payne has already waived the hearing and agreed to proceed to trial."

Ben spun around and faced Payne. "Is that true?"

Payne grinned sheepishly. "Did I do bad?"

Ben slapped his palm against his forehead. "I don't believe this. . . ."

"I thought it would help move matters along. . . ."

"Judge," Ben said, "I was retained to advise Mr. Payne on criminal procedure. If you aren't going to follow the procedures, then I'm of no use to him. I'll have to withdraw from the case."

"That motion will be overruled."

"I beg your pardon?"

"You heard me. You asked to be admitted and I allowed it. I'll not permit you to turn around a few minutes later and withdraw. What is this, some kind of game to you? In, out, in, out. I don't allow lawyers to do the hokey-pokey in my courtroom."

"You can't force me to stay on this case!"

"Mr. Kincaid, I suggest that you refrain from telling me what I can and cannot do. If you do not proceed with this case to the full extent of your abilities, I will hold you in contempt of court. And let me inform you that our sheriff takes my contempt orders very seriously. Got it?"

Ben bit down on his lower lip. "Got it."

"Now let's not have any more of these improprieties."

"Improprieties? From *me*?" Ben knew he should remain silent, but he just couldn't. "I came here expecting an impartial hearing, and instead I got a judge who won't follow procedure and a DA who's baby-sitting!"

Tyler's jaw clenched tightly shut, but he still managed to speak. "Let me put a bug in your ear, Mr. Kincaid. You may think we're just a bunch of hicks out here. You may think I'm some redneck judge who doesn't know what he's doing. Well, I went to law school just like you, mister. I run a clean courtroom, and your boy's going to get a fair trial, whether I particularly care for him or not."

"I never meant to suggest—"

"Let me tell you something else. This town wasn't always the happy hamlet I've lived in the past thirty years. Back in the Fifties and Sixties, we had the KKK crawling all over us—protests, race riots, lynchings. It was a hellhole. Town barely survived."

Judge Tyler swiveled his chair around and gazed out the window. "Maybe I wasn't as strong back then as I should've been. Maybe I didn't do all I could've done. Well, I'm not making that mistake twice. I'm not letting this . . . ASP gang tear apart my town. I'm—"

"ASP is not on trial, Judge—"

Tyler rose to his feet. "Mr. Kincaid, do not interrupt me again!" He allowed an uncomfortable silence to pass before he returned to his seat. "Since your client's friends came to town, they've been terrorizing folks and frightening everyone half to death. If this continues, pretty soon Silver Springs won't be a safe place to raise precious little girls like Amber anymore. Well, I'm not going to let that happen. Not again. Do you understand?"

Ben nodded. He sure as hell did.

* 5 *

Colonel Nguyen sat on the makeshift porch of his home in Coi Than Tien and gazed up at the stars. The sentinels of the night. So calm, so unchanging. When he was younger, he knew the names of all the constellations. He knew where to find the brightest stars in the sky and how to follow their progress. Now he had no time for such amusements. Now when he looked at the sky, it was only to wonder if there could really be someone up there, someone overseeing this cruel and bitter world.

He glanced at his wife, Lan, and their eighteen-month-old daughter, Thuy, whom they called Mary. Their four-year-old, Huong (Holly), was already asleep. Lan held Mary in her lap and rocked her gently. Mary's tiny eyelids were fluttering; soon she would be in the land of dreams. Her face was the very image of contentment; it made Nguyen's heart swell. If only life could always be thus. If only contentment was not merely for those blissfully unaware.

The porch wasn't much of a porch, just as their home wasn't much of a home. It was a Quonset hut, actually, bolted together from surplus corrugated metal. The porch was no more than a thin stretch of dirt; Nguyen had built a wooden railing around it to create the illusion of a real porch.

It embarrassed the Colonel to have his wife and children live in such conditions. Back in the homeland, his family had been wealthy, important. They had the best of everything. But that was a different country, a country that no longer existed. And it was a long time ago. So long now that, as he gazed at the stars and cast his mind back, he could barely remember it.

Lan eased out of her rocking chair. Mary's soft, rhythmic breathing assured them she was soundly sleeping. Lan tiptoed inside the hut to put her down for the night. Nguyen couldn't help but smile; he loved nothing more than watching his wife and daughters. When he recalled how close he had come to losing his wife, to never having any children at all, he shuddered.

Back in Vietnam, Nguyen had been one of the most important men in the South Vietnamese army. He had personally served in the Airborne and in Special Forces; he had commanded a unit of over twenty thousand combat troops. His men had seen some of the bloodiest action in the entire bloody war. Many of the most critical South Vietnamese victories came as a direct result of Nguyen and his soldiers.

When Saigon fell to the North Vietnamese, Nguyen reluctantly fled the country. He hated the thought of leaving his homeland; he could not imagine being separated from the soil of his birth. But the North Vietnamese had not hidden the fact that they intended to "chastise" high-ranking South Vietnamese officers, particularly those responsible for critical military victories. Nguyen had two choices: flee Vietnam or face incarceration, torture, and death.

The Americans were precious little help. Nguyen didn't blame them personally. They were caught short like everyone else when Saigon fell, as their many plans and schemes were destroyed. In the utter turmoil and chaos that followed, he was separated from Lan. He managed to get out before the fall; she didn't.

Colonel Nguyen made his way to America and took a series of hard-labor jobs—sweeping floors, washing dishes, shoveling out horse stalls. Most of his spare time was devoted to trying to get Lan to America. He contacted all the proper agencies and authorities; no one could offer any assistance. He became more and more despondent as he became more and more afraid he would never see her again.

In the meantime Lan had somehow managed to evade the Vietcong rover packs more than ready to exact revenge upon the families of high-ranking officers who had slipped through their fingers. In time, she managed to fight her way onto a boat full of refugees. *Boat* was a generous description given by the press; *raft* would have been more accurate. She was shoulder-to-shoulder with a hundred castaways desperate to escape Vietnam or the harsh refugee camps established in Thailand and other Asian countries. But Lan never complained. She was certain that the boat, any boat, would take her to her husband. To freedom.

She was bitterly disappointed. Her boat drifted up one coast and down another. No one would take them in. They were shunned as if they were lepers or murderers. She could not understand it; she had committed no crime. She was trapped offshore, with no money and no means to contact her husband, even if she knew where he was. She became bitterly sick and filled with despair. She was ready to die.

Finally, the American government agreed to accept a limited number of the refugees. Lan's boat was brought in and its occupants were identified. One of the agencies Nguyen regularly visited contacted him. He flew to Florida to meet her. Since he was by that time already an American citizen, she was able to enter the United States. He immediately took her to a Miami hospital—just in time. According to the doctors, if she had not received medical treatment, she would have soon died of pneumonia.

Lan returned from the house and snuggled close to her husband. "She's asleep."

"Good." He put his arm around her. "I am so happy that we are together."

"As I am, my husband."

Those were more than just pleasantries to Nguyen and his wife. To people who had been separated so long and so horribly, the words had real meaning.

For years, the Nguyens drifted from one temporary home to another, finally settling on the Gulf Coast in Porto Cristo. A number of Vietnamese had emigrated there and become shrimp fishers. Lan loved the idea; the climate and terrain reminded her of the homeland they both missed so dearly. After more than a year, and countless troubles, they began to make a go of it. The business actually showed a profit.

That's when the trouble began.

At first it was just locals—white fishermen whose income diminished as a result of the increased competition. They complained that the Vietnamese *stole* shrimp by violating fishing regulations. The charges were not altogether unfounded. The Vietnamese did not at first understand the complex regulations, and couldn't always afford to comply when they did. Meetings between the various factions were held, but no agreements were reached. It seemed the white men would accept nothing less than total withdrawal by the Vietnamese. Finally, when Nguyen and the others wouldn't agree to abandon their new home and livelihood, someone called in the KKK.

It began with threats—frightening, yes, but no cause to leave their homes and a business just beginning to be successful. Then came the vandalism—fishing equipment stolen or destroyed, boats sunk. Homes painted with swastikas or sprayed USS VIETCONG. The KKK began to patrol the waters, theoretically helping the Coast Guard watch for violations of the coastal fishing regulations. But Nguyen and his friends knew what they were really looking for.

A week later two Vietnamese fishermen were killed. Their boat was found adrift; there were no traces of the assailants. The KKK denied all responsibility and there was no physical evidence to connect them with the crime. The DA refused to prosecute. That night Nguyen and several others found crosses burning in their front yards.

A council of the elders was held. Resistance seemed futile—the KKK was better organized, better armed. Some of the men were willing to fight, but they were not willing to put their entire families on the firing line. Colonel Nguyen hated to run, but Lan had just delivered Mary, and he couldn't bear to see them endangered. With deep regret he agreed to leave Porto Cristo. Their home away from home.

One of the other men came up with the idea of jointly purchasing a broken-down chicken farm and settling in the Ouachitas. Here, so far from the Gulf Coast, they thought trouble could not find them. Coi Than Tien would be their new paradise—that's what the name meant.

They soon learned that chicken farming was far more difficult than any of them had imagined. After they bought a small stretch of land, they couldn't even afford chickens. They arranged for a major food distributor to buy (and own) ten thousand fryers; the Vietnamese would simply be paid a fee for services until the mature chickens were returned to the company for processing. In effect, they were chicken sharecroppers.

The work itself was grueling. It was beyond difficult—almost subhuman. Rising with the sun, back-breaking labor, twelve-hour days. The chickens had to be fed, watered, cleaned. Every morning the dead chickens (and there were many) had to be removed. Unlike cattle, chickens couldn't be left alone periodically to fend for themselves. They had to be cared for constantly.

The work was harder than shrimp fishing, and considerably more time-consuming. But at least they had made a fresh start. And, they thought, they were safe.

They were wrong. Less than a year after they arrived, when the chicken farm was barely operational, local competitors began to complain. Three months later ASP arrived and established a paramilitary camp outside Silver Springs. They bought a church not a hundred feet from the perimeter of Coi Than Tien. From his porch Colonel Nguyen could hear them pray to God to "drive out the infidel."

Random fires had been set—no serious damage thus far, but the shacks and huts of Coi Than Tien were a tinderbox and it wouldn't take much to send the entire settlement up in flames. Acts of vandalism followed, and the ASP soldiers began executing military maneuvers just outside Coi Than Tien. A car parked on the street was firebombed; a young man walking home one night was beaten. And then, worst of all, Tommy Vuong was brutally murdered. A campaign of terror was in full force.

Nguyen had hoped the arrest of that ASP member for Tommy's murder would cool ASP off, but it appeared to have only intensified their antagonism. Colonel

Nguyen did not think the man the sheriff arrested was the murderer. He was too tall, too broad-shouldered. He was not the figure Nguyen had seen silhouetted in the flames. But he could not contact the sheriff without admitting he had been at the scene of the murder. And if he did that, he might be arrested for leaving the scene and withholding evidence, or even charged with the crime himself.

Nguyen had shown no one the papers he found at the murder scene. If those papers got out, and ASP learned he was a witness, Nguyen was certain all hell would break loose. Everyone would be in danger—including Lan, and Holly, and Mary.

He would not let anything happen to them. Not again. No matter what compromise he had to make with himself.

"What do you think we should do, my darling?" he asked Lan. Her head was tucked affectionately under his arm.

"I trust you to make the right decision," she said simply.

"But you must have an opinion."

She smiled. "My opinion is that you will do what is right."

"How can you be sure? Perhaps I will be influenced by my own petty concerns. Perhaps I am not so brave as you think."

She stroked his black-and-gray-flecked hair. "It takes a brave man to know when to show his back to the enemy."

So that was it. She wanted to leave. Or perhaps she was just giving him the option, opening the door so he wouldn't feel ashamed if he wanted to move on. She was such a delicate, noble creature. He cherished her. That was why it hurt him so to see her living in fear, in constant uncertainty. That was why he wanted her to be safe.

The squealing of tires took them by surprise. Nguyen peered down the central road that ended in a circular cul-de-sac defined by the shacks and huts of Coi Than Tien. It was a large black pickup, smoked-glass windows rolled up, no one in the back. The truck was moving far too fast for such a tight, restricted area.

Nguyen removed his arm. "Go inside."

"Why?" Lan asked. "What is happening?"

"Go inside now." He gently but firmly pushed her through the door and closed it behind her.

The pickup made a sharp ninety-degree turn just in front of Nguyen's home. The tires kicked up a cloud of dirt so dense it obscured his vision. He coughed, wiping his eyes. He heard another squealing noise and saw the back of the truck moving toward him. It sideswiped his wooden porch railing and crushed it to the ground.

"Who are you?" Nguyen shouted. "What are you doing?"

His response came in the form of a descending window on the driver's side of the truck. Nguyen strained his eyes but could not see the driver inside. He did, however, see the barrel of the shotgun that emerged from the window.

The first blast was to Nguyen's immediate right. He heard the shots fly past, then ricochet on the corrugated metal. Nguyen dropped to the ground. Several more shots followed, bouncing off his home. Even if the driver didn't intentionally aim at Nguyen, a deflected pellet could kill him. Or anyone else in range.

He crawled forward on his elbows and knees, trying to get clear of the dirt cloud. Another blast fired, this one so close it sent splintered wood chips flying into his face. He froze, his heart racing. He had faced gunfire before. He had been shot at before. But never like this. Never in front of his own home, with his family just inside.

He heard laughter emanate from the truck. Gritting his teeth, he crawled over the now destroyed railing toward them. Three more blasts rang out and shattered the front windows of his home. The metal overhang of the porch clattered to the ground, smashing the chairs beneath. The laughter pealed out again, even louder than before.

Just as Nguyen reached the back of the truck, the wheels spun and it lurched forward. Nguyen dove for the tailgate, missing it by inches. The truck whirled around the cul-de-sac, taking potshots at other houses. Fortunately, no one else was stargazing tonight.

After the truck completed a full circle, it headed back toward Nguyen. An arm stretched out the window, and a red, glowing object burned across the night sky. The truck raced down the road just as fast as it had come and disappeared in the darkness.

Nguyen ran to see what had been thrown. It was a flaming torch, a club wrapped with bandages and probably soaked in gasoline. The flames had caught the grass and ignited the shack of his neighbors, the Phams. If the fire caught on, he knew all of Coi Than Tien could go up in smoke.

Nguyen ripped off his jacket and wrapped it around the torch. Ignoring the intense heat, he rolled the torch in the dirt till the flames died out.

The fire was spreading around the base of the Phams' home. Desperately he kicked and stomped the wooden planks, threw dirt on the flames, then pressed his body against the wall to kill the blaze.

The last spark snuffed out. Nguyen fell onto the ground, exhausted by his brief ordeal. He saw his neighbors emerging from their homes. They were coming to help—too late. If he hadn't been awake and outside tonight, all their homes would have been destroyed.

They would have to begin assigning guard duty in rotating shifts. He would seek the council's approval. It had been suggested before; that should be no problem. Something else bothered Nguyen, though. A far more pressing concern.

The driver of the truck had made token assaults on the rest of the community, but the bulk of the attack was focused on him. Was it coincidence—merely because he happened to be outside tonight? Or did someone know he had glimpsed Tommy's killer?

Was this just another random assault on Coi Than Tien?

Or was the killer looking for him?

* 6 *

Ben arrived in Silver Springs bright and early. He planned to spend the day talking to people and finding out what they knew about the murder. It was a small town, after all. If he spoke to enough people, he was bound to find someone who knew something of value—someone who saw Vick's fight or someone who knew why Vick wouldn't cooperate.

Ben realized that Vick never said he killed Vuong—only that he wanted to plead guilty. That raised several suspicions in Ben's brain.

He strolled down Main Street, taking inventory of various possible sources of information. He spotted another local restaurant—one that *didn't* serve barbecue. Clyde and Claire's Café. The card in the window proudly described their limited menu. The aroma of biscuits and gravy floating through the front door was tempting, but Ben decided to pass. Maybe if he got time, he'd come back for chicken fried steak and fried okra at lunch.

A pickup headed the other direction, executed a one-eighty in the middle of the road, swerved around, and parked on the side of the street, just in front of Ben. The pickup was a souped-up, custom-built set of wheels with a rebel flag draped across the rear window.

Two occupants emerged from the pickup, young men

no more than seventeen or eighteen. Both were dressed in bib overalls and baseball caps. One cap advertised John Deere tractors, the other Shakespeare fishing gear. They were both lean and muscular—local toughs.

"You the big-city lawyer?" one of them asked.

"I'm Ben Kincaid. Who are you?"

"Name's Garth Amick. Thought you were the one." He stepped closer to Ben. "I'd like a few words with you."

"Okay, shoot."

"I don't much hold with people coming to our town and stirring up trouble."

"I don't blame you. And I assure you I have no intention of stirring up—"

"I'll admit I wasn't crazy about it when those Vietnamese set up shop outside town. But since then, I've gotten to know some of them, and they're good, honest people. I've made some friends out there. Then these ASP thugs start setting fires and scaring everybody outta their wits. And then one of my friends is killed." He drew back his shoulders. "Well, anybody who kills one of my friends is going to pay the price."

"I agree entirely—"

"But instead of facing the music, what happens? ASP brings in an outsider, some hotshot lawyer who'll probably get Vick off on some technicality so he and his murdering buddies can go on hassling and hurting my friends."

"Look, I don't have any intention of—"

Garth thumped Ben on the chest, shoving him back. "We're tired of outsiders, Mr. Kincaid. Sick and tired."

Just what he needed. An overprotective teen with too much testosterone. "What's your point?"

"I want you to leave town. Now."

"I can't leave. I've been appointed by the court to—"

Garth grabbed Ben's shirt and twisted it around his fist. "Maybe you didn't hear me right. I want you to take an extended vacation. For your health."

"I'm already on vacation, and my health is just fine, thank you."

In the blink of an eye, the second boy ran behind Ben and grabbed his arms, pinning them behind his back. Garth reared back his fist and delivered it to the pit of Ben's stomach.

"*Oof!*" Ben doubled over, wincing in pain.

"How's your health now, Mr. Kincaid?"

* 7 *

Garth delivered another blow to the same soft spot in Ben's stomach. Both boys grinned. They slapped each other's palms in a high five.

Ben fell to the sidewalk, pressing his hand against his abdomen. "Why don't we stay calm and talk—"

His entreaty was interrupted by a swift kick to his chest. Ben doubled over, then fell on all fours to the pavement. This one was going to be harder to shrug off.

He tried to catch his breath. "Look—let's just—"

Garth wasn't listening. He slid a pair of brass knuckles over his fingers, then cocked his arm back to deliver another blow.

"What the hell is going on here?"

Garth froze.

"Is this Kincaid?"

Ben wheeled around and saw three men standing behind him. They were large men, broad-chested, well muscled. All three were dressed in identical outfits—blue jeans and camouflage green shirts with the emblem of a burning cross over the heart. ASP leisure wear.

"I'm Kincaid." Ben tried to straighten, but his stomach muscles protested mightily.

"I'm Sonny Banner. You're representing Donny?"

Ben nodded.

50

"That figures." Banner stepped between Ben and the two locals. "Trying to beat up a duly appointed lawyer. Typical gook-lover trick."

"Go back to your camp and shoot some more scarecrows," Garth sneered. "This doesn't concern you."

"Like hell it doesn't. You and everyone else in this jerkwater town got all the lawyers too scared to represent Donny. Then, when we dig up an out-of-towner, you try to run him off."

"We just don't like outsiders."

"Oh, yeah? I don't see you beating up on those Vietcong-loving lawyers down the street." He nodded toward an office at the next corner.

"You don't scare me," Garth said. "I got friends. Lots of 'em."

"We know all about you," Banner replied, hovering over Garth. "We know where you and your scrawny pals meet. We know how many of you there are. We know you're all enemies of God and the Aryan race."

"You're crazy," Garth scoffed. "Fuckin' lunatic."

"And we know that you're out to make sure Donny doesn't get a fair shake."

"Bullshit. We just want to make sure hateful bastards like you don't kill off everyone in town!"

Banner's neck muscles tightened. His fingers curled into a fist.

"Major!" one of his friends barked.

"Yes, soldier?"

"In private, sir." The man whispered, but not so low that Ben couldn't hear what he was saying. "Sir, we're attracting attention from the locals. The Grand Dragon specifically said—"

"I don't need you to remind me of my orders, soldier." Banner squared his shoulders and looked down at

Garth. "You—will—*leave*," he spat. "And you will leave Mr. Kincaid alone."

"Oh, will I?"

Banner's two soldiers closed on either side. "Yes," he said. "You will."

The two boys exchanged a glance. They were outnumbered and outmuscled. "We'll leave," Garth said finally. "But this is just a postponement. To be continued." The two boys strode back to their pickup and drove away.

After they left, Banner helped Ben to his feet. "I'm sorry that had to happen."

"Not your fault. Appreciate the assist. Lucky you happened by."

"It wasn't luck. We've been assigned to protect you."

"Assigned?"

"By Grand Dragon Dunagan. He knew they'd try something like this. And if not them, someone else. Unfortunately, Mr. Kincaid, you made many enemies when you took Donny's case."

So he was learning. "Well, anyway, thanks. See you later."

"Oh, no," Banner explained. "I don't think you understand. We're supposed to stick to you like glue. We're your bodyguards."

"My—" Ben tried not to react visibly. "Look, I'm grateful, but I need to conduct some interviews this morning. I don't think anyone's going to talk to me if I'm surrounded by three huge ASP men."

"Oh, you might be surprised," Banner said, pounding a fist into his palm. "We can be very persuasive."

"That kind of persuasion I don't need. Uh—because it could get my evidence tossed out by the judge," he added quickly. "Look, why don't you gentlemen relax in that bar across the street. The Bluebell. Stretch out, have a drink or two. If I need help, I'll know where to find you."

"Well . . ." Ben could almost see the gears turning in Banner's brain. "I suppose that would be all right. If you're sure that's what you want."

"I'm sure. And hey, thanks again."

Ben watched as his bodyguards crossed the street. Good God, he told himself. I voted for Clinton. I'm a member of the ACLU. And now I have bodyguards assigned by the Anglo-Saxon Patrol.

It was then that the full irony of his situation hit Ben like a thunderbolt. As a result of this case, his entire world had turned topsy-turvy. The people he found reprehensible were his friends. The people he sympathized with were his enemies. Correction: they were the opposition.

He was the enemy.

* 8 *

Ben thought it might be prudent to get off the streets for a while, just to make sure Garth and company had cooled off. Following the hint his ASP bodyguard had provided, he decided to pay a visit to the "Vietcong-loving lawyers down the street." He sprinted to the corner and turned into their streetfront office.

The office was small and barely decorated at all—just a few desks and card tables. The walls displayed posters and the tables were topped with brochures. Boldface print demanded AN END TO HATE and STOP ORGANIZED EVIL. It looked more like a lobbyist's office than a lawyer's. Ben expected someone to shove a petition in his face and ask for a dollar.

"May I help you please?"

Ben saw a brunette head rise over one of the desks in the back. He approached; the woman met him halfway.

She was on the tall side—taller than Ben actually, as he noticed almost immediately. Her hair was cropped at the shoulders; her trim figure indicated that she didn't spend her entire life behind a desk. And she was extremely attractive.

"I'm Ben Kincaid," he said, extending his hand. "Is this the Hatewatch office?"

"Can there be any doubt?" She grinned, gesturing toward the propaganda on the walls and tables. Her

54

sweet southern accent told Ben she was not an Arkansas native. "I'm Belinda Hamilton. I'm in charge here. I don't do the decorating, however. My two assistants get overzealous at times."

She shook his hand firmly. "You don't look like a Silver Springs native."

"I'm not," Ben answered. "I live in Tulsa—I'm on vacation. I'm a lawyer, and when I heard about what was going on—"

"You decided to drop by and check us out. Great. I can use all the help I can get."

She hadn't understood at all, but Ben decided to leave it alone for the moment. "Are you assisting the prosecution with the Vick case?"

"I'm planning to conduct my own independent investigation. The prosecution has not requested our assistance. They seem to think they have the case under control."

"Really," Ben said, trying not to sound too interested. "They have strong evidence against this kid?"

"So I've been told. Vick's hatred of the Vietnamese is a matter of public record. He's been at that ASP paramilitary camp for months running combat maneuvers. He was seen the afternoon before the murder picking a fight with the murder victim. Just before he was thrown out of the bar, he shouted, 'I'm gonna kill you, you perverted Vietcong bastard.' Plus I've been told trace evidence found at the scene of the crime links him to the killing."

"If the prosecutor has the case under control, why is Hatewatch here?"

"The murder trial didn't bring us. We came because ASP is here. We try to provide support for victims of racially motivated crimes, and to file civil suits to prevent or punish the terrorist tactics ASP uses to intimidate the Vietnamese and their supporters."

"Sounds like dangerous work. Aren't you concerned they might come after you?"

"I've been threatened often enough." She tried to make light of it, but Ben sensed she wasn't quite as nonchalant as she sounded. "Once a few years ago they—well, never mind. So far no one's hit the office with a bucket of napalm. I'm not going to let them scare me."

Ben suspected they would scare him whether he let them or not. He realized he was talking to one seriously courageous woman. "How'd you get assigned to this trouble spot?"

"To tell you the truth ... I assigned myself. See, I run Hatewatch, from our Montgomery headquarters. In fact, I founded the organization."

"You—" Ben's embarrassment was palpable. "I'm sorry. I—"

She laughed. "Don't worry about it. Everyone makes the same mistake."

"Well—" Ben floundered, trying to save himself. "You don't seem old enough to be in charge of an organization like Hatewatch."

"Or male enough, eh?"

"No, no, I didn't mean that—"

"I know you didn't. At least not consciously. Don't worry about it." She touched him lightly on the shoulder.

Ben brightened immediately. He fleetingly fantasized that she was as interested in him as he was in her. Was it possible ... ? No, he told himself—climb back down to earth. A world-class woman like this would never give you the time of day.

"I just remembered." She snapped her fingers. "Ben

Kincaid. In Tulsa. You were involved in the investigation and capture of a serial killer several months ago. Right?"

"Well . . . yes." He forced his tongue into action. This was not the time for false modesty. "You heard about that?"

"Heard about it? I monitored the situation very closely. Anytime some wacko—or a group of them—starts systematically slaughtering women, alarms go off in my head. Hatewatch confronts organized hatred in all its shapes and permutations. I was planning to send a task force to Tulsa to assist. But that turned out to be unnecessary." She took a step closer to him. "Since you resolved the whole case before I had a chance."

Ben stared at the floor and shuffled his feet. Her hazel eyes were dazzling. "I had first-rate help. . . ."

"Don't try to bamboozle me, Ben. I've read the files. You were instrumental in solving that case. And you put your own life on the line to do it. If it hadn't been for you, more people would have died." She glanced back at her desk. "You know, I have several reports and letters I need to finish. But I'd welcome the opportunity to talk with you in more detail."

Ben took a deep breath and swallowed. "And I'd enjoy learning more about Hatewatch. . . ."

"I'll tell you whatever you want to know. You'd be a magnificent addition to our organization." She tilted her head to one side, causing her bobbed hair to sway enticingly. "But more than that, I'd like the opportunity to find out more about *you*."

Ben's heart felt as if it might palpitate out of his chest. "We could probably arrange that. . . ."

"Will you be in town for a while?"

"Definitely." His head was reeling. This never happened. Anytime he was attracted to a woman, she was inevitably married, diseased, or not remotely connected to this solar system. But this time the attraction appeared to be mutual. And possible. "I could stop by later. That is, if you're free tonight."

"Splendid. I usually don't leave until nine or ten, but I can make an exception. Could you pick me up around seven?"

"I could do that," Ben said, perhaps a little too quickly. "That would be fine. Belinda."

"I'll look forward to it. Till then—"

Ben was distracted by a noise from the back of the office. Someone was coming in the back door. "That must be one of your—"

Ben glanced over Belinda's shoulder. A man was crouched behind the rearmost desk. To his astonishment, Ben saw that the man was holding a gun. And the gun was trained on Ben's face.

"Freeze!"

* 9 *

"What in the—!" Ben ducked behind a card table.

Belinda didn't budge an inch. "Frank, what in God's name are you doing?"

"Protecting you!" the man shouted from the back of the office.

Ben peered out between the legs of the card table. Who the hell was Frank? Another Silver Springs hothead?

"Put that gun away right now!" Belinda commanded.

Frank emerged from behind the desk. "But you said we weren't letting those bastards anywhere near our office."

"Frank, get a grip! This man has come to help us!"

Frank stared back at her. "That man is trying to get that ASP murderer off the hook!"

Belinda's eyes crinkled. "What?"

"The word is all around town. He's been hired to represent Vick."

Belinda walked back to where Ben had ducked for cover. Ben brushed himself off and rose to his full, not very formidable, stature. He kept a wary eye on Frank. "Is that true?" she asked.

There was no future in lying, Ben realized. Especially with trigger-happy Frank hovering in the background. "It's true. I'm representing Vick on the murder charge."

Belinda was stunned. "The man who brought down the Kindergarten Killer is helping . . . *them*?"

"I was appointed by the court."

"They wouldn't appoint an out-of-town lawyer without his consent."

Ben nodded regretfully. "True."

"Why didn't you tell me?"

"I—I thought—"

"You thought I might feed you inside information if I mistook you—as I did—for a halfway decent guy instead of a—a—"

"Hatemongering bastard," Frank offered.

Thank you so much, Frank. "I never meant to mislead you," Ben said.

"Right. You just accidentally forgot to level with me about why you're here. And we were going to dinner together!"

Another man entered through the front door. He had wavy dark hair and a build somewhat less imposing than Frank's. He quickly surveyed the scene. "What's going on, Belinda? Trouble?"

"I'm not sure." Belinda frowned. "Ben, this is John Pfeiffer. John, Ben Kincaid."

John tentatively offered his hand. "You're the man they brought in to represent Vick."

"Does everyone in town know about this? Is it in the morning paper or something?"

"Well, as a matter of fact, yes," John replied. "*The Silver Springs Herald*. This rag only comes out twice a week, Monday and Thursday, but almost everyone in town reads it. You got front-page coverage. I guess no one could believe someone would really represent that despicable punk."

"How did the *Herald* find out so soon?"

"Can't say for sure. But I know the editor, Harold

McGuiness, makes a point of stopping by the sheriff's office and the courthouse before he puts an edition to bed. It's not easy to find news in a small town like this."

"Great," Ben muttered. "Just great."

"To complete the intros," Belinda said, "the man with the gun is Frank Carroll."

Ben extended his hand, but received nothing in return.

"We can't take any chances," Frank offered by way of explanation. "Not after what happened in Birmingham."

"What happened?"

"Some of Dunagan's goons grabbed Belinda one night outside her office," John explained. "They—"

"I don't think we need to go into the details," Belinda said, cutting him off.

"If Frank hadn't saved her," John said, "there's no telling what might've happened to her."

"Dunagan," Ben murmured. "He came in from Birmingham, then?"

"As if you didn't know," Frank grunted. "He's the man signing your paycheck."

"The man signing my paycheck is Uncle Sam. No one else."

"That doesn't make it okay. You're still—"

"I'm still an attorney handling a case no one else had the guts to take!"

Frank gritted his teeth. "You're a sleazebag shyster trying to put scum back on the streets."

"I resent that! You don't know anything about me!"

Frank grabbed him by the lapels. "I know someone ought to rub you and your kind off the face of the earth!"

"Frank! Stop it!" Belinda tried to edge in between

them. She broke Frank's grip and pushed Ben away. "You'll have to excuse Frank. He has . . . personal feelings about ASP. And a very volatile temper."

"Yeah, but—"

"Ben, this would be a smart time for you to go."

"I don't see why—"

"Really. It's for the best."

"But what about—"

"Ben, just *leave!*" Belinda pulled back suddenly, as if startled by the strength of her own voice. "It's best for everyone."

Ben held his breath. "What about tonight?"

"Tonight? You have the audacity to think— Forget it."

"But—"

"I'm sorry. You may have all your rationalizations down pat. But I can't condone what you're doing. And I can't socialize with someone who's helping those people."

"Oh." Ben shoved his hands in his pockets. "Then I'll go."

"And Ben." Belinda walked to the door with him. "Don't come back."

"If you do," Frank added, "I'll be waiting. You've been warned."

Ben clamped his jaw shut and pushed himself out the door.

* 10 *

About an hour later Ben arrived at the Sleepy Hollow Inn. From polite inquiries directed at people who hadn't read the morning *Herald* yet, he had learned that the Sleepy Hollow was the best, the finest, and incidentally, the only hotel in town. It was an oversized house basically, a bright yellow Victorian A-frame. It couldn't possibly have more than ten rooms, but then, unless the Virgin Mary was spotted at the Bluebell Bar, Ben doubted it would ever need more than ten rooms.

A bell rang as Ben passed through the front door and approached the registration desk. The man sitting on a stool behind the counter appeared to be in his late sixties. He wore gold-rimmed bifocals that threatened to drop off the edge of his nose at any moment. Ben saw to his dismay that the man was reading *The Silver Springs Herald*.

"Excuse me," Ben said. "I'd like a room for—"

"You're the one!" the elderly man said. He slid off the stool, then flipped back to check the front-page photo. "You're that young lawyer fella on the front page."

"Lucky me."

The man made a snorting noise and tossed the paper down on the counter. "I've lived in Silver Springs for sixty-seven years, and I ain't *never* had my picture in the paper. Much less on page one."

"Go to law school," Ben suggested. "It happens to me all the time." He glanced at the *Herald*. "They must've gotten my photo out of the bar directory. I never liked that picture."

"Too late to complain," the man pronounced, hooking his thumbs under his suspenders. "Everyone in town's seen it by now."

"Swell. Look, I'd like a room for the night. In fact, I may need it for a week or two."

The clerk made a tsking noise with his tongue and teeth. "Sorry, son. Can't do that."

"You're full up?"

"Oh, no. Haven't been full since that Bigfoot sighting in seventy-two. But I can't let a room to you. Everyone in town would take my head off."

"I'm not asking you to help me overthrow the government. I just want a place to spend the night."

"No can do. Maybe you should set up at a campsite in the hills."

"I already have a campsite. I need in-town accommodations."

"Sorry. If I put you up, I'll start getting the Silver Springs brush-off. No one will stay with me, and no one will trade with me. Can't run a hotel without supplies."

"I can't believe an entire town would be so narrow-minded—"

Ben saw the man's face scrunch together; his shoulders rose half a foot. "Lookee here, son. This is a good town, and don't you be sayin' otherwise. We never asked for all this trouble. We never asked your people to come in with their big guns and bombs and—"

"They're not my people," Ben said adamantly. "I'm

just a lawyer who made the mistake of taking a case in this two-bit town."

"This—!" The clerk's wheezing became more rapid. "Until your people came here, we all lived quiet, peaceful little lives. Nothin' too excitin', mebbe, but we liked it. Even after they showed up, we tried to be friendly; Mary Sue took some of them into her boardinghouse on Maple. Pretty soon we got graffiti, and fires, and brawls. And now murder." The clerk licked his lips. "We just don't like all this trouble, see? So you ain't going to be very popular in this town."

"But—I didn't kill Vuong!"

"Maybe not, but you're sure as tarnation going to try every trick in the book to set the killer free."

"That's not true."

"Oh?" The clerk grabbed the paper and spread it across the counter. He pointed to the page-one article below Ben's picture and read. " 'District Attorney Swain said he would make every effort to circumvent the courtroom antics and big-city maneuvers of lawyer Benjamin Kincaid, who was quoted as saying that he would try every trick in the book to put Donald Vick back on the streets.' "

Ben snatched the paper away from him. "I never said that. I've never even met this reporter."

"The papers don't lie," the clerk said indignantly.

Ben raised an eyebrow. "So there's a town the *National Enquirer* doesn't reach. That's reassuring."

"Get on out of my place, son. I don't have room for you. And I never will."

"But this is the only hotel for sixty miles!"

"Git!" The man's entire torso shook as he pointed toward the door.

"I'm going, I'm going." Ben flung open the door, ringing the bell. "Have a nice day."

* 11 *

It took him almost an hour, but eventually Ben managed to find Mary Sue's boardinghouse. It was a two-story Victorian home, with bright blue shutters and gingerbread gables. A sign on the front porch confirmed Ben's belief that she would have rooms to let. There should be at least one vacancy now that Vick had taken up residence in the city slammer. And that gave Ben two reasons to be here.

Ben knocked, then pushed open the front door. He saw an interior Dutch door that restricted access to the parlor—probably the hostess's version of a registration desk.

Ben glanced up the staircase and, to his surprise, saw Christina standing at the head of the stairs. "Christina! What are you doing here?"

"I've taken a room." Her face was stiff and solemn. "I don't feel safe out at the campsite."

"You're afraid of muggers?"

"No, I'm afraid you'll bring your Nazi pal back for a client conference."

"Then you're sticking around for a while?"

She folded her arms across her chest. "I'm not going to let you ruin *my* vacation."

"Boy ... if you're going to be in the neighborhood anyway ... I could really use some help with—"

"Forget it." She turned and marched away from the staircase.

Ben sighed. He rang a small bell on a table in the foyer. A few moments later a petite woman in a pink frock came to the other side of the Dutch door. She was wiping her hands on her apron; she looked as if she had been baking. Ben assumed this was Mary Sue.

" 'Morning," Ben said, putting on his best smile. "I see you have rooms to let."

"Indeed we do. Will you be staying long?"

"Probably a couple of weeks," Ben said. "Maybe more." Thank goodness. She didn't appear to recognize him.

He spotted the morning *Herald*, folded down the middle, on an end table by the Dutch door. His likeness was facing straight up, although the paper did not appear to have been opened. All the better. Now, if he could only keep her from looking at it for another two minutes.

"Bunch of trouble in town these days," Ben said casually.

"Don't you know it," Mary Sue replied. "Sometimes it seems more than a body can bear." She leaned conspiratorially across the Dutch door. "He stayed here, you know."

Bingo. "You mean ... ?"

She nodded. "Donald Vick. Took the room at the top of the stairs. Of course, I had no idea."

"No. Of course not. Was he ... difficult?"

"Oh, no. He was the nicest boy you could imagine. Sometimes I forgot he was from out of town. Very polite, well mannered. Opened the door for the ladies. Never took seconds. Respected the other tenants' privacy. In fact, he rarely spoke to anyone."

"Well," Ben said, "it's always the quiet ones."

"Isn't that the truth? You know, it wasn't until the last

week—the week before the, well, you know—that he even had visitors."

"Is that a fact?"

"Yes, sir. That was when I got my first hint that he might be planning something. 'Course I never guessed—"

"No. Who could've?"

"Normally I don't even take notice of my tenants' visitors. But when that woman came by"—she raised her chin—"well, that was a different kettle of fish."

"I can imagine."

"If Donald Vick thought I was going to let him go sparkin' with that woman in *my* boardinghouse, well, he had another think coming. I don't run that kind of place."

"I'm sure."

"I was prepared to march right in there and boot her out myself if necessary. Fortunately she left on her own just a little after eleven." Mary Sue took a white guest book from the end table and opened it to the current page. "If you'll just sign in, please."

Ben took the feather pen and signed.

" 'Course, I will have to ask for some . . . you know . . . in advance. Since we don't know each other."

"Naturally." Ben reached into his wallet and withdrew a fistful of twenties. "Will this do?"

"Oh, my, yes." Mary Sue reached eagerly for the money, but one of the bills slipped through her fingers. A draft from the front window caught it, nudging it to her side of the Dutch door. It slowly drifted downward . . . and lighted on the end table on top of the morning *Herald*.

Don't look! Ben found himself issuing mental commands, for all the good it would do. Just pick up the money and—

"Oh, my gracious. Is this you?"

Ben's eyes rolled to the back of his head.

Mary Sue picked up the newspaper and unfolded it. "You're this—Benjamin Kincaid?"

Ben briefly considered a story about an evil twin, but decided it was probably futile. "It's me."

Mary Sue scanned the article. "Then you're—good Lord!" She threw down the paper. "Why didn't you tell me?"

Ben shrugged. "It didn't come up. . . ."

"You're one of them!"

"I'm not one of anything. I'm just a lawyer—"

"Do you have any idea what you people have done to this town? I don't feel safe walking the streets anymore."

"I'm just representing a man I believe may be innocent—"

"Innocent!"

"You know Donald. You know how harmless he is."

"I saw him nearly beat a man senseless!"

That slowed Ben down. "What?"

"I was at the Bluebell Bar that afternoon, before the murder. I was shocked; I had never seen Donald act like that. For no apparent reason, he attacked that poor Vietnamese boy. From behind, with no warning. He liked to have killed the boy before he even knew what was happening. A few of the boy's friends pulled Donald away, then laid into him. When they threw Donald out, he was bleeding in half a dozen places, screaming about how he was going to kill him. And the next morning that Vietnamese boy was dead. That's pretty conclusive evidence as far as I'm concerned."

"That's strictly circumstantial—"

"Circumstantial? What's that—some big-city lawyer word?" She threw Ben's money back at him. "You just get on out of here. I don't want anything to do with you and your kind."

"Please listen to me, ma'am—"

Mary Sue bent down, then came up with a double-barreled shotgun almost as big as she was. "You get on out of here, understand? Now!"

She held the shotgun steady and ready; Ben didn't doubt for an instant that she knew how to use it.

"Last chance! *Scram!*"

Ben knew it was pointless to argue, and probably highly dangerous. He grabbed his money and hurried out the front door.

* 12 *

Hours later all Ben had accomplished was several repetitions of the same old scene. No matter where he went, *The Silver Springs Herald* had been there first. No one would talk to him; no one would even take his money. Overnight he'd become a local pariah.

By nine P.M., Ben had covered both Main and Maple streets from one end to the other and managed to find absolutely no one who would talk. They didn't pretend that they didn't know anything; they just weren't telling him. What Judge Tyler had said was absolutely true; the whole town was on edge—expecting the ticking time bomb to explode at any moment.

The only lights on Main Street that still flickered were the ones inside the Bluebell Bar. A red neon sign in the front window boldly announced that they had Coors on tap. At this point Ben was ready for a drink. And more importantly, he recalled that this was where the fight between Vick and Vuong took place on the afternoon before the murder.

Ben spotted a scuffle in the alley just outside the bar. Both combatants were beefy, tough-looking men in blue jeans and T-shirts. Fortunately they appeared to have imbibed a fair amount of beer. More punches were connecting with empty air than any part of either body.

Ben pushed open the front door and stepped inside.

The Bluebell was small, simple, laid-back—and packed. The bar had six stools, all but one of them currently occupied. A pool table in the corner was flanked by two pinball machines, both of which Ben judged to be at least fifteen years old. Four booths in the back provided space for couples who wanted to get snuggly.

Ben took the available bar stool and flagged the bartender. The jukebox was wailing a country-western tune, a bit of homespun philosophy courtesy of Mary-Chapin Carpenter. "Sometimes you're the windshield," she sang, "sometimes you're the bug. . . ."

"I'll have a longneck," Ben said, pointing at the label on a bar coaster.

The bartender peered at him, eyes narrowed. He was an older man, but the pronounced wrinkles lent his face an air of distinction and world-weariness. "You're the lawyer."

Ben had heard it too many times today to be surprised. "That's right. And now that the introductions are out of the way, could I have my beer?"

The bartender hesitated. "I don't want no trouble in my place."

"I don't plan to cause any," Ben replied. "Unless you don't get me that beer."

The bartender gave a small, lopsided grin. "What the hell! I suppose Satan himself has to take a drink now and again."

He pulled a Bud out of the ice. The song changed; now Mary-Chapin Carpenter was singing a slow sad song about being haunted by the past, and finding the courage to love again after "the first time you lose." Carpenter's voice was barely more than a whisper. "Come on, come on . . . it's getting late now. . . ."

While he waited Ben scanned a copy of the *Herald* lying on the bar. It appeared that District Attorney

Swain was trying his case in the morning edition and polarizing public opinion by making the "big-city lawyer" the bad guy. Ben learned that Sheriff Collier had found the murder weapon, a twenty-four-inch Carvelle crossbow. Swain claimed that tests run by the forensic office in Little Rock conclusively linked the crossbow to Donald Vick.

"My name's Mac." The bartender pushed a beer and a bottle opener across the bar.

"I'm Ben. But you probably already know that." Ben opened the beer and downed a good long gulp. He wasn't that fond of Budweiser, but since the man had apparently compromised his virtue by serving it, Ben wasn't about to appear ungrateful. "Nice place."

"Thanks," Mac said. His pride was evident. "Had the bar shipped in from St. Louis the day the county voted to go wet. Stools, too."

"I guess this is where it happened," Ben commented.

"What's that?"

"The big fight. Vick and Vuong."

"Oh, yeah. Right here."

At long last. Someone was actually talking to him. "Must've been a hell of a fight."

"You better believe it. Kicked the hell out of my best pinball machine."

Ben saw that the head glass on one of the pinball machines was shattered, just over the picture of a fiery red cyclone. "You were here that night?"

"Of course. I'm here every night."

"What happened?"

"Well, that Vietnamese fella was minding his own business, sitting just where you are, when in walks Vick. They talk a little bit, and then he up and says, 'You—' "

To Ben's dismay, Mac stopped suddenly, just as the

story was becoming interesting. "Maybe I shouldn't say any more."

"Don't stop now!"

"No, no." Mac picked up a bar rag and began polishing the woodwork. "I've said too much already."

"Mac, I have to prepare a man's defense. This is a capital crime. You have to help me!"

"Like hell I do."

Ben leaned across the bar. "Look, I'm desperate. You've gotta see that—"

Ben felt two hands slap down harshly on his shoulders, shoving him back onto his stool. Before he had a chance to become curious about who it was, the hands whirled him around.

It was the two local boys who had accosted him that morning, Garth Amick and his tough-looking friend. Except now they had a third friend, who looked even older and meaner than the first two.

Garth—still the group spokesperson—leaned into Ben's face. "I thought I told you to get out of town."

"I think you did. So?"

"You talk pretty tough for a big-city lawyer who's about to get the hell beaten out of him." The smell of beer on his breath was thick and nauseating.

"Why don't you just go back to your beer and leave me alone?"

"I've got somethin' else in mind. Hold him, boys." Garth's two friends each grabbed one of Ben's arms.

"Kincaid!" It was Mac. He'd raced around the side of the bar. At first, Ben thought Mac had come to his rescue. He was quickly disillusioned. "I thought I told you I didn't want any trouble!"

"Me? Why are you telling me? I was just sitting here minding my own business."

"Should've minded it somewhere else." Garth drew back his fist.

"Garth!" Mac yelled. "Take it outside. I don't want any more damage to my place."

"Fine." Garth grabbed Ben by the shirt collar and jerked him toward the front door. His two friends held tight to Ben's arms.

They made it to the door just at the same split second that Sonny Banner and his two bodyguard buddies came in. Banner and Garth almost bumped heads.

"Banner! Thank goodness!" So this was what it had come to, Ben thought grimly. He was overjoyed to see a bunch of white supremacist headbashers saunter in. "What are you doing here?"

"This wath where you thold uth to wait, 'member?" The thickness of his tongue left Ben little doubt about what the boys had been doing all day. He began to have serious doubts about the imminence of his rescue. "What the hell ith going on?"

"None of your goddamn business," Garth barked. "Just get out of our way."

Banner inflated his chest. "Not till I get thome answers."

"We're just going out for a chat." Ben felt the hands on his arms tightening.

"Zat right?"

Ben shook his head. "They're taking me outside, to use their own words, to beat the hell out of me."

"Zat so? Three against one? Figures. Vietcong-loving punkth."

"Screw off, you redneck freak," Garth said. "I don't have to take—"

The first punch landed squarely on Garth's jaw and sent him reeling. Ben felt both of Garth's friends release his arms. They raised their fists to defend themselves.

"Take it outside!" Mac shouted from behind them. "Take it—"

It was too late. Ben ducked out of the way and the three locals took on the three ASP men one-on-one. Garth and his crew were spirited and resilient, but they were outmatched in weight and skill. The three ASPers were a bit sluggish, but they were still more than able to hold their own.

Ben watched Banner spin Garth through the bar, punch by punch, while one of his friends delivered a swift kick to a townboy's groin. The stylish fighting moves came more naturally to the ASPers. Ben supposed that was understandable. This was what they trained for every day, after all. This was what they lived for.

The brawlers flew back and forth across the tiny bar, smashing and clattering as they went. Ben considered jumping into the fray to help; the question was—whom would he help?

Banner had Garth in a headlock and was banging his face against a beer-stained table. Garth's shouts were silenced by the repeated pummeling and the viselike grip around his throat. For a moment Ben was afraid Banner was going to kill him. Then, to his amazement, he saw Banner literally lift Garth off the ground and throw him across the bar. Garth landed on the cyclone pinball machine, shattering the glass.

Mac was not going to be happy.

Ben saw that Garth's two friends were similarly on the bad end of major-league beatings. Just as he began to be concerned for their long-term health, he heard a siren wailing down Main Street. A quick peek out the window confirmed it—the sheriff was paying them a visit. Mac must've called.

Ben crawled back to his bar stool and took another drink of his beer. It looked like it was going to be a long night.

* 13 *

As Ben had noticed during his earlier visit, there were only three cells in the Silver Springs jail, and Donald Vick already occupied one, so Sheriff Collier was forced to divide everyone up into their respective teams: the locals in one cell, the ASPers in the other. With their best buddy Ben, of course.

Ben had protested his innocence to both Sheriff Collier and Deputy Gustafson ever since they picked him up, based on Mac's identification of Ben as the "instigator." The sheriff was not impressed. And Gustafson was treating Ben even more coldly than he had when they met.

After delivering a stern lecture on the evils of drinking and carousing, Sheriff Collier excused himself and left Deputy Gustafson to handle the actual incarceration. Vick eyed Ben as he passed down the corridor, but he remained silent. What must be going through the kid's mind? Ben wondered. Just when you think it can't get any worse, you see the deputy putting your lawyer behind bars.

Gustafson locked the locals in one of the vacant cells, then put the ASP men in the other. To Ben's surprise, Gustafson closed the door to the cell and locked it while Ben was still outside.

Maybe there was hope yet. "Does this mean you're letting me go?"

"Dream on," Gustafson said curtly.

"Can you at least undo my handcuffs?"

"No." Gustafson's face was like a rock. No sign of warmth or humanity was apparent.

"You know, I didn't lay a hand on anyone," Ben said. "I had nothing to do with that fight."

"That's not what Mac said."

"Mac was too busy crying over his pinball machine to get his story straight. I'm telling you, I'm innocent. And I can't afford to spend all my time before the Vick trial in jail."

"Don't sweat it. The sheriff'll let everyone out in the morning. After you've had a chance to sleep it off."

"Sleep what off? I never finished my first beer."

Gustafson whirled Ben around and grabbed him by the throat. "Look, you piece of crap, I'm doing the best I can to control my temper. So just shut up and don't try my patience." He shoved Ben down the corridor and out of sight of the cells.

"I don't understand. What have I ever done to you?"

Ben could see right off the bat that he should have remained silent. Gustafson was seething; his rage was already on the verge of boiling over. "You remember that car your boys torched two months ago because you mistakenly thought it belonged to the Vietnamese?"

"I don't know what you're—"

"Well, my little sister was on the sidewalk beside the car. Got caught in the explosion. She almost died—been having health problems ever since. Her face was ruined."

"But that wasn't me!" Ben protested.

"When something horrible like that happens to your sister, it just does something to you. Tears you apart.

Makes you go a little crazy." He looked up at Ben. "Makes you want to kill the man responsible."

"I'm telling you, I never hurt—"

"She was beautiful," Gustafson said, stony-eyed. "But now she's—" With the sudden fury of a hurricane, Gustafson whipped out his billy club and pounded Ben on the back. The sudden pain was so shattering that Ben found he couldn't make a sound. His knees weakened; his back felt paralyzed.

"My little sister never hurt anyone. That's for god-damn sure. So don't come crying to me for sympathy."

Ben leaned against the wall for support. "But I . . . wasn't involved . . . didn't even know . . ."

"Liar." Gustafson pounded him again, this time on the rib cage. "Admit it. Admit you knew about the fire-bombing!"

"I'm just"—Ben gasped—"a lawyer."

Gustafson spun him around and shoved him face-first into the wall. Ben's cheek scraped against the speckled concrete. "All the worse, as far as I'm concerned. At least the boys in Cell Block B believe in what they're doing. You're just in it for the money."

Ben's reply was smothered as Gustafson jerked him away from the wall. The next blow from the billy club caught Ben on the side of the head. He fell to the floor in a crumpled heap.

Gustafson rammed the club under Ben's throat, drove his knee into Ben's spine, and pulled upward. His knee burrowed into Ben's back while the club flattened his larynx.

Then, abruptly, Gustafson removed the club and let Ben's head fall to the floor. Ben braced himself for the next blow, but it never came. Instead he heard the sound of Gustafson's boots moving down the corridor.

Wasn't he afraid Ben would try to escape? Ben almost laughed. He couldn't even move. The thought of trying to stand up hurt him more than he could bear.

He heard Gustafson open the door and leave the cell corridor. Ben lay there on the floor, unable to move, unable to help himself, racked with pain.

And he realized, with sudden and terrible certainty, that he was absolutely, totally—

Alone.

* 14 *

Colonel Nguyen sat in the center of the chicken barn that served as Coi Than Tien's town hall. On his left, his old friend Duong Dang sat with the council of elders, the nominal governing body of their community. On his right, "Dan" Pham sat with his followers, principally the younger members of the settlement.

The two groups could not have been more polarized. It was the old guard versus the young Turks, the voice of conciliation pitted against the voice of resistance. And there seemed to be no middle ground that either side could accept.

Dang tapped a small gavel. "Now that we have resolved the guard-duty issue, we will address Dinh Pham's suggestions about a possible response to last night's incident."

Pham leaped to his feet. "We must fight back! We must retaliate!"

Dang pounded his gavel. "You have not been properly recognized."

"Everyone knows who I am."

"That is not the point. It is a matter of courtesy, of tradition—"

"I'm not interested in traditions. I'm interested in retaliation."

"There are proper ways to proceed—"

"My grandmother was shot!" Pham shouted. His voice echoed through the barn, rattling the rafters on the roof. A horrible silence blanketed the barn.

Colonel Nguyen closed his eyes. As he had learned last night after the black pickup disappeared, some of the ricocheting pellets had pierced a window and struck Pham's elderly grandmother. Although the injury was not itself terminal, at her age, any wound could be life threatening.

Dang stroked his white beard. "We all grieve with you for Xuan's injury."

"Grieving is not enough. It is time for action!"

Nguyen shook his head. There was such a difference between Pham and Dang. Dang still spoke in the old traditional ways; Pham had fully assimilated the slang and rhetoric of his adopted country. And what they said was as different as the way they said it. Dang spoke with caution, with concern for all possible ramifications. He was slow to anger, and equally slow to take action. Pham was younger in spirit and temperament; he was unwilling to accept the world as it was. There was more of America about him than of Vietnam.

Pham turned to address the entire assembly. "A gentle woman in her seventies who has never done harm to anyone was struck by a shotgun blast to her shoulder blade. What are we going to do about it?"

Nguyen watched Pham as he made his appeal to the masses. He was impressed with Pham's bearing, his strength, his natural aptitude for leadership. At the same time Pham's words filled him with apprehension. Nguyen knew Pham's inflammatory speech could only lead Coi Than Tien in one direction.

Another elder, Vanh Truong, intervened. "I am told that your grandmother will recover."

"Her shoulder blade is shattered!" Pham spat out. "This is intolerable!"

"It seems to me," Dang said, "that we have a choice."

"We must choose to fight!" Pham yelled, interrupting Dang. A spattering of cheers punctuated his cry, mostly from the younger men in the barn.

"That is not among the choices," Dang said, maintaining a calm, even voice. "The choice is whether we remain and endure, or whether we move on."

"Whether we *run*! That's what you mean. Whether we run like cowards as we did before. Well, I for one will not run!" More cheers and applause followed, even stronger than before. His support was growing.

"If we remain here," Truong said, "we risk continued harassment." He looked directly at Pham. "If we fight, we risk extermination."

"And where will you go when there is nowhere left to run?" Pham demanded. "When the forces of hate have hounded us to the ends of the earth. What then?"

Dang waved his hands. "The decision to leave has not yet been made. This is simply an open discussion. We must consider our options."

"I will not accept an option without *honor*!"

A smart boy, Nguyen thought. Pham was reaching out now, sounding a chord that would appeal to the older members of the community as well as the young. This was the turning point. If Nguyen was going to speak, he could delay no longer.

"Excuse me, Elder Dang." Colonel Nguyen quietly interjected himself into the debate. "It is possible that honor can be found in all options."

Pham looked at him with dismay and disappointment. "Colonel Nguyen! Surely a warrior such as yourself does not say we should run."

Nguyen averted his eyes. "A brave man knows when to show his back to the enemy."

"And what does that mean?"

He hesitated. "It means there is no honor in fighting if it costs us our souls. Or our families."

"I cannot accept this. I cannot believe the great Colonel Nguyen would say these words."

"What would you have us do, Pham? Would you have us kill someone? Exact your vengeance? We do not know who shot your grandmother."

"Of course we do. It was those murderers from ASP. The pious assassins who go to church under our noses on Sunday morning, then set fire to our homes on Sunday night."

Nguyen felt the heat radiating from all sections of the barn. "We do not know that for certain. It is conceivable that . . . there could be other motivations for last night's attack."

"Such as what?" Pham demanded.

Nguyen paused. It would be so easy, so much simpler if he could just tell them what he knew, what he had seen.

He glanced back at Lan, who was sitting with Mary and Holly. No. They would all be placed in danger. And Coi Than Tien couldn't protect them. Coi Than Tien couldn't protect anyone.

"I do not know," Nguyen answered. "But there are many motives for violence. Hatred is only one of them."

"Colonel Nguyen," Pham said. "I mean you no disrespect. But you are wrong. You speak the words of a coward."

"Pham!" Dang said harshly. "Think what you are saying! Colonel Nguyen is one of our most honored citizens. He is your elder."

"Yes," Pham growled. "And his elder wisdom got Tommy Vuong killed!"

There was an audible gasp, followed by a suspended silence. The unspeakable had been spoken.

"Pham," Dang said, "you bring shame on us all. You do not know what you say."

"I know what I know!" Pham fired back. "I know Colonel Nguyen was the last to see Tommy alive. I know he counseled Tommy to suppress his anger, to turn the other cheek. And look what happened."

All heads turned toward Colonel Nguyen, obviously awaiting a reply. But none was forthcoming. The Colonel retook his seat. He did not like what Pham had said, but he would not dispute it. How could he? He *had* advised Tommy not to seek retribution against the man who attacked him in the bar. He had left Tommy just when he needed him most. If anyone could have saved Tommy, it was him. And he failed.

"Dinh Pham, you have disgraced this assembly," Dang pronounced. "We must ask you to leave—"

"Fine. I'll leave. But I won't leave alone." Again Pham turned to face the crowd. "Who is with me?"

The response was slow at first, just a few young men who were known to be Pham's close friends. But then Thung Hieu, a man in his mid-fifties with three children, joined him. Then Elder Tran, whom the Colonel had known all his life. They were joined by women, mothers, even children. The sentiment spread like a dandelion in the wind. Pham's isolated few became a majority, a defiant congregation that would not be driven from their homes again.

Pham marched proudly out the barn door. Over half of those in attendance followed.

Dang tapped his gavel faintly on his table. The sadness in his eyes was unmistakable. "Under these circumstances," he said, "I see no reason to continue this meeting."

Nguyen knew the significance of these events as well as Dang. All chance of solidarity, as well as all chance of negotiating a peaceful solution, was lost. Pham was the real leader of Coi Than Tien now. And he would lead his followers into direct confrontation with ASP. A confrontation that could only lead to death, mostly on the side of Coi Than Tien. All the valor in the world could not mitigate the effectiveness of well-organized hate.

Nguyen followed Dang and the remaining few out of the barn. He knew now that violence was inevitable. And at least in part, it was his fault.

* 15 *

"What the hell happened to you?"

Ben staggered into the Hatewatch office, clutching his side. Belinda jumped up from her desk when she saw him and helped him to a chair.

"I've had a tough night," Ben mumbled.

"No kidding." Belinda took his head in her hands. His face was bruised and his left eye was swollen shut. A long red laceration highlighted his eyebrow. "Where'd you spend the night, a trash compactor?"

"Close. City jail."

"Jail? *You?* What was the charge?"

"Drunk and disorderly." Ben grimaced; talking only exacerbated the aching in his side. "I'm . . . sorry, Belinda . . . I know you didn't want me back here . . ."

"Don't be stupid. You're hurt."

"But what if Frank and—"

"Frank and John will be out all morning."

"It's just—" Another sharp shot of pain blazed through his rib cage. "Didn't . . . think I could make it back to the campsite, and I didn't have anywhere else to go."

"I said, don't worry about it. Who did this to you?"

"The Right Honorable Deputy Gustafson."

"Oh, God. Why was he after you?"

Ben rubbed the soreness in his side. "Wanted me to admit I was in on an ASP firebombing."

"Why the hell didn't you? It's not as if you were under oath."

Ben shrugged. "Principle of the thing."

Belinda shook her head. If Ben wasn't mistaken, just the tiniest trace of admiration crept back into her eyes. "Principles can get you beaten up badly with a redneck like Gustafson."

"You know him?"

"He's come around here a few times, trying to get us to do some stupid thing or another. Did he tell you about his sister?"

"I believe he mentioned her, yes. Although he let his club do most of the talking."

"How long did he beat you?"

"I'm not entirely sure. I kind of faded out there toward the end. When he was done, he just left me lying on the stone floor. I couldn't move a muscle. About an hour later he dragged me into Cell Block B. With three members of ASP."

"Out of the frying pan and into the fire. Did they hurt you?"

"No, worse." Ben touched the cut on his face gingerly. "They were nice to me."

A faint smile played on Belinda's lips. "You poor kid. Let me get a first-aid kit." She ran to a room in the back of the office, then returned with the kit and a washcloth. She applied a medicated Q-Tip to the cut over Ben's eye.

"Ow!" he said. "That stings."

"Don't complain. It's good for you."

"Haven't I been tortured enough?"

Belinda ignored him and continued dressing his wounds. She was being extremely kind, Ben thought.

Was it possible his first impression hadn't been altogether wrong? Was it possible that there might still be some attraction—?

"How was your bed?" Belinda asked.

"No beds. No cots, no metal bunks. We slept on the floor. Which became particularly unpleasant after my drunken roommates began vomiting all over the place."

She lifted his shirt and examined the ugly blue-black bruise on the side of his rib cage. "My God, that's terrible. Did he break a rib?"

"I don't think so. He seemed to be pretty good at inflicting pain but stopping short of any permanent damage."

"Permanent damage leads to lawsuits. A few bruises can be written off to an alleged escape attempt. You are going to sue, aren't you?"

"No way."

"Ben, he violated your civil rights!"

"What else is new?"

"If it's a question of money, Hatewatch could subsidize the expenses—"

"No. I've got enough problems without any new lawsuits."

She removed a gauze bandage from the kit and wrapped it around his chest. "Vick case not going well?"

Ben watched as she expertly tended to his wounds and abrasions. She obviously had some medical training. Which was not surprising. Given her choice of vocation, she probably came face-to-face with violence on a regular basis. "The Vick case isn't going at all. No one will talk to me. No one will help me. My own legal assistant won't help. I can't even get a room for the night."

Belinda finished wrapping his chest and pulled down

his shirt. "Can't say I feel sorry for you. Your client is pond scum, Ben."

Ben tucked in his shirt. "C'mon, Belinda, you're a lawyer. You know the process doesn't work unless both sides are represented."

"True. But that doesn't mean you have to represent every dirtbag on earth."

"No one competent would represent this dirtbag. It was either me or a probate attorney who doesn't know abstracts from arraignments."

"Still—"

"If we're not going to give the man a fair trial, we might as well not give him a trial at all. Is that what you want? Conviction without a fair trial?"

"In the case of Donald Vick, I won't shed any tears."

"Then you need to ask yourself if the ASP members are the only fascists around here."

Belinda frowned. She packed up her first-aid kit, then placed it on her desk.

Ben reached out and took her wrist. "Belinda, I'm desperate."

She tried to shrug him away.

Ben turned her head with his finger and made her look at him. "I need your help. I can't do this alone."

Her movements slowed; her face showed her confusion. Ben noticed, however, that she did not remove his hand. "I'm not going to help you get a murderer off the hook."

"I'm not asking you to. I just want you to help me investigate. You were planning to investigate the case anyway; you told me so. We might as well do it together."

"I'm not sure that's wise. We're not on the same side."

"We both want the same thing. The truth." He looked at her pointedly. "Isn't that right?"

Belinda thought for a long time before answering. "I suppose if I accompanied you, people might be more willing to talk."

Ben quietly released his breath. "That's the spirit."

"But I warn you, if we uncover any evidence that incriminates your client, I'm going straight to the DA with it."

"Understood." He leaned back in the chair, careful not to strain any sensitive muscles.

Belinda rubbed her hands together. "Let me take care of a few emergencies, then we can get started. If you're up to it."

"I will be. Just give me a minute to pull myself together."

"Fine. Anything else I can do for you?"

Ben tried to open his swollen eye. "Well ... you could uncancel our dinner date. . . ."

* 16 *

Belinda agreed to drive Ben back to the campsite so he could change clothes and collect some supplies. During the drive over, Ben saw Christina from the road; she was in the middle of the lake fishing. She must've left Mary Sue's early to launch another assault on the local fish stock.

She had seen him, too, not that it made any difference. She glanced up briefly, then returned her attention to the fish.

Ben crawled into his tent, changed clothes, and retrieved enough supplies to get him through the day. On his way out, a sudden burst of wind whipped across the campsite. The gust was so strong it made Ben lean to one side.

"Is a tornado approaching?" he asked Belinda.

"I don't think so."

The wind intensified, blowing dirt and debris into their faces. Ben heard a steady, rhythmic chopping noise. It seemed to be coming from the sky.

"Up there!" Belinda shouted, pointing just over their heads. "It's a helicopter!"

"More than that," Ben added. "It's a police helicopter."

"Why is it flying so low?"

Ben squinted into the sun. "I think it's coming in for a landing."

"Why would a police helicopter be landing here?"

"Guess I should've paid those parking tickets."

They watched as the helicopter descended into a large clearing near the lake. The aircraft touched down and the whirring blades slowed. The insistent chopping noise gradually faded. Just as the copter was almost still, Ben heard a loud internal crash, followed by the sound of metal grinding against metal. Finally the helicopter coughed and sputtered to silence.

"I think that chopper is due for an overhaul," Belinda commented. "Any idea who the pilot is?"

"Well," Ben said as he ran toward it, "I only know one guy who's certified to fly these buggies. . . ."

The tall, dark-haired man who clambered out of the cockpit was wearing an unseasonably heavy overcoat and flight goggles. A cross between Sam Spade and Junior Birdman. Undeniably, it was Homicide Detective Mike Morelli. Ben's friend. And ex-brother-in-law. To the extent the two descriptions weren't mutually exclusive.

"Damn, damn, damn."

"Mike! What are you doing here? Is something wrong?"

"Yeah. I think my copter blew a fuse."

"I don't mean—I mean, is there an emergency?"

"Well, I heard a rumor that you were in a spot of trouble. So I took a leave of absence. And here we are."

"We?"

As if on cue, Jones and Loving crawled out of the back of the helicopter.

"Jones!" Ben cried.

"In the flesh."

Ben gestured toward Belinda. "Belinda, this is Jones. Back at my Tulsa office, he's my secretary."

"Executive assistant," Jones corrected. "Say cheese." He pointed a black, handheld video camera at Ben's face. "I've been trying out this minicam I got for Christmas. I recorded the whole flight down here."

"If you're going to continue filming," Ben said, "let me give you a tip. You're shooting into the sun."

"Details, details."

"Also, the lens cap is on." Loving jumped out of the backseat. "Belinda, this is Loving, my investigator."

She extended her hand. "Ben, why is it none of your staff members have first names?"

"Don't ask me. They came that way. Loving, say hello to Belinda Hamilton."

"Hell-*o*!" Loving eyed Belinda appreciatively. "I dropped everything and flew out with Morelli as soon as I heard you were in trouble, Skipper. Although you look like you're doing just fine to me."

Ben turned his attention back to Mike, who had opened the cowling above and behind the passenger area and was tinkering around with the engine. "How'd you get a helicopter? You didn't steal it from the traffic division, did you?"

"Of course not. After ten years of devoted service the department put her up for auction. Five of my cop buddies and I pooled our bucks and bought her."

"But—why?"

"To fly, of course. I've had my copter certification for years, but in the past I've always had to go out to Allied Helicopter or Riverside Airport and rent one just to get in some fly time. Now I have my own Hiller 12SL4."

"You know, Mike, I humored you when you bought

the Trans Am. I remained silent when you bought all that hang-gliding equipment. But a helicopter?"

"What's wrong with that?"

"Shouldn't you at least remove the police-department seals? Since it's no longer in official service?"

Mike shrugged. "I haven't been able to bring myself to do it. They look really cool, don't you think? And it makes it much easier to get a parking space."

"Don't you have to file a flight plan, or maintain radio contact with a control tower?"

"Not out here. I just stick to the VFR—Visual Flight Rules—cruise at about fifteen hundred feet, and keep my eyes open." He grinned. "It's easy. Want to go for a ride?"

"No thanks. I don't fly in reputable airplanes, much less that bucket of bolts."

"Portia could use a bit of work here and there, but she's not a bucket of bolts," Mike protested. "That landing did sound bad, though. I think I need to replace her engine block."

"Portia? You've given your helicopter a name? You really have gone off the deep end, Mike. Even your Trans Am didn't have a pet name."

"Don't strain your quality of mercy. It's a perfectly ordinary name."

"Spare me the Shakespearean allusions." Ben leaned over Mike's shoulder and tried to see what he was doing. "I didn't know you were mechanically inclined. I thought you spent all your spare time reading the classics."

"If you can't repair your own bird, you shouldn't be flying it. That's my motto. Mechanics aren't going to give your baby the tender loving care it deserves. You can't just treat it like so much metal, you know." He patted the windshield. "You have to caress it like a woman."

"I had no idea engine repair could be so sensual," Belinda said.

Mike grinned. "Now you know." He closed the cowling. "Portia is going to need spare parts, Ben. Is there a place in town?"

"That carries helicopter parts? Not likely. I think I recall seeing an auto-parts store."

"That might do, if I use some creativity. I'll check it out later—" Mike stood up and, for the first time, took a close look at Ben. "What in God's name happened to you?"

Ben touched his swollen eye. "I had a disagreement with some of the townsfolk. Most of them, actually."

"Want to tell us about it?"

"Like you wouldn't believe. I'm thrilled to see you all here. But I'm afraid the vacation is already over. We've got work to do."

Ben gathered Belinda and his staff in a circle around the dead campfire and summarized all he knew about the case to date. While they talked Christina returned from her fishing expedition.

"Jones! Loving!" She dropped her fishing paraphernalia and ran to greet them. Loving spread open his arms to give her a great big bear hug. Since Loving weighed two hundred and fifty pounds and was built like a brick factory, Christina disappeared within his embrace.

Jones, always the cooler head, offered Christina a handshake. He was wearing khaki shorts, knee-high socks, and a photojournalist jacket with a million pockets. "Nice to see you looking well," he told her. "By the way, you smell of trout."

She tweaked his cheek. "Jones, you old charmer, you." She gave Mike a quick hug, then found herself face-to-face with Ben.

They glared at each other for a protracted moment. Christina glanced at Belinda, then turned away.

Great, Ben thought. He'd been gone all night, and had returned with a woman she'd never seen before. And she didn't even appear interested.

Ben began planning their pretrial strategy. "Since it doesn't look as if we can expect much help from our client, I think we should do everything we can privately to learn more about Donald Vick and his activities since he came to Silver Springs."

"Does that mean checkin' out ASP?" Loving asked.

"I'm afraid so."

"They ain't gonna like being investigated, Skipper," Loving replied. " 'Specially since they think you're their best buddy and all."

"Granted," Ben said. "But we have to try."

"I'll do it, then. I'm the only one who has half a chance of coming out of a scrape with those goons with his head still attached."

Ben wasn't about to argue with him.

"I'll hang out at the bars and pool halls—see what I can learn. If I get them gabbing, maybe I can pick up some useful info."

"Sounds good to me," Ben concurred.

"How's the forensic evidence look?" Mike asked.

"I don't know any details," Ben answered. "But the DA told Belinda he thought it was conclusive, and he was bragging about it to the newspaper. I plan to go by his office as soon as I finish here."

Mike stroked his chin thoughtfully. "Good plan, but as you well know, prosecutors tend not to tell the defense anything they aren't legally obligated to reveal. Is the DA's office near the auto-parts shop?"

"Within walking distance."

"I might wander over there myself. Since I'm going that way. See what I can scrounge up. I'll flash my badge around and play the visiting law-enforcement officer. They might be willing to tell me something they wouldn't tell you."

"Worth a try," Ben said eagerly. What a comfort to have his friends and associates helping him again. Except Christina, of course. She wasn't even looking at him, much less talking to him.

"Anyone in town have a computer?" Jones asked.

Ben thought for a moment. Jones wasn't the most skilled legal secretary in Tulsa, but he was a whiz with computers. "Haven't seen one. Wouldn't hold my breath."

"We have one in the Hatewatch office," Belinda offered. "A Gateway 2000 IBM-compatible."

"Connected to a modem?"

"You bet—9600 baud."

"Great." Jones clapped his hands. "That's where I'll start. Let me investigate ASP on-line. I might run a search on Mr. Vuong, too, and some of the other members of Coi Than Tien."

"That sounds great," Ben said.

"And it'll give me an opportunity to film downtown Silver Springs—a rural paradise in America's heartland."

Ben hoped Jones spent more time punching the computer keyboard than he did shutterbugging. "And what about you, Christina?"

Christina gave him a stony glare.

"What can you contribute to the investigation?"

Christina's lips pursed, and her face became almost

as red as her hair. She pushed herself to her feet and stormed off without saying a word.

Ben frowned. Bad move. "Excuse me," he said awkwardly. "I think I'd like to talk to Christina in private." As if he had any choice.

He followed Christina to her tent and invited himself inside.

"What do you want?" she said icily.

"Christina, I know you didn't want me involved in this case. Maybe you were right—it's certainly become more of a headache than I ever dreamed. But the fact is, I accepted the responsibility, and now I need my whole staff behind me or I'm going to get creamed."

Christina's expression did not change. "I told you I wasn't going to help you, and I meant it."

"Christina—" He looked at her with pleading eyes. "I *need* you."

"You should have thought of that before you accepted the case."

"What am I supposed to do, ask for your permission before I take on a client?"

"In some instances, yes. You have an admirable sense of ethics, Ben. But sometimes you lack common sense."

"Someone had to represent Vick."

"Yeah—but why you?" She stood and looked him square in the eyes. "I'd do almost anything for you, Ben. You know I would. I certainly have in the past. Because I thought I understood you . . . because I thought you believed in the same principles I believed in. Now I feel like I don't know you at all." She inhaled deeply. "I will not help this . . . racist redneck Rambo. Not in any way."

"That's your final word, then?"

"Yes. It is."

"Fine." He pushed open the tent flaps. "I thought I

could count on you, Christina. I guess I was wrong." He marched outside.

Ben stood in the glaring sunlight and kicked at the dirt. Why had he done that? Christina didn't deserve to be treated so harshly, even if she wasn't cooperating.

He turned back toward her tent, then froze just outside the entrance. He heard a soft trembling inside. Was she crying? Oh, no . . . He moved in closer.

Christina nearly knocked him onto the ground. "Get out of my way." She marched past him carrying her rod and reel.

"Christina, wait—"

"Bug off, Ben. I'm going fishing." She kept on walking without looking back until she was out of sight.

* 17 *

Belinda dropped Ben off outside the DA's office on the far end of Main Street. Swain's office differed from the DA offices with which Ben was familiar in two principal respects: first, Swain didn't have a secretary or receptionist, and second, he had a portable playpen set up behind his desk.

Swain didn't see Ben come in because he was busy reading a story, or describing it anyway, to his daughter.

"See, Amber," Swain said, "Carl takes the baby and the puppy to play in the flowers." He turned the page. "And—oh, no!—the puppy squirts Carl with the garden hose!"

Amber pointed at the picture in the book and giggled.

Ben glanced over Swain's shoulder and saw that the Carl in question was a huge black dog. "Every baby should have a rottweiler for a playmate," he said.

Swain turned around. "Mr. Kincaid! I didn't hear you come in."

"Don't let me interrupt."

"Oh, no. It's office hours. I just—" He suddenly became embarrassed. "My wife Marjorie works part-time at the hardware store, so I keep Amber on Tuesdays and Thursdays."

"That must make it hard to get any legal work done."

"You ain't kiddin'. Fortunately there isn't that much

to do. We've never had much trouble in Silver Springs. At least not until your boy and his buddies came to town."

"Do you mind if we discuss this case?" Ben tilted his head toward the back of the office. "It might be best if we talked in private."

"Oh. Right. Of course." Swain smiled down at Amber. "Honey, Daddy has to talk to this nice man. Why don't you look at the book by yourself for a minute?"

Amber's lower lip protruded. "Wead."

"I will, honey. As soon as we finish talking, I'll read it to you. Twice, if you like."

"No!" Amber said emphatically. "Wead!"

"Honey, I can't."

"Wead! Wead! Wead!"

"Honey, no."

Amber ran to the side of the playpen and pressed her face against the white mesh like a pint-sized prisoner of Alcatraz. She began to wail at an earsplitting pitch. *"Weeeeead!"*

"Honey!" Swain leaned in close to her. "If you'll be good for a few minutes, I'll give you a nice bottle of milk."

"No!" she screamed back. Her face was a puffy crimson. "Wead!"

Swain looked at Ben and shrugged helplessly. "Okay, if you don't want milk, I'll give you some apple juice."

"Wahhh!" Amber wasn't even responding now. She just wailed.

"Okay, okay. If you'll just be good for a minute, I'll let you have some"—his voice dropped to a whisper—"Coca-Cola."

As abruptly as it had begun, the caterwauling ceased. Swain turned around quickly and checked Ben's reaction. Ben did his best to look as if he hadn't heard.

Swain sprinted to the mini-refrigerator in the back of his office and took out an aluminum can of Coke Classic. "Normally, of course, I would never let her near this stuff."

"Of course not," Ben said. "That's why you keep a case of it in your office."

"Well ... I drink it, too."

While Swain emptied the can into a plastic bottle, Ben checked the contents of the cupboard. Chocolate-chip cookies, graham crackers, cheese puffs, and Honey-nut Cheerios. "I guess this nutritious stuff is for you, too?"

"Sometimes I get hungry during the workday," Swain murmured. He passed the soda-filled bottle to Amber. She snatched it eagerly, popped it in her mouth, and nestled down in the playpen with her book.

"Whew." Swain wiped his forehead. "Well, that'll keep her occupied for two or three minutes, anyway. What did you have on your mind, Mr. Kincaid?"

"I'd like to see the evidence you have against my client. If you'd like, I can file a motion to produce—"

"Oh, that won't be necessary. I'll show you my whole case file." Swain went to his desk and opened the topmost drawer. "What do you want to know?"

"Well, for starters," Ben said, "what's this over-whelming evidence you alluded to in yesterday's *Herald*?"

"Ah. Well, you know the sheriff found the crossbow used to kill Vuong."

"I read it in the paper."

"It's true. Found it shortly after the murder took place, about half a mile from where Vuong was killed."

"And there's no doubt that it's the crossbow used to kill Vuong?"

"Not in my mind. How many industrial-strength

crossbows do you think there are around here? That's a pretty rarefied piece of equipment. Big mother, too. I'd find it difficult to believe anyone had one in these parts, if we hadn't had professional killers move into the neighborhood."

Ben decided to let that pass. "What's the forensic evidence that links Vick to the crossbow?"

"The hairs. Two hairs, to be specific, caught in the firing mechanism of the crossbow."

"Surely that's not enough to bring charges on."

"The state labs say it is. They've run tests and compared the hairs to exemplars taken from your client. They say they're his. I don't know all the scientific lingo, but they say their conclusion is one hundred percent certain."

Sounded like a DNA matchup, Ben mused. Not at all good news. "And I expect you asked Mr. Payne's permission before you took the exemplar from Vick?"

"Of course. He had no objection. He's been very cooperative."

I'll bet. That's probably why he was chosen. "What else have you got?"

Swain hedged. "Well, our investigation is still ongoing. . . ."

"What about fingerprints?"

"We didn't find any on the crossbow."

"That in itself must be unusual."

Swain shrugged. "If the killer watches TV, he would know to wipe his prints off the crossbow. But he might not notice a stray hair."

"Have you checked out Vick's alibi?"

"You call that an alibi? He says he was walking out near the lake when the sheriff found him about an hour after the murder. No one was with him. He had both the time and the opportunity to kill Vuong.

"Frankly," Swain continued, "I was expecting to have to bust an alibi when I heard about the arrest. Regardless of what really happened, I figured Vick would get a bunch of his ASP buddies to leap to his defense and claim they were with him at the time of the murder. But that didn't happen. I get the impression Vick wasn't all that popular, even with his own people."

Now that was interesting. "I've heard Vick had some visitors the week before the murder. Any idea who they were?"

"Why don't you just ask your client?"

Ben shrugged awkwardly. "I—uh—just wanted to see what you already know. So I don't waste time with unimportant witnesses."

"Well, I don't have any idea who visited Vick. It's not something anyone in this town is likely to admit voluntarily. And the ASP people won't talk to me at all. I was planning to go out to that ASP camp with some subpoena, but given this forensic evidence, I don't see the point. We've got your man dead to rights. And if I don't have to go there again, I won't."

"Then you've visited the ASP encampment?"

" 'Fraid so. I've been out a few times on some disorderly-conduct reports—and I didn't enjoy it. That place gives me the creeps. It's like, one minute you're in an Ouachita paradise, and the next minute you're in hell."

"Can you tell me how to get there?"

"Better yet, I'll draw you a map." Swain ripped off a sheet of legal paper and sketched a map of the roads between Silver Springs and the ASP camp.

"Don't they have any lodgings out there? On campus, so to speak."

"Oh, yeah. Couple of barracks. Why?"

"It just seems odd. If Vick could've stayed there, why did he have a place in town?"

"It wasn't just him. Several of them did. At least, until the killing. Now no one will take them in. But before this happened, the town was a bit more tolerant. Some of the ASP men slept at the camp, but others, the more social ones, I guess, kept a place in town."

It chilled Ben to think of Donald Vick as one of the more social ones. "Does Vick have any friends? Family?"

"One assumes even white supremacists have mothers. But if Vick has family or friends, none of them have come forward. I doubt if he has any around here."

Ben nodded. He would ask Jones to check that out later. "I'm sure you realize I'm going to file a motion in limine to exclude evidence of Vick's alleged threat made at the Bluebell Bar."

Swain grinned. "Well, Mr. Kincaid, you feel free to file whatever you like, for all the good it will do you. We're not as fond of those motions as you city boys are."

"The law is the law," Ben replied. "Wherever you are."

"Well . . ." Swain chuckled amiably. "We'll just see."

Ben couldn't think of any more intelligent questions. He couldn't fault Swain in terms of fair play; as far as he could tell, Swain had told him all he knew. Unfortunately it hadn't helped a bit. "If you discover any exculpatory evidence, I'll expect to be informed."

"Of course. Where can I contact you?"

"I—I'll just drop by periodically."

"Suit yourself."

Ben walked toward the playpen. "That'll give me a chance to visit Amber." He crouched down and waved at her. "Bye-bye, Amber."

Amber removed the bottle from her mouth, then burped very loudly.

"Oh, sweetie," Swain said, covering his face. "How unladylike."

* 18 *

Loving stepped through the front door of the Bluebell Bar. He knew everyone in the joint was giving him the once-over, so he figured he might as well hold still and let them get it over with. Come to think of it, he could use the time to give them the once-over, too.

It was still early evening, but a crowd had already formed. Judging by the prefixes on the license plates outside, folks came from miles around to wet their whistles at the Bluebell. And judging by the accents he heard from the boys gathered around the pool table, some of them had come a lot farther than the neighboring counties. Those were the ones he wanted to chat with.

Loving grinned. He might not have a couple of college degrees like the Skipper, but he sure as hell knew his way around a bar.

He strolled casually to the pool table and laid a quarter on the bank just above the coin slot. "Mind if I play?"

The man holding the cue stick barely looked up. "Suit yourself." He was broad-shouldered with blond curly hair—exactly as Ben had described Sonny Banner.

"You Banner?" Loving barked, just at the instant Banner decided to shoot. The tip of the cue shot up into the air; the cue ball rolled just enough to cost him his turn.

"Goddamn you!" Banner threw his cue down on the table. "Don't you know better than to talk when a man is taking his shot?"

"Sorry, pal. You were going to scratch, anyway." Loving cut him off before he exploded. "Does this mean you're Banner?"

"Who wants to know?"

"Name's Loving. I'd like to join ASP."

Banner placed his hands on his hips. "You think we'd take some asswipe who can't keep his goddamn mouth shut when a man is takin' his turn?"

Loving slapped him on the shoulder. "Let me make it up to you. I'll buy the next round. What're you drinking?"

Banner softened a bit. "Coors, of course. So are my buddies."

"Right." Loving motioned to the bartender. "Get me three Coors and a Michelob Light."

"Michelob Light?" Banner guffawed. "Wassa matter, pretty boy? You on a diet?"

Loving took four bottles of beer and a bottle opener from the bartender. "Well, I could stand to lose a pound or two."

"You know what I think?" Banner was right in Loving's face. His breath indicated this was not his first beer of the evening. "I think you must be a sissy boy."

Banner's friends whooped and hollered. "Sissy boy," they chanted with amusement. "Mama's little sweetheart."

"Do tell." Loving nodded calmly. "You gonna open your beer with the bottle opener or your teeth?"

Banner's eyebrows moved closer together. "Are you

crazy? You can't open a beer bottle with your teeth. You'll kill yourself."

With a patently bored expression, Loving placed the top of the bottle in his mouth. He clamped his teeth down on the cap, made a great show of grunting and groaning, then jerked his head back. The bottle cap popped off.

Loving held the cap between his teeth, then poked it out with his tongue. "Piece of cake."

Banner's face was transfixed with admiration. "Wuh—what'd ya want to talk to us about?"

"Let's just say I'm an upstandin' citizen who doesn't always like what he sees happenin' in this country, and I'd like to talk to you boys about joining ASP. Even if some of the members do appear to be sissies."

Banner glanced at his two friends. "Takes a month to get in. We have to quiz you first. Make sure you're not some Vietcong sympathizer tryin' to infiltrate us."

"Can you quiz me while we shoot pool?"

Banner shrugged. "I don't see why not."

"Good. Rack 'em up."

Loving suppressed a grin as he watched Banner round up the balls. They wouldn't tell him anything at first, natch. It would take a while. But he was definitely off to a good start.

It was amazing what you could accomplish with a good barroom stunt. Since these boys made it clear they never drank Michelob Light, they didn't realize it came in a bottle with a twist-off cap. And they didn't see him untwist the cap most of the way off before he put it in his mouth.

* 19 *

Nhung Vu crept through the pitch-black night behind Pham and the other four men, careful to make no noise, no sound whatsoever. He knew some of them were watching him, hoping he would do something wrong. He had to make sure that didn't happen. He had to make sure he didn't let Pham down.

Many of Pham's men had thought it foolhardy to include Nhung in their group. He's only fifteen, they had insisted. He's only a boy. But Pham had waved their concerns away. This is a battle of the young, Pham said. The elders will not help us. There is no guarantee the job will be completed soon. The young are our future.

And so Nhung had been permitted to join them, to attend their meetings, to share in their plans. And most importantly he had been allowed to be part of the select group making this midnight raid—their first organized act of resistance against ASP.

It was a momentous occasion, made all the more special by the fact that Pham had permitted—in fact, practically invited—him to come. Dan Pham was Nhung's hero. He was the only man with the courage to speak out against the elders, to force them to take action against these killers. Whatever Pham wanted Nhung to do, he would do.

Crouching close to the ground, they crept over the

crest of the last hill and saw the ASP camp in the valley below. A barbed-wire fence surrounded the encampment. Nhung had expected it to be patrolled, but there was no sign of a guard. It would seem ASP wasn't expecting any trouble.

Their mistake.

Pham's group crept down the hill toward the camp. Nhung watched Pham remove the components of the firebomb from his backpack and carefully assemble them. Pham had learned that one of the barracks in the camp was the armory, the place where weapons were kept. And explosives. That would be their target. No one knew how Pham came by this knowledge. He seemed to have an undisclosed source of inside information about ASP. His secrecy had created some dissension in the ranks. But when all was said and done, Pham's information was usually correct.

Pham stuffed an oily rag down the delivery case. He was preparing to light the fuse when Nhung felt a strong arm wrap around his throat.

"Pha—" He tried to warn someone, but a hand clamped over his mouth.

Pham heard the noise. He whirled around, then froze.

Nhung saw the barrel of an automatic weapon protrude over his shoulder.

"You gook boys are coming with me," the voice behind Nhung said. "We're going to have a little talk with the Grand Dragon. And if you don't cooperate, I'll kill you like the stupid ape-bastards you are."

"Then you'll hang for our murders," Pham said.

"Shit." The man holding Nhung laughed. "We'll kill you, skin you, then bury you on the premises. No one will ever know a damn thing about it."

"We have committed no crime against you," Pham said.

"No, not yet," the guard hissed. "But only because you're dumbfuck Vietcong niggers who let yourself get caught."

Pham's face burned with rage. "Your raiders shot my grandmother!"

"Now ain't that too fuckin' bad." He shoved Nhung toward the compound. "That'll be a picnic compared to what we're gonna do to you."

Nhung could see the worry in Pham's eyes. It was Pham's first strike, the assault the Colonel and so many others had urged him not to make. And it was turning into a disaster. The resistance was being squelched before it had even begun.

He had to do something.

Nhung rammed his elbow back into the guard's gut, then thrust the gun barrel upward. The gun fired into the air, splitting the silence of the night. Pham and two others rushed forward, fists clenched. Seconds later the guard tumbled to the ground, unconscious.

Lights came on in the compound, followed by shouts and movement.

"Come on!" Nhung said.

"Not yet." Pham lit the rag, reared back his arm, and tossed the firebomb into the camp. It soared through the air like a glowing orange meteor, then struck the side of one of the barracks. A second later the north wall of the building burst into flame.

Nhung followed the rest of Pham's men back over the hill. It was a long run to the place where they had left the car, but they would make it. Since the ASP men were awake and alerted, they would probably be able to put out the fire before it consumed the camp. But that would keep ASP from following them. They would be able to get away. They would escape the wrath of ASP.

At least for the moment.

* 20 *

The next day was heaven-sent—not a cloud over the hilltops—so Ben and Belinda decided to walk to Mary Sue's boardinghouse. As they strolled down Maple together, Ben took the opportunity to learn what he could about his newfound companion.

"So tell me about yourself. What was it like growing up in—what was it, Montgomery?"

"Right. Well, the poor country on the outskirts of Montgomery, actually. Both my parents were killed in a car wreck when I was eight. My sister and I were shipped off to live with my aunt, my mother's sister. Her husband had a small piece of land he sharecropped. They had four kids already and barely enough to go around. They didn't need two more."

"But they took you in?"

"Didn't have too much choice, really. I got my first job when I was ten, sweeping out stores after hours. I spent most of my time trying to help make ends meet. And trying to keep my younger sister out of trouble."

"How much younger?"

"We're four years apart. Cindy Jo was a handful. Was—still is. Any kind of trouble you can think of, she's probably been in it. And I was always the one who had to come in and try to make it better. Nothing against my aunt, but I took care of Cindy Jo."

"And now you take care of everyone," Ben commented.

"I suppose that's one way of looking at it. Not that that makes me anything special. Jones told me you've been known to do some legal do-gooding yourself."

"I went to law school because I wanted to be in a position to help other people. In between keeping my head above water and trying to ward off starvation, I try to remember that."

Belinda beamed. "I went into law for exactly the same reasons. I think many people do. But most of them won't admit it." She jostled his shoulder affectionately. "Maybe you're not such a bad sort after all, Kincaid."

Ben led Belinda to Mary Sue's front door. The sign on the porch still indicated that she had vacancies, although Ben doubted she would be any more willing to extend one to him than she had been the day before.

They slipped into the foyer together. Mary Sue was not at the Dutch door, although a clattering in the kitchen suggested she was home.

"I'd better handle this one," Belinda said. She directed Ben to stand against the wall in the hallway. "You just stay out of sight."

"All right." Ben glanced up the staircase. Christina was nowhere in sight. He pressed against the wall so he could see Belinda and hear what was said without being seen by Mary Sue. "But watch out for her shotgun. She's not quite the Donna Reed clone she appears to be."

"Point taken." Belinda rang the bell on the table.

A few moments later Mary Sue emerged from the kitchen. She was wearing a blue dress this morning, but she still had the apron tied around her waist. Her movements were slow and halting; her eyes seemed unfocused. She paused in the middle of the living room, as if momentarily unsure how to find her way to the Dutch door.

"May I help you?"

"Yes. I'd like to take a room, if that's possible."

"Of course." Mary Sue brought out her guest book and opened it to the proper page. "How long will you be staying?"

"I'm not sure. At least a week."

"That'll do fine. We'll just take it one week at a time." Mary Sue offered Belinda the feather pen, then brought it back suddenly. "You're not"—her voice dropped to a whisper—"a *lawyer*, are you?" She pronounced the word as if it were a synonym for *child molester*.

"Why, yes," Belinda said. "Why do you ask?"

"Are you associated with Donald Vick?"

"In a sense."

Mary Sue withdrew the pen and closed the book.

"I'm with an organization called Hatewatch," Belinda explained. "We investigate hate crimes and file lawsuits to make groups like ASP financially responsible for their actions."

"Oh!" A relieved expression washed over Mary Sue's face. "Then you're not with that other gentleman."

"Other gentleman?"

"Well, I use the term lightly. The Tulsa lawyer. He came here, you know."

"No!"

"Oh, yes. Wanted a room. Practically demanded it."

"How awful. What did you do?"

"I told him in no uncertain terms that I didn't permit his kind of riffraff in my boardinghouse. And when he wouldn't take no for an answer, I brought Old Sally into the discussion."

Belinda didn't have to ask who—or what—Old Sally was. "My office is not connected to Mr. Vick's defense," she explained. "In fact, most people would say we're on the opposite side."

"Oh, well then. That's all right." She handed Belinda the pen and reopened the book.

"I understand Vick lived here."

"That's right. He was my tenant. Room six."

"Did he cause any trouble?"

"Not at all. Quiet as a church mouse. Only saw him in the evenings. Most nights he didn't even come to dinner. By the way, I'll need a first night's deposit."

To give herself more time for casual questioning, Belinda slowed the check-in process as much as possible. "Of course. Did Vick get many visitors?"

"Only in the last week. Before that, he had been quite the loner."

"I don't suppose you remember who his visitors were?"

"I didn't know who they were at the time. Didn't know it was going to be important."

"Probably men from that awful training camp outside of town."

"No," Mary Sue replied. "You'd be amazed—the man who came to see him two nights before the murder was Vietnamese."

Belinda's eyes widened. "You're certain?"

"Of course. How could I mistake something like that? I thought it was a hopeful sign—maybe the two groups were finally learning to get along. And then tragedy struck."

"Do you think you would recognize this Vietnamese man if you saw him again?"

Mary Sue reflected for a moment. "I don't know. Just

between us chickens, those Vietnamese all look the same to me."

Belinda reached into her purse and made a slow show of counting out the first night's rent. "Do you remember anything distinctive about Vick's other visitors?"

Mary Sue hiccuped. "Excuse me. Well, of course, his caller the night before the murder was a woman."

Belinda became intensely interested. "A woman! Can you describe her?"

"Oh, dark hair, slim figure. Sorta like you. Maybe a tad shorter."

"Why was she seeing Vick?"

"Well, I was afraid"—her neck stiffened—"that something not quite proper was taking place. But it turned out I was wrong. They talked for about half an hour. Then she left."

Belinda phrased her next question delicately. "You're certain they just . . . talked?"

Mary Sue's darting eyes moved over Belinda's head and up the stairs. "I happened to be in the hallway outside his room. I overheard them talking."

"Did you overhear what they were saying?"

"Of course not. What do you take me for, a busybody?"

Ben suppressed a guffaw.

"I do remember this," Mary Sue said. "The woman's voice was almost hysterical. She was crying, gasping words between sobs. I became concerned and listened more carefully. I heard her say, 'I don't know what to do,' and then, not too long after that, I heard a sentence that ended with, 'a baby.'"

Ben committed the remarks to memory.

"Sounded to me like they had done something they shouldn't and Donald was pressuring her to—well, you know. Men are like that. Only one thing on their minds, and once they've had it, they don't care what happens to you."

"Did you hear anything else?"

"No. After that, I went downstairs for Old Sally. I figured the two of us would intercede before he compromised that poor girl any further. But by the time I got back upstairs, it was too late. I heard a banging noise, and for the first time ever I heard Donald raise his voice. And then the woman left. Went flying out of his room, ran down the stairs, and disappeared."

"Have you seen this woman since that time?"

"Nope. Never saw her before, never seen her since. Don't know where she went."

Well, Ben thought, they would just have to find out.

"I don't suppose you were at the fight the next day," Belinda asked. "At the Bluebell Bar?"

"Indeed I was. Quite an eye-opener."

"Would you mind telling me what happened?"

"It was pretty much like the paper described it. The *Herald* don't make many mistakes." Ben attempted to contain himself. "There was one detail they left out, though."

"What was that?"

"Well, the article made it sound as if Donald just walked up to Vuong and started slugging. Not so. Believe me, I was there, and I watched them the whole time. Donald talked to Vuong for two or three minutes first. They were whispering, but I could tell it was a heated conversation all the same."

"And then?"

"I guess Vuong said something Donald didn't like. I never saw anything like it before. Donald's face just changed—it was like Jekyll turning into Hyde. He became enraged. Grabbed Vuong by the collar and slung him across the bar. That's how the fight began."

Belinda nodded. "Thank you so much for your kindness. I'll be in late tonight, probably after dinnertime."

"That's all right, sweetheart. I'll put a cold plate in the fridge for you."

"That would be wonderful. Say, is something in the kitchen burning?"

"Oh my!" Mary Sue skittered back toward the kitchen, banging her leg on the coffee table on her way. Belinda took advantage of her absence to grab Ben and pull him out the door.

* 21 *

"Good work," Ben said as they walked down Maple together. "You got a lot more out of Mary Sue than I did. Despite the fact that you're"—he lowered his voice to a hush—"a *lawyer*."

Belinda laughed. "Mary Sue certainly has been taking an active interest in the affairs of her lodgers. I'm not sure how reliable her information is, though."

"Why is that?"

"Surely you noticed. Mary Sue is an alcoholic."

"What? How can you tell?"

"Didn't have much choice. I smelled her breath. Plus, I saw her tentative stride, her glazed eyes. She'd definitely had a few."

"That doesn't necessarily make her an alcoholic."

"It's still morning, Ben. No one drinks this time of day unless they need it. And let's not forget she was at the Bluebell Bar when the big fight occurred. In the afternoon."

"Perhaps you're right. Still, she couldn't have imagined that entire story about the woman who visited Vick."

"No. Pity we don't know who the woman was."

"Agreed. I'll ask Vick, but I don't think he'll tell me." Ben thought for a moment. "I wonder if any of Vick's comrades-in-hate would know?"

"It's possible. Especially if she was a woman they were passing around."

"That settles it. I'm going to pay the ASP camp a visit."

"Ben—no!" Belinda reached out and pressed her hand against his shoulder. "Those men are killers. Every one of them."

"The fact that they belong to a repellent organization doesn't necessarily make them killers."

"Ben, believe me. I've been tracking these creeps for years. They've left a trail of bodies in their wake a mile long. They're remorseless."

"Don't worry. I can take care of myself."

Belinda shook her head. "You remind me so much of myself it's scary. You sound just like I did two years ago. Before I learned better." She turned away and gazed up at the clear blue sky. "You remember John mentioning that ASP came after me, in Birmingham."

Ben's eyebrows knitted together. "He said Frank saved you."

"Eventually, yes. After they'd held me captive over four hours." Despite the brightness of the sun, her eyes became dark and clouded. "I was leaving Hatewatch late one night, alone. They grabbed me outside my office. Four of them. All wearing hoods. Twisted my arms behind my back, tied a gag so tight it cut my face. They threw me in the back of my car and pinned me down with a boot in my back."

Instinctively Ben reached out and took her hand.

"After over an hour's drive we arrived at their secret meeting place. At least fifty of them were there, all hiding beneath hoods. They dragged me to the center of a field—by my hair. Tore big chunks of it out of my scalp. Then they tied me to a wooden cross surrounded by kindling and wrapped a rope around my neck. Made me think they were going to burn me alive. Or hang me. Or both."

She inhaled deeply. "Then the leader approached me. With a knife."

Ben squeezed her hand tighter.

"He pressed the knife against my neck, my face. He toyed with me. Of course, it was Grand Dragon Dunagan, but I'll never be able to prove it. He hooked the knife inside the collar of my blouse ..." She looked down at the ground and covered her eyes. ". . . then cut the blouse off my body. Then he cut loose my skirt. Underclothes, too. Bra, panties. I was tied to that cross, stark naked, clothes dangling from my wrists and around my ankles."

Ben's hands trembled. "Did—did they . . . ?"

"Rape? No, that wasn't the first item on his agenda. He ran the blade all over my body, threatening me. Fondling me with his knife. Then he put it down and took up a bullwhip."

"My God! They didn't—"

"They did. Twenty-five times." Her eyes began to well up. "I've still got the scars to prove it. They might still be beating me if Frank hadn't shown up with the cops. Although I think they had something else planned for me later."

Ben took her into his arms and pressed her head against his shoulder.

"The ASPers got away, but at least Frank rescued me before—" Her voice choked. "Before it was too late."

"And after all that," he murmured, "you're still fighting them."

"More than ever," she said solemnly. "So you see how dangerous it would be for you to go to that camp."

Ben embraced her tightly. She didn't seem uncomfortable, and he certainly wasn't going to be the one to end it. "Well, at the moment they seem to be my friends."

"That won't last long once you start asking the hard questions. Ben, this is not a smart idea."

"I'm sorry. I have to."

Belinda gripped his arm. "You don't know what you're getting into. I don't want you to—I—" She stopped, reformulated her sentence. "Ben, don't do it."

They looked at one another, their lips barely inches apart. "I don't have any choice," Ben said. He stroked her cheek. "But thanks for being concerned. It's a refreshing change."

* 22 *

Finding the ASP encampment deep in the Ouachita Mountains was not easy for Ben, but then, Ben was not great with directions. Geographically challenged, Christina called him. Being male, of course he didn't ask for help. Not that there was anyone to ask on this particular occasion.

The map he had obtained from District Attorney Swain got him to the end of the dirt road, but from there he had to walk an additional half mile on foot. Honda Accords were not generally considered all-terrain vehicles. The journey was an exhausting series of ascents and descents. Ben felt winded after the first fifteen minutes. There was no point in kidding himself; he wasn't in shape for this sort of exertion.

Finally Ben topped the final hill and saw the ASP camp in the valley below. The encampment was surrounded by a barbed-wire fence. To his relief, he didn't see anyone on duty at the sentry posts. He had a hunch visitors weren't greeted with open arms.

Attempting to look casual, Ben pushed open the heavy metal gate bearing a friendly sign that said TRES-PASSERS WILL BE SHOT. In a clearing, perhaps a hundred yards away, he saw about fifty men running through field maneuvers. They were dressed in camouflage-green fatigues, heavy boots, web gear, and matching caps. They were all carrying weapons; from where Ben stood, they looked like assault rifles.

A brief glance was sufficient to tell Ben that these men took what they were doing very seriously. Their expressions were determined and they rarely missed a step. Two men stood apart from the rest, barking out commands. Drill sergeants, apparently. He heard one of them shouting about *kill zones*.

This explained why no one was guarding the front door, Ben thought. They were all out in the field high-stepping through tires and crawling under wires on their elbows. He was relieved, although he realized this could make it difficult for him to interview anyone. On the other hand, it could give him an unexpected opportunity to survey the grounds unrestricted.

Four barrackslike buildings were positioned in the center of the encampment. They were cheap, portable, prefab constructions that kept the rain off your head and not much else. Two were considerably larger than the others. One of them was blackened on the north side, as if it had been subjected to a mild fire.

Ben stretched up on his tiptoes and peered through the window of the building closest to him, one of the large ones. The main interior room was filled with cots lined so close together they almost touched. These two buildings must be where the men slept, Ben realized. At least, those who didn't have a place in town like Vick.

Ben assumed that one of the other two buildings performed an administrative function. And that meant, with any luck, he might find files. Records. Maybe the answers to a few of his hundred or so questions about Donald Vick.

Ben was just rounding the building and heading toward the door when he heard a loud voice directly behind him.

"Intruder!"

Before Ben had a chance to react, someone knocked his feet out from under him. He slammed into the side of the building, then thudded down on the ground.

He shook his head, trying to regain his bearings. He rolled over onto his back, just in time to get the business end of an M-16 poked directly into his face.

* 23 *

"Wait a minute!" Ben shouted. "Don't shoot!"

"Shut your goddamn mouth!" the soldier hovering over him growled.

Two other men appeared on either side of the first, seemingly from nowhere. They were all dressed in standard ASP drill uniforms. They even had black charcoal smeared on their faces.

"Report, private!" one of the newcomers shouted.

"Sir, yes, sir!" The young man raised his gun and stood at attention. Ben took the opportunity to climb back to his feet. "Found the intruder sneaking around the barracks. Saw him looking through the window. He must be the one. Sir!"

The leader, a brown-haired man only marginally older than his so-called private, glared at Ben. "I'm Corporal Holloway. Do you have a pass?"

Ben swallowed. "Well, no . . ."

Corporal Holloway grabbed Ben by the neck and shoved him back down on the ground. Ben fell to his knees and caught himself by his hands, but a swift kick from one of the men's boots flattened him. His chin pounded against the dirt.

"Search him, privates!"

Ben felt four hands roaming all over his backside. He

didn't care much for the sensation, but under the circumstances, he decided not to complain.

After the search was completed, Holloway pried the butt of his rifle under Ben's ribs and rolled him onto his back. One of the privates clamped his hand down on Ben's throat, securely pinning him to the ground.

"Who authorized your presence?" Corporal Holloway barked.

Ben didn't feel lying would improve his standing in the community. "No one."

"State your business!"

Where to begin. "Well," Ben said hoarsely, "I came for information—"

"*Spy!*" The private squeezed his throat.

"Look—" The grip on Ben's larynx was so tight he could barely whisper. "I'm not any kind of—"

"Who sent you?"

"No one sent me."

Holloway drove a boot into Ben's ribs. The kick would have smarted under the best of circumstances, but in this case, it landed in the area already softened up by Deputy Gustafson's pummeling the night before last.

"Let's try it again," Holloway said, teeth clenched. "Who sent you? Hatewatch, or the gooks?"

Ben tried to focus on the question, but he kept thinking: Belinda was right. When would he learn to rely on the sound advice of people with common sense? "I'm here for Donald Vick, actually."

"Stupid choice." Another kick to his ribs. This time the impact was so violent it knocked the air out of his lungs. Ben wasn't sure he would be able to breathe anymore. "Stupid spy. You chose the only member of the camp who isn't here anymore."

Ben felt a sudden wave of nausea so great it was almost impossible for him to speak. No great loss. Everything he said only made matters worse.

"We'll put him in detention," Holloway said. It was an order, not a suggestion. "Till the Grand Dragon has a chance to interrogate him."

"Sir. Where should we put him, sir?"

"I think the Box would be a good place for this spy," Holloway said. "Especially on a hot summer day like today. After a few hours in there, he'll be begging to talk to us. Ripley, Short! Take the prisoner to the Box." He paused. "See that he comes to some harm along the way."

"Yes, sir!" they answered in unison.

"What the *hell* is going on here?"

It was a familiar shout. Corporal Holloway suddenly stood at attention. "Sir. We found the spy surveying the grounds, sir!"

"Your alleged spy is Ben Kincaid, Holloway!" It was Sonny Banner, the leader of Ben's ASP bodyguards. Ben hadn't seen him since he got out of jail. "He's the man who's representing Private Vick."

"He's the mouthpiece?" Holloway's demeanor slipped, if only for a second. "We didn't know. Sir. I mean—"

"Did you ask him to identify himself?" Banner demanded.

"Of course. He—"

"Did he tell you he represented Private Vick?"

"Sir. I—" Holloway paused. "Well, he mentioned Vick's name—"

"Consider yourself on report!" Banner barked. "I'll fill out the paperwork when I have time. You can count on it." He extended his hand to Ben.

Who, me? Ben thought. And just when the dirt was starting to feel comfy. They clasped hands. Ben's ribs had no desire to be elevated, but he let himself be pulled upright nonetheless.

"This man is more valuable to us than you will ever be, Holloway," Banner said sharply. Poor Holloway— Ben was almost starting to feel sorry for him.

Banner straightened Ben up and brushed off his shirt. "Are you all right?"

"I think I can walk. . . ."

"Good man." He slapped Ben on the back. The slap was almost as painful as Holloway's kicks. "What can I do for you?"

Ben thought quickly. "I'd like to speak to the Grand Dragon. It's about the case."

"Of course. I'll arrange it immediately." Banner turned back for a parting shot. "I'll be speaking to the Grand Dragon about you, also, Corporal Holloway. I wonder if you shouldn't spend some time in the Box yourself."

Holloway didn't respond, but the terrified expression on his face spoke volumes.

"Come on, Ben." Banner clamped his thick arm around Ben's shoulders. "I hope you can forget what happened here. This was inexcusable. You're a VIP—a Very Important Person—to the members of ASP. From now on I guarantee you'll be given the respect you deserve."

Ben wasn't sure which sickened him more—the way Holloway treated him, or the way Banner did.

* 24 *

Ben was escorted into the smallest of the ASP buildings. It appeared to be their strategic command post.
The outer room was filled with charts and maps, many
with colored pins stuck in the various places. Ben might
be geographically challenged, but he could still tell the
maps were of the surrounding countryside, including
Coi Than Tien.

Banner let Ben wait in the outer room with the two
privates while he stepped inside. Ben scanned the papers on the desks and table and glanced nonchalantly
into the file cabinets. The immensity of the paperwork
astounded him. He doubted if the volume of reporting
and memo writing could be much greater at the Penta-
gon. That in itself was sobering—what were these people planning in such minute detail? He would love a
chance to sort through these files at his leisure, but
since the privates were standing nearby, desperate for a
chance to redeem themselves, he decided to keep his
curiosity in check.

In a side room, Ben found a printing press that was
furiously spitting out paper. He picked up two fliers
bundled on the floor. One announced that SCIENTISTS
SAY GOOKS STILL IN APE STAGE. The front of the other displayed a comic-book drawing of an Asian male with a

leering, malevolent expression on his face. The headline read: THE ONLY GOOD GOOK IS A DEAD GOOK.

Ben opened the flier. "A yellow thieving baboon," the interior text read. "He will steal your job, your wife, your daughter. He will live on welfare while taking everything you have. He is the enemy."

"The Grand Dragon will see you now," Banner announced.

Ben dropped the flier on the floor with the others. As they crossed the hall Banner whispered, "You don't know how lucky you are. The Grand Dragon is a very busy man."

"He certainly generates a tremendous amount of paperwork."

"Big plans in the works," Banner said ominously. "Big plans. The Grand Dragon hasn't taken a visitor in weeks. Totally blew off that DA schmuck the other day. But when I told him you were here, he put down what he was doing and told me to bring you in immediately."

"I'm honored."

They entered an inner office in the back of the barracks, with the two privates close behind. "Ben, this is Grand Dragon Dunagan."

Dunagan rose from his chair, removed his glasses, and approached Ben, arm outstretched. He was a short man, balding, with the last remnants of his red hair clinging to either side of his bald head. He had a generally healthy, ruddy appearance, although his beltline showed some middle-aged spread. No more so than usual for a man Ben judged to be in his early fifties.

Ben had expected the physical incarnation of evil, and instead he found himself greeted by a man who could only be described as perfectly ordinary.

"Pleased to meet you, Mr. Kincaid." Dunagan had the

vigorous handshake of a Baptist preacher. "This is a great task you've taken on. A noble deed."

"Call me Ben. I didn't have much choice, to be honest."

"Don't soft-soap me, Ben. You're a brave man to accept this challenge when the forces of Satan gather all around us. Banner and the other boys told me about the beating you took at the jailhouse from that gook-loving deputy. Around here you're a hero."

"It was nothing. Really. All I did was lie on the floor and try not to bleed too much."

Dunagan shook his head. "It's a shame, you know, how those gooks have got everyone in this town on edge."

"You blame the civil unrest on the Vietnamese?"

"Damn right. They were the ones who invaded this peaceful country. They slashed their prices and agreed to work for the big chicken-processing outfits for next to nothing. Made it damn near impossible for the white man to compete."

"Sounds like they're guilty of being shrewd businessmen."

"It isn't just that. They've been stirring up trouble since we arrived. Did you see that scorching on the barracks where we store our weapons?"

Ben nodded.

"Firebomb. In the middle of the night. We put it out before it caused much damage, but what if we hadn't? That whole building would've gone up in an explosion you'd hear from here to Branson." Dunagan folded his arms across his chest. "You tell me who did that, if not the Vietnamese."

"I'm afraid I don't know," Ben said. "This is the first I've heard of it."

"Hell. I'm sorry to get on my soapbox like that. You

didn't come all the way out here to listen to my problems." Dunagan pulled a chair out from under a table and gestured for Ben to sit. "What can I do for you?"

Ben settled himself in the chair. "For starters, I'd like as much background information as I can get about Donald Vick. I've spoken to Donald, but he hasn't been very communicative."

"Hmmm." Something seemed to be bothering Dunagan, but he didn't say what it was. "Well, you've come to the right place. I've known Donny for years."

"He's been a member of your ... organization for some time, then?"

"Donny? No, he's only twenty-one. We don't take them much younger than that. But his father was a lifetime member, just like his father before him."

"Runs in the family."

"Exactly. Back in Alabama, people have strongly held beliefs, and they tend to pass those beliefs from one generation to the next. Hell, in today's world, when children are bombarded with all kinds of crap by television and movies and the left-wing press, a father has to do whatever he can to set his kids straight. Otherwise the poor bastards become totally screwed up."

The Grand Dragon as Dr. Spock. Interesting. "So Vick's father brought him into the organization."

"Hell, yes. Like father, like son. Frankly we don't care much for people who stand off to the side and let others do what needs to be done. You're either with us, or against us. That's how I look at it."

"So Donald grew up under the loving arm of the Klan."

"Now wait a minute—we're not the Klan. We're not unfriendly to the Klan, mind you, but we're our own separate organization." He winked jovially. "As a lawyer, I'm sure you understand the importance of maintaining these distinctions."

Principally the importance of avoiding liability for civil lawsuits filed against the Klan, Ben surmised. What a great bunch of people.

"But yes," Dunagan continued, "I've known Donny since he was knee-high to a billy goat. A fine boy. Raised right. Loves the Lord God Almighty and is willing to fight for him, too. Bit on the quiet side, but there's no law against that, is there?"

"No," Ben said, not that he thought Dunagan was overly concerned about the prohibitions of law. "So Donald is fulfilling familial expectations?"

"Very much so. I knew Donny's pappy, Lou. He was a tough man. A little hard on Donny, but it was for his own good. He let the boy know what he expected in no uncertain terms. Nothing wrong with that. The world would be a better place if more fathers weren't afraid to be fathers."

"You used the past tense," Ben said. "Has Donald's father died?"

"Oh, yes. He passed on three, four years ago. Lung cancer got him, rest his soul. Since his pappy died, Donny's been the man of the family. It's important that he act like it."

"If he's the head of a household, I'm surprised he would leave home and come out here."

"I'm sure he wasn't happy about it," Dunagan replied, "but a man has obligations. When the war is on, a man has to leave the comforts of home behind and do his duty."

When the war is on? Ben decided to let it slide for the moment. "Just exactly . . . how far does Donald's duty extend?"

"Ben, I'm an honest man. I don't tell lies. If you've got a question to ask, just ask it."

"Okay. Did you order Donald to kill Vuong?"

"Absolutely not."

"Did anyone else in ASP?"

"Again, no. I can't say I was particularly distraught about that gook's death, but no one ordered it. Donny was acting on his own initiative." He grinned. "Looks to me like Donny had a little too much to drink and let his righteous anger go to his head."

"I see. Is Donald . . . fond of you?"

Dunagan twisted his shoulders. "What in hell are you insinuating?"

"You said you've known him for years. Are you close?"

"I suppose so. In the manner totally appropriate for two men. What are you getting at?"

"Donald isn't telling me all he knows about this case. It occurred to me he might be protecting someone."

"And you think it's me? I sure as hell didn't kill that Vietconger."

"I didn't say you did. As Donald's lawyer, though, I have to explore all the possibilities."

"I guess so. Still, I don't know of anyone he's protecting. I think Donny got into this on his own authority. And Jesus Christ's, of course."

That would make for an interesting co-conspirator indictment. "Does Donald have any friends here?"

"Not really. There are other men in his platoon, of course. But they aren't what you would call friends. Donny is kinda shy. Always has been. Doesn't socialize much with the other men."

"What about women? Girls. Was he dating anyone?"

"I'm not sure." He snapped his fingers. "Except, now

that you mention it, I do seem to recall hearing about him being involved with some girl from town."

Ben wondered if it was the same woman who visited him at Mary Sue's boardinghouse. "Do you know who she was?"

"Sorry, no."

"Who told you about this?"

Dunagan reflected for a moment. "I can't remember. To tell the truth, I can't remember any more about it than I've already told you."

"Do you know how Donald met Vuong?"

"I assume they bumped heads at that bar where they had the big bust-up."

"I have reason to believe they knew each other before that night."

"I don't think so," Dunagan said firmly. "We don't allow fraternization with the chinks."

"Still," Ben said, "Donald was staying in town. . . ."

"That doesn't mean anything!" Irritation tinged Dunagan's voice. "He's just the kind of boy who prefers to keep his own company. Whose side are you on, anyway?"

"Donald's. I want to represent him to the best of my ability. What do you know about the murder?"

"Just what I read in the papers."

"You haven't heard any inside information from your men? Suggestions? Rumors? Gossip?"

"I don't gossip. Bearing false witness is a crime against God."

"You've heard how the murder was committed?"

Dunagan nodded.

"You said that building outside is stockpiled with weapons. Are you by any chance stocking . . . crossbows?"

"As a matter of fact, we are. Crossbows are a critical

survival weapon. Rifles run out of ammunition and eventually become useless. But as long as you take care of the bow and retrieve the bolts, a crossbow can be used forever."

Ben decided to be bold. "Do you mind if I check your supplies? I'd like to see if the weapons you're keeping are compatible with the murder weapon."

"Too late. The DA's already done it."

"Oh?" Ben was surprised, although he realized he shouldn't be. He knew Swain had been out here. "What did he say?"

"Said the crossbow was swiped from our armory. But the funny thing is—we don't stock the bolts for it. We've tried, but we've never been able to locate bolts for that particular model. I don't know where the killer got them."

"Do you mind if I examine your purchase orders or supply invoices?"

"I don't have any."

"What?"

"Don't keep up with that trash. Don't have enough room for it. And I don't need any more paperwork."

Ben tried another tack. "Do you mind if I have a word with some of your men?"

"Of course not. Feel free. I want to support you in any way I can. Remember, Ben, this is a holy crusade. When the war's on, we all have to hang together."

Or we'll surely hang separately, Ben thought grimly. "All this planning is impressive, but . . . there isn't any war on, is there?"

"Depends on how you look at it," Dunagan said. "Some people think there is."

"I don't know what you mean."

Dunagan leaned over the edge of his desk. "Ben, how

long do you think this country can go on the way it is now?"

"I'm not sure what—"

"Street gangs. Race riots. Crime, rape, sodomy—most of it committed by members of the nonwhite races. Biracial marriages tainting the gene pool. You saw what happened in L.A. a while back. It happens on a smaller scale every day. Hell, stuff goes on in Alabama that would curdle your blood. And it rarely makes the papers."

"Unreported crimes?"

"Oh, they're reported—the papers just won't print it. They're all controlled by left-wingers." He leaned in closer. "This country is teetering on the edge of total chaos. Thank goodness we don't have the Russkies to worry about anymore—but we have another threat that's even more dangerous. A threat from within."

"You're hypothesizing about . . . a race war?"

"Ain't nothing hypothetical about it. It's gonna happen. I give this country about five more years—on the outside. Maybe less. Then all hell breaks loose. Communication lines break down, transportation systems crash. The world in turmoil."

Ben was beginning to get the drift. "That's when this camp comes into play, right?"

"This isn't the only one. We've got camps in five different states. We only set up this camp when we were called to serve the cause here a few months ago. But you're right. When the end comes, we'll be ready. We've got everything we need here—food, water, clothing, ammunition."

"So this is not only a training camp, but a survivalist camp."

"The ASP camps will be a sanctuary—the vanguard of the future for the Aryan race. The men of ASP will be the pale riders, leading the survivors to a brave new world. While all the minorities butcher one another, we'll rope off our own territory and wait for the holocaust to end."

"So you'll hole up in your camps till the heat passes?"

Dunagan smiled. The smile sent chills down Ben's spine. "I expect our territory to expand over time. After all, we'll be better armed, and better prepared, than anyone else. And we'll have the righteous favor of God on our side."

"So you're going to take over?"

"In time, perhaps. Most importantly the scourge must be eradicated. The impure races must be expunged." He gripped Ben by the shoulders. "We must provide a better world for our children. Don't you agree?"

"Well, yes, but—"

"We cannot back away from the challenge God has placed before us. We must be ready to stare Satan in the eye." Dunagan rose to his feet, his eyes glowing. "We must be willing to put our lives on the line. We must be willing to fight. Fight, fight, *fight!*"

To Ben's amazement, the other three ASP men in the room joined in the chant. "Fight! Fight! *Fight!*"

"Blood!" Dunagan shouted.

"Blood! Blood! *Blood!*" the men chanted. "Fight! Fight! *Fight!*"

"Kill the enemy!" Dunagan shouted.

"Fight! Fight! Fight! Kill! Kill! Kill!" The men's voices grew louder with each chant. *"Blood! Blood! Blood!"*

Horrified, Ben edged toward the door. And then, just as suddenly as it had begun, the chanting stopped.

Dunagan wrapped his arm around Ben's shoulder. "I'm sorry, Ben. We tend to get emotional around here. We take what we do very seriously."

Ben couldn't seem to frame a reply. His hands were shaking. He wanted Dunagan to remove his arm in the worst way.

"We should get together again. Maybe someplace more social."

Ben hoped his head appeared to be nodding, not trembling.

"Why don't you come to church Sunday morning? We worship at a little place a few miles from here. Used to be a Methodist church; we took it over and converted it to our own use. I'm afraid it's near the Vietcong settlement, but as long as you come in from the north, you'll never notice. We're upwind."

The other men in the room laughed heartily.

Ben steadied himself long enough to shake Dunagan's hand and murmur some meaningless pleasantry. Then he made a beeline for the front door and didn't stop until the ASP camp was far behind him.

* 25 *

Nhung Vu set the three boxes down and searched his pockets for the keys to the broken-down '68 Oldsmobile communally owned by Coi Than Tien. The car was a relic, an embarrassment, but it was all that was available to him today. They only had two cars, and Elder Dang had taken the other for the day. Come to that, the '74 Ford Pinto might be worse than the Oldsmobile.

Nhung slid the first box of supplies into the front seat, careful not to break or spill anything. He didn't want Pham to be angry with him. Many of Pham's followers still did not want Nhung included in their group, even after he proved himself during the midnight raid. He was too young, they said. Too green.

For the time being, Pham had restricted Nhung to supply runs and similar unimportant tasks. Nhung didn't care. He would do whatever he could for Pham. And when the time came for Pham to give him a more important duty to perform, he would be ready.

Nhung shoved the second box into the car. He had to hurry. The supply run had taken far longer than he anticipated. Pham was meeting with his key followers at six. Nhung didn't want to miss it. They would surely discuss the midnight raid, as well as their plans for the future.

Nhung had hoped the firebomb would scorch ASP off

the face of the earth, but it hadn't. At the very least, though, maybe now they would leave Coi Than Tien alone. Maybe now the violence would end. Maybe now—

"All by yourself, gook?"

Nhung dropped the third box onto the concrete. Bottles shattered, spilling their liquid contents.

"Clumsy little nigger, ain'tcha?"

There were four of them, and they had him surrounded. They weren't wearing their ASP uniforms, but he knew who they were, just the same.

One of them peered down at Nhung, leering. It was the guard. The one Nhung and the others had fought during the midnight raid.

"Please, sirs," Nhung said. To his embarrassment, his voice broke. "I must take these supplies back to my family. They are hungry and my sister is very ill."

The ASP guard appeared to be the group leader. He dipped his finger in the spillage. "Your family eats combustible chemicals, I see. Don't you dumb gooks know that's dangerous? Probably not very tasty, either."

The other three ASP men laughed. Nhung tried to bolt through their ranks, but they grabbed him and shoved him back against the car. His chin bashed against the hood.

The leader ripped the car keys out of Nhung's hands. He opened the back door and shoved Nhung inside. The ASPers sat on either side of him while the leader drove. They pulled out of the parking lot and headed toward Maple.

Nhung looked desperately all around him. What would these men do? How much did they know? Through the car window, he saw a man he recognized from town, the editor of the newspaper, walking down the street. Nhung flung himself against the car window and shouted at the top of his lungs.

The driver floored the accelerator, and the man sitting next to Nhung yanked him back into his seat. Before Nhung could speak again, the man slapped him brutally across the face. Nhung cried out, this time in pain. Apparently his ASP host didn't know the difference. He hit Nhung again, with a clenched fist. Nhung's head thudded back against the car seat.

Nhung didn't remember much else about the drive. The sun set and it soon became dark. He couldn't tell where he was or where he was going. He was dazed; his mind seemed to flicker in and out of consciousness. His mouth and jaw ached, and two of his teeth felt as if they had been knocked loose. He wanted to run, but there was nowhere to go. He wanted to cry, but he knew it would only make matters worse.

The car stopped finally and they hauled Nhung out. Many more ASPers were assembled in a clearing in full regalia, including hoods. They hauled Nhung past a blazing campfire toward a wooden post in the center of the assemblage.

No—it wasn't a post, Nhung realized. It was a cross.

They wrapped a thin cord around his hands and feet, then tied him to the cross. The ASP men moved closer, encircling him, none of them speaking. The field of green hoods filled Nhung with terror.

One of them approached. He was shorter and larger than the man who had beaten him in the car. This man stared at Nhung for a long moment, then walked behind him. A moment later, Nhung felt his shirt being ripped off his back.

Another man in green advanced. He was cracking a bullwhip over his head.

Nhung wanted to be brave, but it was too hard, too

impossible. He clenched his eyelids shut and cried. "Please don't," he whispered. "Please don't—"

The tail of the whip smacked his exposed back. Nhung screamed, a loud high-pitched wail. He felt as if his back had been split open, as if the skin had been ripped off and the soft wet underflesh left exposed.

The whip cracked again. The nerve-shattering pain pierced his back like a dagger. He was certain he could not bear it any longer. And then they hit him again.

His knees weakened. If he had not been tied to the cross, he would have collapsed. The man wielding the whip was quite skilled; each blow landed in almost exactly the same place as the previous one, deepening the wound, intensifying the agony.

The whip sounded again and again and again. Nhung's vision began to blur. He felt his consciousness fading.

And then, as abruptly as it had begun, the whipping stopped. The wind whistled through the trees, stinging Nhung's back, licking at the open wound. But the whip did not crack.

The ASP men were moving away from him, huddling around the campfire. They worked busily at some task, but Nhung couldn't tell what it was. He heard a few chuckles, then some malevolent laughter.

He became very scared.

The ASP huddle parted, and through wet and blurry eyes Nhung saw what they were doing. The short man, the one who had torn his shirt, was in the center, stoking the fire. No, that wasn't it. He was holding something in the flames. Something long and thin, like a poker.

The man raised the iron object high above his head. Now Nhung could see it clearly. It wasn't a poker.

It was a branding iron.

The hooded men on all sides began to chant. "Blood, blood, *blood*," they cried. "Death, death, *death*."

"We will strike back against the enemy," the man with the iron cried out. "We will fight and fight until the land is pure once more!"

"Please don't do this," Nhung begged them. "Oh, God! Please no. Please no!"

"Death, death, *death*," they chanted, even louder than before. *"Kill, kill, kill!"*

The short man held the glowing iron an inch from Nhung's face. The heat emanating from it stung Nhung's eyes. The brand was in the shape of a cross.

The short man ripped the drooping tatters of Nhung's shirt off his chest.

"No," Nhung whimpered, over and over. "I'll do anything. Please. *Please*—"

He heard a hideous hissing noise, followed by the most searing pain he had ever felt, had ever imagined. It burned through his chest and ignited every nerve in his body. His agonized shout reverberated through the twilight. And to his horror, he found that when the iron was removed, his suffering was even greater.

The only mercy was that he fell into deep unconsciousness and, as a result, wasn't aware of what they did to him next.

* 26 *

Ben was gratified to find that Deputy Gustafson was not on duty when he arrived at the jailhouse the next morning. Sheriff Collier waved Ben through, never once making eye contact with him. Ben wondered how much he knew about the beating Gustafson had dished out when Ben was here before. More than he cared to acknowledge, Ben guessed.

Vick was the only inmate of the county jail that afternoon, which Ben realized had probably been true for most of the time Vick had spent behind bars. That had to get lonely, day after day. Ben only hoped the mounting loneliness would make Vick more talkative than he had been last time around.

Vick rose from his cot when he saw Ben come down the hallway. "Are you here for a visit," he asked, "or are you staying the night?"

"I'm definitely not staying the night," Ben answered. "Ever again, if I can help it."

Vick grabbed the cell bars. "What makes you think you can spring me from this hellhole when you can't keep yourself out?"

"That night was no party for me," Ben said. "But you'll notice that I'm free now and you're still behind bars."

"Good point." For a fleeting moment, Vick's lips

149

formed something that might have been a smile, or at least a smirk. "How's the eye?"

"Much better, thanks."

"What ticked off Gustafson so bad?"

"Principally the fact that I'm representing you."

"Oh." That caused Vick to reflect for a moment. Good. Ben was more than willing to let Vick be motivated by guilt. "Guess this was a bad career move for you."

"Guess so. Mind if I ask you a few questions?"

Vick instantly pushed away from the bars. "About what?"

"This case, of course. How can I represent you without any facts?"

"I told you I want to plead—"

"Nonetheless I can't handle this case without more information. You think I can just make the facts up as I go along?"

"I wouldn't be surprised."

Ben decided to move on to the questions. "I've been to the boardinghouse where you were staying, and I've talked to Mary Sue. She says you had some visitors shortly before the murder."

Vick didn't respond.

"Mary Sue described one of your visitors as Vietnamese. That wouldn't have been Tommy Vuong by any chance, would it?"

A deep furrow formed over Vick's eyes. "Why would I meet with him?"

"I can't imagine. But I don't think you met him for the first time in that bar. I think you two had some history."

"Well, you're dead wrong."

"Am I?" Ben took a few steps down the hallway. "If it wasn't Vuong, who was it?"

"I don't know what Mary Sue's talking about. She has a tendency to drink more than she should. She probably hallucinated it."

"Imagined a Vietnamese visitor to a member of a white-supremacist group? Seems unlikely."

"Maybe he was visiting someone else in the house. She had several tenants."

Ben decided to move on. It was better to keep him talking, even if he was lying, than to tick him off and cause him to clam up. "Mary Sue also said someone else dropped by to see you, the night before the murder. A woman."

Vick's eyes widened ever so slightly.

"Don't deny it," Ben said. "I can already see that it's true."

"What's she accusing me of? Fornicating with the whore of Babylon?"

"Nothing quite that serious. Actually she seemed to think you just talked. At least on this particular occasion. Who was she?"

"I—I—" Vick looked away suddenly. "I can't tell you."

"Why not?" Ben clung to the bars that separated them. "Donald, I'm your lawyer. I'm on your side."

"I—" Vick averted his eyes. "I'm sorry. I made a promise."

"A promise? To whom?"

"I—can't say."

"Mary Sue said she overheard the woman mention—"

"I said I can't talk about it!"

"Donald, would you please screw your head back on? How can I represent you if you won't even tell me what you know?"

Vick folded his arms across his chest and turned away.

"Is this related to the fight at the Bluebell Bar? Or was that about something else?"

Vick didn't honor Ben's inquiry with a reply.

"What was the point of that fistfight, anyway? I can't believe you went after Vuong just because he was Vietnamese."

"He and his friends outnumbered me," Vick snapped. "They all attacked at once."

"They didn't gang up on you just for the hell of it. I heard you started the fight."

"Nonetheless, they—"

"*Why*, Donald? Everyone keeps telling me you're the quiet, soft-spoken type. From what I hear, you didn't even drink, much less hang out in bars. I think you must've gone there looking for Vuong. *Why?*"

Vick didn't respond. He sat down on his cot and faced the wall.

"Donald, answer my question!"

No change.

"Is Dunagan the one you're protecting?"

Vick's head jerked around, his eyes fierce and narrowed. After a long moment he slowly turned back toward the wall. He wasn't taking the bait.

"I know you've known Dunagan all your life and that he's an old family friend and all that crap. I also know you had a tough father with high expectations who passed away before you had a chance to satisfy him. Assuming that was possible." Ben paused. "I have some understanding of that situation myself. My guess is that your involvement with these ASP goons is part of some cockeyed plan to please your father."

Ben could see the muscles in Vick's neck tightening.

"Is that it, Donald? Are you taking the rap to protect your daddy's buddy, the Imperial Grand Dragon?"

Ben waited a long time, but no answer came.

Under different circumstances, Ben might've been willing to take Vick's silence as confirmation, but here, he just wasn't sure. There was so much he was uncertain of, so much he didn't know yet. Most of his theories were flying off his tongue as soon as he thought of them.

"Are you aware that the DA found hairs on the murder weapon? Hairs he has matched to yours."

No response.

"What about it, Donald? Have you been shedding around any crossbows lately?"

Nothing at all.

"I know they stock crossbows at the ASP training camp. I've been there."

Silence. No reply.

"Do you know what's happened to this town? It's in an uproar. Everyone's scared to death that today will be the day the fuse on the powder keg ignites and all hell breaks loose. They want your blood, Donald. They're going to give you the death penalty because they're hoping that will be enough to put Silver Springs back the way it was before you and ASP came to town. You're going to take the rap for the whole club.

"But I know they're wrong," Ben continued. "I know this town will never be the same until we find out who really killed Tommy Vuong. Can't you help me do that? Can't you help me keep your miserable butt alive?"

Not a word. Not even a twitch.

"Fine." Ben marched down the corridor, away from Vick's cell. "I just hope to hell you *don't* get what you deserve."

* 27 *

By late afternoon Ben was back at the campsite. Both Jones and Loving were gone. Ben hoped they were burrowing into their respective assignments and uncovering useful information about Donald Vick, Tommy Vuong, and ASP.

Christina was there, but she was still giving Ben the cold shoulder. Cold wasn't a strong enough adjective—glacial might be more appropriate. Subzero.

Mike was on top of his helicopter—at least Ben assumed it was Mike. All he could actually see was the top of his head. A vast array of tools and machine parts were spread on the grass around him. "What are you doing?"

Mike tried to answer, but his response was incomprehensible. After he took the wrench out of his mouth, it was better. "I'm installing some of these parts I got in Silver Springs."

"Do they fit?"

"They do after I solder them in." Mike's hand fumbled around in the grass for a tool. "My principal concern is these spark plugs. They're really meant for tractors."

"Oh, well," Ben said. "Tractors, helicopters. How different can they be?"

"Right." Mike pushed himself off and opened the

door to the cockpit. "I'm going to start her up. Will you crawl on top of the engine and tell me what happens?"

"You must be joking."

"Just tell me if the spark plugs spark. And if you spot anything else rattling loose or flying out of its housing, that would be good to know, too."

"You're out of your mind. I won't be anywhere near that bucket of bolts when you start it."

"Don't be such a chicken. I'm just going to turn over the engine. What could happen?"

"Soldered spark plugs could ignite my flesh. Aerial scrap metal could fly like shrapnel into my face."

Mike patted the hull. "I don't think you should refer to Portia as aerial scrap metal. You might hurt her feelings. Are you sure you won't keep an eye on the engine while I start it?"

"Not unless I can do it from the other side of the lake."

"My hero! By the way, while I was in town this afternoon I got the scoop on the prosecution's case. They've found the murder weapon."

"Yeah, yeah, yeah. Crossbow near the scene of the crime. Hairs in the firing mechanism. I've heard all about it."

"Is that a fact?" Mike stroked his chin. "Then you know about the bloodstain?"

"Bloodstain?" Ben said blankly.

"That's what I figured. It's the kind of zinger prosecutors like to keep to themselves until trial, if at all possible."

"But Swain told me about the hairs."

"Right. That's the straw man. He's hoping you'll expend all your energy—and cross-ex time—trying to convince the jury that the hairs don't necessarily incriminate your client. And when you've finished, Swain will stroll calmly to the podium for redirect and tell the jury about the bloodstain."

"On the crossbow?"

"You got it. And it's Vick's blood type. You might be able to talk your way out of a hair or two, but two hairs and a blood blot make for a pretty damning combination."

"Blast." Ben bit his knuckle. "And they're sure the blood is Vick's?"

"Like I said, the types match. I doubt if this burg is equipped to run microscopic analyses. But I would be"—he glanced at Portia—"if I could get back to Tulsa."

"What is this, blackmail? I'm not crawling on top of that alleged flying machine and that's final."

"Suit yourself. But I really could get some tests run. I think the lab tech in town would give me a sample from the bloodstain." He shook his head. "Sure is a long walk back to Tulsa, though."

"Mike, be reasonable!"

"I think I'm being perfectly reasonable."

"How about a compromise? I'll stand between the tents. I'll still have a clear view of the helicopter, but I'll be far enough away that the chances of being pelted by flying debris will be, oh, no better than one in two."

"I'll take what I can get. Agreed."

Mike climbed into the cockpit. Ben scurried to the relative safety afforded by the tents. Mike started the engine.

At least, that's what Ben thought Mike was doing. He had to assume Mike wasn't killing a cat, although that was more what it sounded like. There was a painfully high-pitched screeching, followed by the excruciating sound of metal grinding against metal. Not quite as bad as fingers on the chalkboard, but close. There were a few final clattering noises, followed by a loud thump from the engine casing.

Ben didn't need a close-up view to tell him that Portia was not taking off. "I don't think it's working," he shouted.

Mike turned off the power and fell dejectedly out of the cockpit. "Damn. I thought I had it that time."

"Evidently not."

"Did you hear that crash? I think the entire engine fell. It's in worse shape now than it was before."

Ben was forced to agree.

Mike shoved his hands into his pockets. "Looks like I'll be sending your blood samples to Tulsa by Federal Express, Ben." He thought for a moment. "I wonder if they can deliver helicopter parts?"

* 28 *

Belinda was already at Coi Than Tien when Ben arrived just after sunset. They had decided earlier it might be best if she went in first and prepared the way. Several members of the community had previously met her or one of her Hatewatch associates and were aware of their good works. Some of the older members probably thought Hatewatch stirred up trouble, but they were more likely to befriend her than the man who was representing Donald Vick.

Ben parked his car outside the rickety assembly of warped wood and cardboard that constituted the boundary fence of Coi Than Tien. It was a moonless night, but Ben managed to find his way to the front gates.

The largest building inside Coi Than Tien was the barn, a long rectangular structure centrally located beside two other storage buildings. The barn appeared to hold equipment and supplies. Ben couldn't see inside the two other similar but smaller buildings, but in previous years he'd had a bit of experience with chickens, and the clucking and squawking inside told him that was where the principal assets of any chicken farm were housed.

Scattered in a rough semicircle around the storage facilities were the residences of Coi Than Tien. Ben was shocked at the impoverished conditions; they were even poorer than he had imagined. Most of the homes were little better than shacks. The better ones had a few walls or perhaps a roof made of corrugated metal. Despite the obvious poverty, however, there was no squalor; on the contrary, Ben got the impression that the homes were well cared for. Some of them even had small makeshift gardens. The residents appeared to be doing the best they could with what little they had.

Ben found Belinda on the porch of one of the homes. She was sitting next to a much older Vietnamese man. The porch was dark as the night; only the glow from a thin, long-stemmed pipe provided illumination.

Belinda identified the man as Duong Dang.

"Pleased to meet you," Ben said. He wondered if she had explained what Ben's role was in the current drama. Well, he wasn't going to be the one to bring it up.

"Elder Dang is the leader of this community," Belinda explained.

"Was," Dang corrected. "I am no longer. My people will not listen."

"There's been a schism of sorts," Belinda explained. "Elder Dang and his council have always followed the path of peace and reason. But there is another faction within the community led by a young man named Dan Pham. He favors a more . . . aggressive approach. Active resistance. First-strike assaults. He's rounding up all the support he can find."

"How successful has he been?" Ben asked.

"Much too successful," Dang replied. "More than half our people now follow him."

"What exactly does Pham want to do?" Ben asked.

"Fight fire with fire," Belinda replied. "Meet the terrorist activities of ASP head-on."

"Counterterrorism?" Ben said. "Against those maniacs? Surely he knows he hasn't got a chance."

"He cannot see the truth of our situation," Dang said sadly. "He wants to be a crusader, a hero. He wants to save his people. He is blind to the realities."

"If he takes on ASP, he'll be made aware of the realities pretty damn fast," Ben said. "Maybe this is all just bluster."

Dang and Belinda exchanged a glance. "Someone tossed a firebomb into the ASP encampment," Belinda said.

"I know," Ben replied. "I saw the scorched building. You think Pham was behind that?"

"I cannot say with certainty," Dang replied. "But who else would run such a risk?"

"We've heard it didn't cause much damage," Belinda said.

"True," Ben replied. "But it could've. The bomb hit the ASP ammunition stockpile. If the fire had burned much longer, there would've been a major explosion. Fortunately that didn't happen. No one was hurt."

"No," Dang said. "But their retaliation has nonetheless been swift and brutal. One of our two automobiles was stolen this morning. And a fifteen-year-old boy, Nhung Vu, was attacked and severely beaten. Two of his teeth were knocked out. And—" Dang hesitated. His eyes closed. "They branded him. With the sign of the cross. After he was unconscious, they pounded his face, like it was a piece of meat. There may be permanent damage to his right eye."

"Have you reported this to the sheriff?"

"Of course. But what can he do? There were no witnesses. Nhung did not know his attackers. Most of them were hooded. ASP is very careful."

"You need to corner this Pham kid and tell him to cool it," Ben said. "More violence will only make matters worse for Coi Than Tien."

"It may be too late," Dang said gravely. "There are rumors that the ASP men are not finished, that they plan retaliation in even greater measure in the near future."

That was certainly bad news. Ben didn't think Coi Than Tien could withstand a full-out frontal assault by ASP. But then, who could?

"Has Belinda asked you about Tommy Vuong?" Ben asked.

"I have known Tommy for many years," Dang replied. "He came from a good and honorable family. A bit wild, but that was not unusual given his youth and vigor."

"I heard he was in some legal trouble about a year ago. Do you know anything about that?"

"He was investigated by the sheriff. Apparently a woman accused him of . . . forcing his affections upon her."

"You didn't believe the charges?"

"It is a common occurrence," Dang said gravely. "Two young people of different races fall in love. All is well until the families discover their relationship. Then stories must be created, lies must be told. Loving relationships may be turned into criminal acts."

"Then you don't believe it was rape?" Belinda asked.

Dang looked at him thoughtfully. "I know the district attorney decided not to prosecute. Given the ill will of much of Silver Springs toward Coi Than Tien, I believe that if there was any proof of her accusations, he would have arrested Tommy."

Probably right, Ben mused. Unless, of course, the DA was busy baby-sitting that night.

"Did you know of Vuong's connection to Donald Vick?"

"No," Dang said, frowning. "I very much doubt that

there was any connection before the fatal incident at the bar."

"Some Vietnamese man visited Vick shortly before the murder occurred. Do you know who that might have been?"

"I find it difficult to believe that any resident of Coi Than Tien would visit such a man for even the most desperate of reasons."

"And you don't know what Vick and Vuong fought about?"

"The men of ASP need no excuse to fight. Their hate drives them far further than any logical motive could do."

Ben tried to contain his frustration. This wasn't getting him anywhere. "Do you know why Vuong was in that bar that afternoon?"

Dang's head fell. "Alas, to my eternal regret, I do. I sent him there."

Belinda was as surprised as Ben. "You did? Why?"

"Coi Than Tien orders a small quantity of various alcoholic beverages from the Bluebell Bar on a regular basis. We use it for ceremonial purposes and, on occasion, to soothe worried brows. The owner of the bar, a man named Mac, is kind enough to order it at wholesale rates and to supply it to us at cost. In that manner, we can obtain what we need in a less expensive ... and safer manner."

"So you sent Vuong to pick up the shipment."

"Exactly. I sent him with three other young men from the settlement. I thought he would be safe." He looked down at his long, thin hands. "And now Tommy Vuong is dead."

* 29 *

Ben realized it was pointless to tell Dang not to blame himself. "I have one favor to ask. Do you think it would be possible for me to talk to this Pham fellow?"

"I can introduce you," Dang said. "Whether he will talk to you is quite another matter."

Dang led them down the dark path that lined the shacks and Quonset huts. A few minutes later they reached the Pham residence. Dang led them through the front garden and knocked on the door.

Ben noticed an older man sitting on the porch of the house next door. He appeared to be using a flashlight to read a book, but at the moment his eyes were fixed on Ben and Belinda. He was watching them carefully.

The door opened. A young Vietnamese man stood in the doorway. He glared at Elder Dang. "I told you I have no wish to continue our previous conversation!"

"I have not come to attempt to persuade you," Dang said. "I fear you have already gone so far you cannot hear the voice of reason."

Pham made no reply, but his irritation was evident.

"These kind people wish to speak to you." With that introduction of sorts completed, Dang left the porch.

"I'm Belinda Hamilton," she said. "I'm with Hate-watch."

Pham nodded politely.

"This is Ben Kincaid. He's with me." She left it at that. Ben just hoped Pham didn't read *The Silver Springs Herald.*

Apparently he didn't. "I am honored to meet you," he said. "How can I serve you?"

"We're investigating the Donald Vick case," Belinda explained.

"He must be brought to justice!" Pham said emphatically. "He must be punished for his crime."

"I'm sure we all agree," Belinda said hurriedly. "If he's guilty."

"If these men are not stopped, they will continue until we have all been killed. Did you hear what they did to young Nhung Vu?"

"I'm afraid so."

"They must be taught that they cannot treat us with such contempt. In the only way they understand."

"Are you responsible for the firebombing at the ASP encampment?" Ben asked.

Pham eyed Ben carefully. "I do not know that there was any firebombing. The camp still stands."

"The fact that the attack was unsuccessful doesn't mean it didn't happen," Ben said. "Besides, you haven't answered my question."

"We are not sheep!" Pham's voice soared. "We will not stand idly by while our families are slaughtered!"

"Well, let's not exaggerate. No families have actually been slaughtered."

"My grandmother is in the hospital! A seventy-six-year-old woman—shot by a vicious sniper. They strike our old. They strike our young. We must take action!"

Belinda dealt herself back into the conversation. "What we really wanted to know was whether you had any information about what passed between Tommy Vuong and Donald Vick."

"Tommy was a brave man," Pham answered. "He was willing to fight for his people."

"Did you ever see him with Vick? Or hear him mention Vick?"

"Of course not," Pham said. "He would not descend to the company of such swine."

"Apparently he did," Ben replied. "I think they may have met before the incident in the bar."

"I cannot believe it. Even setting aside the shame and dishonor of such a meeting, it would be suicide."

"We understand Vuong was making a supply run to the bar the afternoon of the fight. Were you one of the men who accompanied him?"

"I was not. If I had been, the result might have been different."

"I didn't get the impression Vuong needed any more muscle. Apparently they thoroughly trounced Vick."

"But they let him live." A cold glint reflected from Pham's eyes.

"Are you saying they should have *executed* him?"

"If they had, Tommy Vuong would still be alive. And my grandmother would not be in the hospital. And Nhung Vu would still have his face."

Ben felt a shudder creep up the back of his neck. Pham was obviously on the verge of some major violence. And according to Dang, he represented many others who felt the same way and were willing to do whatever Pham wanted done. "Were you the last to see Tommy alive?"

"No." Pham stepped through the door and looked to the porch of the neighboring home. "That honor fell to Colonel Nguyen."

The man on the next porch set down his book and

flashlight. He paused for a moment, then came to meet them.

Despite the man's relative shortness he had a dignity and bearing that immediately impressed Ben. His hair was cut short; flecks of gray highlighted the temples.

"Colonel Nguyen is a great war hero," Pham said. "He commanded thousands of South Vietnamese in the Great War. He led our people to many of their greatest victories."

"Not great enough," Nguyen said gruffly.

"The outcome of that war was not your fault," Pham said. "You served your country bravely and well. I only wish you would do the same in the current war."

"There is no war," Nguyen said firmly.

"There is." Disappointment clouded Pham's eyes. "I only wish you had not lost your taste for battle."

"I have lost nothing," Nguyen said. "I have only gained an understanding of the importance of caution."

Ben tried to derail what was obviously an ongoing argument and to return to the matter at hand. "I understand you were the last to see Tommy Vuong before he was killed."

"That is so. We walked together from Silver Springs back to Coi Than Tien. We only have two automobiles—one now—which we all share, so it is frequently necessary that we walk."

"Did Vuong seem unusually nervous? Scared? Edgy?"

"Only a fool would not be frightened when death is all around us." Nguyen hesitated a moment. "But there was something . . . unusual about Tommy that night. Some feeling of foreboding."

Now that was interesting. "Do you have any idea why he felt that way?"

"No. At the time I assumed he was simply expressing

the anxiety we all feel here. It was only after he was dead that I wondered if the words had more meaning."

"Did you see anything—or anyone—unusual during the walk home?"

"No. We parted just outside the fence. I returned to my home and—I assumed he would return to his."

"Then you weren't at the actual scene of the murder."

There was only the slightest hesitation. "No."

"And you didn't see what happened."

Colonel Nguyen gazed into Ben's eyes. "No."

"And you don't have any other information about the murder?"

"I—no. Nothing more than what I have already told you."

Ben couldn't put his finger on it, but for some reason, he was almost certain Colonel Nguyen was holding something back. But what reason could he have to lie?

Ben shifted the focus to Pham. "Are you planning any more attacks on the ASP encampment?"

Pham stared at him coldly. "I am not at liberty to discuss our plans."

"I know you have only good intentions," Ben said. "But your recklessness could hurt people."

"If we do not act, these killers will force us out of our homes."

"If you start a confrontation with ASP, you could destroy Coi Than Tien. And perhaps Silver Springs as well."

"We will not submit—"

A thunderous noise curtailed their debate. All four of them whirled toward the sound, just in time to see a blaze erupt about a hundred feet away. The impenetrable darkness was now illuminated by flame.

Coi Than Tien was on fire.

* 30 *

"The Truong home!" Colonel Nguyen shouted.

The wooden shack was ablaze. In the space of a second it was engulfed in flames.

The four of them ran toward the conflagration. Ben saw what looked like a black pickup truck speeding away, past the barn and through the central gates. It was too dark to get a license plate number, even if there was one.

By the time they arrived, a solid wall of fire separated them from the house. The Truong home was one of the largest in Coi Than Tien, but it was now entirely obscured. Black smoke billowed outward, choking them as they approached.

Ben shielded his eyes from the intense brightness of the flames. "Do you have any telephones here?"

Colonel Nguyen shook his head gravely. "And the nearest fire department is in the next county."

The fire raged, towering over their heads. The radiating heat was intense; it drew beads of sweat from Ben's forehead.

Ben suspected there was little chance of saving the house. They had to make sure no one was inside and, furthermore, had to make sure it didn't spread throughout the entire settlement. But how?

Ben pounded his fists together. They needed to do something, and quick. He just didn't know what.

"Didn't I see a well on my way in here?" Belinda asked. Her face was illuminated by the flickering flames.

"Yes!" the Colonel said. "Just north of the barn. And there are buckets inside the barn door."

"Ben and I will start the water brigade. You two make sure no one is trapped inside."

Colonel Nguyen nodded. Without further discussion Ben followed Belinda back to the barn.

They found the well without any trouble. The light of the blaze made the area almost as bright as day. Inside the barn, they found several dozen wooden buckets stacked against the wall.

The water in the well was easy to reach. Ben filled a bucket. Straining every muscle, he hoisted it out of the well and carried it back to the Truong home, sloshing and spilling all the way.

He threw the remaining water into the spreading flames. The fire consumed the water as if it were air. At this rate, it would burn forever.

Ben ran back to the well. By this time several Coi Than Tien citizens had emerged from their homes. Most of them had moved directly toward the well. Belinda put two strong men at the wellhead to fill the buckets. She organized everyone else in a line stretching from the well to the fire. One by one they passed the water-filled buckets down the line.

Water still sloshed out along the way, but not as much as when Ben had carried his bucket solo. Each bucketful had only minimal impact on the blaze, but a minimal impact was still an impact. Belinda's brigade delivered the water quickly and consistently. At least the fire wasn't getting any worse. It was just possible they might get it under control.

Ben started back toward the fire and saw Colonel Nguyen staggering from the flames. He was walking erratically and coughing. As he cleared the smoke Ben saw Nguyen was carrying a woman over his shoulder.

Ben ran out to help him. Together they gently lowered the woman to the ground.

Ben took one look at the unconscious woman, then quickly turned away. She was alive, but burned horribly.

"Are you all right?" Ben asked Colonel Nguyen.

Nguyen coughed loud and harshly. Seconds passed as he was unable to stop coughing. Ben feared he had severe smoke inhalation—or worse. Finally Nguyen drank in a deep gulp of air.

"Went around back," Nguyen said. "Climbed up to the nearest window, looked inside." He started coughing again.

"Take it easy," Ben said. "Breathe slow and regular."

"Wall collapsed. Fell on top of me. Burning."

Ben saw that the left side of his clothes were singed.

"Heard a scream from inside," Nguyen continued. His eyelids drooped. He was struggling to retain consciousness. "Had to get her out—" The raspy choking swallowed his voice.

"Don't try to talk," Ben said. "Just rest."

The Colonel nodded.

Ben brought Colonel Nguyen some water and put a wet cloth on the woman's forehead. She was still unconscious. Ben felt certain her burns needed medical attention. He called for help; a man from the brigade line stepped forward and huddled over the woman's body.

A piercing scream riveted Ben's attention. A woman near the end of the brigade line had dropped her bucket and clutched her face.

"What is it?" Ben asked.

Her face was distorted by the shadows cast by the blaze. Ben couldn't understand what she said. But she pointed toward the burning house.

Inside the dense smoke, Ben saw a dark silhouette hugging the ground. It moved.

Ben heard a horrible gasping and choking noise. Then it was gone.

Someone else was trapped in there.

Ben looked around for help. The brigade line was back in action, but it was stretched to its maximum capacity. They couldn't afford to lose another body. It was him or no one.

He started toward the smoke.

The woman shouted, "Wait!"

Ben turned and the woman threw a bucketful of water, drenching him. He removed his windbreaker, then inhaled and exhaled rapidly, filling his lungs. He held the jacket over his eyes and mouth and plunged into the dense gray cloud.

Ben felt the smoke burning his eyes. He had to resist the temptation to breathe. If he took smoke into his lungs, he was history.

He made his way to the body lying on the ground just outside the front door of the house. The heat was searing; he felt as if he had stepped into the sun.

It was a woman, a young one. Ben rolled her over onto her back. It was difficult to see her face clearly in the smoke, but to his surprise, he found she was not Vietnamese. A slim figure, white face, dark hair. For a brief, horrifying moment he thought it was Belinda.

No. As the smoke cleared he saw she was shorter, more angular, and had an entirely different hairstyle. But whoever she was, she was in trouble. The fire consumed the house not five feet away from them.

Ben wrapped his arms around her and lifted her into the air. She was a small woman, but the sudden weight bore down on his ribs, still tender from their recent pounding. The residual air burst out of his lungs. Ben clamped his lips shut and ordered himself not to breathe.

After what seemed an eternity, he emerged from the cloud of smoke. He laid the woman on the ground and gasped for air. It flooded into his lungs, making him woozy and nauseated all at once.

Ben braced himself against the ground. As soon as he felt relatively stable, he examined the woman. He was no medic, but she wasn't burned and she appeared to be breathing regularly. He didn't know why she had fallen unconscious. She had probably taken in too much smoke or fainted from the heat.

Her eyelids began to flutter.

"Are you all right?" Ben asked.

The woman blinked rapidly. Then, suddenly she sat up straight, eyes widened desperately, and screamed.

The cry was loud and bloodcurdling. Ben had never heard any sound so horrible in his entire life. The woman reached out toward the flames, shouting words he could not understand. Eventually her breath gave out and her screams were washed away by uncontrolled sobbing.

"What's wrong?" Ben held her by the shoulders. "What's the matter?"

The woman shook her head back and forth, crying and moaning. Tears streamed from her eyes.

"Ben!"

Ben looked back over his shoulder. It was Belinda. She was running past the burning house, searching for him.

Ben ran to her. The instant she saw him, she opened her arms and hugged him.

"My God," she said. "Someone told me you ran into the fire."

"I did. But I'm all right."

"Thank God." She clutched him so tightly Ben wondered if she would ever let go. He hoped she didn't.

He gazed over her shoulder at the Truong home. The fire was finally dying out. Only a few flames on the north side remained, and they would soon be gone. Belinda's brigade had saved the day. The woman he now held in his arms had taken charge of a desperate crisis situation and saved both homes and lives.

He squeezed her all the tighter. She was incredible. With the lingering wisps of smoke swirling around them, their lips pressed tightly together.

"Why did you go into the fire?" Belinda asked, after they parted.

"There was a woman trapped in the smoke, trying to get out."

The woman in the brigade line who had first alerted Ben to the situation interrupted. "You're wrong. She wasn't trying to get out. She was trying to get in."

Ben stared at her. *"What?"*

"I saw it. She came out of nowhere, took one look at the burning house, screamed, and ran into the flames. I thought she was crazy."

"Where is this woman?" Belinda asked. "I want to talk to her."

"She's right—" Ben turned toward the area where he had left her. "She was right here."

He ran back to the now empty place, then looked in all directions, but found nothing.

"She's gone!"

PART TWO

* *

The Silent Sentinels

* 31 *

In the orange glow cast by the sun rising over the Ouachitas, Ben and Mike surveyed the damage to Coi Than Tien. The Truong home was gone; nothing remained but charred wood and rubble. Substantial portions of the homes on both sides were also burned. The entire settlement reeked of smoke.

After Sheriff Collier finally arrived, he took Colonel Nguyen and Maria Truong, the woman Nguyen had pulled from the burning home, to a clinic in town, along with several others suffering from smoke inhalation. They never found the woman Ben had rescued. She had disappeared without a trace; no one seemed to know who she was or where she had gone.

As Ben and Mike approached the charred ruins Sheriff Collier was standing outside, scribbling in a notepad.

" 'Morning, Kincaid," Collier said, without looking up. "Glad to see you again when you're not behind bars."

Not as glad as I am, Ben thought. "Find anything interesting?"

"Lot of wasted firewood," Collier muttered. "Few personal possessions. Not much else."

"Have you determined what started the fire?"

"What am I, a fortune-teller?" the sheriff said irritably.

Ben glanced at Mike, then decided he'd better take the lead in this conversation. If Mike started lecturing the sheriff about arson, Collier would probably go off the deep end.

"Did you find any evidence of an incendiary device? Perhaps some fire-resistant casing? Maybe something as simple as a book of matches for a fuse."

Sheriff Collier eyed him suspiciously. "What makes you so sure a book of matches started the fire?"

"I'm not. I'm hypothesizing."

"Look, mister, these shacks are firetraps. No two ways about it. Probably one of these folks was smoking one of those funny pipes in bed, or trying to light a Chinese lantern, and the place caught fire."

"No way," Ben said firmly. "I was here when it happened. This was no gradual fire. We heard a loud noise, and then, a second later, the house erupted into flames. I saw a black pickup speeding away. Someone intentionally torched the house. We need to determine how they did it."

"I'll be damned if I'm going to root around in that trash heap," Collier said. "What's your interest in this, anyway? What's the connection between this fire and your boy's case?"

"I don't know," Ben answered. "But I can't help but think there is one."

Sheriff Collier closed his notepad and started toward his silver pickup. "If you're looking for some convoluted story to get your client off the hook, you might as well forget it. We're simple folk here in Silver Springs. We don't get ourselves caught up in a lot of nonsense."

"If it's all nonsense," Ben said, "you won't mind if we look through the ruins ourselves?"

Collier frowned. It was obvious he did mind, but didn't think he was in a position to offer any objection.

"Suit yourself, but if you find any evidence, I expect to hear about it."

"Believe me, you will." The sheriff drove away.

"Good work, kemo sabe," Mike said. "You played him like a violin."

"Yeah, right." He entered the ruins of the Truong home. "Aren't you an arson expert?"

"Well, I worked arson cases for two years, if that's what you mean."

"Good enough. You're in charge. How shall we proceed?"

Mike pointed toward the north end of the house. "You take that end; I'll take this end."

Ben started on the outside perimeter and slowly moved inward. He was glad he brought some gloves; these charred embers were still hot. He pulled out some tattered clothes and a few bits of plastic that might have once been records or tools or someone's favorite toy. How awful to have your home consumed by fire, he thought. To have everything you hold most dear go up in smoke.

"I don't really know what I'm looking for," Ben admitted. "You're the expert, Mike. Clue me in."

"Well, the first item on an arson investigator's wish list is evidence of a criminal design. Proof that the fire was not an accident."

"Are we looking for liquids . . . solids . . . ?"

"Both. Or neither. A liquid inflammatory agent is probably most likely here. They're cheap and easy to come by. Alcohol. Kerosene. Ether. Gasoline."

"What would a solid inflammatory agent be?"

"Well, there are dozens, but one I've seen in good supply around this town is coal dust. Mix it with air and ignite it and that'll start a fire in nothing flat. Some grains will do the job, too."

"What about chemicals?"

"Harder to come by, but not impossible, even in Silver Springs."

"ASP probably keeps a stockpile in their ammunition dump."

"Probably so. Sodium and potassium are both common chemicals, and both ignite upon contact with water. ASP could claim they keep them for, oh, excavation purposes, and then use them to make a heck of a good bomb."

"Any news on that blood sample you sent in for testing?"

"I FedEx'd it to Tulsa and asked the lab to give it Priority One treatment. Even so, it'll be several days before we get the results."

"Okay." Ben paused. "You're a real friend in need, Mike. I appreciate your help."

"Don't mention it."

"This is way beyond the call of friendship—"

"When I said, don't mention it, I meant, don't mention it!"

"Okay, okay." Ben resumed his search. "Sorry. Didn't mean to suggest you might have a sensitive side."

"I don't. By the way, did I tell you I saw your sister last week?"

"No, you didn't."

"Yeah. Julia and I had a long talk. Well, longer than a minute, anyway."

"For you two, that's an eternity."

"She has a baby now. By her second husband."

"So I hear."

"But she's divorcing him. The husband, I mean."

"Seems to be a habit with Julia."

"Yeah. I told her you were on vacation. She was glad you were getting away for a while."

"That's nice."

"Then I told her you went camping. And she just started laughing hysterically."

Ben concentrated on his examination of the debris. "Julia always did have an odd sense of humor."

"Yeah. She was real nice to me, though."

"Well, hot dog. Maybe you two will patch it up yet."

"Oh, don't be stupid. I don't give a flip about her anymore."

"Uh-huh. That's why you get all moony-eyed and morose every time her name comes up. Even after she divorced you."

"You should talk. You've been all screwed up about Ellen for years! That's—" He stopped himself in midsentence.

A deadly silence descended upon them.

"Hey, I'm sorry, Ben. I shouldn't have brought that up—"

"Just forget it," Ben said, not looking at him.

"Right. Sorry."

Ben didn't say anything for a long time.

Half an hour later Ben shouted, "Hey, I think I found something!"

Mike ran over to examine Ben's discovery. It was a broken glass Coke bottle, blackened and charred, but still recognizable.

Mike took the bottle shard and held it up to the light.

"Is that what started the fire?" Ben asked. "Or just leftovers from the Truongs' lunch?"

"Dollars to doughnuts, this bottle delivered a liquid inflammatory agent." He held the bottle to his eye and peered inside. "I can't believe you found it so soon."

"It's a gift," Ben said modestly. "You should treat me with more respect."

"I'll bear that in mind." He handed the bottle back to Ben. "Notice the charring on the inside. If the fire had started from a pipe, or any other external agent, the outside of the bottle would be blackened, but not the interior. That tells me the fire started right in there. It was probably filled with gasoline. A Molotov cocktail. It's easy enough to make. Now we look for the wick or fuse, if it still exists. Probably an oily rag, or perhaps wadded paper. If we can find that, we'll have a case of arson."

Ben resumed the search.

The combination of the morning sun and the heat rising from the charred ruins made the search increasingly unpleasant. Time after time Ben wiped sweat off his brow and out of his eyes.

After a while he lost track of the time. Providence appeared to be balancing the scales. Since he had found the bottle almost immediately, it was going to take him forever to find the fuse. The black soot rubbed off on his clothes and face; soon he was covered.

Ben began to wonder if this was even possible. He couldn't identify most of the debris he sorted through. He could be holding the fuse in his hand and never know it.

"What if the fuse was made of paper? Wouldn't it have been consumed in the fire?"

"Possibly," Mike answered. "Even then, though, we should be able to find—"

Midsentence, Mike's voice simply disappeared. There was no interruption. He just wasn't talking anymore, as if the air had suddenly been sucked out of his throat.

"Mike?"

Ben glanced back over his shoulder. Mike was still there, but his face was pale. "What's wrong? Did you find the fuse?"

"I found—" Mike pressed the back of his hand against his lips. "Not the fuse," he whispered. "A body."

"Oh—God. *No.*" Ben was torn between wanting to ask and not wanting to know. "A . . . body?"

Mike nodded. He looked as if he might be sick at any moment. "What's left of it. Skeleton, mostly."

Ben eased to his feet. So they didn't get everyone out after all. What a hideous way to die. "A man? Woman?"

Ben was astonished to see tears spring from Mike's eyes. He shook his head slowly back and forth.

"A baby."

* 32 *

Belinda was introducing Jones to the computer setup in the Hatewatch office. "Now, I think this gizmo is the disk drive. . . ."

Jones waved her away. "Thanks, I can take it from here." He booted up the computer and accessed the communications program stored on the hard drive. "I don't suppose you know what your communications protocol is?"

"Well . . . actually, John handles most of the computer work."

"No sweat. I'll work it out." He tapped a few more keys, then pulled up a blue screen with PROCOMM in big red letters. "Here we go."

"I should warn you," Belinda said. "We've tried to get documents from ASP before in litigation discovery. They claim they lost almost everything in a fire. They claim an electromagnetic discharge erased all their computer disks. To make a long story short, they never have anything you want."

Jones noted, "So we won't waste time asking them."

"Maybe I'm not making myself clear. If they won't produce the documents during a lawsuit, when a judge is breathing down their necks, I don't think you're going to find them in a computer database."

"How much do you think it cost Dunagan to move all

these men out here and set up that camp?" Jones said abruptly.

"I don't know. Twenty, maybe thirty thousand dollars."

"You think Dunagan has that much loot at his personal disposal?"

"I'd be very much surprised."

"Then he had to take out a loan. And bank records can be accessed."

"What good will that do you?"

"The loan records will tell me how much money they got, and who the sureties were. I can use that to trace credit records, for ASP and Dunagan and any other principals. Keep following those leads, and I'll soon have a financial trail that will tell me who ASP is, how much money they have at their disposal, where they spend it, and what they spend it on."

"You're kidding."

"Nope. It's time-consuming, but it works. And I can tie the financial records to parallel cities in newspaper and magazine databases. When I'm done, I'll be able to give Ben a reasonably accurate account of every major ASP activity for the last three years."

"You're amazing."

"Well, yes." Jones punched a few more keys. "I need to know all the names ASP does business under, and all the officers who represent ASP. I'm going to enter a legal database."

Belinda laid her hand on the terminal. "Oh, sorry. We don't subscribe. Those pricey legal services aren't in the Hatewatch budget."

"They're not in the Ben Kincaid budget, either. But I know a few tricks."

"A few—" Belinda watched admiringly as Jones continued to work. "Wait a minute. This doesn't involve anything illegal, does it?"

"Do you really want to know?"

"Well ... as an officer of the court, I suppose I should ask if this activity violates the lawyer's Rules of Professional Conduct."

Jones hit Enter and brought up the Secretary of State's records on the Anglo-Saxon Patrol. "Beats me," he answered. "I'm just a secretary. Excuse me. Executive assistant."

* 33 *

Colonel Nguyen quietly approached the chicken house in the center of Coi Than Tien. Although he had been released from the clinic, he was still shaky and short of breath, and his head throbbed as if a dozen men were pounding it with sledgehammers.

Getting too old for these childish heroics, he told himself. And yet, what was he supposed to do? If he had not gone into the home, Maria Truong would be dead.

He had visited Maria on his way out of the clinic. It might have been better if he had let her die.

Lan had stayed at the hospital with him all night, after leaving the children with a friend whose home was not harmed by the fire. Lan said little, and she would not permit herself to cry, but her feelings were clearly expressed just the same. She was deeply worried about all the threats, all the danger—and the fact that whenever danger struck, her husband always seemed to be in the middle of it.

Each time the evil came a little closer to him, and as a result, a little closer to his family.

If some harm came to their daughters, Lan's life would be over. She would never forgive him. He knew that now, with crystal clarity.

That night, as she had watched over him in the hospital, he had suspected for the first time that she realized he knew more about Tommy Vuong's death than he had admitted. Had she found the papers? No, he checked as soon as he returned to his home—they were still where he had hidden them. Lan was very smart; she had simply figured it out.

And it worried her.

Colonel Nguyen eased through the entry doors and into the storage building where the chickens were kept. Dan Pham was there, with five of his closest followers huddled around him. Usually they held these meetings in the barn, but the barn was now a refugee camp, providing shelter to those the fire had left homeless until other arrangements could be made.

Nguyen couldn't hear what they were saying, but it didn't take a genius to determine the topic of conversation. Pham would not be cowed by this latest onslaught. He would never admit that they were outstripped, outmatched. He would retaliate.

Nguyen stole closer to them. The chickens clucked as he passed, but it was a sound they had all long since learned to ignore. From his new vantage point, he managed to overhear a few words. "Parade," he heard Pham say several times. What could he possibly be referring to? "Surprise," someone else said, followed by muffled laughter. Then he heard Pham distinctly pronounce the word *attack*.

"Have you come to join us, Colonel Nguyen?"

He looked up and saw Pham staring directly at him. There was no point in pretending he was doing anything other than what he obviously was doing.

He walked into their midst and sat between Pham and his followers. "I have not."

"Is it your assistance you offer? Your experience in battle?"

"I wish to know your plans."

"I do not think that would be wise."

"I must know if Coi Than Tien is in danger. Think of the others in our community, Pham. Think of our families." His eyes narrowed. "Think of your grandmother."

Pham's face became rigid. "It grieves me to be unable to assent to any request from a great man such as yourself. But if you will not join us, I believe it is best we keep our plans to ourselves."

"Your plans will bring great danger down upon us. And our families."

"You do not speak the words of a great war hero." Pham laughed derisively. "You sound more like the white meddler who came last night to pry into our affairs."

Nguyen knew to whom Pham was referring. The white meddler—the lawyer. The one Nguyen had lied to. Or at the very least, had withheld the truth from.

Nguyen knew who the lawyer was, of course. The nimble words of the woman from Hatewatch had not fooled him. Unlike most in Coi Than Tien, the Colonel went into Silver Springs every day, and he usually read the newspaper as well. The white man was the attorney representing Donald Vick, the man accused of killing Tommy Vuong.

The man Colonel Nguyen was almost certain had not committed the crime.

The lawyer was undoubtedly seeking information to help his client, engaged as he was in the noble cause of seeking justice for an innocent man.

And Nguyen had refused to tell him what he knew.

"The young man who visited us last night was right when he said that violence only begets violence. Terrorism is no solution. It only fans the flames of hate."

"Take your homilies and go," Pham said bitterly.

"Will you not even hear me out?"

"The time for words has passed. It is time for action!"

"Will you not let your friends speak for themselves? We are in America now. Let us put it to a vote."

"I speak for my people!" Pham jumped to his feet. "Fine. We'll put it to a vote then. Who favors including the great Colonel Nguyen in our plans?"

The five other men looked among themselves. No one's hand rose.

"There is your vote, Colonel Nguyen. Now leave."

Regretfully Nguyen left the chicken house. It was pointless to attempt to reason with Pham now. Nothing would stop him, not until he had brought the full fury of ASP down upon them and Coi Than Tien was utterly destroyed.

He considered gathering his family and their meager belongings and leaving, now, in the dead of the night.

He felt ashamed. If he did that, Pham would be right. He would be a coward. There had to be another way.

He would go into Silver Springs, as he did every day. He would try to find some meaning to *parade* and *surprise*. He would try to stop Pham and his men before the final die was cast.

Before it was too late for them all.

* 34 *

"Is she conscious?" Ben asked.

The doctor nodded. "In and out. We have a catheter connected to the base of her spine feeding her painkillers. Tends to make her sleepy. Which is for the best, under these circumstances."

Ben and Belinda were at the emergency treatment clinic in Silver Springs, in an examining room that had been converted to a makeshift burn treatment center for Maria Truong. Ben was consulting with the doctor in residence, Harvey Patterson, a tall man in his midforties.

"How bad are her burns?" Belinda asked.

"Severe, I'm afraid. If they were any worse, she wouldn't be alive. She's got scorched lungs and third-degree burns all over her body. Her hands are useless, virtually gone."

"You said she's on painkillers?"

"Yes. Some of her burns are so profound she's suffered nerve damage, so she doesn't feel the pain there. Some of the lesser-degree burns are still stinging, though. It's ironic—the least critical burns are the ones that are causing her so much misery; the ones she can't feel are the ones that may kill her."

"Then you think she's—"

"We have a guideline known as the Rule of Nines.

It's a shorthand method for determining the percentage of the body that's been burned. She scores over seventy percent. And that's mostly third-degree burns." He paused, then looked down at his clipboard. "Burn victims with greater than sixty-percent burns rarely survive. And even if they do—" His voice choked; he never finished the sentence.

"Is there anything we can do?" Belinda asked.

"We've done all we can for her here, and we've called for transportation to a burn center in Little Rock. She'll get all the best treatment. If that's what she wants."

"What do you mean?"

Dr. Patterson shifted his eyes to his patient. "At the burn center they can run tests and try grafts and plastic surgery, but it won't do much good. Look at her hands, her face. Even if she survives, what kind of life will she have? She won't be able to function; she'll be in constant agony."

The doctor dropped heavily into a nearby chair. "I've been working all night and day, doing everything I can think of to save her." His voice lowered. "But the whole time I've been wondering if I should."

"You're doing the right thing," Ben said. He hoped he sounded confident. He wasn't. "Is it all right if I speak to her?"

"I don't see that it can do her much harm. But remember, she's heavily medicated. I can't vouch for the quality of her answers."

Together Ben and Belinda approached the side of Maria's bed. "Mrs. Truong?"

The top of her head was wrapped in bandages. Her eyes seemed unnaturally wide and hollow; after a moment Ben realized it was because her eyebrows and eyelashes were gone.

Slowly her eyelids opened. "Yes?"

"Ma'am, my name is Ben Kincaid."

"Are you the one"—her voice was broken and hesitant—"in the fire—"

"No. That was Colonel Nguyen. He carried you out. Saved your life."

"The Colonel. Yes." She wet her lips with her tongue. "A great man."

"Ma'am, I'd like to ask you a few questions. I've already spoken to the rest of your family, but they didn't have much to tell me. I thought you might have seen someone, or might know something, about what happened last night. If you don't feel up to it, though, just tell me and I'll stop."

Maria tried to nod, but found it difficult to move her neck. Her skin was thick and leathery; her burns were hardening to eschar.

Belinda reached across the bed and gently raised the woman's pillow. Maria smiled appreciatively.

"Did you see what happened last night?"

"Truck," Maria whispered. "Black. Threw something . . ."

"Did you see what was thrown?"

She shook her head.

"Did you see who was in the truck?"

Again she indicated that she did not.

"Do you have any idea why they would single out your house?"

She didn't. Her eyes became watery. She moved her arm toward Ben, but it was restricted by the IV.

Ben untangled the IV tube. He reached out to take her hand, then froze. It was not a hand at all. Not anymore.

He touched her shoulder lightly and hoped she had not noticed. "My understanding is that you lived with your husband and your ten-year-old son. Is that correct?"

"Yes. Are they—"

"They're fine, ma'am. The boy's a little shaken up, but he's not hurt."

"And Vanh?"

"He's fine, too. They visited you while you were sleeping. I'm sure they'll be in again soon."

"That is . . . good."

"Do you know why—" How should he put it? He didn't know. It was best to just get it over with. "Do you know why a baby would be in your home?"

Even given the limited powers of expression her charred facial skin allowed her, Ben could tell she had no idea what he was talking about.

"Is there anyone who might leave a baby with you? A friend? Or a relative, perhaps?"

"A baby," Maria repeated. "I always wanted a baby. Tim is my stepson. He was five when I married his father."

"Do you know where a baby might've come from?" Ben repeated.

"No idea." A horrified expression passed across her face. "Was the baby—"

"No," Ben said quickly. "The baby is fine. Everyone else got out without injury." So call him a liar. This woman had enough pain in her life.

Maria tried to roll over on one side, but her burns were too sensitive. She gasped suddenly, then released a small, stifled cry. She rolled onto her back, her face contorted in agony.

Ben fought back his tears. Burns had to be the worst kind of suffering. The absolute worst.

"Can you think of anything else that might help us determine who set this fire?" Ben asked.

He could tell Maria was trying to think, but nothing came to mind. She probably had more pressing concerns.

"Thank you for your help," Ben said. "I understand they're arranging transportation to take you to the burn center—"

"No!" Maria said suddenly. "No more . . . treatments."

"Ma'am, they can help you—"

"No." She held up her hands and gazed at the charred, misshapen stubs that remained. "I'm done."

Ben looked to Belinda for help. On his own he couldn't find the words.

"Mrs. Truong," Belinda said, "you have our deepest sympathy for your misfortune."

"Not so bad," she whispered. "My boy is fine. My husband . . . also." Her eyelids slowly closed. "That is enough."

* 35 *

The next day Ben rose shortly after the sun did. His usual Sunday morning routine was to tumble out of bed, feed his cat, pour a heaping bowl of Cap'n Crunch cereal, and work the *Tulsa World* crossword. This morning, unfortunately, he had no cat, no cereal, and no crossword. He would have to settle for a quick wash and a shave in the lake.

He'd had a good night's sleep, all things considered. He only dreamed about the fire twice. Dreams— nightmares actually. Horrible nightmares. Ben hoped he never came anywhere near fire again.

He brushed his teeth and tried to shift mental gears. He had several tasks he wanted to accomplish today, and several people he needed to talk to before the trial began.

After he was dressed, he took a powdered doughnut from a plastic bag in his tent and waited for the rest of his staff to assemble. To his surprise, Christina was the first to arrive.

" 'Morning," he said. They had not spoken since their previous argument. "Thought you were staying at Mary Sue's."

"I am," she said flatly. "I came out early to catch the bass while they were still sleepy." She took a Coke from a cooler and popped it open. "I hear you're going to church this morning."

"Seems appropriate," Ben said. "After all, it is Sunday."

"And you're taking . . . that woman."

"Belinda?" He raised an eyebrow. "Yeah. She should be here any minute."

"You two have been spending a fair amount of time together."

"That's true." He coughed. For some reason, he was suddenly uncomfortable. "She's a very brave woman. Smart, too."

"I see." Christina stared at her Coke can. "Why are you taking her to church?"

"It would be stupid to go alone." He looked up suddenly. "And you won't come."

"Ben, I—"

"It's not too late, Christina. The trial hasn't started yet. I need a legal assistant." He brushed the doughnut crumbs off his lap. "That isn't quite true. I need you."

"Ben—" She pressed the Coke can against her forehead. "I can't do that. If I did, I don't know how I could sleep at night. I don't know how you—" She shook her head.

"Of all the people in the world," Ben said quietly, "I thought you would understand."

She turned away. "You were wrong."

Fortunately at that moment Jones emerged from his tent and joined them. "Did you get that report I left you, Boss?"

Jones had pieced together a bundle of information on ASP financing and ASP activities, both official and unofficial, during the last three years. He gave Ben the lowdown on the survival camps, the scare tactics, the outright terrorism in Montgomery and Birmingham and elsewhere. Ben suspected it would be helpful at trial.

"Thanks," Ben replied. "I appreciate your hard work."

"I live to please, Boss."

"Nice to hear that someone does," Ben commented. "I have a new assignment for you, Jones."

"Shoot."

"I pulled a woman out of the fire the other night at Coi Than Tien. Slim, maybe a hundred and ten pounds, dark hair. White. I think. It was very dark and smoky— I can't be certain I saw her clearly."

"Okay. What about her?"

"I want to know who she is, and why she was there."

"Why didn't you ask her?"

"She disappeared before I had a chance."

"Know anything else about her?"

" 'Fraid not."

"That doesn't give me much to go on. But I'll do my best. Mind if I use Loving?"

"Of course not. If he can spare the time."

"I think he can. Most of the thugs he's working on don't come out until after dark. Kind of like vampires."

Ben spotted Mike approaching from the riverbank. "Where have you been?"

"Just out for a bit of exercise," Mike said, "and to commune with nature. You know, doing the Thoreau bit."

"Natch. Got Portia working yet?"

Mike sullenly grabbed the doughnut bag. "No comment." He took two doughnuts, one for each hand, and alternated bites from each.

"Find out anything about the infant?" Ben asked. It sickened him just to raise the topic.

"Um-hm," Mike answered, wiping the powdered sugar from his mouth. "Baby girl. Newborn."

"Anyone claimed her?"

"Not yet. And no one knows who she is, or how she got there."

"Including the Truongs," Ben said. "I've talked to them."

"That's hard to imagine."

"Granted. But I believe them. After all, they got themselves to safety. It wouldn't have been that hard to carry a six-pound baby with them. If they'd known she was there."

"This is one strange case, Ben. Hell of a way to spend a vacation." He shoved the rest of both doughnuts into his mouth.

Ben agreed. "Normal cases start to unravel as you acquire more information. The more we learn about this case, though, the more tangled it becomes."

A car drove up the dirt road beside the campsite, then honked twice.

"Sounds like my ride," Ben said. "See you later. I'm off to church."

"Church?" Mike almost choked on his doughnuts. *"You?"*

"Well, of course. It's Sunday, isn't it?"

"And," Jones added with a wink, "he's taking Belinda."

"Is that a fact? How romantic."

"See you goons later." Ben stood, then hesitated a moment. "So long, Christina. We'll continue this discussion later, okay?"

Christina looked up, but didn't say a word.

* 36 *

Belinda pulled her Jeep Cherokee into the space cleared away for parking in front of the Aryan Christian Church. It was an old-fashioned wooden church building with a tall steeple and an iron bell. A smaller separate structure—a garage, probably—was in the back. Attached to the church was a smaller house—preacher's quarters, Ben guessed. And beside the quarters was a wire-enclosed kennel with five barking bird dogs inside.

"Looks like the preacher is a hunting man," Ben commented.

"Not surprising," Belinda replied. "Men in these parts take their hunting very seriously. When deer season is on, you can't find a blue-collar worker for a hundred miles around."

"They hunt deer with dogs?"

"No. The preacher must go after ducks. Or maybe raccoons." She turned off the ignition, then turned to face Ben. "Are you sure we should be doing this?"

"Hey, I was invited."

"I wasn't. When they see me, they'll pitch a fit."

"I need your help, Belinda. You have far more background and experience with ASP than I do."

"Granted. Maybe neither of us should go in there."

Ben touched Belinda's shoulder. "I have an obligation to defend my client to the best of my ability. The trial starts Monday afternoon. I can't let pass an opportunity to talk to people who may well have been responsible for the crime my client is accused of committing."

"I suppose you're right. I just—" She looked down at his hand on her shoulder, then placed her hand over his. "When you ran into the flames the other night to save that woman, I—I was so scared. I didn't know whether you'd ever come out again. I—"

She moved closer to him. "I know we've had our differences, Ben. But I don't want anything to happen to you." Her lips moved toward his. The kiss was at first tentative, then assured and lingering. Their bodies pressed close against each other.

"We'll never get into that church at this rate," Ben said. "Let's postpone this to a later date and a more private environment." Reluctantly, he pulled away from her. "Don't worry about me, Belinda. I'll be fine."

"Still—take care."

They jumped out of her Jeep and walked toward the church. "It's hard to believe this place is less than a hundred yards from Coi Than Tien," Belinda said. "Spooky coincidence."

"Hardly a coincidence. More likely it's an ASP intimidation tactic."

As Belinda passed by the kennel two of the largest of the bird dogs leaped up on the wire fence and barked loudly.

"Animal magnetism," Ben commented.

"Ha-ha." She watched them carefully. "Those poor dogs look underfed."

"They probably are. Some people do that, you know. To make them mean and eager to attack. I've handled several cases for an animal-rights group in

Tulsa. I could tell you stories that would break your heart."

"You don't suppose those dogs can escape, do you?"

Ben examined the sturdy wire fence and gate. "Not unless someone slips them some wire cutters. The gate appears to be electric. There's probably a control switch inside."

They walked up the front steps of the church and entered. The interior was plain and largely unornamented; a far cry from the Episcopal church Ben grew up in. He saw a panel with lighted buttons on one wall—probably controlled the kennel.

The services had already started. Ben and Belinda slid into a pew in the back.

The first part of the service was much like any other fundamentalist Christian service Ben had ever attended. The congregation sang "Rock of Ages" and "Amazing Grace"; they recited the Lord's Prayer. The preacher, a man called Brother Curtis, was wearing a full-length black robe and appeared to be packing a gun underneath. Other than that, it was church as usual.

It was only when the sermon started that Ben observed major differences. Brother Curtis's message was a call to arms, but not to Christianity—at least not as Ben had ever heard it explained before. Curtis defined Armageddon in terms of an imminent worldwide race war that only the Anglo-Saxon race would survive; apparently this was part of the Aryan Christian Church's official doctrine. It seemed the Second Coming was a Caucasians-only affair.

"This government shall perish in flames," Curtis intoned. "It has betrayed the faith of those who created it. It is controlled by the Jews, the blacks, the Hispanics, the Asians"—a loud murmur of assent—"the Communists, the Catholics, and all those peoples whose avowed goal is the destruction of America as we know it."

His proclamation was followed by a chorus of *amens* and *praise Gods*.

"The Jews are not the chosen. It is we, the Aryan people, who are the chosen race." Another loud chorus of approval. "The inferior races are the descendants of Satan. They are devils." He prolonged the final *s* to a hissing noise. "They have stolen our birthright. But the time has come to take it back."

He pounded on the podium. "We must fight those who would deprive us of our rightful heritage. We must fight the infidels who tarnish our land. We must fight the demon warriors who stand in our way. We must fight the demon lawyers who pervert our righteous cause."

Ben looked absently over his shoulder. Demon lawyers? Where?

"We must fight and fight and fight, until no obstacle remains between us and the one true church, the New Nation. An all-white nation, founded with our sweat, our toil, and our blood!"

Amidst the chorus of cheers and hallelujahs, Ben whispered to Belinda, "I can't stand much more of this."

"This?" She shrugged. "This is mild. You should hear them when they really get revved up."

Ben grimaced. He already hated everything these people stood for, but if possible, he hated them even worse now for this act of sacrilege. What could be worse than prostituting the church to serve your own self-centered hate-filled goals?

Brother Curtis called for another hymn, this one out

of a mimeographed pamphlet. Ben read the words as the congregation sang the dirgelike tune:

White and proud,
That's what I am,
Storming the streets,
Getting rid of the trash.
What's wrong with knowing your race is strong?
Aryan people unite against:
Drugs, race mixing, and crime.
Brothers and sisters, stand by my side,
Join the fight for what's right.

Ben read in the notes beneath the lyrics that the song had been written by a twelve-year-old girl.

He threw down the pamphlet and settled back into his pew. He only hoped that when he finally got the chance to talk to some of these people, he would be able to carry on a civil conversation.

* 37 *

After the service concluded, most of the congregation milled about in the reception area.

"Ben! I wasn't expecting to see you here."

It was Sonny Banner, dressed in his Sunday best—a blue sport jacket with khaki pants. His necktie had a small gold emblem near the tip—a shield with a burning cross. As Ben looked around he noticed most of the men in the lobby were similarly adorned.

"Grand Dragon Dunagan invited me to today's service."

"That's great." Banner whispered into Ben's ear. "Don't worry about security during the trial. We've got the whole matter taken care of."

Ben didn't much care for the sound of that. "What do you mean?"

"I'll be inside the courtroom at all times, with at least two others. Plus we'll have men posted at both exits, all day long. If anyone tries to start trouble, we'll snuff it out."

Ben wished he had chosen a different verb.

"And if that isn't enough to quiet the rabble," Banner continued, "the parade will be."

"I'm not anticipating any violent demonstrations. . . ."

"It's best to be certain," Banner declared. "I've heard

rumors that the gooks are planning major violence. Especially after that fire at Coi Than Tien."

"Speaking of which," Ben said, "I don't suppose you know who started it."

"No, I don't. It wasn't an ASP operation."

"How can you be certain?"

"Grand Dragon Dunagan has released a public statement."

"Well, you could hardly expect him to admit it."

Banner seemed taken back. "Grand Dragon Dunagan does not lie."

"Not even for the cause?"

"Our cause is a noble crusade. We have no need for lies or deception."

Ben could tell he was getting Banner's dander up. Much as it gave him personal satisfaction, he figured it was probably not a particularly smart tactic. "By the way, does anyone in this group drive a black pickup?"

Banner shrugged. "I expect several of us do, including myself. That's the most common vehicle for this country. Why do you ask?"

"Idle curiosity."

Ben felt a sudden slap on his back. "So you came after all, Ben. I'm genuinely pleased."

It was His Exalted Grand Dragon Dunagan. For the services, he had tucked his short round little self into a brown sport coat and the club tie. "Have any trouble finding us?"

"No. We just turned left before the entrance to Coi Than Tien."

An eyebrow rose. "You've been to Coi Than Tien?"

"Of course. As part of my investigation."

"I see. . . ."

"In fact, I was there when the fire started."

Dunagan nodded. "Terrible tragedy, that. Of course, I

don't think those people belong here in the first place, but I hated to see that happen. I suppose I'm not surprised, though. Those who play with fire will perish in the flames."

"Is that from the Bible?" Ben asked.

"Actually, that's my own."

"Ah. I understand you issued a public statement disavowing any responsibility for the attack on Coi Than Tien."

"True. If it was an attack. From what I hear, someone may have been smoking one of those weird chink pipes in bed."

"The preliminary investigation indicates arson."

"Really? I hadn't heard that." Dunagan stroked his chin. "I'm surprised anyone around here is sophisticated enough to make that kind of determination."

Ben wondered if he was counting on that. "So you don't have any idea who did it?"

"Of course not. Ben, we wouldn't set someone's house on fire. Especially on the eve of your trial. I like to think I'm a little smarter than that. I don't want to see Lou Vick's boy executed."

Ben just hoped that was right. But for some reason, he was starting to wonder. "Do you know who the baby was?"

Dunagan's face wrinkled. "The baby?"

"The baby who died in the fire."

"They let a little baby burn to death?" Dunagan's head shook with sudden rage. "Those goddamn godless heathens! Some people shouldn't be permitted to have children."

"Apparently the baby didn't belong—"

"This is an outrage. They should lock up whoever was smoking that goddamn pipe and throw away the key!"

The Grand Dragon's shouting was attracting attention. "Calm down, sir. The sheriff has the matter—"

"Who let her in here?" Dunagan suddenly demanded. Ben whirled around and saw that he was talking about Belinda.

Belinda approached them. "Good morning, Mr. Dunagan. Nice to see you again. You look better without the hood."

"Demon Hamilton!" he shouted back at her. "How dare you show yourself on these holy premises!"

"I invited her," Ben interjected.

"You . . . *what*?" Dunagan stared at him as if he was lower than a worm. "What in the name of Christ did you think you were doing?"

"Ms. Hamilton has been very helpful to my investigation."

"Demon Hamilton is Satan's bitch!" Dunagan spit back. "Tainted Jezebel! Whore of Babylon!"

"Now wait a minute," Ben said. "There's no need for that kind of talk."

"This woman and her malignant friends have interfered with our righteous cause for the past five years!"

Belinda did not back off. "We've tried to prevent you from stomping all over poor and defenseless minorities, if that's what you mean."

"This woman had the audacity to bring a civil lawsuit in Birmingham. Against *me*!"

"Yes. And you sent some of your goons out to beat and humiliate me. I'd say we're about even."

Dunagan's eyes flared. "Get thee away, Lucifer!" He motioned to Banner. "I want this woman removed."

Before Banner could act, Brother Curtis stepped into the fray. "Just a minute, my son."

"Brother Curtis, don't interfere." Dunagan pushed him away. "I'm taking care of this."

"This is my church, and my flock," Brother Curtis said. "And what goes on here is my concern."

"She's an infidel. An unbeliever."

Brother Curtis gave Belinda a head-to-toe examination. "She does not appear to be a member of one of the inferior races."

"She's a sympathizer."

"Then it is all the better that she attend our services."

Dunagan spoke through gritted teeth. "I don't *want* her here!"

"It is God's will we must be concerned with," Curtis said. "Not yours. God has brought her here. We cannot subvert His will to serve our own petty goals." On that note, he turned and walked toward the pulpit, apparently confident that his will—and God's—would be obeyed.

Dunagan stood toe to toe with Ben and glared up into his face. "I won't forget this," he growled. *"Demon Kincaid!"*

Dunagan whirled around and stomped upstairs.

As they were leaving, Belinda whispered into Ben's ear, "I'm afraid you've lost the Aryan seal of approval."

Ben nodded. "I'm afraid you're right."

* 38 *

Colonel Nguyen strode to the back of the barn. There was no need for stealth this time; they undoubtedly knew he was coming and he knew exactly where they were. All he had to do was follow the noise of the hammers, the chain saws, and the electric drills.

There was no longer any pretense that Pham led a secret resistance; the ground swell of support he had received since the torching of the Truongs' home gave him the confidence to act openly.

The largest inner room of the barn was used as a storage and construction facility. Today, the large swinging double doors were closed, and Pham and one of his followers stood guard outside.

Colonel Nguyen tried to push past them without comment, but they closed shoulders and blocked his passage.

"Let me through, Pham," Nguyen said.

"I regret that I cannot," Pham replied. His face was stony and impassive.

"I want to know what you are doing in there."

"And I would like to show you. But under the circumstances, how can I? You have made it clear that you oppose me."

"I oppose bloodshed, if that is what you mean. I oppose the wasted loss of lives. And families."

"As do I," Pham said solemnly.

"Don't you see you're leading all of Coi Than Tien on a path of destruction?"

"I believe I offer Coi Than Tien a chance to live with honor. Where we choose to live."

This was pointless. They had had this debate a thousand times, and he had yet to make the slightest dent in Pham's thick head. "What are your men doing?"

"We are . . . building," Pham said.

"That much I know already. What are you building?"

Pham's lips remained closed.

"Is it for the *parade*?"

Pham's eyes widened in reaction to the last word.

"For weeks now, you have been extremely well informed about ASP's activities, both past and future," Nguyen said. "What is your source of this information?"

"I am more interested in learning how much you know, Colonel Nguyen."

"I know you plan some sort of disruption. A surprise."

"A warning," Pham replied.

"You are so eager to issue warnings, yet you yourself have ignored all those we have been given."

"What warnings?"

"What happened to Nhung Vu was a warning. What happened to your grandmother was a warning. Don't be a *fool*!" He shoved Pham aside and started for the door. As he fumbled with the latch Pham's partner pushed him back. He stood between Nguyen and the door, fists raised.

Pham scrambled back to his feet and positioned himself behind Nguyen, sandwiching him in. All three waited to see who would make the first move.

Colonel Nguyen felt his entire body stiffen. It was a

familiar reaction; even subconsciously, he was preparing for combat. "Do not presume to fight me," Nguyen said, barely audibly.

"You leave me no choice," Pham answered.

"I would not welcome combat with my own people."

"Nor I. It is possible that a warrior such as yourself would be able to defeat both me and my companion. But remember—there are twenty more of us just inside these doors."

Nguyen had to remind himself that this boy was not the enemy, not really. He had to control his temper. A fistfight in the barn would accomplish nothing.

"I beg you to reconsider," Nguyen said. "For all our sakes."

Pham repositioned himself in front of the doors. "I am afraid that once again I must decline. Please go."

Colonel Nguyen slowly pulled away from the barn doors.

"You will see, Colonel Nguyen," Pham shouted as he departed. "One day you will see that I was right. Tomorrow will begin a new era!"

Yes, Nguyen thought as he walked into the harsh glare of the noonday sun. That much he believed.

Starting tomorrow, everything would change.

* 39 *

Ben arrived at the Silver Springs courthouse at nine o'clock sharp. He found Judge Tyler, District Attorney Swain, and Ben's alleged co-counsel, Harlan Payne, in the judge's closetlike chambers. The air in the tiny room had a boozy smell; Ben suspected the bottle in the judge's bottom drawer had made a few trips around before he arrived.

He squeezed into a seat between the DA and Payne. "Where's Amber?" Ben asked Swain.

"Marjorie has her today." He appeared faintly embarrassed.

"That's a shame," Ben said. "I was hoping to hear you sing 'Rock-a-bye Baby' in the courtroom."

Judge Tyler smiled wryly. "That little Amber is welcome in my courtroom anytime, Mr. Swain. Your singing, however, is not. Shall we get to it, gentlemen?"

Both attorneys announced that they were ready to proceed.

"Now, let's use this time productively and work out our problems in advance so this trial can move along as smoothly as possible. I'm anticipating a large turnout for this trial, and we don't want everyone to think we're a bunch of stupid hicks like Mr. Kincaid does."

"Your honor," Ben protested, "I never said—"

"Never mind that," Judge Tyler said. "What can I do for you?"

"Well," Ben said, "I've had a few discovery problems."

"Like what?"

"The prosecution has not given me a witness list."

Judge Tyler addressed Swain. "That true?"

Swain chuckled. "I hardly see what difference it's going to make. Vick's guilty as sin."

Ben leaned forward. "Your honor—"

"Not necessary," the judge said, holding up his hands. "Mr. Swain, regardless of your private assessment of the defendant, we're going to run a good clean trial. So give Mr. Kincaid a list."

"Yes, sir."

"And you will make your witnesses available to Mr. Kincaid if he wishes to chat with them before they take the stand."

"Yes, sir," Swain agreed. "I will."

"Now see," Tyler said, peering across at Ben. "Maybe we hicks know how to run a trial after all. What else can I do for you?"

"I'd like to see all his exhibits," Ben said. "Before trial."

"Well now," Tyler replied, "I believe you're only entitled to see evidence deemed exculpatory."

"Swain doesn't consider anything exculpatory, since he's certain my client is guilty as sin."

Judge Tyler tapped his pencil impatiently. "Mr. Swain, I believe it might be best if you provided copies of all your exhibits to Mr. Kincaid."

"But, sir!"

"I think you can probably have those ready for him by noon, don't you?"

Swain swallowed. "I'll . . . do my best, sir."

"Good. I'll have Mabel drop by your office just to make sure you haven't forgotten."

"Uh ... that'll be great, sir."

"I'm glad we got that taken care of. What else can I do for you gentlemen? Any motions I need to consider?"

"Yes, your honor," Ben said. "I have two."

"Two?" Tyler wiped his brow. "Great balls of fire. I sometimes go months without hearing a motion. I've tried entire cases that never had any motions. And you waltz in here with two!"

"I think they're important, your honor."

"No doubt. You big-city lawyers are scads more creative than us dumb country boys."

Ben tried to ignore the jab. "First I have a motion in limine."

The judge blinked. "Say what?"

"A ... motion to exclude certain evidence."

"I know what a motion in limine is, counselor."

"He wants to keep out evidence that incriminates his client," Swain explained.

"Well, wouldn't we all?" Judge Tyler peered down at Ben. "Just what is it you wish to exclude?"

"A hearsay statement allegedly made by my client at the Bluebell Bar after a fight."

Swain piped up. "My witness will testify that Vick said, 'I'll get you, you perverted little Vietnamese gook.' "

"The statement has no probative value," Ben insisted, "but it would prejudice my client's case. And it's hearsay testimony. No question about it."

"Well, maybe so," the judge said. "But wouldn't it also be an admission against interest? And as such admissible as an exception to the hearsay rule?"

"My thoughts exactly," Swain said.

"No," Ben said. "How could it be an admission? An admission of what? That Vuong was a perverted gook? It's just name-calling."

"Ah," Swain said. "But that's the point, your honor. It shows Vick hated Vuong. It proves his motive."

"Thank you," Ben said. "Mr. Swain has just confessed that he wants to admit this statement to prove the truth of the matter asserted—that Vick planned to kill Vuong. It is therefore by definition hearsay and cannot be admitted."

The judge pursed his lips. "Any response, Mr. Swain?"

"Uh, no, your honor."

"Mr. Kincaid," the judge said slowly, "your motion will be granted."

Swain was all eyeballs. *"What?"*

"I think you heard me."

Ben was almost as astonished as Swain. He had felt obligated to make the argument, but he hadn't expected to win. Wonders never ceased.

"Wait a minute, Judge," Swain said. "I need that testimony. It's practically a confession!"

"I've already ruled, counsel. Anything else?"

"I have another motion," Ben said. Why quit when he was on a winning streak? "For a change of venue. I want this case transferred somewhere else."

"Now, why would you want to do that? Don't you like our fair city?"

"It isn't—"

"Are you hoping to cut a few of your city-slicker lawyer friends in on this case? Maybe split some fees?"

"No, Judge. I just don't think Donald Vick can get a fair trial in Silver Springs. You said it yourself last week—this town is a powder keg. Everyone's running scared. A jury elected from this pool might convict my client just in the hope that it would set the world right again. Whether they're convinced of his guilt beyond a reasonable doubt or not."

"Got any evidence to support this theory of yours, Mr. Kincaid?"

"Well, how could I? I haven't taken a poll."

"Anybody come up to you and say they were going to convict your man no matter what?"

"Of course not."

"You'll have the chance to voir dire every prospective juror just like everyone else. If you find anyone who's biased, you may excuse them."

"Your honor, no one is likely to admit that they favor a quick conviction just because they're frightened."

"Then what am I supposed to rule upon? Your motion is denied."

"Judge, that was only my first ground for a change of venue." Ben had hoped he wouldn't need the second. But now it appeared he was going to have to go all the way. "The second reason for a transfer is the trial judge's obvious bias against my client."

"What? How *dare* you—!"

"Judge, you told me yourself you read the DA's file on the case. That's improper. You said the evidence against my client looked pretty bad. You've already made up your mind."

The judge rose halfway out of his chair. "I was simply stating facts!"

"The jury is supposed to determine the facts," Ben said. "Not the judge. I want a transfer."

"Mr. Kincaid, I am beginning to understand why you've had such a hard time holding down a job! I have served on this bench for twenty-eight years, and never—*never!*—have I been accused of being unfair!"

"You may not be conscious of it, sir, but you're still—"

"Be quiet!" He pounded his fist on his desk. "I heard you out, now you listen to me. You're right about one thing. I don't like your client. And I'm starting to like you even less. But my likes and dislikes are irrelevant. Justice is what matters. And this court will serve justice—perfect justice—to the best of my ability.

"Your client will have a fair trial. And if he loses, it will be because the evidence was against him and he was found guilty by a jury of his peers. And for no other reason. Do you understand me?"

"Yes, sir." There was nothing else to say.

"Very good. Your motion is denied. Understood?"

Ben nodded.

"Anything further?"

All attorneys present shook their heads.

"Very good, gentlemen. See you in court."

* 40 *

Vick was hunched over the exposed sink in the middle of his cell when Ben arrived. He was splashing water on his face, wiping the sleep from his eyes. He didn't look as if he had been up long.

" 'Morning," Ben said amiably.

Vick peered out over his wash towel, then went on with what he was doing.

"This will probably be our last chance to talk before the trial."

Vick threw down his towel. "Why is there going to be a trial? I thought I told you I wanted to plead guilty?"

Ben chose his words carefully. "The DA didn't give me a deal." Not that he asked for one.

"I don't give a damn. I'm pleading guilty."

"Look, Vick. I know you're young, inexperienced, and not incredibly . . . worldly-wise. Let me explain the facts of life to you. This case is going to trial, whether you like it or not. Therefore you have fulfilled your goal of protecting whoever it is you're determined to protect. Maybe you're concerned that if the jury finds you not guilty, the prosecution will go on trying people until they get a conviction. Wrong. Prosecutors bet all their chips on the first trial. If they win, great. If they lose, they complain that they were screwed by the judge or the lawyers or the press. They almost never bring charges against a second defendant following an acquittal. After all, to do so would be to admit they made a mistake."

"I don't need your—"

"Just shut up and listen. Given that this trial is going forward, and given that no one else will ever be tried for this crime unless he confesses his guilt on national television, the only remaining question is what the outcome of your trial will be. Will I get you off, or will you be on the receiving end of a lethal injection?"

Vick stepped away from the iron bars.

"It isn't going to make a bit of difference to anyone else. Only to you. So what's it going to be? Will you let me try to save you?"

Vick walked back to his cot, then seated himself on the edge. His eyes remained locked on Ben.

"I made a promise," he said finally.

"Fine. Keep your goddamn promise. We'll work around it."

Eventually Vick's head began to nod. "What do you want to know?"

Hallelujah. "They found a bloodstain on the crossbow. They say the blood is your type. Any idea how it got there? I thought possibly you were practicing with the crossbow out at the ASP camp one day and cut your finger. Then maybe someone else picked up the crossbow and used it to kill Vuong."

"I don't think so."

"Forensic evidence doesn't lie," Ben said. "If I can't come up with an explanation for how your hair and blood got on that crossbow, the prosecution will ram it down our throats."

"Nothing like that ever happened," Vick said.

Oh, well. It was worth a try.

Vick's answers were largely useless, but Ben was nonetheless encouraged. Vick hadn't actually proclaimed his innocence, but he was at least expressing interest in something other than a one-way ticket to death row. "Have you heard about the fire? At Coi Than Tien."

"I read the paper the sheriff gave me."

"Was this an ASP operation?"

"How would I know? I've been locked up in here for weeks. Was the fire . . . bad?"

"Destroyed one home, damaged two others."

"Anyone hurt?"

"A few people with scorched lungs or smoke inhalation. One woman was burned severely. We don't know if she's going to live."

Vick looked down at his hands. His sorrow appeared genuine.

"So," Ben continued, "if you know who set the fire—"

"I don't," Vick said firmly. "No idea at all."

Ben hated to add to Vick's already hefty guilt load. On the other hand, if there was any chance he might have information about the night of the fire . . .

"There was a baby in the burned home," Ben said softly. "We found her in the ruins. Her remains, anyway."

Vick stared up at him, his eyes wide. "A"—his voice choked—"baby?" He barely got the word out.

"Yeah. Newborn. We don't know who she was or where she came from. Do you?"

"Of course not."

"I just thought that since you're—"

"I said I don't know anything about it!" Vick's voice echoed down the narrow stone corridor. "What the hell does it have to do with Vuong's murder, anyway?"

"I think there's a connection," Ben said, "although I'm not sure what it is. But I can tell you this for certain. Everyone in town thinks ASP is responsible for the fire, just as they think ASP is responsible for this murder. And those people are going to be your jurors."

"Maybe you should talk to someone at the camp."

"I've tried," Ben said. "Without any luck. But speaking of your friends at the camp, I gather you weren't all that friendly with them. Any reason in particular?"

Vick looked away. "I'm new to the club. Relatively. Takes a while to make friends."

Ben suspected Vick could have been in this club for decades and never made any friends. He just didn't belong. It was as if ASP was a gigantic "What's wrong with this picture?" puzzle, and the answer was *Donald Vick*. "You wouldn't have fallen in with these people if not for your father, right?"

Vick didn't answer him.

"Donald, there comes a time when you have to shake loose of the person your parents want you to be. You have to be yourself." Ben stopped and listened to his own words. Good advice, Ben. Good advice.

"Donald," Ben said, "your father is dead. If this ASP crap isn't for you, shake loose of it."

Vick's head turned up slowly. His face was almost smiling. "A little too late, isn't it?"

Ben only hoped Vick was wrong.

* 41 *

On his way out of the jailhouse, Ben was greeted by the sound of tinny, blaring music. It seemed to be coming from the north end of Main Street.

Ben saw something moving his way, but he couldn't make out what it was. A field of green, creating a strange shimmering sensation just over the pavement.

He felt a chill creep down his spine.

As they approached, Ben determined that the music was martial—a John Philip Sousa flag-waving special. And then he saw the camouflage uniforms, and the wooden cross towering over them.

Dozens of them, six across, several rows deep.

ASP was on the march.

They were in full regalia: green fatigues with the burning-cross emblem over their breasts. Several marchers were carrying placards. RELEASE DONNY VICK read one; JUSTICE FOR ALL read another. A large banner was emblazoned with AN ENEMY OF ONE IS AN ENEMY OF ALL.

No doubt about it—this was a pretrial protest parade. A public demonstration designed to inform all prospective jurors that a guilty verdict could bring the wrath of ASP down on their heads.

Ben noticed that Jones and Loving were standing

near him on the sidewalk. Jones was taping the event with his video camera.

"What are you doing here?" Ben asked.

"Recording this for posterity," Jones said. "I love a parade."

"Been hearing about this for days at the Bluebell," Loving said. "Supposed to be quite a show."

Ben ground his teeth together. "I can't believe Judge Tyler denied my request for a change of venue. This is outrageous."

"What are you complaining about?" Jones asked. "If they scare all the jurors to death, that's got to work in your favor at trial."

"I wonder," Ben said. "I think this town is sick and tired of being bullied."

The ASP rally marched down Main Street at a slow, steady pace. They were ensuring that everyone had an opportunity to see them. As they crested the hill Ben saw there was more to the procession than just the marchers and the cross. A gigantic gallows on wheels was being pushed along behind the procession. On the platform several figures in effigy swung from nooses. A large sign nailed to the gallows identified the figures as THE ENEMY.

Ben was able to identify three of the figures almost immediately. They were the Hatewatch volunteers, Demon Carroll and Demon Pfeiffer. And of course, next to them, a slender brunette figure in a stylish blue dress.

"Darn. I knew I shouldn't have worn that dress." Ben turned to see Belinda standing behind him, watching the parade. "I look much better in red, don't you agree?"

Ben took her hand. Any woman who could make

jokes while being hung in effigy was his kind of woman.

"You realize they're trying to screw the trial?"

Ben nodded.

"Think it'll work?"

"I doubt it. The DA will use voir dire to—"

Ben was startled by the sound of music—different music—coming from the other end of Main Street. This wasn't coming out of any boom box, though. This was being sung, or chanted. Live.

Ben and Belinda pushed forward to see what was happening. There was another assemblage on the other end of the street, marching head-on toward the ASP group. And they were all Vietnamese.

Ben spotted Dan Pham at the head of the group, chanting and shouting at the top of his lungs. His group was carrying placards, too. They all said RESISTANCE.

The ASP marchers spotted them. At first they slowed; then a figure at the front waved everyone ahead. It was Grand Dragon Dunagan. And he wasn't backing down.

The two groups advanced on a collision course. Ben now saw that the Pham contingent had visual aids, too.

Theirs was a tank.

A paper tank, to be sure. It had been constructed around a broken-down Oldsmobile, Coi Than Tien's last remaining vehicle. The tank was made of napkins and chicken wire, like a homecoming float. From an artistic standpoint, pretty sorry. But from the standpoint of conveying a message, not bad at all.

Dunagan kept motioning for his men to march on, but the procession was definitely slowing. The ASPers had probably been expecting a pleasant walk in the noonday sun, not a head-on confrontation with their sworn enemies.

The ASP parade ground to a halt. A few seconds later the Vietnamese group also stopped. They were barely twenty feet apart, on opposite sides of the street.

"We don't want any trouble!" Dunagan shouted.

"Neither do we!" Pham shouted back. *"Ever."*

There was a silence. The sidewalks were now filled with bystanders. Everyone waited to see what would happen next. The tension was palpable.

"We have a permit to march today," Dunagan said finally. "Do you?"

"How like you," Pham replied, "to hide behind laws. And lawyers."

Ben noticed numerous heads on both sides of the street turning to look at him. In most of their minds, Ben realized, he might as well have been standing with the rest of ASP in a green uniform. Only he knew about their falling-out the day before.

"Our permit allows us to march down Main, then turn east on Maple and march to the city limits. So get out of our way."

"I care nothing for your permit!" Pham shouted back.

At that moment a tremendous boom sent tremors through the crowd. Ben wasn't sure where it came from. But he was certain of the result.

The ASP gallows was ablaze.

"Fire!" Dunagan shouted. His men rushed back toward the wooden gallows. One of his men, who was standing too close when the fire erupted, hit the pavement, trying to extinguish the flames that had caught on his shirt.

Another firebomb, Ben thought. Like the one that hit the ASP munitions building a few days before.

Since there was nothing they could do to quell the fire, the ASP men turned their attention to the other end of the street. They surged toward the ranks of the Vietnamese. The Vietnamese stood ready, wielding sticks and knives and anything else that was available.

"Someone stop them!" Ben shouted, but no one heard. The deathly stillness of a few moments before was now replaced by chaos. Screams. Running. Clenched fists. Terror. What they had all dreaded was actually happening. The race war was upon them.

The front lines of ASP met Pham's group and fists began to fly. Ben saw two Vietnamese collapse; he also saw Pham duck under someone's swing and rush at Dunagan.

Main Street became a combat zone. Smoke from the fire filled the air, obscuring vision, making the scene even more confused. Ben heard shouts of fear and howls of pain splitting the thick sooty smoke. Sticks and rocks flew through the air. A billy club rose above the billowing black cloud, then descended with a sickening thud.

Bodies crumbled to the pavement. Through the haze, Ben saw a two-by-four smash into the base of a Vietnamese skull. A few locals ran in from the sidewalks to try to break it up, only to be rewarded by a punch in the gut or a club to the head. Ben recognized Dr. Patterson trying to tend to some of the fallen. The impact of a brick to the back of the doctor's head brought a premature end to his relief efforts. He fell on top of the man he was tending. Two ASP men ran over him, trampling his body underfoot. A group of six or seven young men on the other side of the street charged into the fray. Ben recognized Garth Amick and some of his chums. Apparently they weren't going to let this riot pass without busting some heads themselves.

Several more Vietnamese men were knocked to the pavement. A young man Ben remembered from the bucket-brigade line ran out from under the tank float. He was carrying a baseball bat. He ran up behind a green-fatigued figure and swung the bat across his back. Ben could hear the man's piercing cry as clearly as if he were standing right beside him.

Ben was watching the riot so intently he didn't see the man who tackled him. All he knew was his feet were not beneath him anymore. He fell butt-first onto the pavement.

"Son of a bitch. I got a bone to pick with you."

It was Garth, of course. Ben tried to be sympathetic; after all, under different circumstances it might've been him trying to defend his friends in this misguided manner. On the other hand, he wasn't going to just sit there while Garth took potshots at his face.

Garth's fist came torpedoing toward Ben. Ben grabbed it in midswing. He held Garth's fist with both hands, pushing back as hard as he could. Garth pushed, too. And Garth had leverage on his side.

In a few seconds Ben was flat on the sidewalk and Garth was hovering over him. Bystanders were all around, but no one came to Ben's aid. He continued to grapple with Garth's left hand, and as a result, he didn't see Garth's right coming.

Garth's right fist, the one encased in brass knuckles, smashed into Ben's chin. Ben felt as if his jaw had been separated from his skull. The back of his head thudded against the concrete, leaving him dazed and disoriented. He was just able to perceive Garth swooping around for another blow.

And then, as if by magic, Garth rose off the ground. His fists swung at empty air.

Ben pushed himself up. What on earth . . . ?

It was Loving. He had hoisted Garth up by his belt and flopped him onto the sidewalk. Garth squirmed, arms and legs flailing, but Loving pinned him down like a bug.

"Want me to put 'im outta commission, Skipper?" Loving growled.

"No." Ben rubbed his jaw. It was probably still connected, but it hurt like hell to talk. Precisely what he needed on the first day of a big trial. "Just tie him up or dump him in a trash can."

"Got it." Loving hauled Garth back into the air and started down the sidewalk.

By the time he was back on his feet, Ben was relieved to see that Sheriff Collier and four of his deputies had arrived. Collier fired his revolver several times into the air. Many combatants from both camps scattered. A few isolated fistfights remained, but the peace officers were gradually breaking them up. The man who had wielded the baseball bat was cuffed to a street lamp. The crowd was dispersing.

There were over a dozen figures lying motionless in the street, two in green, ten from Pham's group. A few bystanders. They lay in twisted, unnatural positions. Many of them were bleeding profusely. Ben hoped to God everyone was still breathing. But it was hard to tell.

The fire on the ASP gallows had burned itself out. There was nothing left but a charred post and a platform bearing the stuffed remains of the figures in effigy. John and Frank. Belinda. Several Vietnamese. And—what?

Ben advanced slowly toward the platform. There was another figure there, one that had been blocked from his view before by the others.

It wasn't of Madame Tussaud's quality, but it was

good enough. Medium height, brown hair, on the slender side. Like looking in the mirror.

Ben brushed away the soot on the singed sign below the figure.

DEMON KINCAID.

* 42 *

When Ben reached the courtroom, it was a madhouse. The gallery was filled to twice its capacity; people were standing in the back and sitting in the aisle. At first, he thought some people must have taken refuge from the parade and the resultant brawl, but there was no sign that anyone was leaving. They were here for the show.

Ben struggled past the squatters and tried not to be concerned. Silver Springs hadn't had a murder in—what did Judge Tyler say?—twelve years. It was only natural that this trial would be a major event.

Just as Ben reached the front of the courtroom, a flashbulb exploded in his face. Ben covered his eyes. Was that a reporter from *The Silver Springs Herald*? Because if it was . . .

The face behind the camera belonged to a small boy aged, perhaps, ten. "A souvenir for your scrapbook?" Ben asked.

The boy blanched, then turned and skittered away.

Great, Ben thought. Now I've acquired the ability to strike terror in the hearts of ten-year-olds. He wondered if that was the result of what the *Herald* was saying about him, or what the boy's parents were saying about him. Or both. What a wonderful vacation this had turned out to be. He hadn't caught any fish, but he had managed to become the Silver Springs bogeyman.

Swain came in the back door and made his way to the prosecution table. He was wearing a sport coat and slacks, suspenders, and a bolo tie. A sharp contrast to Ben's three-piece suit (flown in courtesy of Jones). Which was probably exactly what Swain wanted. I'm one of you, Swain was subliminally telling the jury; Kincaid isn't.

Ben went to the defendant's table and began preparing his notes. To his surprise, Swain walked over to talk to him.

"Got a deal for you, Kincaid."

"Bit late, isn't it?" Ben gazed out at the audience. "I think the good citizens of Silver Springs have come to see a trial."

"It's not a trial they want, Kincaid. It's a hanging. That's my whole point. I saw what happened on the street today and it scared me to death. If I can, I want to keep this town from coming unglued." He poked a finger beneath his tie and unfastened the top button. "Also, I'm having a hell of a time finding a baby-sitter."

"What is it you had in mind?"

"You plead guilty; the judge gives you life imprisonment."

"Life! You call that a deal?"

"It's a hell of an improvement over death, that's for damn sure. With good behavior and all that rot, your man could be out in nine years."

"And all he has to do is plead guilty to a crime he didn't commit."

Swain plopped his briefcase on Ben's table. "Kincaid, I know you haven't had time to get up to speed on this case, much less prepare a defense. Let me tell you— we've got more than enough to put your boy away. I'm not trying to buffalo you. I wouldn't say it if it wasn't true. My only concern is that while we're in here playing lawyer games, Silver Springs is going up in smoke."

"Sorry, Swain. My client says he wants a trial." Thank goodness that was finally true.

"Once the trial begins, my offer is off the table. Once this circus is under way, it can't be stopped until your man has a death sentence hanging over his head."

"Thanks for the early warning, Mr. Swain. Now if you'll excuse me, I need to prepare for trial."

Swain left, shaking his head as if Ben had single-handedly ushered in the end of civilization. Ben only hoped he hadn't made a tragic mistake for Donald Vick, either. He hated to see a man plead guilty to a crime he didn't commit. But twentieth-century plea bargaining turned criminal justice into a high-stakes dice game. And if Ben crapped out at trial, the penalty for Donald Vick would be stiff indeed.

Payne was already seated at defendant's table. He wasn't planning to contribute, but he had to be there to maintain the facade of being co-counsel. And, Ben figured, it couldn't hurt to have a trusted townie sitting at his table. There would certainly be plenty of locals sitting with Swain.

Two deputies escorted Donald Vick into the courtroom. They handcuffed him to the defendant's table. In Tulsa, Ben always had the opportunity to clean up his defendants—get them a haircut, put them in a respectable suit of clothes. Not here. Vick was wearing jail-house-gray coveralls. He was going to appear to the jury to be exactly what he was: an accused man who had spent the last several weeks behind bars.

"How do you feel?" Ben asked him. It was an inane question, but it was all he could contrive at the moment.

"I've felt better," Vick replied. His nervousness was etched all over his face.

"The DA has offered us a plea bargain. You plead guilty, he'll give you life. A long tour of duty, but preferable to death."

"What'd you tell him?"

"I told him you wanted your day in court. But it's not too late to accept his offer."

Vick's brain appeared to be working double time. "Well," he said, after a long pause, "when's this show get on the road?"

A few minutes later Judge Tyler entered the courtroom in his long black robe. The courtroom hushed instantly; he didn't have to touch his gavel. The bailiff called the case and Tyler noted that all parties were present and represented by counsel.

"*State versus Donald Vick* will now commence," the bailiff solemnly intoned. "All those who have business before this honorable court will come forward."

"Gentlemen," Judge Tyler said, peering down at Ben and his client, "this trial begins now."

* 43 *

"Mr. Kincaid," Judge Tyler continued. "I read your statement in the morning paper."

"Statement? I never—"

"Let me tell you right up front—I don't appreciate disrespectful comments about this Court being published in the press. If you have a problem with me, you can say it to my face. And by the way, I've never let my cases be decided on the basis of legal trickery, and I don't intend to start now."

"Your honor, I assure you—"

"That's enough. A word to the wise is sufficient. Now then, we need to select a jury. Bailiff, call the veniremen."

The bailiff began drawing names out of a metal cage that looked like an old-time bingo hopper. The selected people walked, some hesitantly, all nervously, to the jury box. Once the required number of bodies was seated, Judge Tyler instructed Swain to begin voir dire.

"Thank you, your honor." Swain stood directly in front of the jury box, his arms spread wide, a warm and friendly smile on his face. "Ladies and gentlemen, we have assembled today in the midst of a great conflict. A festering cauldron of hate has spawned the most sinful of crimes—the wrongful taking of a man's life. I don't need to tell you the importance of the task that lies before us. I will just ask you this. Is there anyone here to-day that for any reason believes he cannot do his duty to God and this court of law?"

Not surprisingly no hands were raised.

"If we prove the defendant's guilt beyond a reasonable doubt, and we will—is there anyone here who would be unable to apply the maximum sentence mandated by law for this heinous crime?"

No hands. But just in case there was some doubt about the sentence to which the DA was referring . . .

"Is there anyone here who feels he or she might be unable to issue a sentence of death, if the law and the circumstances commanded it?"

After a long pause one young man on the far end of the first row raised his hand.

"Mr. Clemons," Swain said.

How did Swain know his name? Ben wondered. He couldn't have memorized them all when the names were called. No—small town, Ben reminded himself. Small town.

"Mr. Clemons, would you be able to issue a sentence of death?"

"Well . . . I just don't know," Clemons said awkwardly. He was aware that half the town was watching him. "I mean . . . *death*—that's an awful harsh sentence. I just—I just don't know if I could do that or not."

"I see," Swain intoned. His disapproval was evident. "I appreciate your honesty." He glanced at the judge. Swain wouldn't ask for Clemons to be removed now, with everyone listening in, but as soon as they were in chambers, Clemons was a goner. "Anyone else?"

Apparently the possibility of becoming executioners didn't trouble anyone else enough to speak up.

"Very well," Swain said. " 'Preciate your cooperation." He returned to his table.

What is this? Ben wondered. He's done? Jury selection in capital cases often went on for days. Sometimes selecting the jury took longer than the trial. Swain had barely been up there for five minutes.

Definitely not a good sign. Either Swain knew the jurors personally and believed they were already predisposed in his favor, or he considered his case so strong he didn't care who sat on the jury. Or both.

"Mr. Kincaid," Judge Tyler said, "you may inquire."

"Thank you." Ben scrambled to the podium. "Ladies and gentlemen of the jury, you are probably familiar with the words District Attorney Swain just used—beyond a reasonable doubt. That's the standard he has to meet. If you don't think he's proved his case *beyond* a reasonable doubt, you must find my client, Donald Vick, not guilty."

"Counsel," Judge Tyler interrupted, "this isn't closing argument. Get on with the voir dire."

"That's what I'm doing," Ben assured him.

"Well, maybe they allow you to plead your whole case during jury selection over in Tulsa County," he said sternly, "but I don't."

A small tittering emerged from the gallery. And just in case the jurors didn't already know Ben was the out-of-towner, the fact was now abundantly clear.

Ben approached the jury box. It was hard to know where to stand. He tried to position himself as close to them as Swain had been, but when he did, he saw the front row of jurors instinctively shrink back in their chairs. They didn't want him that close; he was invading their personal space. The message was obvious: Swain was their friend; Ben wasn't.

"My first question is this," Ben said. "Do you feel that if you are called to this jury, you will be able to apply the reasonable-doubt standard?"

No hands. No reactions.

"Perhaps I should explain what I mean by that. Beyond a reasonable doubt means—"

"Now I'll object to that," Swain said. He popped a suspender for effect. "He's not allowed to define *reasonable doubt*. He can't even do that in closing argument. That's your honor's job."

"The objection will be sustained," Judge Tyler pronounced.

Ben frowned. He was getting nowhere fast. "Let me try it this way. How many of you have heard or read anything about this murder case?"

Eighteen hands shot into the air.

"Your honor," Ben said. "Under these circumstances, my motion for change of venue—"

"Will be denied. Proceed, counsel."

Ben sighed. "Well, how many of you have already made up your mind about what happened?"

Eighteen hands fell. Which made sense, of course. This was an exciting case. These people wanted to sit on the jury, except perhaps Clemons. They weren't about to admit they were prejudiced.

"Do any of you know the defendant? Have you had any contact with him at all?"

Only a middle-aged woman in the third row raised her hand.

"Thank you," Ben said. "And you would be Ms. . . ."

"That's Mrs. Conrad," Swain informed him.

Thanks, Mr. District Attorney, for reminding us that you know everyone here and I don't. "Mrs. Conrad. How do you know Donald Vick?"

"Well, it's like this," she explained carefully. "After that tornado last spring took the north wall off my house, I moved into a boardinghouse where this man was also staying."

"I see," Ben said. "Would that be Mary Sue's place?"

"Why—yes," she said, obviously surprised. Score one for the out-of-towner.

"Did you get to know Mr. Vick during that time?"

"Well, not too much. He was a quiet one. Kept to himself. Rather morose. Always seemed like he was . . . thinking. Or planning—"

"Thank you very much, Mrs. Conrad, I think I've got the idea. Anyone else?"

Ben continued voir-diring the veniremen for another half hour, but he acquired no fresh information. All of them knew enough about the case to have preconceived conclusions, but no one would admit it. Ben would have to proceed on instinct.

Unfortunately Ben knew his instincts were lousy. This was a part of the trial where he typically depended on Christina. She had a knack for puncturing the subterfuge and perceiving what was really on people's minds. But Christina wasn't helping today. She wasn't even in the courtroom.

In chambers, Swain used only one of his preemptory challenges, to take Mr. Clemons off the jury. Ben removed Mrs. Conrad and four other older women. Older women tended to be harsher judges and to give harsher sentences. A statistical generalization, to be sure. Barely better than a stereotype. But at the moment it was all Ben had.

And that left twelve jurors. No recalls were necessary. In barely more than an hour they had selected the twelve men and women who would decide Donald Vick's fate.

The judge and lawyers returned to the courtroom. Judge Tyler charged the final twelve jurors.

"I'm glad we got that taken care of," Tyler said.

"Lawyers tend to be a long-winded bunch. Anytime we can select a jury in less than a day, I feel accomplished. The rest of the veniremen in the courtroom are dismissed."

Tyler glanced at his watch. "We'll call it quits for the day and let you all get home and make the necessary arrangements with your employers and families. Be back at the courthouse at nine o'clock tomorrow morning."

Tyler glanced at the counsel tables. "That includes you gentlemen, too, of course. Have your opening statements ready, and let's keep them down to half an hour, tops. And then, ladies and gentlemen, we shall see what we shall see."

* 44 *

"Don't forget dinner," Belinda said as she and Ben left the courtroom. "You promised."

"And it's a promise I don't intend to break," Ben replied. "But I have tons of work to do before the trial resumes tomorrow. And there's another stop I want to make before it's too late."

"How about you pick me up outside the Hatewatch office around eight-thirty?"

"Deal."

Ben walked three blocks down Main Street, past the auto-parts store, Ed's Gas'M'Up, and the Bluebell Bar. He resisted the temptation to stop in and chat with Mac. He had a hunch Mac wouldn't be that happy to see him; in fact, he might try to bill Ben for the damage to his pinball machine. Instead Ben kept walking until he arrived at the offices of *The Silver Springs Herald*.

Unfortunately the *Herald* saw him coming. As he approached the streetfront window, a middle-aged man in a tweed suit jumped up and made a beeline for the entrance. Ben managed to get his foot in the door just before it was shut.

"Sorry," the man said. "We're closed."

"I want to speak to the editor," Ben said.

"He's not in!" the man insisted. He was wearing a name tag: HAROLD MCGUINESS—EDITOR.

"You're McGuiness!" Ben shouted. "You're the man who keeps writing about me. I have a bone to pick with you."

"I write *all* the articles for the *Herald*. What of it? We're still closed." McGuiness tugged on the doorknob, trying to pull it shut.

"My name is Ben Kincaid."

"You think I don't know that? You think I don't read my own paper?"

"I've been misquoted in your distinguished journal. Repeatedly. I want you to print a retraction."

"Sorry. Can't be done. Now, if you'll kindly remove your foot—"

"I'll remove my foot when you agree to print the retraction. Bad enough you've convinced everyone in town I'm a sleazebag. Now you've got the judge thinking I'm bad-mouthing him. I never uttered a single syllable that you attributed to me."

"Never said you did." McGuiness yanked the door so hard the glass rattled in its frame. "Now get out of here."

"I could sue you for libel. You put quotation marks around a statement I didn't make."

"That doesn't mean it's an exact quote. Least that's what the United States Supreme Court says. And as long as I didn't act with malice, I'm well within the bounds of the law."

Unfortunately, Ben was familiar with the current case law on libel. "Look, I don't want to sue anyone. I merely want to set the record straight. Why don't you interview me—"

"Thanks, don't care to. Got what I need from secondary sources."

"You've ruined my reputation. Everyone in town

thinks I'm going to use city-slicker tricks to put a murderer back on the street."

"Well, aren't you?"

"My goal is to see that Vick gets a fair trial. And your newspaper is making that almost impossible."

"If that's supposed to make me shed tears for your client, it doesn't." He kicked Ben in the shin. Ben's foot involuntarily drew back and McGuiness slammed the door shut.

Ben picked up Belinda around nine, and together they walked arm in arm to Bo-Bo's Chinese Restaurant. It was the only place still open other than the Bluebell, and Ben definitely wasn't taking her there. He did have some doubts about Bo-Bo's authenticity, however. First, there was the question of the owner's name. Second, Bo-Bo's was the first Oriental restaurant Ben recalled that also served red beans and rice, grits, and fatback.

As Ben and Belinda waited to be seated they stood behind a middle-aged Vietnamese woman who was picking up a carryout order. The teenage girl who was supposed to be the cashier was standing in the doorway to the kitchen fighting off (not very hard) the amorous advances of a boy about her age in a chef's cap. Eventually the Vietnamese woman captured her attention. The girl passed the woman a plastic-wrapped bundle of cardboard cartons, still giggling at the boy in the back.

"Seventeen fifty-two, please."

The Vietnamese woman passed a bill across the counter.

"Seventeen fifty-two out of twenty. Your change will be two forty-eight." The girl pulled two ones out of the cash register and counted them into the Vietnamese woman's hand. "That's one, two—"

She glanced down at the register. "Wait a minute. You gave me a ten, not a twenty."

The Vietnamese woman stared blankly at the girl.

"What are you trying to pull? You can't take seventeen outta ten."

"Seven dollar," the Vietnamese woman said. "Paid." She reached out for her ten, still lying on top of the cash drawer.

"Oh, no you don't." The girl slammed the drawer shut. "Now give me back that food."

The woman clutched the food package tightly in her arms. "Paid already."

"My daddy was right," the girl said. "He told me you people have to be watched every single second. Sneaky gooks. Barbara!"

An older woman with a beehive hairdo emerged from the back of the restaurant. "What's going on?"

"This lady tried to pass a ten off as a twenty. Now she won't give back the food."

The older woman frowned. "I'll call Sheriff Collier."

"Now just a minute," Belinda said, interrupting. "This poor woman didn't try to pass off anything. She obviously barely knows the language and probably misunderstood you."

The teenage girl pressed her fists against her hips, annoyed at this interloper. "She tried to pass off a ten—"

"She thought you asked for seven dollars, not seventeen. You assumed she would give you a twenty and didn't notice when she didn't."

"Who do you think you are telling me—"

"The fact is, you were flirting with that boy in the kitchen and you weren't paying enough attention to your job. And now you're trying to make this innocent woman take the blame for your screwup."

The teenage girl shot daggers at Belinda with her

eyes. "I don't understand why you're sticking up for this stupid chink."

Barbara, the older woman, pushed the girl aside. "The lady still owes us seven dollars and fifty-two cents. Do you have that much, ma'am?"

The Vietnamese woman stared back expressionlessly. It was obvious she wasn't following any of this.

"Here's ten more bucks," Belinda said, tossing the bill across the counter. "Keep the change."

The teenage girl stomped back into the kitchen.

After they were given a chilly seating by Barbara, Ben said, "Well, that was disturbing."

"That," Belinda said, "was the entire race-hatred problem in a nutshell. It starts as a stupid misunderstanding. The stranger makes a mistake, the local makes a mistake. It's a minor incident. But tonight that teenage girl will tell her daddy about how that Vietnamese lady tried to rob the restaurant, and how she got in trouble with her boss as a result. Daddy will say, yeah, I'm not getting paid as much for my chickens as I used to, either. Pretty soon, every time something goes wrong in their lives, it'll be the fault of the Vietnamese."

"And then ASP gets invited to town."

Belinda nodded. "That's about the size of it."

Ben and Belinda maintained an animated conversation all through dinner. He was amazed at how much he had to say to her—and how easily the words came. He was not normally a smoothie with the fair sex; on the contrary, he was prone to stutter, trip over the carpet, and inadvertently insult his date's mother, all in the first minute. But tonight seemed to be going fine. He and Belinda liked all the same books (*Bleak House*, *Wuthering Heights*) and the same movies (*Twelve Angry Men*, *To Kill a Mockingbird*). They believed in the same things.

They liked each other.

Ben was halfway through dinner before he noticed Christina was sitting two tables away from them. She was with a large group of people—fellow boarders at Mary Sue's, probably. Contrary to his own chilly reception from Silver Springs, Christina appeared to be getting along famously with the local populace. They were chatting amiably, laughing at her jokes.

The kid sitting next to Christina looked familiar. Ben stretched forward to get a clearer view. It was Garth Amick!—the kid who slid on the brass knuckles every time Ben came into view. It seemed Christina had no such problem.

After finishing cashew chicken that contained more celery than cashews or chicken, and moo goo gai pan that was mostly rice, Ben and Belinda called for coffee.

"Actually that wasn't bad," Ben said, "although it wasn't Ri Le's. When you come to Tulsa, I'll take you there."

"I'd like that."

The waiter returned with coffee and fortune cookies. "Can I take your plate?" he asked Belinda.

"Oh, not yet. I want to save the leftovers."

"I'll bring you a doggie bag."

"Never mind. I have my own." She opened her purse, withdrew one of several small plastic bags, and scraped in the leftover moo goo gai pan.

"You carry your own doggie bags with you?" Ben asked.

"Waste not, want not. That's what my aunt always said. I suppose I don't really have to do this anymore, but old habits die hard." She filled the bag, sealed it, and carefully put it back in her purse. "Deep down I guess I'm always afraid I'll go bust, and I'll be back to stealing candy bars from Mr. Carney's drugstore just to get through the night."

"You didn't really do that, did you?"

"I'm pleading the fifth." She stirred her slow-drip coffee and poured it over ice.

Ben followed suit. "How did you come to found Hatewatch?"

"After I managed to get through law school and survive my first marriage—which was a major-league disaster—I started looking for ways to use my degree to make a meaningful contribution. I'd seen how bad life was for some people, and I was determined to do what I could to make life better for them. I started at the Southern Poverty Law Center, then worked for some other organizations that are fighting hate groups and organized racism. I actually met Morris Dees—now there's a modern-day hero if ever there was one. He does great work, but he can't do it all alone. That's why I started Hatewatch five years ago."

"Only five years ago? For such a relatively new organization, it's been amazingly successful."

"Too successful, as far as some people are concerned. Such as Grand Dragon Dunagan. The Supreme Court said penalty enhancement for hate crimes was constitutional in *Wisconsin versus Mitchell*, and we've made the most of that in criminal and civil cases. This is the third time Hatewatch has come up against one of Dunagan's little hate camps. ASP has gone after Hispanics in Florida, blacks in Birmingham, and now the Vietnamese. Torture, rape, murder—they've done it all. Not exactly boy scouts. Hey, I haven't opened my fortune cookie yet."

She broke the shell and read the message. " 'Soon you will cross over the great waters.' " She frowned. "Well, I don't care much for the sound of that."

"Relax," Ben assured her. "Probably means you're going to Bermuda." He cracked open his own cookie. " 'Birds are entangled by their feet, and men by their hearts.' " Ben grimaced. "I think these cookies came from the Transylvania factory. I'm surprised the management permits this. Restaurants usually screen out anything that might possibly upset the clientele."

"Did you major in restaurateuring?"

"Music, actually. How about you?"

"Funny you should ask." A delightful smile played upon her lips. "Why don't you come up to my place, and I'll give you a demonstration?"

Ben looked at her warily. "Is this dangerous?"

"No." She took his hand in hers. "The dangerous part will be sneaking you into my room while Mary Sue isn't watching."

"Are you sure about this?" Ben said through the bathroom door.

"Positive," Belinda replied. "Get out here."

"Well . . . turn down the light."

"They're down. I can barely see the table."

"And you're looking the other way?"

"And my eyes are shut—cross my heart and hope to die. Would you get out here already?"

Ben opened the bathroom door slightly and confirmed that she was looking the other way. He tiptoed out of the bathroom. He had stripped down to his boxer shorts. Actually Belinda had instructed him to strip, *period*, but there was no way he was parting with his shorts. A boy had to have some modesty.

He lay flat on the table and pulled the towel over him. "Okay. I'm in position."

"Good." Belinda turned around and smiled. "Cute boxers."

"How . . . ?" Ben yanked the corner of the towel over his rear. "I never met anyone who majored in massage therapy before."

"Well, you're in for a treat." She placed her hands on his shoulders. "Didn't I say I wanted to make a meaningful contribution to the world? Now, this is an example of a Swedish massage."

"Perfect," Ben murmured as she soothed his neck and shoulders. "I'm feeling very Swedish tonight."

"The Swedish massage derives from Chinese techniques of physical manipulation. It's composed of five basic strokes—the effleurage, the petrissage, friction, tapotement, and vibration."

"A massage *and* a lecture," Ben said. "Such a deal."

She began the effleurage, which, she explained, involved long, gliding strokes in the direction of the heart. "Boy, are you tense!" She moved her hands systematically down his back. "Your muscles are really knotted up."

"Well, it's been a tense week."

"Lucky I got you on this table before you exploded in the middle of the courtroom."

She took him through her repertoire of strokes—kneading, pressing, tapping, and vibrating. "Of course, this is just one example of each stroke. There are several variants."

"I think we should try them all," Ben murmured.

"This is the Anara massage technique."

Ben could tell the movements of her hands had changed, not that it made much difference. It all felt delicious.

She started working on his thighs. "Strong legs for a desk jockey," she commented.

"I get plenty of exercise chasing my cat."

"Who's looking after her while you're on this extended vacation?"

"My landlady, Mrs. Marmelstein. She's always happy to help out. Cat-sitting gives her an excuse to go through my closets."

Belinda continued moving down his legs. "Man, you are just unbelievably tense. You keep it all locked up inside, don't you?"

Ben chose not to comment.

"Now, this is an example of the Shiatsu massage technique."

To Ben's surprise, her fingertips danced lightly over the soles of his feet. "Hey, that tickles."

"So there's life in you after all." She used her thumb and forefinger to rub out the tension in his feet. "Finally I want to demonstrate the famed Montgomery massage."

"The Montgomery massage?"

"Right." She began lightly kissing his back, then worked her way up the nape of his neck. Goose bumps rose on his skin. "Does this tickle?"

"That's one way of putting it." Ben rolled over and took Belinda into his arms. "Can I play?"

"Please do." The first kiss was followed by several others, each more passionate than the first.

Belinda pulled away for a moment and reached behind her back. A second later her business suit lay in a pile on the floor.

Ben felt his heart palpitating. "You're beautiful," he murmured.

Belinda lay down beside him. She kissed him again on the lips, then let her own lips roam where they would. "I'm not sure, but I think you're becoming less tense," she said quietly. Her fingers ran up his chest and through his hair.

Ben explored the soft contours of her perfect body. "Did you really major in massage therapy?"

She smiled, then rolled over on top of him. "Nah. But I thought it was a great way to sneak a peek at your boxer shorts."

* 45 *

The next morning Ben made it to the Silver Springs courthouse well before nine and began reviewing his notes. He'd had a great night's sleep. Once he and Belinda finally got around to sleeping.

Two deputies brought Vick back to the defendant's table and the crowd began to flood into the courtroom gallery. Most of the people he had recognized the day before had returned. Plus Grand Dragon Dunagan and a small coterie of ASP muscle.

"What brings you here?" Ben asked as he passed by them.

"Came to keep a close eye on you," Dunagan said.

"I thought you considered me lead counsel for the forces of goodness and light."

"That was before I found out you were a Vietcong sympathizer," Dunagan spat out. "Before I found out you were in league with that demon whore Hamilton."

Ben's jaw clenched. "You have no business talking about Belinda like that."

"I know what she is!" Fortunately the drone of the crowded courtroom muffled his shout. "And I know what you are now, too."

"You hateful—" Ben swallowed the expletive on the tip of his tongue. He turned his back on Dunagan and walked away. He noticed that Colonel Nguyen from Coi

Than Tien was in the gallery. And in the front row, Belinda sat beside her associates Frank Carroll and John Pfeiffer.

Judge Tyler entered the courtroom and the crowd was silenced. "Opening statements, gentlemen. Mr. Prosecutor, would you like to begin?"

"Thank you, your honor." Swain planted himself in his intimate, up-front position inches away from the jury.

"Thuy Quang Vuong—known by his friends as Tommy—was a Vietnamese American. But that isn't what this case is about. He was a young man, and subject to many of the troubles most young men face. That isn't what this case is about either. Tommy Vuong was a living, breathing human being, with as much right to live his life as any one of you sitting in this jury box."

Swain leaned forward and made eye contact with each of the jurors. "And *that's* what this case is about. Because you see, ladies and gentlemen of the jury, Tommy Vuong wasn't permitted to live. He wasn't permitted to marry, or to have children, or to experience any of the quiet, simple joys most of us take for granted. Because on July twenty-fifth, on a hot summer night, someone ripped his life away by firing two metal crossbow bolts at close range into his chest and his neck."

He glanced at Vick, an unmistakable bit of nonverbal communication. "And then the killer planted a burning cross over Tommy's bleeding head."

A discernible tremor passed through the courtroom. That was a detail that had been withheld from the press; most people didn't know about it. Unfortunately it was also a detail that appeared to confirm Vick's guilt.

"You might think," Swain continued, "that two crossbow bolts would produce a quick death. You would be wrong. Tommy Vuong's life drained away, slowly and painfully, as his blood poured from his veins. And as if that wasn't enough, the cross caught Tommy's clothing on fire. And he began to *burn*."

Another shudder passed through the gallery. Ben felt a bit of a shudder himself.

Ben could object; this dramatic recitation was hardly likely to aid the jury in their fact-finding mission. But he knew it would be pointless. Every prosecutor had the inherent right to portray the facts as melodramatically as possible. Swain was trying to stir up sympathy for the victim—and hatred for the defendant. And he was doing a commendable job. The jury already disliked Vick; Ben could see them sneaking peeks at him, then quickly averting their eyes. And they had yet to encounter a single bit of evidence that indicated he was guilty.

"Not just anyone could commit a crime like that," Swain continued. "Not just anyone could be so . . . cold. So utterly devoid of feeling. So heartless. No, it took a special kind of man to commit this crime. A man with hatred burning in his gut." He turned and stood squarely before Vick. "Ladies and gentlemen, the evidence we will present will prove beyond a reasonable doubt that the man who committed this horrible deed was the defendant—Donald Vick."

Swain and Vick made eye contact. It was like a contest of wills; neither wanted to be the first to flinch. Eventually Swain turned away and continued his opening.

Swain provided few clues about the testimony he would be presenting. Perhaps, Ben mused, the evidence wasn't as strong as Swain had been suggesting. More likely he just didn't want to give Ben any advance notice. Swain made passing references to trace evidence on the crossbow and Vick's fight with Vuong, and a purported confession. What concerned Ben most was

Swain's elliptical reference to "Vick's fatal mistake—the selection of the deadly and exotic crossbow as his instrument of death."

Swain finished his performance and reclaimed his seat.

"Would you care to give your opening statement now, Mr. Kincaid," Judge Tyler inquired, "or to reserve it until the start of the defendant's case-in-chief?"

"I'll go now," Ben said, rising to his feet. It was crazy to reserve opening until later. The jury could sit for days without hearing any version of the facts other than the prosecutor's.

Ben suspected he could never match Swain's histrionic flair, and given his position in the case, it would be stupid to try. Instead he would maintain a calm, reasoned approach. He would remind the jury why they were here.

"Serving as a juror is one of the greatest honors that can be bestowed on a citizen in a free democracy," Ben began. "But like all honors, it comes with responsibilities. And duties. Your duty as jurors is to ensure that your decision, whatever it may be, is not based on passion or prejudice, but is based solely and without exception on the facts presented to you during the trial. That is the promise you make when you sit in that box. That is your sacred obligation."

It was worth a try. In Ben's experience, most jurors took their position seriously and endeavored to do the job right.

"District Attorney Swain has told you, in great and grisly detail, how Tommy Vuong was killed. About those facts, there is no controversy. We do not dispute how he was killed, and we do not dispute that it was a horrible tragedy. We only dispute one issue: who did it. Because Donald Vick did not kill Tommy Vuong."

Ben scanned the jurors' faces. If their minds were already made up, he probably wasn't changing them. But at least they were listening.

"The prosecution will present a variety of evidence to you in an effort to convict the wrong man of this crime. But as you sift through the evidence laid before you, ask yourself one question: does this evidence prove that Donald Vick did in fact kill Tommy Vuong, or that he *might* have killed Tommy Vuong. Because you see, ladies and gentlemen, any number of people *might* have killed Tommy Vuong. But you can only find Donald Vick guilty if the prosecution has proven beyond a reasonable doubt that Donald Vick *did* kill Tommy Vuong. That it was absolutely, positively Donald Vick—and no one else. The burden of proof is on the prosecution, and if they do not meet it, then Judge Tyler will instruct you that you must find Donald Vick not guilty."

Ben talked a bit more about the prosecution evidence. His remarks were necessarily vague; he had only the barest glimmer of an idea what the prosecution was going to say, much less what his response would be. And as far as he knew, the defendant's only witness was the defendant.

A man who refused to talk.

Ben finished his opening. He gave Vick a friendly, confident smile that everyone could see, then sat down beside him. Some lawyers clapped their defendants on the back, or offered them a Life Saver, just to show the jury that they liked them. That struck Ben as a bit extreme under the circumstances; Vick would have to make do with a smile.

"Very good," Judge Tyler pronounced. "Looks like we still have time for some testimony before lunch. Mr. Swain, call your first witness."

* 46 *

Swain led with his forensic testimony. It was a standard technique—get the boring stuff out of the way while the jury is still fresh and slightly less likely to nod off.

His first witness was the county coroner, David Douglas, who was called to testify that Tommy Vuong was in fact dead. Hardly startling information, but a necessary prerequisite to a prosecution for murder.

Douglas was somewhat uncertain about the cause of death. Was it the crossbow that killed Vuong or the fire? Or a combination of both? Under Ben's cross-examination, he admitted that he suspected Vuong died from loss of blood due to the crossbow bolts, but it was impossible to be certain. Not that it mattered very much. Either way, Vuong was dead.

Next, Ben was disturbed to hear Swain call a lab technician from Little Rock, a man named Darryl Stephens. Stephens would undoubtedly testify about the trace evidence found on the crossbow. Mike was expecting the results of his own tests today and was waiting at the post office for them to arrive. He promised to come directly to the courthouse as soon as they did. So far, though, Mike hadn't appeared.

After establishing Stephens's credentials, Swain questioned him about the crossbow found near the murder site. "Have you had an opportunity to examine the bolts extracted from the dead man's body?"

"Indeed I have."

"And were you able to compare those bolts to the crossbow itself?"

Stephens folded his hands across his lap. "Yes, sir."

"Did you obtain any information from this comparison?"

"Yes." Stephens leaned forward. Ben knew the signs; he was about to go into his *teaching* mode. "Crossbows and their bolts can be analyzed in much the same way the science of ballistics studies guns and bullets. Just as every gun leaves unique markings on the bullets it fires, so a crossbow marks each shaft fired from its triggering mechanism. The markings are harder to spot, but it can be done."

"That's fascinating," Swain said. "I didn't know that."

I'll just bet, Ben thought.

"Were you able to draw any conclusions about the crossbow and bolts you examined?"

"Yes. The same markings found on both bolts extracted from Vuong's body were also found on test bolts we fired in the lab from the crossbow found near the crime scene. There's no doubt about it. This crossbow fired those bolts."

"I see," Swain said, holding the crossbow up high so the jury could see it. "So this crossbow is definitely the murder weapon. Well, we'll be talking about that some more later. Tell me, sir. Did you find any trace evidence on the crossbow when it was first brought to you?"

"Yes, I did." Stephens glanced at Swain, then continued. Ben got the impression this testimony had been rehearsed many times beforehand. "I found two hairs caught in the mechanism of the crossbow."

"Really?" Swain said in mock surprise. "Did you run any tests on the hairs?"

"Yes. I conducted a spectroscopic analysis, and compared them to two exemplars removed from the defendant's head."

"And?"

"The hairs in the crossbow matched those taken from Donald Vick."

"I see," Swain said. "That's all for now, your honor."

"Mr. Kincaid," Judge Tyler said. "Any questions?"

Ben checked the gallery—Mike still wasn't here. Blast. He would have to wing it without him.

Ben positioned himself at the far side of the courtroom from the jury, one sure way to prevent eye contact between jury and witness. "Quite a coincidence, don't you think?"

Stephens's forehead wrinkled. "I . . . don't quite follow you."

"Don't you think it's an amazing coincidence?"

"Think . . . what is?"

"The hairs in the crossbow." Ben pivoted and posed his question as much to the jury as the witness. "How did they ever get in the crossbow mechanism?"

Stephens recrossed his legs. "Presumably they fell from the killer's head—"

"And just happened to get caught in the workings of the crossbow? Now that's what I call a coincidence." He checked the jurors for their reaction. "I would think it amazing if *one* hair managed to fall just perfectly so as to get trapped in the firing mechanism. And your testimony is that *two* hairs fell there."

"Well . . . yes."

"Sir, doesn't that strike you as somewhat incredible?"

"Sometimes unusual events occur. . . ."

"Sir." Ben approached the witness and hovered over

him. "Isn't it much more likely that someone *put* those hairs in the mechanism?"

The jury stirred audibly.

"I . . . suppose that's within the realm of possibility."

"And if that happened, Donald Vick might not have even been there at the time, right?"

"Well . . . I suppose . . . theoretically . . ."

"Now, you testified that the hairs in the crossbow *matched* those taken from Donald Vick. What exactly do you mean by *matched*?"

"Matched means matched. Same texture, same color, same race . . ."

"Sir, isn't it true that at this time there is no absolutely certain method of establishing that a hair came from a particular person?"

The witness squirmed. "We've been working with new DNA analysis techniques—"

"Did either of the hairs you found have a live hair bulb?"

"A—what?"

"Hair bulb. You know, the root."

"Uh, no."

"But, sir, you can't take a DNA fingerprint of the hair itself, because the hair is dead, right?"

"I—suppose."

"And even if the bulb hadn't rotted, you said it wasn't intact."

"That's true."

"Well then, isn't it also true that you cannot say with medical certainty that the hairs in the crossbow came from Donald Vick's head?"

The witness glared at Ben. "That's true. When you put it like that."

"Thank you, sir. No more questions."

"Redirect?" Judge Tyler asked.

"Definitely," Swain said. "Mr. Stephens, let's talk about the scenario Mr. Kincaid just proposed. Do you believe that Donald Vick never came near that cross-bow?"

"No. I *know* he did."

"How do you know?"

"The hairs weren't the only trace evidence I found. There was also a bloodstain."

"A bloodstain!" Swain whirled to face Ben, obviously expecting to see a look of astonishment or surprise. He was greatly disappointed. Thanks to Mike, Ben had seen this one coming a mile away.

"Did you run any tests on the bloodstain?" Swain continued.

"Of course. We typed the blood, then compared it to a sample taken from Donald Vick. They matched."

"Indeed. And what is Mr. Vick's blood type?"

"B negative."

"Is that a common blood type?"

"Not at all."

"So the crossbow has Donald Vick's hair and Donald Vick's blood. Did you find trace evidence belonging to anyone else?"

"No, sir."

"I guess that's it, then. No more questions."

Judge Tyler made a bridge with his hands and rested his chin upon it. "Back to you, Mr. Kincaid."

"Right." Ben approached the witness. "Mr. Stephens, you said B negative is an uncommon blood type. Just how uncommon is it?"

Stephens obviously liked having a chance to display his erudition. "About ten percent of the population has B negative blood."

"And how many people live in Silver Springs?"

"Counting the surrounding country? Oh, I'd say about three thousand."

"And ten percent of three thousand is how many?"

Stephens coughed. "Well . . . math was never my best subject . . . but that would be three hundred."

"So when you say the blood on the crossbow was Donald Vick's type, you're really saying that it was the type of about three hundred people in the immediate area, one of whom was Donald Vick. Right?"

"I suppose you could look at it that way."

Ben heard a noise in the back of the courtroom. He turned and saw Mike entering the gallery. Mike was motioning to him, but Ben knew Judge Tyler wouldn't permit a recess at this critical juncture.

"Did you run any other tests on the blood?" Ben asked Stephens.

"As a matter of fact, I did."

"You did?"

"Yes. We performed a microscopic analysis of the blood cells. Just got the equipment this year," he added proudly.

"What were the results?" Just as he finished the question he noticed Mike waving frantically from the back of the courtroom. His message was absolutely clear: *Don't ask that question.*

Too late. "The tests showed that the blood on the crossbow was Donald Vick's. Not that it came from one of three hundred people. That it came from Donald Vick. Beyond any question."

Ben saw Mike slump down into his seat. The Tulsa tests must have produced the same result.

Ben saw Swain grinning through the hand across his mouth. Swain had suckered him in, and his witness had delivered the punch. Ben knew he was only getting what he deserved. He had violated the cardinal rule of cross-examination: if you don't know the answer, don't ask the question.

"Thank you," Ben said quietly. "No more questions."

"Any further redirect?" Judge Tyler asked.

"Oh, no," Swain said happily. "I think everyone understands the forensic evidence just fine now."

"Very well. Mr. Stephens, you are excused. Ladies and gentlemen"—his stoic face shifted to a sly grin—"I'm hungry. Let's get some lunch. This trial will resume at one-thirty."

* 47 *

After the lunch break Swain called to the stand Mary
Sue Mullins, sole proprietor of Mary Sue's boardinghouse. Mary Sue was dressed in a bright green dress
with a lace collar—undoubtedly her Sunday best. She
left her apron at home.

As she passed Ben on her way to the witness stand,
he noticed she was trembling slightly. Nervous? About
cross-examination? Or perhaps she just didn't like ap-
pearing in public without Old Sally.

Swain extracted a bit of background from Mary Sue,
including the critical fact that she ran a boardinghouse
on Maple Street. He didn't waste much time. Ben had
the feeling everyone on the jury—probably everyone in
town—already knew who she was.

"Do you know the defendant?" Swain asked.

"Oh, yes. I've known Donald for several months."

"And how do you know him?"

"He took a room in my house. Room six. At the top
of the stairs."

"Did you see much of him?"

"Well, a bit. 'Course, he was gone during the daylight
hours. Out at that camp running maneuvers, I'd imagine."

"Objection," Ben said. "She's speculating."

264

Tyler nodded. "Sustained. The witness will confine herself to the events she has seen or heard."

Mary Sue looked stung, but she managed to carry on. "He came back most evenings for supper. Then he'd go up to his room for the night."

"So there's no question in your mind but that you know who Donald Vick is?" Swain asked.

"Not the least bit. He's sitting right over there in the gray coveralls."

Swain nodded. "Where were you on the afternoon of July twenty-fifth?"

"At Mac's place. You know, the Bluebell Bar."

"Was anyone else there?"

"Yes. Tommy Vuong was there. With three of his friends."

"Do you know the friends' names?"

"No. But they were all Vietnamese. Coi Than Tien people, I assumed."

"What happened when Donald Vick came into the bar?"

"Objection," Ben said. "Assumes facts not in evidence."

Swain didn't respond verbally; instead he gave the judge a roll of the eyes and a do-I-really-have-to? look.

Judge Tyler licked his lips. "Sorry, Mister Prosecutor. He's right. Let's do it by the book."

"All right," Swain said. His tone made it clear he considered Ben's objection a trivial annoyance that prevented him from unearthing the truth. "Let me try it this way. Did anyone enter the bar while you were there?"

"Yes. Donald Vick."

"What a surprise." He shared a smile with the jury. "Did Mr. Vick stop and chat with you?"

"Oh, no." She folded her hands over her purse and leaned toward the jury. It was as if she was sharing a bit of gossip on the back porch. "He made a beeline for Tommy Vuong."

"And then what happened?"

"Donald raised his hands like this"—she locked her fists together—"and clubbed Vuong right on the back. Without any warning. He was like a savage beast, just pounding and pounding him, without a shred of mercy."

"That sounds horrible," Swain said. "What happened to Vuong?"

"He didn't know what hit him. He just kinda slumped over the bar. Didn't move a muscle. But that didn't matter to Donald Vick. He kept on hurting him. I thought he was going to beat the poor boy senseless."

"Is that what happened?"

"No. Fortunately Vuong's friends came to his rescue. They pushed Vick away, then overpowered him. Vick wasn't so tough once the tables were turned. I have to say, they did some serious pounding of their own. Vick's face was cut and bleeding, and the rest of him didn't look any too healthy."

"What happened next?"

"They tossed him right out the door." She had apparently been coached not to repeat the hearsay statement Judge Tyler had excluded. "That was the last we saw of him. I figured we'd probably never hear from him again. I had no idea. . . ."

"I'm sure you didn't, Mary Sue. No more questions, your honor."

"Mr. Kincaid?"

Ben walked slowly to the witness stand, carefully considering his strategy. Whether he believed her testimony or not, Mary Sue was an older woman and a respected member of the community. Treating her like the enemy would be a big mistake.

Ben reintroduced himself and tossed her a few softballs, easy questions intended to ease into the cross-examination. But eventually, before the jury got too bored with the chitchat, he knew he had to get to what really mattered.

"Now, ma'am, prior to that night at the bar, did Donald Vick strike you as a hothead?"

"Oh, no. Anything but. He was a quiet fellow. Timid almost. But you know"—her voice dropped to a whisper—"it's always the quiet ones."

"Move to strike," Ben said. When would he learn to keep his clever comments to himself? "Donald never picked a fight at your house, did he, ma'am?"

"Oh, no!"

"Never threatened you, did he?"

"No, no. Of course, I'm not Vietnamese."

"Now that's an interesting suggestion." Ben walked slowly back to defendant's table, drawing the jury's eyes away from the witness. "Donald actually had some Vietnamese friends, didn't he?"

"I'd be very much surprised."

"Didn't you yourself admit a Vietnamese visitor to Donald's room two nights before the murder?"

"Well . . . that's true."

"Who was the visitor?"

"I don't know."

"Was it Tommy Vuong?"

"Absolutely not."

"Was it anyone in the courtroom?"

Mary Sue scanned the faces in the gallery. "I don't think so."

"What about Donald's other visitor?" Ben paused dramatically. "The woman."

"I—I don't—"

"Didn't a woman come to visit Donald Vick the night before the murder?"

"Well . . . yes . . ."

"And didn't she enter Donald's room while he was there?"

Heads turned in the jury box. Ben was afraid the reputation of Mary Sue's boardinghouse would be tarnished for some time to come.

"Y-yes."

"Do you know who the woman was?"

"Never saw her before."

"Was she Vietnamese?"

"No. White."

"Would you recognize her if you saw her again?"

"I think so."

"Is she in the courtroom today?"

Mary Sue took a quick look. "I don't see her."

"Did Donald have any other Vietnamese visitors?"

"Not that I noticed—"

"Is it possible that he had some visitors when you weren't around?"

"Well . . . I suppose it's possible."

Ben had made his point. It was time to move on. "Let's turn to the following afternoon, at the Bluebell Bar. You say Donald walked up and started pounding Tommy Vuong. But, ma'am—wasn't there a bit of conversation before the pounding started?"

"Uh—conversation?"

"Right. Between Vick and Vuong?"

Mary Sue frowned. "They did talk. . . ."

"Vuong talked to Vick?"

"Mostly the other way around, as I recall."

"Did you hear what they said?"

"No. He's your client. Why don't you just ask him what they said?"

Would that it were so simple. "How long did this conversation last?"

"Well, I wasn't timing it. About a minute, I'd guess."

"Did any of Vuong's friends overhear the conversation?"

"I doubt it. The bar was quite noisy."

"And then what happened?"

"Vuong turned his back while Donald was still talking. Just ignored him."

"And that's when Donald hit him?"

"I guess that's right."

"So the fight emerged from the discussion. Argument, probably. Possibly an argument begun two nights before at your boardinghouse."

"I said it wasn't Tommy Vuong that came to visit Vick!"

"Are you sure?"

"I am. With God as my witness, I'm sure."

Ben slowly crossed the courtroom. "Ma'am, I don't want to be indelicate. But isn't it true that you have a drinking problem?"

"I beg your pardon!"

"I don't mean to embarrass you, ma'am. But you are fond of the bottle, aren't you?"

"I . . . occasionally take a small glass of sherry just before bed."

"Well . . . according to your testimony, on the day of the murder, you were in the Bluebell Bar. In the middle of the afternoon. Right?"

Mary Sue lifted her head indignantly. "True."

"And you weren't there just to play pinball, were you?"

Mary Sue looked down at her hands.

"Ma'am, the jury is waiting for your answer."

"No," she said quietly. "I wasn't there just to play pinball."

"In fact, you sometimes take a drink or two in the morning. Right?"

Her eyes began to well up. "It's just so hard some mornings . . . since Joe passed on and . . . and—"

"My point is this," Ben interrupted, hoping to make this easier for her. "Drinking affects your vision, doesn't it?"

"Well, I don't know . . . I guess it could."

"Ma'am, had you been drinking two nights before the murder?"

"I . . . suppose I might've done . . ."

"Are you sure it wasn't Tommy Vuong who came to your house to see Donald Vick two nights before the murder?"

"I told you it wasn't!"

"True." Ben slowly turned toward the jury. "But haven't you also said that all those Vietnamese look alike to you?"

Mary Sue's lips parted, then froze. Her mouth worked wordlessly for a few moments.

"Thank you," Ben said, walking back to defendant's table. "No more questions."

* 48 *

Ben was in the back of the Hatewatch office, in a smallish cubbyhole he had transformed into his War Room. He was poring over his notes for the next day's trial when Mike and Jones entered.

"Nice work on that boardinghouse lady," Mike said. "I think you seriously impeached the veracity of her identification."

"That's true," Ben agreed. "But that doesn't alter the fact that Donald picked a fight with Vuong a few hours before he was killed. That combination of inconvenient facts is going to be very hard for the jury to forget."

"I expect so." Mike noticed that Ben was craning his neck, peering over Mike's shoulder. "Looking for something?"

"Oh . . . not really. I just thought . . . maybe . . ."

"Christina? Sorry. I did see her in town today. I think she was going on a picnic. It's amazing how well she gets on with the locals. You could take some lessons from her. Haven't seen her around here, though."

"Oh." Ben glanced down at his notes. "It's not important. I just thought perhaps she might have . . ."

"Changed her mind?" Jones said. "Christina? Don't count on it, Boss."

"Yeah. Stupid of me. I have other problems to worry

about anyway." He dropped his pencil. "But I sure could use a good legal assistant."

Jones pulled some papers out of his satchel. "Here's some research I did this afternoon on the admissibility of confessions. Should come in handy tomorrow."

"Thanks."

"Sorry I didn't get back from the post office sooner," Mike said. "My lab people back in Tulsa reached the same conclusion, though. They're absolutely certain the blood on the crossbow came from Donald Vick. How much longer do you think the trial will last?"

"Two or three days. Why?"

"After yesterday's riot, it's just a matter of time before the FBI descends on this town. This is becoming a major civil rights situation." Mike grimaced. "If you think things are bad now, wait till the FeeBees arrive."

"Swell. What are you doing tomorrow?"

"If there's some way I can help," Mike replied, "let me know. Otherwise I'm going out of town to try to scrounge up helicopter parts. If I don't replace most of Portia's engine, I'll never get her off the ground again."

"That's fine," Ben said. "There's no point in your hanging around the courtroom watching me get slaughtered."

"Try to cheer up, Ben. If—"

The bell over the front door rang. All heads turned as Belinda bounced into the office.

"Jones," Mike said, "don't we need to be somewhere about now?"

"Not that I can—*oof!*" Mike's elbow in his stomach seemed to jog his memory. "Oh, right. Now I remember."

"C'mon," Mike said, grabbing Jones by the arm. "I'll buy you a drink at the world-famous Bluebell Bar."

After they left, Belinda sat next to Ben, grinning happily. "How's it coming, lover boy?"

"Not well, I fear."

"Nice work in the courtroom today."

"Thanks. But I bet it wasn't good enough."

"Ben . . . you know how I feel about this trial. I—" She paused, then reformulated her sentence. "I don't know why I'm saying this. But I don't want to see an innocent man go to prison. Or worse. There's something you should know."

Ben looked at her, puzzled. "What is it?"

"Mary Sue's testimony wasn't entirely accurate. The conversation at the Bluebell between Vuong and Vick lasted more than a minute or so. It was at least five minutes. Maybe longer. And it wasn't just Vick getting upset. It was both of them."

"How do you know?"

"I was there."

"Wha—!" Ben sat up straight in his seat. "You?"

"Yes. John and I had decided to get out of the office for a bit, so we walked down to the Bluebell for a drink."

"And you saw them talk? And fight?"

"Couldn't miss it. During the fight, Vick's head got slammed down in the middle of our table."

"Why didn't you tell me before now?"

"I told the DA. I didn't know it would be important to your case. Frankly I thought you'd want to mention that fight as little as possible."

Ben nodded. "If I were smarter, you'd probably be right. But that's a big *if.*"

Belinda glanced at the papers scattered across his desk. "Do you have much more trial prep to do?"

"Tons. I keep bashing my head up against the same

unanswered questions. There's too much I don't know. I haven't had the time I need to investigate this mess."

Belinda took his hand and pressed it to her breast. "I don't suppose you'd be interested in taking a little break. . . ."

Ben removed his hand. "Belinda . . . I'm really swamped."

She put her head in the crook of his neck and nuzzled his earlobes. "Not even a little break . . . ?"

Ben pushed her head away. "I don't think that's wise."

Belinda tried not to look hurt. "Have I done something . . . wrong?"

"Have you—? Of course not."

"You seem different today."

"How?"

"I don't know. You seem . . . withdrawn."

Ben looked away. "Belinda . . . last night . . . was . . ."

"So that's how it is." She rose suddenly. "Don't bother trying to let me down easy. I know how to take a hint."

"Belinda, wait."

"Have fun with your trial prep. Lock up when you're done." She strode out of the office.

Ben emitted a long sigh. What the hell was wrong with him? Belinda was a spectacular woman and he was—

That was the problem, of course. As strong as his feelings for Belinda were, they only served to remind him of what had gone before. The specters of the past.

And suddenly he was back in Toronto again, and the snow was on the ground and he was bundled to the hilt and he was with—

Ellen. And he was in love.

The images flashed through his head like a montage from an old black-and-white movie. Queen's College, the church, the exchange student from Scotland, the snowball fight in the quad. And the futon in the attic and the ring and Ellen's radiant brown hair.

He closed his eyes, trying to stop the flow of images, but they just kept coming. Finals, big plans, the Harbourfront carnival. And then he was at the subway station, and there were tears and shouts and blood was everywhere and—

Ben pressed his hand against his face. Tragedy beyond imagining. And worst of all, he had not kept his promise. He had failed her.

He stood up and kicked the desk. It was *years* ago, he told himself. Grow up already! Get over it!

He'd been telling himself that for a long, long time, though, and it hadn't worked yet.

But it would. He pounded the desk, clearing the clutter from his brain. He closed his eyes again and mentally erased all the horrible images, all the wasted moments, all the inescapable consequences from his brain.

He didn't have time for this. He had to get on with this trial.

And he had to get on with his life.

* 49 *

Colonel Nguyen found his way home by starlight, following the path illuminated by the twinkling sentinels of the night. In the old days, he recalled, he used to look to them for guidance, for a sense of permanence, for answers. Now they were just white lights in the sky. Silent. Unresponsive. Nothing more.

Lan sat on the front porch Nguyen had only recently reconstructed. Her feet were propped against the railing; her eyes gazed up toward the heavens.

She was as beautiful as the Vietnamese flower for which she was named. Her smooth, tranquil face warmed his heart. It was almost as if there were no danger at all, as if that same porch had not been riddled with gunfire only a few days before.

He sneaked behind her and kissed her lightly on the cheek. "The children?"

"In bed." She took his arm and pulled it close around her.

"Was it difficult?"

"It is worse every night. They are afraid monsters will come in the night. And what can I tell them?" She shook her head sadly. "The monsters do come in the night."

"How did you get them to sleep?"

276

"I told them their father would protect them, of course. As he has always done. As he always will do."

"Perhaps the monsters will not come tonight," Nguyen said as he sat beside her in the same chair. "Perhaps tonight will be calm."

"Why do you say that? What have you been doing?"

He paused a moment, then decided it would be better to tell her than to let her imagine something worse. "I strung a trip wire across the entrance to Coi Than Tien."

"Do you think that will stop them?"

It would be so much easier to lie to her. But he found he could not do it. "No. But at least now, if the black pickup returns, we will hear it coming."

"Perhaps the conflict is over. Perhaps they will let it die."

"No," Nguyen said. "I have overheard Dan Pham and his associates. I do not know exactly what they plan, or when they plan to do it. But I know they contemplate another assault on ASP."

"Perhaps this trial will quiet their fever."

"How so?"

"Perhaps the trial will make Dan realize we are not alone, not so desperate as he thinks. Perhaps the trial will make the men of ASP realize they cannot commit these atrocities without paying a price." She paused, then slowly brought her vivid brown eyes to meet his. "If Vick is convicted."

Colonel Nguyen looked away. "You think he will be convicted?"

Lan's face became resolute. "I pray to God that he will be."

Nguyen gazed out into space, into the immutable tranquillity of the stars. How he wished to be among them, to be soaring through the void, to be anywhere but where he was. "It would be wrong to convict an innocent man."

"I know nothing of this," Lan said. "But I know what is best for my children. And my friends. And my husband."

She could not have stated it any plainer. There was nothing else for them to say, then. Nothing else at all.

"You will go to watch the trial again tomorrow, my husband?"

He took her hands. "I feel I must."

"Do you not have duties at the farm?"

"The farm will survive without me for a few days."

She nodded slightly, then removed her hands from his. "I will await your return in the evening. We all will."

Without even thinking, Nguyen took his wife into his arms and placed his head upon her chest. She was so warm, so good. He would be nothing without her.

"I only wish . . . to do what is right," he said, after a long time.

"You will," Lan replied. "You always do."

"I am not so sure."

"You are a fine man. Your heart is good."

"Even a good man can grow . . . old. Tired."

"Is this the hero of the 112th National Brigade? Is this the man who saved Maria Truong so recently?"

"Still, I worry. . . . I am not sure I can trust myself."

"Trust me, then. I know you will do what is best. Best for me. And your children. Best for us all."

Colonel Nguyen stared up into the blackness, unanswering. A cold wind blasted his face, stinging his eyes. If only he could be certain. If only he could know. If only—

He hugged his wife close to him, and braced himself against the long cold night.

* 50 *

The crowd in the courtroom the next morning had not diminished in the least. Apparently the first two days had only whetted their appetites. Most of the faces Ben identified the day before had returned for Day Three.

Vick was escorted into the courtroom by four deputies. Ben wondered if a particular event had inspired the sheriff to beef up security, or if the lawmen were just having a slow day. Fortunately none of the escorts was his good friend Deputy Gustafson.

As Vick walked down the main aisle, Ben heard a crash. A window shattered into tiny pieces that crumbled to the floor. A few seconds later a large rock sailed through the new opening. The crowd shrieked and ducked.

Whoever threw it had a strong arm and good aim; it just barely missed Vick's head.

Ben ran to the window and saw two figures in bib overalls racing around the corner. Given the distance and the fact that he only saw them from the back, it was impossible for him to be certain who they were. But one of them bore a sharp resemblance to Garth Amick.

The bailiff swept the debris away and the crowd gradually quieted. But whatever false sense of security the courtroom may once have conveyed was shattered along with the window.

A few minutes later Judge Tyler reentered the courtroom and the trial resumed. Swain called Sheriff Collier to the stand.

After Collier was sworn, Swain identified him as the local sheriff and laid the proper foundations for his testimony.

"When did you first learn of Tommy Vuong's death?"

"Almost immediately after it happened. We got lucky that night," Collier said, although his manner suggested that more than mere luck was involved. "Two of my deputies were patrolling out that way and spotted the smoke rising from that burning cross. They drove in and investigated." Collier described the crime scene for the jury. "Soon as my men saw the body, they got on the radio and called me."

"What did you instruct them to do?"

"Well, first of all, I told them to put out the damn fire, which they did. Then they determined that the victim was dead. By the time I arrived, they had pried the man's wallet out of his pocket. Luckily the boy had a tough cowhide wallet and his driver's license wasn't entirely incinerated. The writing was all melted, but I could still make out the picture. I recognized Vuong, of course, from that trouble he was in last year."

"Yes, well, tell us how your investigation proceeded," Swain said hastily. Naturally he didn't want anyone suggesting that the victim was anything less than saintly.

"Since I knew Vuong lived out at Coi Than Tien, we banged on some doors and talked to some of them folks. None of them seemed to have much to tell us, though."

"What led you to the defendant?"

The corners of the sheriff's lips turned upward slightly. "In a sense, he led himself to us. We were driving back to town and I saw him wandering around on the side of the road. I asked him what he was doing out at that time of night."

"And what was Mr. Vick's alibi?"

"Objection." Ben jumped to his feet. "The use of the word *alibi* suggests that the statement was false and that—"

"Oh, fine," Swain said testily. He rolled his eyes so the jury could see. He was working double time to portray himself as the seeker of truth and Ben as the man hiding it. "I'll rephrase. What was Mr. Vick's explanation for his presence not far from the murder scene shortly after it occurred?"

Thanks, Ben thought. Much better.

Collier faced the jury. "He said he was out getting some mountain air." Several jurors smiled. One flat out chuckled. Their thinking was obvious: only a liar would have such a lame alibi. Ben was apparently the only one in the courtroom who thought its very lameness probably proved it hadn't been invented.

"Why are they laughing?" Vick asked. Ben was startled; it was the first time Vick had spoken to him since the trial began. "I was just out walking. I did that every night."

"We'll bring that out later," Ben assured him. Not that anyone was likely to believe it.

"Was there anything unusual about the defendant's appearance?" Swain asked.

"You better believe it. While we were talking I noticed a big splattering of blood on his shirt."

The crowd stirred. Another previously unrevealed piece of incriminating evidence.

"What did you do then?"

"Well, I figured I needed to ask the boy a few questions. I said, 'Vick, I just found out Tommy Vuong is dead.' That seemed to take him by surprise; I expect he didn't think we'd find the body so fast. Then I said, 'Vuong is dead, and here I find you wandering around in the middle of the night with blood on your shirt. Did you kill him?' "

Swain took his time with the next question. "And what was Vick's response?"

"Well, there was this long silence. I didn't think he was going to answer at all. And then, out of the blue, real sudden like, he up and says, 'Vuong deserved to die.' "

The jurors' heads turned, checking one another's expression. Swain paused, protracting the silence as long as possible.

"That's all I have," Swain said. "Pass the witness."

Ben took his time approaching the witness stand. It seemed like a good strategy—build up some anticipation, make him seem confident and unconcerned. Also, it would give him a chance to figure out what the hell he was going to ask the man.

"Did you read my client his rights before you initiated the interrogation?" Ben asked.

"Hell, no," Collier said. "I was just shooting the breeze with him. I had no idea he was going to up and confess."

"Well, now wait a minute," Ben said. "He didn't actually confess, did he?"

"Sure as shootin' sounded like it to me."

"Did he say, 'I killed Vuong'?"

"Not in as many words."

"Not in any words, right?"

"Not as such, no. But why else would he say that Vuong deserved to die?"

"Many people probably deserve to die, but that doesn't mean Donald Vick killed them, does it?"

"Depends on whether I find their blood on his shirt," Collier said defiantly.

"Well, let's talk about that now. Did you run any tests on the bloodstain?"

"No. Why bother?"

"So you don't actually know whose blood was on his shirt, right?"

"Who the hell else's could it be? Unless your boy killed two people that night!"

"Move to strike," Ben said. "Request that the jury be instructed to disregard."

Judge Tyler promptly did so.

"Did Donald Vick say anything else to you that night?"

"Not a word. Totally clammed up."

"So you've been claiming for weeks that Donald confessed, when in fact all he did was say that he didn't like Vuong very much."

"That's not how I—"

"Thank you," Ben said. "I have no more questions." Ben suspected he had done all he could do with this witness who obviously sympathized with the prosecution. It was best to get him off the stand before he caused any more damage.

There was no redirect. For some reason, Swain was procrastinating about calling his next witness.

"Have you any other witnesses?" Judge Tyler finally asked.

"Yes," Swain said. He rose, then turned to face the gallery. "The prosecution calls Daniel Dunagan to the stand."

* 51 *

There had been a few gasps and twitters from the gallery before, but nothing compared to the stunned reaction that occurred now. Grand Dragon Dunagan was going to testify—*against* one of his own?

Ben had to amend his initial observation. Everyone in the gallery seemed surprised—except Grand Dragon Dunagan. He walked calmly to the front of the courtroom and took his seat in the witness stand. He closed his eyes as the bailiff read the oath, then answered in a booming voice, "So help me God."

Swain made his way quickly through the preliminaries and established that Dunagan was the Grand Dragon of ASP.

"Now that's kind of a funny title," Swain said. "Why do they call you that?"

"It's a million years old," Dunagan said. He seemed embarrassed. "In the early days, all the Anglo-Saxon organizations used titles like that. Frankly I've been trying to get them to call me *President* Dunagan for years. But old habits die hard."

Swain was nodding, as if he really bought into this. "You know, I think there may be some misunderstandings about what ASP is. Can you give the jury some background?"

284

"ASP is a legitimate, fully registered, lobbying organization designed to promote political change."

"What changes do you advocate?"

"First let me tell you what we *don't* advocate. We don't advocate any laws that would hurt the non-Anglo-Saxon races. My motto is 'live and let live.' All we favor is separation, letting people work and play among their own. I know that may not be politically correct, but it's the way this country worked for a good long time, and frankly most people think the world was better then than it is today."

"How do you pursue your political goals?"

"By lobbying the government. And by establishing camps where people can get away and live among their own kind."

"Do these camps stockpile weapons?"

"Yes. And we train our people how to use them, too. But only for defensive purposes. When you live out in the wild like that, with no easy access to law enforcement, you have to learn how to take care of yourself. But we absolutely do not engage in aggressive, violent, or terroristic acts!"

"Then ASP wouldn't, for instance, firebomb a car?"

Ben couldn't believe it. Swain was actually going along with this whitewash. He must've wanted Dunagan's testimony in a big way.

"Absolutely not. We had no part in that."

"And ASP wouldn't set fire to someone's home?"

"Of course not. I thought what happened out at Coi Than Tien the other night was tragic. Hell, I approve of Coi Than Tien—a community where the members of a single race live among their own. I think there should be more like them."

"Was there anyone at ASP who felt differently about the use of violence?"

Dunagan took a deep breath, then slowly released it. "Well ... I hate to talk about my own men. ..."

"You're under oath," Swain reminded him.

"Right. Well ... there was the defendant. Donald Vick."

In the corner of his eye, Ben could see the jurors leaning forward, straining to pick up each word.

"Vick favored the use of violence?"

"Vick is a hothead. Always was. I've known him for years, and he's always been the same."

Ben stared at Dunagan in disbelief. What on earth was going on? Dunagan was selling his old buddy Lou Vick's boy right down the river.

"What did Vick want to do?"

"Oh, there were so many nasty cockeyed ideas. ... Let me think." He paused for a moment. "Well, he was a big fan of planting burning crosses in Vietnamese front yards."

The connection wasn't lost on the jury. The murderer was fond of burning crosses, too.

"What else?"

"He was always picking fights. Like he did with this Vuong fella. For no reason at all. He was just a mean SOB, to tell the truth. He liked to toss a Molotov cocktail or two, also."

"Like the one that exploded a car on Maple and burned three people?"

"Well ..." Dunagan said slowly. "Since that happened ... I've had to wonder. ..."

Swain returned to counsel table and thumbed through his legal pad. Ben knew he didn't need to check his notes. He was just taking his time, letting all this sink in before he moved on to the next topic.

"Mr. Dunagan, do you know where Donald Vick was on the night of the murder?"

"No." He folded his hands calmly. "He left the camp early that afternoon. Told some of the boys he had something to do. Didn't specify—acted real mysterious about it. Of course, now I realize he was going to pick that fight in the bar—"

"Objection!" Ben interrupted. "Lack of personal knowledge."

"Right, right," Judge Tyler said. "Sustained."

Swain picked up right where he left off. "Mr. Dunagan, do you stock crossbows at your camp?"

"Oh, yes. As I said, we have to defend ourselves."

"Have you seen the particular crossbow that has been identified as the murder weapon in this case?"

"Yes, I have."

"Do you have an opinion as to where that crossbow came from?"

"I'm afraid I do." He sighed, then looked directly at Vick. "It came out of our armory."

"And who would have access to your armory?"

"It's not a prison camp. Anyone could get in if they really wanted to."

Swain leaned in for the clincher. "Including Donald Vick?"

Dunagan looked as if his answer filled him with regret. "Including Donald Vick."

Ben saw the jurors settle back in their seats. He had the disturbing feeling they thought they had heard enough.

"Thank you, Mr. Dunagan." Swain turned toward Ben and smiled. "Your witness, Mr. Kincaid. Good luck."

* 52 *

Ben considered waiving cross-examination altogether. Dunagan apparently was determined to destroy Donald Vick, and if that was the case, the sooner he was off the stand, the better. But Ben had to try to keep the jurors from making up their minds before the defense called its first witness.

On the other hand, there was no point in pretending he was friendly with this man. So he didn't.

"Are you trying to tell this jury that ASP is just a peace-loving, civic-minded bunch of regular guys? Kind of like the Peace Corps? Or the Boy Scouts?"

"Well," Dunagan said, "I see no cause for sarcasm."

"Grand Dragon Dunagan, isn't the ASP motto 'The only good gook is a dead gook'?"

"I don't know what you're talking about." And of course, Ben couldn't prove he was lying, since he hadn't pocketed any of the man's propaganda.

"Isn't it true that you and your followers are expecting a big race war any day now?"

"Some people do believe that will happen, including people who are not members of ASP. I just hope it doesn't come to pass."

"Come on now. Isn't it true you're setting up all these armed camps so that when the big war hits, you can take over and turn the South into a gigantic whites-only country club?"

"Your honor," Swain complained, "I don't see the relevance of this. Mr. Dunagan is not on trial."

"Agreed. Move on, counsel."

"Your honor," Ben said. "Mr. Swain opened the door to this line of questioning. It goes to the witness's credibility."

"I said move on, counsel!" Tyler's bushy eyebrows moved together till they formed a straight line across his face.

Ben gritted his teeth and changed the subject. "Didn't you tell me that your armory didn't have any bolts that fit the crossbow that was stolen?"

"It seems I was mistaken. After I talked to you, I was informed that—"

"I don't want to hear any hearsay," Ben said, cutting him off. He didn't know what Dunagan was about to say, but it didn't sound helpful. "Is a crossbow difficult to fire?"

"Hell, no. All you do is point it and pull the trigger. A five-year-old could do it."

"Do you train your men in the use of the crossbow?"

"Of course. Including Donald Vick."

"Despite your haste to single out Donald, the fact is, all your men had access to the crossbow and knew how to use it, right?"

"That's true."

"Thank you. I have—"

"But of course, all the other men were in camp, where they were supposed to be, at the time of the murder. The only man missing was Donald Vick."

Ben squeezed his eyes tightly closed. It would be pointless to object. The jury had already heard it.

He couldn't think of any more questions to ask. And

every second Dunagan remained on the stand, prospects looked a little dimmer for Donald Vick. "No more questions, your honor."

Ben returned to his seat at defendant's table. He just hoped that he had sewn enough seeds of uncertainty to keep the jury from making up their minds.

But he doubted it.

•

* 53 *

After lunch, the courtroom reassembled itself with relative calm. Or at any rate, this time no rocks came through the windows.

"Any further testimony from the prosecution?" Judge Tyler asked.

"One more witness," Swain said. "But he'll be brief. The State calls Richard Litz."

Richard Litz was a nondescript man with brown curly hair and a bushy brown mustache. He was wearing glasses with tinted lenses. Ben didn't have a clue who the man was. And judging from the expressions on the other faces in the courtroom, neither did anyone else.

Except Henry Swain. "Mr. Litz, would you please tell the jury what you do for a living?"

"I'm the order clerk for Domestic Soldier in Hot Springs."

"And what is Domestic Soldier?"

"Domestic Soldier is a mail-order supplier of equipment for outdoorsmen. Tents, compasses, hiking boots. You name it, we carry it."

"Would your inventory include weapons?"

"Yes, it would."

"Crossbows?"

"Definitely. All shapes and sizes."

"And bolts?"

"Wouldn't be much point in selling the crossbows without the bolts, would there?" He chuckled at his own little joke.

"Have you ever supplied any equipment to the ASP camp just outside of Silver Springs?"

Ben was beginning to see where this testimony was leading. And he didn't like it a bit.

"Yes, many times. They're regular customers."

"Do you carry the bolts for the"—he held up Exhibit A and read the label—"KL-44 Carvelle crossbow?"

"Yes. We're one of the few in this country that do. It's a fairly rare item."

"Do you sell those bolts to the ASP camp?"

"Normally not. But we did get an order from them for that item just a few weeks ago. First and last time ever."

"Now, this is important, sir, so please take your time before answering." Of course, Swain wasn't really telling the witness this next bit was important; he was telling the jury. "When did this order come in?"

"July twenty-first. They were delivered on the twenty-fourth."

"Right. And the crossbow murder occurred on the twenty-fifth." Swain nodded thoughtfully, then returned to counsel table. He was almost there when he suddenly stopped and pivoted around to face the witness. "One last question, Mr. Litz. Who placed the order for the crossbow bolts on the twenty-first?"

"A man named Donald Vick."

The murmur in the courtroom crescendoed. Judge Tyler banged his gavel and demanded silence.

"That's all," Swain said. "Pass the witness."

Ben strolled to the witness box, thinking all the way. "You take phone orders for a mail-order company, right?"

"That's what I said."

"So you didn't actually see Mr. Vick when he ordered?"

"True . . ."

"He was just a voice on the telephone."

"That's true, but—"

"Then it could've been anyone," Ben said. "Anyone could've claimed to be Donald Vick."

"I guess that's true," Litz said. "But I know who picked the order up."

"What? I thought you said you delivered them."

"Right. I delivered them to the ASP man who came for them on the twenty-fourth. And that was the man sitting right there in the gray coveralls." He pointed directly at Vick. "I saw him with my own eyes."

Swain jumped to his feet. "Let the record reflect that the witness has indicated that the pickup man was Donald Vick."

"It will so reflect," Judge Tyler intoned. "Anything else, Mr. Kincaid?"

Damn. Ben hated to end his cross on such a negative note. But he wasn't prepared for a follow-up question. The coffin was nailed tightly shut.

"No, your honor."

"Redirect?"

"I see no need," Swain said, displaying his understandable confidence to the jury. "And the prosecution rests."

"Very well," the judge said. "We'll start up again tomorrow afternoon at one o'clock with the defense case. Court is dismissed."

He banged his gavel, and instantaneously the silence was broken. The exodus from the gallery was swift. Only the jury remained seated. And their eyes, Ben noticed, all twenty-four of them, were focused on Donald Vick.

Ben leaned forward, blocking the jury's view, and whispered into Vick's ear. "Why in God's name did you pick up those crossbow bolts?"

"That was my job. I made all the supply runs."

"You did?" If he had known that, he could have brought it out during cross. Now it was too late. "Why you?"

"Who else? Dunagan always gave me the grunt jobs."

Ben observed that Vick invoked the name of the exalted Grand Dragon with somewhat less reverence now. At least he realized what the man had done to him. "I'm going to have to put you on the stand, Donald."

Vick glared at him. "I already told you. I won't talk."

"I won't ask questions about any subjects you don't want to discuss. I won't ask you what you and Vuong fought about. But I have to get you on the stand so the jury can hear you say you didn't kill him." Ben glanced over his shoulder, just to make sure no one else was listening. "Otherwise, frankly, I don't think you have a chance."

Vick stared back at him, his voice caught in his throat. Surely he realized the trial was going badly, but that probably wasn't the same as having his own attorney tell him straight out that he was headed for death row.

"I—I'll think about. I'll let you know."

"I'll be outside your cell tomorrow morning bright and early. So we can prepare your testimony."

Vick nodded, and the deputies took him away.

Ben watched as Vick faded out of the courtroom. Every time Ben saw him, he looked less and less like a hardened hatemonger and more and more like a scared little boy who thought he saw the bogeyman lurking underneath his bed. A terrified youth who didn't know what to do next.

And the tragedy was, his attorney didn't know what to do next either.

* 54 *

Ben reviewed his fifth draft of the direct examination he'd prepared for Donald Vick. He moved his lips as he read, trying each question on for size.

It was the hardest direct he had ever written. Normally he would just take a witness through his story. What could be easier than that? In this case, unfortunately, Vick's story was like a minefield. It was filled with dangerous subjects Vick refused to mention. Ben had to hone his questions to draw out responses on topics Vick would discuss without making the jury wonder about the topics he hadn't.

Jones and Mike dropped by, but neither had any new information to report. They hadn't found a trace of the woman Ben rescued from the burning Truong home, and they hadn't found any witnesses who were willing to testify on Vick's behalf. Loving, they said, was at the Bluebell shooting pool, as he had been for the last several nights. They weren't sure if he was onto something, or if the Bluebell crowd was just his kind of people.

And Christina still adamantly refused to help.

It was almost ten-thirty before Belinda quietly opened the front door and walked to the back desk where Ben was working. She sat in a chair several arm's lengths away from him. It was a long time before she spoke.

"What are you working on?" she asked.

"A direct examination for my client."

"You're going to put him on the stand? Is that wise?"

"Most defense attorneys prefer not to if it can be avoided. But I don't have any choice. Vick doesn't have any other witnesses. Even ASP appears to have turned against him. Our only chance is to put him on the stand and hope the jury believes him."

She nodded. It was obvious she wanted to discuss something other than the case, but couldn't quite bring herself around to it. "Most of the evidence the prosecution put on is circumstantial."

"Most? All." Ben pressed his hand against his forehead. "But there was so much of it. The jury can't overlook so many links between Vick and the crime."

"You think the jury is leaning toward a guilty verdict?"

"I've seen men convicted on less."

"Ben—" She paused, then started over. "Ben, I know you take your work seriously, and I admire that. But don't forget who it is you're representing. This is Donald Vick, the Vietnamese assassin. The man probably responsible for the car bombing that maimed three people. The man who tried to beat Vuong senseless at the Bluebell Bar. Even if he didn't commit this crime, he's probably committed others as bad or worse."

"If he didn't commit this crime, he shouldn't be convicted of it," Ben said flatly.

Belinda sighed. She fidgeted with her hands, turned them over in her lap. "Ben . . . this isn't what I wanted to talk about. I didn't want to be the one to bring it up. I figured, if that's the way you want it, fine. If you already got all you want—"

"Belinda! I promise you, it isn't—"

"But I couldn't let it go. I just couldn't. Maybe you can bury all your feelings. But I can't."

"Belinda—" He gazed across the desk at her. Her eyes were wide and sparkling. "It isn't that at all. It isn't anything to do with you. It's all me. All my problem."

"Then let's at least talk about it!"

Ben reached out and took her hand. "We don't have to. I'm over it. I've decided. I'm not going to allow myself to wallow in the past forever. I'm over it."

"Are you hoping that if you say it often enough it will be true?"

"No. It is true."

Belinda closed her eyes. "I was afraid I had done something wrong. I was afraid I was too aggressive, or too . . . I don't know. Strident. I was afraid I had done something that . . . changed how you feel about me."

"I can't conceive of anything that could make me feel differently about you."

"Really?"

Outside, the red neon Coors sign in the front window of the Bluebell cast colored shadows across the street and through the undraped office window. The faint echo of Mary-Chapin Carpenter seeped through the doors and flowed down Main. Her voice was like the wind whispering in Ben's ear. *Come on, come on . . . it's getting late now. . . .*

Ben pulled Belinda closer. "I love you," he said, in the instant before their lips met.

Twenty minutes passed before either of them thought to pull the drapes.

* 55 *

Ben spent three hours the next morning preparing
Vick to take the stand. He wasn't nearly as concerned
about what Vick would say as how he would say it. His
demeanor was critical. If the jury detected any hesi-
tance, or uncertainty, or equivocation, they would assume the prosecution's version of the facts was correct.

As the jury filed back into the courtroom Ben patted
Vick reassuringly on the shoulder. "Try not to worry,"
he murmured. "You'll be fine."

Vick smiled, but the smile was unconvincing in the
extreme.

Judge Tyler breezed through the preliminaries with
unaccustomed dispatch. He appeared as anxious as everyone else to proceed with the day's programming.

Ben called Donald Vick to the witness stand.

"Would you state your name for the jury?"

"Donald Allan Vick." He spoke in calm, clear tones.
Confident, but not cocky. Honest, but not like he was
working at it. Just as Ben had instructed him.

Ben guided him through a general description of his
background in Alabama: his childhood, his education,
his family life.

"When did you become a member of ASP?"

"When I was eighteen."

"Why did you join?"

Vick tilted his head to one side. "All the Vick men have been ASP members since the organization was first formed a hundred and twenty years ago."

"Sort of a family tradition, then?"

"I guess you could say that."

"Did your father expect you to join ASP?"

Vick nodded. "He insisted on it. If I hadn't, he would've booted me out of the house."

"Do you remember when you joined?"

"Oh, yes. The first day I was able. On my eighteenth birthday. ASP makes a big ceremony of it—putting on uniforms and lighting torches. They talked about how I was making the transition from boyhood to manhood."

"It's sort of a rite of passage for the Vick men, then?"

"Exactly."

"Your honor, I object." Swain rose to his feet. "We've been very patient with this line of questioning, but I don't see what it has to do with this murder case."

He did, of course. He understood its purpose just as well as Ben did. The purpose was for the jury to get to know Donald Vick, the person. For him to become a human being, rather than a cardboard villain.

"Your honor," Ben said. "I needn't remind the court that my client is charged with a capital offense. The jury should have the opportunity to learn all they can about the man whose fate they will determine. I ask for the widest possible latitude."

Judge Tyler frowned, but he overruled Swain's objection.

"How often were you involved in ASP activities?" Ben continued.

"New members are expected to spend their first two years in what amounts to an apprenticeship for ASP." Vick looked at the jury from time to time, establishing an easy rapport. He was so fresh-faced and clean-cut, after all; it was just possible he might turn the jury around. "Personally I had hoped to go to college, but ..." He shrugged. "My father and ASP had other plans."

"What did you do during this ... apprenticeship?"

"At first I handled clerical tasks in the Montgomery office. Busywork, mostly. Then, a few months ago, after this new camp was set up outside Silver Springs, I was transferred here."

"Did your responsibilities change?"

"No. I still handled the clerical chores. Requisitions. Food, supplies. For some reason, Mr. Dunagan never assigned me more challenging duties."

"Did your clerical chores include ordering weaponry?"

"Yes. I did *all* the ordering and the picking up. Not just on those crossbow bolts."

Ben checked the jury reaction. They made the connection. His testimony cast a different light on the evidence.

"Why did you take a room in town? Couldn't you have stayed in the barracks at the ASP camp?"

"Oh, yeah. But—I don't know. I preferred to have some privacy from time to time. I didn't get on all that well with the rest of the ASP guys."

"Why is that?"

"I don't know. I guess we didn't share that many interests."

"What did the ASP members like to do?"

"Oh, drink. Lots of drinking. And talking about women like they were ... well, you know. In a manner I don't find appropriate. And they talked about what they were going to do to those Vietnamese people. Most of them never did anything to any of them and never would. But they loved to talk about it."

Ben stood beside the jury box so Vick could easily look from him to them. "How did you feel when they talked about the Vietnamese?"

"I didn't care much for it."

"Why not? You're a member of ASP, aren't you?"

"Yes ... I'm a member. . . ."

"And you believe in the superiority of the Caucasian race, don't you?"

"I guess. But that doesn't mean we have to go around beating up on all the other races. On the contrary, it seems to me that if we're really all that superior, we should be able to live peacefully with other people."

Ben paused, leaving plenty of time for Vick's words to sink in. The alleged hatemonger was much more the philosopher than anyone the jury had heard from thus far.

"Donald, did you participate in the car bombing on Maple Street several months ago?"

"No. It's true I requisitioned the materials that must have been used, but I didn't know that was going to happen when I ordered them. I was just doing what I was told."

"Told by whom?"

Vick hesitated. "By Mr. Dunagan. He controlled all supply orders. I only made purchases on his instruction."

"Donald, do you remember what you were doing the night of July twenty-fifth?"

"Yes. After dinner, around ten, I went out for a walk."

"That seems odd."

"No, I walked almost every night. It was my habit. Mary Sue could've confirmed that. If anyone had asked her."

Sure, Ben thought, rub it in. "Why did you walk at night?"

"Do I need a reason? It's beautiful country out here, and especially beautiful at night." Good answer; jurors tended to be civic-minded. "Gave me a chance to get away from all the swearing and chanting and plotting. Gave me a chance to think."

"Do you recall your stroll being interrupted by Sheriff Collier?"

"Of course."

"Were you irritated with him?"

"No, he was just doing his job. He was nicer about it than some I've seen."

"What happened?"

"Oh, it was pretty much as Sheriff Collier described it."

"Whose blood was on your shirt?"

The air in the courtroom seemed suspended; at last a question that got to the heart of the matter.

"That was my blood. I got hurt that afternoon at the Bluebell Bar. During the fight. I suppose I should have changed my shirt, but it never occurred to me."

"And since the sheriff never analyzed the bloodstain, he never found out it was your own blood."

"I guess that's right."

"The sheriff also claims that after he told you Vuong was dead, you said, 'He deserved to die.' Is that true?"

Vick paused only a second before answering. "Yes."

"And why would you say that?"

"Because it's true." He directly confronted the jurors. "That's not to say I was glad he was dead. I wouldn't wish that on anyone, especially not the way it happened to him. But he did deserve to die."

"Donald." Ben slowly approached the stand. "Did you kill Tommy Vuong?"

"No. Maybe he deserved to die, but I'm not an executioner. I wouldn't do that. And I didn't."

"Thank you, Donald. No more questions at this time." The jury remained very still as Ben returned to defendant's table. He couldn't be sure, but he thought Vick's earnest testimony had had a real effect on them.

"Fine." Judge Tyler swung around in his big leather chair. He appeared to have been as mesmerized by Vick's testimony as everyone else. "Mr. Swain, you may inquire."

* 56 *

"Well, Mr. Vick," Swain said. "I had no idea you ASPers were so sensitive."

No one so much as smiled. His attempt at sarcasm had fallen flat.

"Was that a question, sir?" Vick asked politely.

"No." Swain cleared his throat. "But this is. You seem to have omitted a very important detail from your story. Where were you on the afternoon before the murder took place? Say around four o'clock."

Damn. Beneath the table and out of sight of the jury, Ben clenched his fists. He had hoped Swain would discuss some of the subjects brought out on direct first. But Swain was going straight for the jugular.

"I was at the Bluebell Bar."

"Just stopped in for a drink?"

"No. Actually I don't drink."

"Oh, of course not." Swain grinned. "You're probably a buttermilk man."

Vick didn't flinch.

"If you don't drink, why were you at the Bluebell Bar?"

"I was looking for someone."

"Who?"

Vick took a deep breath. "Tommy Vuong."

"And why were you looking for him?"

Vick looked across the courtroom at Ben. His mouth remained shut.

Ben jumped to his feet. "Objection!"

Tyler peered down at him. "Got any grounds, counsel, or do you just not want the witness to answer?"

"I object . . . on grounds of relevance, your honor."

Swain piped in. "Of course this is relevant. It goes toward establishing the defendant's motive. It also establishes a predisposition for violence toward the victim."

"We'll stipulate that Donald wasn't fond of the victim, your honor. So the question is unnecessary."

Tyler shook his head. "The objection is overruled."

Ben didn't sit down. "Then I object on grounds of . . . um . . . lack of proper foundation."

Swain's forehead crinkled. "Do I have to respond to that, Judge?"

"No." He pointed his gavel at Ben. "The quality of your objections is quickly deteriorating, counsel. Overruled. I suggest you sit down."

Reluctantly Ben did as the judge told him.

"Let me ask it again," Swain said. "Why were you looking for Tommy Vuong?"

Vick took another deep breath. "I would prefer not to say."

"Is that a fact?" Swain looked to the judge. "Gosh, your honor, the witness would prefer not to say!"

Judge Tyler frowned. "The witness will answer the question."

Vick closed his eyes and swallowed. "I won't."

"What?" Tyler drew himself up like a grizzly bear rearing for an attack. "What do you mean, you won't?"

"I mean, I won't answer the question. I can't."

"Mr. Vick, you took a solemn oath to tell the truth. The whole truth."

"Yes. But long before today I made another promise. And I can't break it."

Tyler peered down at the witness. "If you do not answer the district attorney's question, sir, there will be severe consequences."

"If I do answer the question, someone else's life will be ruined. I won't do that."

Ben could tell the jurors were disturbed by Vick's sudden recalcitrance. Whatever good he had done for Vick during his direct examination was slowly oozing away. "Your honor, perhaps if Mr. Swain could phrase the question differently."

"Okay," Swain said. "I'll play along. What did you say to Tommy Vuong?"

"I—I can't tell you."

"We've heard you two talked for several minutes. What did you talk about?"

"I'm sorry. I can't say."

Swain spread his arms wide. "Your honor . . . what can I do?"

"Once again," the judge said, "I instruct the witness to answer the question!"

"I'm sorry, sir. I mean no disrespect. But I can't do that."

"You *will* do that!" Tyler pounded his gavel. "I will not allow this contempt of court!"

"You'll have to, sir."

"I will insist on an answer if we have to stay here all night!"

"Then I invoke the protection of the Fifth Amendment and respectfully decline to answer."

Ben closed his eyes. It was enough to make a lawyer cry. His defendant agrees to take the stand, only to plead the Fifth and refuse to answer the DA's questions.

It would've been better if Ben had never put him on the stand at all.

"So that's it, then?" Tyler demanded. "You're going to take the Fifth?"

"Yes, sir. I am."

"In that case," Swain said, "what's the point of proceeding? I have no more questions."

And no need to ask them, Ben realized. The expression on the jurors' faces had changed dramatically. There was outright hostility toward Vick now. He was hiding something.

"Very well," Tyler said. "Mr. Vick, you're excused. Get out of here."

Vick scurried out of the box, without once looking back at the jury. It was just as well. He wouldn't have liked what he saw.

"Any further testimony, Mr. Kincaid?"

"No, sir," Ben said regretfully. "Mr. Vick is our only witness."

"Any rebuttal from the prosecution?"

Swain shook his head happily. "I see no need, your honor." And of course, he wanted to rush this trial to its conclusion while the memory of this disaster was still fresh on the jurors' minds.

"Very well. I'll entertain any motions from counsel." He checked his watch. "It looks like we can just squeeze in closing arguments before quitting time. And then," he said to the jury, "this matter will be in your hands."

* 57 *

District Attorney Swain began his closing in a voice so hushed the court reporter had to strain to pick up his words.

"Donald Vick doesn't want you to know the whole story. He only wants you to know pieces of it—the safe parts, the parts he can get away with telling. We, on the other hand, have shown you the whole story. We have shown you all the evidence. We have held nothing back. As a result, I believe that each of you can see what really happened."

He pushed away from the jury box and crossed the courtroom, drawing the jurors' eyes toward the defendant. "We know for a fact that Donald Vick is a member of a hate group called ASP, that he is the sworn enemy of the Vietnamese members of our community, and that he is a hothead who continually agitated for violent attacks against the Vietnamese.

"We know that on the afternoon of July twenty-fifth he sought out Tommy Vuong and found him at the Bluebell Bar. He has admitted this to you. He refused to tell you what they discussed. Witnesses have testified that soon thereafter Vick began beating Vuong with all his might. If it had not been for the intervention of others, Vick might well have killed Vuong then and there.

"We know that Vick had access to the murder

weapon, and that he himself ordered and received the crossbow bolts. We know he used it, too—his hair was caught in the firing mechanism and his blood was smeared on the frame when the weapon was found shortly after the murder occurred. Which was only a few scant hours after Vick attacked Vuong in the Bluebell Bar."

He returned to his original position directly in front of the jury. "I ask you to consider the evidence that has been presented, to consider it with your minds, and your hearts. Is there any other explanation for these facts? Is there any possible conclusion other than the conclusion that Donald Vick fired the fatal shots?"

Swain lowered his hands slowly to his side. "I suggest to you that there is not. We all want to live in a safe place. We want to live where our children can play, where we can raise a family, where our elderly can retire—without fear. Silver Springs used to be like that. But it isn't anymore. Now you can't walk the streets without wondering whether someone might step out of the shadows and put a crossbow bolt in your back."

Ben started to object, then decided against it. Swain's closing was dangerously close to being improperly prejudicial. He was asking the jury to convict in order to purge the community of evil, not because the evidence proved Vick's guilt. But the jury had already heard it, and they were already hostile toward Ben's client. He didn't want to make matters worse by annoying them with a poorly timed objection.

"It doesn't have to be this way," Swain continued. "We can reclaim our town. We can take it back. You— the ladies and gentlemen of this jury—can put out the word that terrorism, and violence, and intolerance will not be condoned any longer.

"We have shown you Donald Vick's motive, his

nonexistent alibi, his access to the murder weapon, and the uncontested trace evidence found on that weapon linking it to Donald Vick. I respectfully submit that we have met our burden. And I request—indeed, for all our sakes, I *urge* you to render a verdict finding Donald Vick guilty as charged."

As soon as Swain reseated himself, Ben slowly rose and approached the jury, well aware that he was about to do more than simply argue for a favorable verdict.

He was pleading for a man's life.

"Ladies and gentlemen of the jury. ASP is not on trial. The future of Silver Springs is not on trial. Donald Vick is on trial. Period. And you are not being asked to determine what's good for the community, or for your children, or for future generations.

"You are not being asked to take a stand against hate groups, or racists, or terrorists. You are only being asked to answer one question: has the prosecution proven that Donald Vick is guilty of murder in the first degree beyond a reasonable doubt? And if your answer is no, then the judge will instruct you that you must, not should, but *must*, render a verdict of not guilty."

Ben returned to counsel table, bringing Vick back into the jurors' field of vision. He wanted to remind them that this was a real living breathing person they were talking about.

"Every piece of evidence presented by the prosecution—without exception—has been circumstantial. None of it directly proves that Donald committed this crime. No one saw him do it, no one heard him do it, no one saw blood on his hands."

Stupid choice of words; the jury would remember the blood on his shirt. Too late now—best to keep moving ahead.

"The prosecution's version of the facts is, at best,

only one possible version of the facts. It is not an inescapable conclusion. Just for a moment let's imagine another possibility. Picture that lonely country road in the middle of the night—only this time let's imagine that it was *you* out for a midnight stroll.

"Let's suppose, just to make it interesting, that you had an argument with someone that afternoon. I'll bet each of you has had a fight with someone at some time in your life. I bet each of you has lost your temper and done something you later regretted. But let's suppose that just after you lose your temper and have that fight, the person you fought with is killed. And when the police come for you, you haven't had the foresight to concoct a clever alibi. So they arrest you. Picture yourself sitting in that chair at the defendant's table. On trial for your life.

"Preposterous, you say? That could never happen?" Ben spread his arms. "But that's what the case against Donald Vick is. The prosecution wants you to convict him because he didn't like Tommy Vuong, because he fought with Tommy Vuong, and because he didn't have an alibi when Tommy was killed. But you say—that could happen to anyone. And I say to you—yes, you're right. And that's exactly the point."

Ben placed his hands on the rail and stood closer to the jury than he had ever dared stand before. "You cannot convict a man of first-degree murder on a possibility. You cannot convict him because he might have done it. You can only convict him if you have eliminated all the other possibilities. You must be certain—certain beyond a reasonable doubt.

"And you know what?" Ben said. "I don't think you are. I don't think you could be. I think each of you has doubts. Maybe they aren't big ones. Maybe it's just one teeny-tiny doubt. But that's enough. As long as that doubt remains, you have no alternative. Enter a verdict finding Donald Vick not guilty."

Ben held their eyes for a few more moments, then returned to his seat.

That had gone well, better than he expected, actually. Unfortunately he didn't get the last word.

"Rebuttal?" Judge Tyler asked.

"I think so." Swain sprang to his feet. He undoubtedly realized the jury was tired of speeches. He was going to say what he had to say and get it over with.

"Well, Mr. Kincaid was very dramatic, wasn't he?"

Now that, Ben thought, was the pot calling the kettle black.

"But he left a few details out. Like, for instance, the fact that Donald Vick had access to the crossbow and personally picked up the bolts the day before the murder. That he was found wandering around the crime scene shortly after the murder occurred—with blood on his shirt."

Swain picked up the crossbow and waved it in the air. "Has Mr. Kincaid forgotten that Vick's own hair and blood was found on this crossbow?" he shouted. "I think not. But he's hoping you will.

"This crime could not have been committed by just anyone. Who else attacked the victim? Who else specially ordered the ammunition? Who else told the sheriff that Tommy Vuong deserved to die? No one else!" He whirled around and pointed at the defendant. "*No one else!* Only Donald Vick!"

Swain returned to counsel table, closed his eyes briefly, then looked one more time at the jury. "There is only one possibility, one alternative, one way to set the world right again. I ask you to find Donald Vick guilty of murder in the first degree."

The judge instructed and cautioned the jury, then the

bailiff led them to a room in the back of the courthouse. Judge Tyler told them to begin deliberating immediately, rather than waiting till the following morning.

It was clear to Ben, from the judge's tone, that he didn't think the deliberation would take long.

PART THREE

* *

The Residue of Hate

* 58 *

Just after sunset Colonel Nguyen and Lan walked hand-in-hand through the loblolly pine trees outside the perimeter of Coi Than Tien. The night was still and peaceful; they could almost forget all the turmoil that surrounded them.

Colonel Nguyen left the courtroom after the jury was dismissed. They still had not returned. Nguyen told himself repeatedly that no one could be certain what the jurors' thoughts were. But the evidence at trial had been strong, almost overwhelming. He had little doubt but that the jury would find him guilty, and the death sentence would be rendered against Donald Vick.

A man he was almost certain had not committed the crime.

"We came here to escape," Lan reminded him. "But I sense your troubles have followed you."

He smiled as best he could. He wondered if all this had not been hardest on her, all his trauma, his moodiness, his indecision. At least he was in control—he could chart his own course. She was at the mercy of the decisions of others.

"Are you still thinking of the trial?"

He nodded.

"Surely they will convict the man. Surely there is no other choice for us. For Coi Than Tien."

There was truth in what she said. Nguyen knew that even as they spoke Dan Pham and his followers were gathered in the barn, waiting for word of the jury's verdict. They had made it clear they expected Vick to receive the maximum sentence. And that if the courts did not deliver justice to their satisfaction, they would do it themselves.

That was the choice that lay before them. A guilty verdict would mean the conviction of an innocent man. And a not guilty verdict would mean strife, violence, rioting—probably death to Coi Than Tien.

Lan took his hand inside hers. "Is there nothing I can do to soothe your worries, husband?"

"No. We will just have to wait and see what—"

He was interrupted by the sound of clattered tin cans inside the fence surrounding Coi Than Tien. Someone had triggered the trip wire he'd strung across the front entrance. A few seconds after that he heard gunshots firing in rapid succession. Automatic weapons.

"Stay here," he told Lan.

Without waiting for a response, Nguyen ran toward Coi Than Tien. It would take him at least another minute to make it to the front gates. Instead he ran to the fence and leaped up against it. He rose at least four feet into the air and was able to grab the top. Pushing against the fence with his feet, he hoisted himself up and swung over into Coi Than Tien.

It was the black pickup with the smoked windows, returned once again to wreak death and destruction on Coi Than Tien. Gun barrels extended from both the driver's and the passenger's windows, spraying a steady stream of bullets in all directions.

Nguyen ran as fast as he could toward the pickup. He passed terrified neighbors running in the other direction, desperately trying to get themselves and their families away from the danger.

He dashed around the barn and bolted toward his home. The pickup spotted him. Its engines roared; it pivoted around and began firing at him. A bullet ricocheted off the porch just inches above his head. Nguyen dropped to the ground, then crawled on his knees and elbows toward the front door. He flung the door open, crawled inside, and slammed the door behind him.

Holly was standing in the living room beside Mary's cradle. Mary was crying loud and hard.

"I stayed with the baby, Daddy," Holly said. Tears were streaming from her eyes. "Just like you said."

"Get down!" Nguyen grabbed his daughter and knocked her against the wooden floor. Another volley of bullets rained through the windows. Holly screamed.

Nguyen took his baby from the cradle and hugged her close to him. He pressed both daughters flat on the planks and prayed that the danger would pass them by. He could hear the pickup moving outside, circling the barn, keeping everyone pinned inside their homes.

Another round of bullets pierced the front door and windows, the ones he had only repaired two days before. Anger boiled up inside Nguyen's breast. To attack them in their own homes—to endanger his children! His body tensed and filled with hate. If he could just get out of here, he would tear them apart. He would destroy them. But he could not leave the children—

"Go," a voice behind him said.

It was Lan. She must've cut through the rear of the settlement and come in the back door.

"I will see to the children. Go."

As soon as he was sure the pickup had momentarily moved away from his home, Nguyen moved a chair beside the bookshelves he had constructed in the front room. From behind two books on the top shelf, where the children could not possibly get it, he withdrew a gun.

The one that had served him so long and so well in his previous life.

It would serve him again.

As he ran out the front door he once more heard the sound of gunfire, but this time from a different quarter. The front doors of the barn were open, and a steady stream of bullets poured out from within.

It must be Pham and his self-styled resistance league. Despite Pham's denials Nguyen had suspected they were stockpiling weapons; now his suspicions were confirmed. Under the circumstances, however, he could hardly complain.

Pham's group did not have automatic weapons, but there appeared to be many of them, and they were well hidden within the dark interior of the barn. The pickup had stopped roving and was now at a stationary location between the barely reconstructed Truong home and the barn.

Colonel Nguyen went down on one knee, held his gun in both hands, and aimed carefully. His first bullet punctured the pickup's left rear tire. Those huge over-sized tires made for an easy target. The second bullet blew out the left front tire.

Someone in the pickup noticed what was happening. The wheels spun as the pickup tried to move away. The pickup lurched into drive, doing a lopsided tilt toward the left and scraping the wheel hubs on the dirt. Just as the pickup began to move, Nguyen fired a third bullet into the rear window. The window shattered as the pickup barreled toward the front gate, leaving a trail of glass shards in its wake.

Nguyen raced after the truck, but it was out of sight

before he had run fifty feet. The black pickup had struck again, and now would disappear without a trace just as it had done so many times before.

Dan Pham emerged from the interior of the barn. "What a marksman you are!" he exclaimed. "The great Colonel Nguyen has once more triumphed against the enemy."

Nguyen's face remained stern. "You told me you were not storing weapons. You lied."

"Yes," Pham admitted, "and you knew I was lying. What of it?"

Pham's followers began to emerge from the barn, many of them carrying their guns.

"Are you still so blind?" Nguyen grabbed Pham by the collar of his jacket. "Don't you see what is happening? With each incident, the destruction escalates. It will never end!"

"It will end," Pham said solemnly. "It will end when ASP has been eliminated!"

His followers cheered. Nguyen scanned their faces. Angry faces, faces of men prepared to do anything, prepared to march on ASP and tear the camp apart board by board. Faces filled with rage.

The same rage he himself had felt only moments ago.

"If you march on the ASP camp," Nguyen said, "they will mow you down like cockroaches."

"I do not doubt that," Pham said. "But that is not our plan. Our intelligence has provided us with an alternative approach. One that will hurt them in a way they will never forget!"

"Don't do this!" Nguyen said, shaking Pham furiously.

"It is too late," Pham said, pushing him away. "We were already planning to strike. We were simply waiting for the outcome of the trial. But no trial has stopped

ASP before—no trial ever will." He turned to face his followers. "It is up to us! We will make our move tonight!"

They cheered again, long and loud.

"This is insane! Suicide!" Nguyen shouted, but few could hear him over the clamor of Pham's warriors. "I will not allow you to do this!"

Suddenly the night was split apart by a piercing scream, so loud it seemed to reverberate through all of Coi Than Tien.

"My God," Nguyen said quietly. "What now?"

The youngest Dang daughter, Cam, ran out the front door of the newly constructed Truong home. Cam was crying and wailing; her hand was pressed against her mouth.

"Why was she in there?" Nguyen wondered aloud. "The house is not yet ready for them." It was not finished; it was simply a wooden framework with a thin layer of boards on all sides.

Nguyen didn't have to wonder long. Cam ran straight to him and buried her head against his shoulder. "I was checking the homes, to make sure no one was injured by the gunfire." She paused and tried to catch her breath. "I don't know why I went in there. I just had . . . a premonition. I wanted to be thorough. And I found—"

Nguyen's eyes expanded with the horrible realization. He passed Cam to one of Pham's men and raced toward the new home. The frame was still visible in many places; it had the fresh yellow coloring of new-cut pine.

He flung open the front door.

A body lay crumpled on the floor. A female body. With a bullet hole in her head.

A puddle of dark blood encircled her head and shoulders. The bullet had left a star-shaped hole about the size of his fist in her skull. Nguyen grabbed her wrist, but he knew he would find no pulse. She was dead; she probably died the second the assassin's bullet struck her skull. The poor Truongs—as if they had not already been cursed enough—

He blinked and wiped the sweat from his eyes.

This woman was not one of the Truong clan. He stared down at her wrist, her hand, her pearl-colored complexion.

She was white.

What would she be doing here? He brushed away her dark hair and examined her face, what was left of it, more closely.

She was definitely white. And for some reason, she looked familiar.

All at once, tears poured out of his eyes. He could not hold them back any longer. For so long, so long, he had not allowed himself to acknowledge his own feelings. Now the tears came whether he wished them or not.

No one was safe. An innocent woman had been killed. In his rage, Pham would kill innocent men, men whose only crime was joining a club that was popular in their hometown. And in retaliation, ASP would destroy Pham and all his men—perhaps all of Coi Than Tien. No one was safe.

And in large part, Nguyen realized, it was his fault. In his concern for his own family, he had crippled the law enforcement efforts to restore peace, had crippled the court's ability to exact justice.

He had caused great harm. And he had prevented nothing. His words had been useless—dust in the wind. The cataclysm between ASP and Coi Than Tien would proceed just as surely as if he had never been here at all.

Nguyen suddenly realized he was still clenching the dead woman's hand, but he did not drop it. He squeezed

it all the tighter. He could do one thing. He could prevent another innocent death, another tragedy like the
one that now lay beneath him soaking in her own blood.

He could do that. And he would.

* 59 *

"Mr. Kincaid. May I have a few words with you?"

Ben and Mike gazed up at the rugged Asian face, the deep-set eyes, the gray-flecked temples. "Of course. This is my friend Lieutenant Mike Morelli. You're Colonel Nguyen, aren't you?"

"Colonel Khue Van Nguyen." He bowed slightly. "You have a good memory."

"I've seen you in the courtroom. You've been watching the trial."

"Yes. Yes I have."

Nguyen was being strangely hesitant, as if he had something important on his mind, but couldn't make himself say it. "Any particular reason?"

"Curiosity. The jury has not yet returned?"

"No. They're taking their own sweet time about it. Looks like it's going to spill over into tomorrow. At least."

"That is unfortunate." Nguyen wrung his hands anxiously.

"Colonel Nguyen, forgive me for being blunt, but I have the distinct feeling there's something you want to tell me."

"There is." Nguyen folded his hands together. "Donald Vick did not kill Tommy Vuong."

"What?" Ben rose out of his chair. "How do you know?"

"Because I was there."

"You mean *you* killed him?"

"No. But I saw it."

"You were with him when he was killed?"

"I arrived less than a minute afterward. The cross was still burning. I heard his last words. I saw the fire consume his body."

Ben reached across the desk and took Nguyen's arm. "Who killed Vuong?"

"That I do not know. I saw the silhouette of a figure moving away from me as I arrived. I could not see it clearly."

"But it wasn't Vick?"

"No. I am certain. The killer was thinner, not as tall. It was someone else."

Ben glanced at Mike. "You're my witness."

"Understood."

"Colonel Nguyen, why didn't you tell me this before the trial was over?"

Nguyen lowered his head. "I was concerned about the possibility of . . . repercussions. Not for myself. But my wife, my children. I could not allow them to come to harm." Nguyen's eyes were filled with shame. "I do not offer that as an excuse. It is simply . . . an explanation."

"What changed your mind?"

"Have you heard what happened at Coi Than Tien tonight?"

"Not another fire?"

"No. An armed attack. Men in a black pickup with automatic weapons."

"ASP?"

"Presumably. But we have no proof. Just like every other time."

Ben nodded grimly. "Was anyone hurt?"

Nguyen's face tightened. "There was one fatality. A white woman."

"At Coi Than Tien? Again?" Ben's eyebrows furrowed. "Who was she?"

"I do not know."

Mike interrupted. "Is someone investigating this crime?"

"Sheriff Collier is there now," Nguyen answered. "But I suspect he has no idea how to proceed."

"Ben," Mike said, "if you don't have any objection, I'm going out there to see if I can help."

"No. Do it. I can wait for the jury by myself."

"Thanks." Mike grabbed his overcoat and bolted out of the office.

"Mike is a homicide detective in Tulsa," Ben explained. "He'll know how to handle the situation."

"That is good."

"Colonel Nguyen, what else can you tell me about Vuong's death?"

Nguyen reached inside his jacket and withdrew a stack of papers about two inches thick. "I found these in the forest less than twenty feet from where Tommy was killed."

Ben took the papers and examined them. It was all hate literature. Pamphlets and comic book tracts. *The Whole White World*, one was called. *Keep Your Neighborhood Pure*, another demanded. All of them bore the imprint of ASP; the stamps on the back indicated that they had been printed at the Birmingham ASP camp.

"Is it possible that these were dropped before the murder occurred?"

"So close to Coi Than Tien? I do not think so."

"And you didn't show these to the sheriff?"

"No. I was concerned . . . since they indicate that the killer is connected to ASP."

"That's what they're supposed to do, anyway," Ben murmured. "But I wonder." He placed the papers inside the desk. "Thank you for your help, Colonel Nguyen. Is there anything I can do for you?"

Nguyen shook his head sadly. "There is nothing anyone can do for me. When Pham learns what I have done, he will surely demand that I leave Coi Than Tien. And when my wife learns . . ." He clasped his head with his hands. "I fear I will be leaving Coi Than Tien—alone."

Loving suddenly burst through the front door. Ben had never seen the heavy-built man move so quickly.

And if that wasn't surprise enough, just as the door closed behind him, Christina pushed it back open.

"Skipper!" Loving shouted. "We gotta talk!"

Ben looked right past him. "Christina!"

"*Skipper!*" Loving said insistently. "We gotta talk—"

"Just a minute. Christina, it's—it's good to see you. I didn't expect—"

"I came to see Loving," she said abruptly. She tossed her strawberry-blond locks behind her shoulders. "I was getting a snack at Bo-Bo's when I saw him run in here. I thought he might be able to give me a lift."

"Oh. Then it wasn't—"

"Skipper, listen up! This is an emergency!"

Ben sadly turned his eyes away from Christina. "What's wrong? What's the big emergency?"

"It's ASP. They're planning something major league. And it's going down tonight!"

"How do you know?"

"Some of the regulars at the Bluebell spilled it. I've been pallin' around with them for days. They think I'm one of them. Hell, they've practically drafted me."

"Are you sure the big event hasn't already happened? They made a raid on Coi Than Tien earlier this evening."

"This is somethin' else. Starts at midnight. A special meeting."

"At their camp?"

"No. Some super-secret meeting place. I don't know where."

"Well, groups like ASP probably hold secret meetings all the time. Why are you so excited about this one?"

"Because the ASP clowns ain't callin' it a meeting."

"Yeah?"

"They're callin' it a *trial*."

* 60 *

"A trial? Of what?"

"I don't know, Skipper. But it's gotta have somethin' to do with Vick. Hell, maybe they're gonna try the guy who really killed Vuong."

"More likely they'd give him a merit badge."

"Perhaps," Colonel Nguyen suggested, "Grand Dragon Dunagan is on trial. For his testimony against one of his own."

"That seems unlikely," Ben said, deep in thought.

"I heard somethin' else about this big meet," Loving added. "The boys at the Bluebell said the armory was open. They're all gunning up. Skipper, this is gonna be big!"

Colonel Nguyen lowered his head. "It is as I feared. Armageddon. They are arming, we are arming. We will destroy one another."

"Did you hear anything else about this meeting?" Ben asked.

"No. That's all I could get out of 'em."

"A *trial*," Ben repeated. "I just don't know what that could mean. But I agree—it must relate to Donald Vick. And it might just fill in the missing pieces and explain what really happened to Tommy Vuong. Thanks for the ace detective work, Loving. If I weren't so busy, I'd give you a kiss."

Loving looked horrified. "Skipper!"

"Stay calm, Loving. Just a joke." Ben took a deep breath. "I'm going to go."

"What? Go where?"

"To the ASP secret meeting."

"You can't! Skipper, those guys'll rip your skull off your shoulders if they see you!"

"I'll have to take that chance."

"Then I'm coming with you."

"No. You take Christina home. And don't leave her alone. If there's trouble tonight, it could spread throughout the entire town."

"But how will you find the meeting place? I told you, it ain't at their camp. I don't know where it is."

"Neither do I," Ben said as he grabbed his windbreaker. "But I know someone who does."

To Ben's dismay, Deputy Gustafson was the only peace officer on duty at the jailhouse.

"I want to see my client," Ben said. "Immediately."

Gustafson's upper lip curled. "Do you, now? Well, that's a shame. Because I don't believe I care to let you in."

"You don't have any choice. He has a constitutional right to counsel."

"During the trial, sure. But as I understand it, the trial is over. All but the fat lady singing, anyway."

"I don't have time for this crap. I want to speak to Sheriff Collier. Where is he?"

"Out at Coi Than Tien. Seems those Vietnamese folks had another spot of trouble out there. He went to investigate. In fact, everyone on duty did." He smiled, baring all his teeth. "Except me."

Ben reached down, grabbed Gustafson's brown tie and twisted it around his fist. "Listen to me, you stupid simpleminded son of a bitch. I've had about as much of you as I can take. You got your licks in on me last week, and I didn't say a word about it afterward."

"Because you were scared shitless."

"Wrong. Because I have a sister, too, and I wouldn't like it if someone hurt her. In fact, I'd be mad as hell and I'd probably want to kill the man who did it. But enough is enough. I didn't have anything to do with that firebombing and I don't have time to screw around with some redneck moron trying to alleviate his guilt by throwing his weight in my way. So give me the goddamn keys!"

Gustafson peered at Ben through narrowed eyes. And a few moments later he slid the metal key chain across his desk.

"Thanks for your cooperation." Ben snatched the key chain and unlocked the back door that led to the cells.

As before, all the cells were empty except for Vick's.

"We've got to talk," Ben said.

Vick's face was lined with concern. "Has the jury returned?"

"They're still deliberating. That's not what I want to talk about. ASP is having some kind of top-secret special meeting tonight in a top-secret special location. And I want to know where it is."

"I've been in this cell for weeks. I don't know—"

"Spare me the ignorance routine. How many special meeting places can they have? You must have some idea where they're gathering."

"M-Mr. Kincaid . . ." He looked down at the floor. "I swore an oath."

"I don't want to hear about it."

"But I promised—"

"And I am sick to death of hearing about your insipid promises! Let me tell you something, pal. I'm the only friend you've got in this town. You were determined to stick your neck in a noose, and for some crazy reason, I was determined to get it out, even if I stuck my own neck in there in the process. I have a chance now to solve this whole gigantic mess, and I'll be damned if I'm going to let it pass just because you swore some stupid ASP oath!"

Ben gripped the metal bars between them. His eyes burned a line straight into Vick's. "I've done the best I could for you. And you haven't done a damn thing for me. But that's going to change. Starting right *now*."

* 61 *

Ben inched through the tall green pines surrounding the Aryan Covenant Church. The forest was dark and almost deathly quiet. But Ben knew the peace was an illusion. Violent forces were at work. All he could hope to do was to avoid them for as long as possible.

The church building was dark; there was no sign of movement inside. But Vick had prepared him for this. He wouldn't be fooled by appearances.

He crept around to the back of the church, between the kennel and the garage. Dried leaves crackled underfoot, reminding him that each step could easily be his last. Despite his anxiousness to get inside, he had to go slow. He had to be careful.

He held his breath as he tiptoed past the dog kennel. Brother Curtis's hunting dogs appeared to be sleeping on the other side of the pen. Lucky break—a chorus of angry barking would bring everyone running.

Ben tiptoed past the garage and headed toward the back of the church. He heard a sudden clattering noise and froze.

He looked all around him. Where had the noise come from? Had he been spotted? He didn't see anyone. Not that he could see much of anything in this pitch blackness.

He wiped his brow and took deep steady breaths, trying to still his racing heartbeat. His hands were shaking and his teeth were rattling. He tried to tell himself to relax, that if the ASPers caught him, they probably wouldn't hurt him. It was useless. He knew better.

Just as he was about to push off, he heard the clattering noise again, this time even louder than before.

It was coming from the garage.

As quietly as humanly possible, he crept to the garage front door, a wide descending door the width of two cars. The door was down, but there was a row of windows across the top, just above Ben's eye level.

Leaning gently against the door, Ben pushed up on his toes and peered through the window. The overhead garage light was off, but a kerosene lamp was lit. There were two men inside. Ben didn't know their names, but he recognized them from the ASP parade. They had been at the front, close to Dunagan.

And now they were standing on opposite sides of a pickup. A black pickup.

At least partially black. One of the men held a paintbrush; the other was wielding a spray gun. They were painting the pickup red.

So that was how it was done. These ASP thugs would make their raids on Coi Than Tien, then retreat to this church garage, barely a hundred yards away. Small wonder they were never caught; they would be safely tucked away long before the sheriff arrived. Then the painting would begin. By the time the sheriff thought to look in the church garage, if he did, the pickup would be painted and all traces of the operation would be washed away.

Ben noticed that the pickup's two left tires were flat, although he saw two new tires nearby. The men would probably put them on as soon as the painting was completed. The rear window had been shattered. That would be harder to replace. It looked like Coi Than Tien got a few good licks in. Neither of the men appeared to be wounded, however.

Pity.

That resolved one mystery, but there was still more Ben wanted to know before he returned to town. He was just about to push away from the garage when he heard a voice behind him.

"Don't move."

Ben jumped a foot into the air. Panicked, he whirled around and saw—

Christina. *Christina!*

"I said, 'Don't move,' " she hissed. "Do you want a *tête-à-tête* with those goons in the garage?"

"Christina!" She was dressed in black from head to toe—black turtleneck, black jeans. She was carrying a satchel over her shoulder.

They moved away from the garage so they wouldn't be heard. "How did you get here?"

"I followed you, obviously."

"But—why?"

"Someone has to keep an eye on you, Ben. Let's face it, you get lost going home from the grocery store. I'm surprised you made it this far."

"But—I mean—you wouldn't help me before—"

"Is that a fact? Who do you think called in Mike and Jones and Loving?"

"I—" Actually he hadn't even thought about it. "But I mean, about the trial—"

"The trial is over. Or all but."

"Yes, but—"

"Look, Ben, I still don't like this a bit. Taking this case was sheer stupidity on your part. And just when I thought you were starting to treat me like an equal partner, you blow me off and decide to represent the local fascist! I didn't understand that at all. I still don't." She paused. "But I won't let you get yourself killed."

Ben bit down on his lip. He wasn't going to spoil the occasion by asking more inane questions. "You know, I'm perfectly capable of taking care of this myself."

"Yeah, right. Let's just get on with it."

"Those men in the garage are the ones who've been terrorizing Coi Than Tien."

"Thanks. I figured that much out for myself."

"I wish I had brought a camera."

"And you think you're perfectly capable of taking care of this yourself." She opened her satchel and pulled out Jones's hand-size video camera. "Here, 007. It's all charged and ready to go."

"Will it shoot in the dark?"

"Well enough. It has a high lux rating."

Ben took the camera and crept back to the garage door. After taking about a minute's worth of footage, he decided he had enough to put them away for a good long time.

"Follow me." Ben led her to the back of the church.

"Surely we're not going to walk in the back door."

"No, we're not." He stopped in front of the sheet-metal cellar doors.

"This big meeting is being held in the cellar?"

"Appearances can be deceiving." Ben opened one of the double doors and stepped down a ladder within.

The room at the bottom was not well lit, but there was enough spillover that Ben could tell this was more than an ordinary cellar. The walls were lined with shelves, and the shelves were filled with papers, plans, and photographs.

"What is this?" Christina whispered.

"Unless I miss my guess, this is the real ASP war room. Where all the nasty plans are made. They probably moved all the incriminating material here so the DA wouldn't find it when he searched the camp. Or maybe it was always here. Much closer to Coi Than Tien, after all."

Christina pointed toward an open doorway. There was some sort of murmuring noise from the next room. Singing? No—*chanting*.

"Is that where the big meeting is?" she asked.

"Let's find out."

Holding his breath and stepping as lightly as possible, Ben passed through the doorway into the next room.

The immediate increase in lighting was blinding at first. This was a much larger room. Ben saw a sign that identified it as FELLOWSHIP HALL. How ironic. He realized they were still below ground level; that's why the lights were not visible from outside.

ASP was congregated at the other end of the hall, huddled in a circle around a long table. Grand Dragon Dunagan stood behind the table in full ASP regalia.

Ben and Christina crept forward and hid behind a tall stack of boxes containing bottled water. They were still out of the ASPers' sight, but close enough to hear what was going on.

Ben poked his head cautiously around the side of the boxes. Fortunately all the ASP men's eyes were trained on Dunagan.

"Has the jury returned a verdict?" Dunagan asked, in deep, solemn tones.

What was this? Had the jury returned while he was out creeping through the forest?

"We have." One of the ASP men approached. Ben could see that he was standing to one side with eleven others. Dunagan wasn't talking about the Vick trial jury; he was talking about a jury of his own.

The man handed Dunagan a small scrap of paper.

Dunagan read it, smiled, then crumpled it in his fist. "The jury finds Donald Vick guilty in absentia of high treason."

The crowd cheered. After thunderous applause and shouting they fell into a chant. "Blood, blood, blood, blood, *blood*!" they shouted, fists raised in the air.

"Donald Vick has committed the cardinal sin," Dunagan proclaimed. "Treason against ASP. For reasons entirely his own, he betrayed us all, disregarding his oath and performing acts at odds with our hallowed goals. His name shall be stricken from the rolls of ASP. It shall be as if he was never there. He is dead."

More cheers. Dunagan's last words echoed in Ben's ears. He wondered if that was a proclamation, or a prediction.

Ben slapped his forehead. "Stupid, stupid, stupid."

Christina frowned. "What?"

"I should've been taping this whole disgusting assembly. Hand me the camcorder."

"Let this be a warning to all our enemies," Dunagan cried out. His voice soared in pitch and volume. "ASP will mete out retribution to those who oppose us, whether they lie without or within."

"Blood, blood, *blood*," the ASP men chanted. "Death, death, *death*!"

The cry filled the room, so loud it made Ben's bones shake. He gripped the camera tightly and tried to prevent his trembling from spoiling the picture.

"They certainly have *esprit de corps*, don't they?" Christina whispered.

"Too much for my taste."

Dunagan continued his sermon. "Those who challenge us will perish as surely as all the godforsaken nonwhite races will die in the flames of Christ's fiery sword. We have slaughtered our enemies before. And we shall do so again."

This time the chanting persisted for more than a full minute. Ben swept the room with his camera, trying to make sure everyone got in the picture. Say cheese, ASP.

Dunagan raised his right hand, and his followers quickly did the same. He began to recite, and every man in the room joined him. They all knew it by heart.

"I am an Aryan. I serve the forces that guard my Aryan race. I am prepared to give my life in defense of my race."

Their voices swelled, chanting in unison. "I am an Aryan. I will never betray other Aryan people. I will fight the enemies of the Aryan race with my dying breath. I will never surrender.

"I am an Aryan," they continued. "If I am incarcerated, I will remember at all times my duty as an Aryan. As a political prisoner of war, I will answer only with my age, name, and address when questioned. I will resist any activity harmful to the Aryan race. I will obey the orders of my superior officers at all times."

The oath continued for three more verses, followed by cheers and shouts. Ben kept the camera rolling. Finally Dunagan waved down the noise. "You may also wish to know that tonight's incursion against the infidels at Coi Than Tien was a complete success."

Another spontaneous cheer, raising the rafters. Ben began to fear the meeting would disintegrate into a riot.

"Every time we act, our enemies become a little weaker, a little less able to resist. Soon they will give up, recognizing defeat. They will leave this place to the Anglo-Saxon races to whom it rightfully belongs. Tonight's operation went entirely as planned, according to my orders."

Ben gripped the camera all the tighter, focusing

tightly on Dunagan's face. Thank you for the confession, Mr. Grand Dragon. I think you just said enough to get yourself convicted of felony murder.

Ben was so focused on Dunagan's confession he didn't hear the sneakered footsteps approaching behind him.

"Intruder!" The shout was long and loud, silencing the assembly.

A pair of hands thudded down on Ben's shoulders, causing him to drop the camera. He tried to break away, but another pair of hands twisted his arms tightly behind his back.

"Christina! Run!"

Too late. They had her. One of them grabbed her satchel, another had an arm around her neck. She fought and kicked, but it was no use. They were much too powerful for her.

"There's two of them!" the man holding Ben shouted.

Dunagan's eyes narrowed when he spotted Ben. When he finally spoke, it was almost like a growl.

"Bring them to me."

* 62 *

The two men holding Ben dragged him through the ranks of ASP to the center table, with Christina close behind. He struggled futilely. He couldn't get away. And even if he could, where would he go? He was surrounded by fifty more just like the two who were holding him.

"Demon Kincaid," Dunagan said through clenched teeth. "How nice to see you again."

"The pleasure isn't mutual."

"I would advise you not to offend me more than you already have," he said ominously. He glanced at Christina. "Who's she? Another Hatewatch whore?"

"She's a member of my staff. An employee. She's only here because I ordered her to be here. Let her go."

"I'm afraid it may be too late for that."

"Don't even think about hurting her, Dunagan. I heard what you said a minute ago. Including your confession that you're behind the attacks on Coi Than Tien."

"Our land must be cleansed."

"Yeah, well, tonight's cleansing resulted in a death, and that means you can be charged with felony murder. That's a capital offense, Dunagan. Just like murder one."

The muscles in Dunagan's face and neck tightened.

"Then I will have to ensure that you never have a chance to tell anyone what you have learned."

Another ASP man broke through the ranks. He was waving the video camera. "The intruders dropped this."

Dunagan snatched the camera away, glaring at Ben the whole time. Unfortunately he knew how camcorders worked. He rewound the tape, then watched it through the viewfinder.

"They are spies!" he shouted. "Enemies!"

The angry snarls and hisses chilled Ben's blood.

"How convenient," Dunagan continued, "that we already have a jury assembled. Gentlemen of the jury, I submit Exhibit A!"

He passed the camera to the man who had submitted the previous verdict, who in turn passed it to the other members of the ASP jury. Some of them looked at the tape; some of them didn't bother.

"Are you able to reach a verdict?" Dunagan asked.

"Wait a minute!" Ben said. "What kind of trial is this? Don't I get an opportunity to be heard?"

Dunagan slapped Ben harshly with the back of his hand. "Your actions have spoken much louder than your words ever could. I ask you again, gentlemen of the jury. Have you reached a verdict?"

The jury huddled for less than ten seconds. "We find the intruders guilty of conspiracy against ASP."

Ben struggled to get free, but his captors held his arms tight. He couldn't even budge. "I'm not intimidated by this sick kangaroo court, Dunagan. You wouldn't know justice if it knocked you in the face."

Dunagan hit Ben again, this time with his fist.

"Very good." Dunagan faced the entire assembly. "The intruders have been found guilty by this tribunal. What shall their sentence be?"

"Death!" one voice shouted, and then the others joined in. "Death, death, death, death, *death*!"

Ben couldn't believe this was happening. It was too fast—too surreal. People didn't really act this way. No one could have so much hate; no one could be so devoid of conscience. Not so many of them. Unfortunately the mob mentality was probably the main problem. Groups were easier to manipulate than individuals. And this group was thoroughly under Dunagan's control.

"Death, death, death, death, *death*!" ASP shouted.

"The jury has spoken," Dunagan solemnly pronounced.

"That's murder you're talking abut, Dunagan. No matter how you dress it up, it's murder!"

Dunagan ignored him. He motioned to one of his assistants.

Before Ben had a chance to react, someone had clamped a damp cloth over his nose and mouth.

Chloroform. Damn! He stopped breathing, but he hadn't had time to inhale first. He knew he wouldn't be able to hold out long.

He twisted his head around. Christina was getting the same treatment. Her eyelids were fluttering. Then they closed.

Ben's own vision was getting foggy. He tried to force his eyes to remain open.

The commotion among the crowd was growing—wait a minute! Something else was happening. People were pointing toward the back, running. . . .

The ASP men were scrambling, deserting the hall. But why? Ben couldn't make out what was going on.

And then, suddenly, the back room exploded into brilliant white light. A hot light. It shimmered and changed shape. It grew.

Ben had seen this before. Much too recently.

Fire.

In the final instant before he passed out, Ben realized the church was burning.

* 63 *

Ben awoke choking. The smoke cast a gray haze through the hall. It was difficult to see more than a few feet away.

He shook his head several times, trying to clear out the cobwebs. He was still in Fellowship Hall. At least he thought he was. It was difficult to be certain. The chloroform had left him with blurred vision and a dull throbbing between his temples. He had to—

Oh my God. Christina!

He shouted out her name, but didn't hear a response. He looked all around, but the smoke obscured his vision. Worse, he could see the blaze billowing out from the ASP war room and spreading into the hall. The fire must've been set in there, probably through the cellar door Ben had left open.

"Christina!"

He ran around the table, trying to find some trace of her. Would they have taken her with them? Why her and not him? It made no sense.

"Christina!"

He tried to remember where he had seen her last. They were holding her over there, behind the table. . . .

He practically stepped on her before he saw her. She was lying on the floor, hands over her head. Her eyes were closed.

"Christina!" He coughed; the smoke was getting to him. He took her head and gently moved it back and forth, calling out her name.

Slowly her eyelids opened. She started to speak, inhaled smoke, and began to cough violently.

Ben helped her sit upright. "What happened?" she gasped.

"Someone set the church on fire. The ASP clan fled. They left us here to die."

"Great. How—" Her voice was consumed by coughing.

"I think you got a bigger dose of chloroform than I did before ASP hightailed it out of here. Can you stand?"

She nodded. Ben helped her to her feet.

"I don't mean to rush you, but the back entrance is already blocked off by fire. We need to get out of here before the front doors are impassable as well."

With his arm around her shoulder, they moved to the stairwell that appeared to lead to the ground floor of the church. The passage was already filled with dark sooty smoke, but they made their way to the top.

The front entrance to the church was consumed in flame.

Ben clenched his teeth. "They must've set a second fire. The arsonist was trying to trap everyone inside."

"It must not have worked," Christina said. A layer of black soot underlined her nose and mouth. "The ASP gang isn't here."

"The back entrance," Ben said, snapping his fingers. "Remember—we passed it on our way to the cellar door. Must be on the other side of the pulpit." He grabbed Christina's hand. "Come on!"

"Wait a minute!"

"What? We don't have time—"

"Listen!"

Ben fell quiet. And a few seconds later he heard it, too, above the roar of the flames.

The whimpers and cries of the dogs.

Christina ran to one of the stained-glass windows in the chapel. The windows were too narrow to squeeze through, even if they knocked the glass out. But the windows did provide a view of the dogs. "The fire has spread to the kennel! They're trapped!"

"I'm sorry," Ben replied, "but we don't have time for this. We have to get out of here!"

"We can't just let those poor dogs burn to death!"

Ben swore silently. "There's a control panel near the front entrance. I saw it when I was here before. It electronically controls the kennel doors."

"Show me."

Ben and Christina ran back to the front entrance. In the space of perhaps a minute, the flames had grown twice as large. Even standing ten feet away, the heat was so searing they couldn't come any closer.

Ben pointed. "It's over there, on the wall. Beside that closet door or whatever it is."

"It's too hot!" she cried. "I can't get to it!"

Ben remembered where the men's room was. He ran in and found to his relief that the faucets were still working. He removed his windbreaker, soaked it thoroughly, and threw it over his head.

"Be careful!" Christina shouted when he emerged.

"I'll do my best." Draped in the wet coat, Ben ran to the control panel. The heat was scalding; he could almost feel his skin melting. The coat provided some protection to his face, but he knew he couldn't count on that for long. Images of Maria Truong flashed in his brain. Please God, he did not want to be burned like that. Please—anything but that.

He had no idea which of the blinking buttons controlled the kennel, so he tried them all in rapid succession. After the third button, he heard Christina shout from inside the chapel.

"That's it! The doors are opening! Get out of there!"

Ben raced away from the control panel, the flames licking at his heels. He felt scorched from head to toe. But he made it out.

He looked through the chapel window and saw the terrified dogs bolting out of the blazing kennel. "Now let's get out of here!"

He grabbed her hand and raced toward the back door. Or as close to it as they could get.

The delay of a few minutes had cost them dearly. The fire in the basement was spreading not only out but up. The flames caught onto the wooden floor and crept all over the north wall.

They couldn't even get close to the door.

"That's it, then," Ben said, staring into the flickering flames. "We're trapped."

* 64 *

Christina pressed close against him. "There must be something we can do."

"Look at the fire spreading," Ben said, almost mesmerized by the red glow. "This wooden church will go up in no time at all."

"I'm not giving up. If we can't get out, we should move up."

The wheels in Ben's head began to turn. "There's a staircase in the front lobby."

"Come on!"

They ran through the chapel to the staircase. Just as they hit the stairs Ben heard a sudden *whoosh!*— followed by an intense flash of heat.

The fire must have hit a gas main or something flammable. The flames had burst forward, filling the chapel.

It was following them.

There was only one room on the second floor. It had no furnishings, but Ben saw many folding chairs and tables stacked against the walls. Probably a social room, or for Sunday school. Smaller groups that didn't need a room the size of Fellowship Hall.

"There are no windows!" Christina exclaimed.

Ben scanned the room quickly. She was right.

"I had hoped there would be some way out—a window or a ventilation duct. Some exit from this death trap. But there isn't."

Ben could see the mounting panic in her eyes. She was out of ideas, and knew better than to look to him for help. He had never been any good in an emergency; she was the one who always saved the day. But this time it seemed even Christina was stumped.

"Maybe I can punch a hole in one of these walls," he said, without much conviction. He covered his fist with his wet coat and gave one a try. He barely left a mark.

"Let's go back down." Ben had barely reached the head of the stairs before he realized that was impossible. The flames filled the ground floor. There was nowhere down there to go but straight into the inferno.

"Ben," Christina said, "I—I don't feel so good." She began to cough violently. She sat down and braced herself against the floor.

She'd taken in too much smoke, Ben realized. Soon she'd be suffering from serious inhalation damage or scorching of her lungs. Or worse.

The fire reached the top of the stairs. It was filling the church, obliterating it. The flames wouldn't stop until the church was utterly destroyed.

And everything in it.

"I need air," Christina gasped, between coughs.

Ben pounded his fists together. There had to be something he could do. There had to be a way. This second-story refuge had become a prison; there was nothing they could do but wait for the fire to reach them. There was no way out. Not in the wall. Or the floor.

But what about the roof? Ben raised his head and looked upward. Yes! There was something up there—a trapdoor, perhaps?

He jumped toward it, but he was too short to reach it. He grabbed one of the folding chairs. They were hot to the touch. Gritting his teeth, he unfolded the chair and stood on it.

He popped open the trapdoor. From the opening he could see the steeple tower. Of course—this was how they rang the bell.

The fire was in the room with them now. They didn't have a second to spare.

Ben scrambled down to Christina's side. "Do you see the opening?"

Her nod was barely perceptible.

"Do you think you can get through?"

She didn't answer, but her eyes told Ben she had serious doubts.

"I'll go through first. If you can just stand on the chair, I'll pull you up. Okay? Will you follow me?"

She smiled weakly. "Don't I always?"

Ben pushed his head through the opening and grabbed the top of the roof. He'd never been very good at chin-ups in school, but it was amazing what you could do when the only alternative was being burned alive.

As soon as he was on the roof, he lay flat and reached down for Christina. She was already standing on the chair, but she was teetering uncertainly. She held out her arms to him.

Ben stretched his arms through the opening. Bloody hell! He would have a legal assistant who was barely five feet tall. Reaching down with all his might, he grabbed her hands and pulled. Once he had her head through, she flattened her arms against the shingles and helped push. A few seconds later she was on the roof.

And not a moment too soon. The fire filled the second-story room.

"We made it," Ben said breathlessly. "Thank God."

Christina drank in deep gulps of fresh—or at least fresher—air. "We made it," she echoed. "But to what?"

Ben knew exactly what she meant. The way this fire was spreading, it would only be a matter of moments before it reached the roof. Or more likely, the flames would eat away at the structural supports and the roof would crash into the blazing cauldron below.

Ben peered uneasily over the edge of the roof. They were much higher up than the usual second-story roof. The chapel was probably designed with a high ceiling. Even if he had been inclined to try to jump to the ground, though, in this case, it would be a suicide plunge. The fire had spread to the surrounding land. He would be jumping to a hellish instant death.

There were no signs of assistance; in fact, there was no sign of anyone. Probably the only ones who had noticed the fire were the residents of Coi Than Tien, and they were hardly likely to mount a rescue.

There was no help from others, and no way they could help themselves. They were surrounded by flames on all sides.

And there was no way out.

* 65 *

Ben sat beside Christina, hopeless and defeated. He had failed miserably. He hadn't saved them. All he had done was buy time, and not much time at that.

Christina's coughing had subsided, but in its place was a deep, rasping noise. Her breathing was heavy and labored. Ben knew she was hurting.

"You did all you could," she managed to say. "Don't blame yourself."

"Why would I?"

Christina tried to smile. "You always blame yourself. For everything."

Ben turned away. He couldn't stand to see her like this. Despite what she said, it was his fault she was here, and he damn well knew it.

He glanced down through the trapdoor. The room below was ablaze; there was nothing left but the yellow flames that destroyed everything in their path. The fire was barely inches away from the roof.

"Christina," he said. "I'm so sorry."

She coughed again, a harsh hacking cough. "Told you not to blame yourself," she whispered.

"It's not that. I'm so screwed up. I should've—"

"You did what you could." Another deep, rasping breath. "You always do."

"But it isn't enough. You deserve better. I—" He

clasped her hand. "I want you to know before it's too late that I—"

He was interrupted by a strange sound, a noise in the background he hadn't heard before. What was it? Some bizarre Ouachita wildlife? It seemed to be coming from the sky. A bird? No, that wasn't it. It was more like—

Like a chopping noise.

Ben pointed toward the clouds. "It's Portia!"

Christina strained to see. "Who?"

A bright headlight shimmered through the smoke clouds. "I mean, it's Mike, *in* Portia. He got the damn thing fixed!"

The chopping and whirring noises grew louder as the helicopter came almost directly overhead.

"That's great," Christina said, watching the flames catch the roof. "But how do we get from here to there?"

As if in answer, the passenger-side door opened and a red rope ladder fell out the side.

"That looks pretty dodgy to me," Christina said.

"Consider the options."

"Yeah, but—"

"Christina, I never cared much for heights, but I'm still going up that ladder. And if I can do it, I know you can!"

"Well, maybe, but—"

"You first."

He walked her to the ladder and placed it in her hands. She slowly stepped up the ladder, one rung at a time. When she was halfway up, Ben stepped onto the ladder. The rungs were soft and they gave much more than he would have liked. But it held him. He was off the roof.

"Get us out of here!"

The helicopter eased away from the blazing church. Ben saw two heads poking out the side of the copter. It was Sheriff Collier—and Loving. The ladder was on a winch and they were reeling it in.

When he was about halfway up, Ben heard a tremendous crash below him.

He knew he shouldn't look down, but he couldn't stop himself. The roof of the church had crashed down into the flames. The entire building was consumed; there was nothing left but a gigantic glowing fireball.

Just in time, Mike. Just in time.

The conflagration had taken more than just the church. As Ben could see from his aerial perch, it had spread in all directions. The familiar loblolly pines were ablaze, as well as the kennel, and the garage that once held all that incriminating evidence.

But most importantly, Ben saw that the fire had spread a hundred yards to the south.

To Coi Than Tien.

* 66 *

The fence surrounding Coi Than Tien, the barn, and most of the shacks, were all in flames. Ben saw people fleeing their homes, their dearest possessions on their backs, their children clutched to their chests. Others scrambled around trying to fight the blaze, to little effect.

Someone on the ground was organizing a bucket-brigade line from the well to the nearest point of fire. He couldn't make out the face on the slender body, but he had a strong hunch who it was.

Sheriff Collier and Loving hauled Ben into the helicopter. It was crowded—five people in a small helicopter—but he wasn't about to complain.

Before Ben could get his bearings, he was astonished to feel Loving wrap his arms around him—and hug him.

"Are you all right, Skipper?" An expression of profound worry crossed his macho brow.

"Yeah, I'm all right," Ben said awkwardly. "But Christina isn't. She needs medical attention."

"No," Christina said. She was staring out the window, watching Coi Than Tien fight the flames. "We have to go down there and help."

"I can't land too close," Mike said. "Portia's blades could fan the flames and make the blaze worse than it already is. But there's a clearing on the other side of the settlement."

Ben protested. "But I still think—"

Christina shook her head. "Take us down."

As Ben suspected, Belinda had organized another brigade to fight the rampaging fire. This fire was several times as great as the one they had fought before, but this time Belinda had many more hands. She had three different lines aimed at different parts of the fire, radiating from the well like spokes from the hub of a wheel.

Most of the residents of Coi Than Tien had returned to fight the blaze, and many citizens of Silver Springs were there as well. Mike explained to Ben that the fire had broken out while he and Sheriff Collier were at Coi Than Tien investigating the latest death. Collier radioed for help. Every officer, off duty or on, turned out, and on their way out of town they raised the alarm at the Bluebell, Hatewatch, and just about every other place they could find people this time of night.

To Ben's amazement, he saw Grand Dragon Dunagan standing on the sidelines with two of his ASP followers. He wasn't helping, and for a reason: he was wearing handcuffs on both wrists.

Ben took a place beside Mike in one of the brigade lines. "How did you find us?" he shouted over the noise and the smoke.

"I got Portia fixed this afternoon," Mike explained, "so I flew her to Coi Than Tien. When the fire broke out, we ran toward the church and saw all these ASP creeps in costume bolting out the back door. Collier and I arrested Dunagan and a couple of the others on suspicion of arson."

"I don't know about that," Ben said, passing another

bucket into Mike's hands, "but I can give you some even juicier charges to work with."

"Great. They wouldn't tell me where you were at first, but after I leaned on one of the sidekicks, he told me you and Christina were still inside the church. I knew I couldn't get through that wall of fire on foot, so I decided to try an aerial rescue."

"How did you get him to talk?"

"Oh, you know. Held his head close to the fire. Threatened to handcuff him to the front door. That's all."

"Oh, well," Ben said. "Nothing the Supreme Court would disapprove of, I'm sure."

The buckets of water continued to fly down the human spokes of Coi Than Tien. The fire had spread to almost all the buildings, but it didn't seem to be getting any worse. At least they were containing it before it devastated the entire countryside.

Ben had been on the line a full fifteen minutes before he noticed that the man passing buckets to him was none other than Sheriff Gustafson. Ben hadn't even noticed. Their eyes met, but neither said a word.

Ben scanned some of the other lines. The other deputies were there, and he saw District Attorney Swain, too. Mac was there along with several of the Bluebell regulars. John Pfeiffer and Frank Carroll were there with Belinda. Pham and his contingent formed an almost continuous line. Colonel Nguyen was helping them, with a boy Mike identified as Nhung Vu. He had a patch over his right eye, but he seemed strong and able.

And then a miracle occurred. Ben heard the wailing of the siren first. The sound grew in pitch and intensity as it Doppler-shifted closer to them.

Ben saw the large red vehicle drive through the entrance gates of Coi Than Tien. It was a fire truck—a real one. And it was carrying ten professional firefighters.

"Thank God," Mike said. "Collier called them in from Yell County."

"You knew they were coming?"

"Yeah. But I was afraid the fire would be out of control before they arrived."

The firefighters unhooked their hoses and started to work. The brigade lines kept going, but they cleared a path and tried not to get in the professionals' way. The truck didn't have access to a hydrant, but they dropped a sump pump in the well and had a limited supply of water on the truck.

It was slow going, but it was making a difference. The citizens had brought the fire under control, and the pros were now extinguishing it. They killed the fire at Coi Than Tien, then put out the remaining flames at the church and the outlying areas. By two in the morning, the fire was gone.

But so was Coi Than Tien. All that was left was black, smoking embers. The barn was the only building still standing, and it had suffered significant damage. The church was gone, all but the charred remains. Worse, the mountain countryside between the two was ruined.

The fire had taken its toll on everyone. And everything.

* 67 *

Ben stood in the center of what was once Coi Than Tien, barely able to contemplate all the waste and mindless destruction. Where would these people go now? he wondered. What would they do? What *could* they do?

Mike approached him, hauling Dunagan along by the short chain of his handcuffs. "You had something you wanted to tell me about this man?"

"Damn straight." Ben continued to gaze at the pitiful ruins. "Well, Dunagan, it looks like your mission is accomplished. I hope you're happy with yourself."

"I don't know what you're talking about. I didn't set this fire."

"Maybe not, but you set into motion the forces that made it inevitable." Ben saw a face he recognized running past. *"Pham!"*

Dan Pham stopped. "What do you want?"

"I'd like a few words with you."

"I have matters to attend to—"

Ben grabbed Pham and pushed him toward Dunagan. "We're all going to talk. And if you won't stay voluntarily, Mike will arrest you on suspicion of arson."

"Arson? What are you talking about? Are you suggesting I set fire to my people's homes?"

"No. But I think you torched the ASP church, and

361

that fire blazed out of control and spread to Coi Than Tien."

Pham folded his arms across his chest. "You have no proof of these accusations."

"You told Colonel Nguyen you planned to retaliate tonight. You must've heard about the ASP meeting just like I did. What I don't know is how you found their secret meeting place."

A tiny smile crept across Pham's countenance. A smile Ben didn't like at all.

"You followed *me*," Ben said. "I led you to it."

"I have had a man following you since you became counsel for that hatemongering killer."

Ben grabbed Pham's shirt and shook him with all his might. "How dare you? How dare you use me to further your terrorism!"

"Terrorism? Are we the terrorists? All I did was defend my home. They are the terrorists!" He pointed an accusing finger at Dunagan. "I saw more than just a church meeting tonight. I saw two men painting a black truck in the church garage. The pickup that has been used to strike against Coi Than Tien time and time again!"

"It's true," Ben told Mike. "I saw it myself."

"These gooks moved in where they don't belong," Dunagan grunted. "They asked for trouble."

"Where we don't belong?" Pham countered. "We were here long before you!"

"No, my *people* were here long before yours." Pham and Dunagan were standing nose to nose. "You declared war on ASP. And that war is going to go on and on until your people crawl back to the rice paddies where they belong!"

"We will not go back!" Pham cried. "We will fight you to the last man!"

"Will you listen to yourselves!" Ben pushed himself between them. "When in God's name will you ever learn? Violence is not the answer. Hate doesn't do anyone any good. One of you swears to fight, the other one swears to retaliate. And look what happens. *Look!*"

Ben grabbed them both by the back of their necks and forced them to look at the smoky remnants of Coi Than Tien, the huddled families that had nothing left and nowhere to go, and at the crest of the hill, the church that was now a waste heap waiting to be shoveled over and forgotten.

"Both of you were determined to hurt your enemy. And both of you ended up hurting yourself. Can't you see how wrong this is?"

Dunagan turned away, his eyes closed. "I never meant for this to happen," he said quietly.

"It's too late for regrets," Ben said. "As soon as I have a conversation with the district attorney, ASP is history. You might as well tell your men to start packing up the camp now. Hate is going out of fashion."

Dunagan's face flushed with fury. "You think that's going to accomplish anything? You think you can stop us? So you run us out of Arkansas. So what? We're everywhere. *Everywhere.* We're in your schools, in your churches. We're in your armies and your police forces. We're the skinheads in Portland. We're the KKK in Corpus Christi. Stopping me won't change anything."

"Mike," Ben said through clenched teeth, "please take this . . . man away."

"Gladly." Mike grabbed Dunagan by the cuffs and hauled him back toward the sheriff's car.

Ben faced Pham. "Once ASP leaves town, you can disband your resistance league."

"We still have many grievances—"

"Who doesn't?" Ben laid a hand on his shoulder.

"You've got to put your hate behind you. And start re-building."

"There is too much to do," Pham said, gazing at the vast destruction. "I cannot possibly—"

"You'll need help. And I know where you can get it." Ben pointed toward the front gates. Colonel Nguyen was heading away from them. Leaving.

"Colonel Nguyen!" Pham shouted.

Nguyen turned and cautiously approached. "I know what you will—"

"You were right," Pham said, interrupting him.

Nguyen fell silent, surprised.

"I was wrong. Armed attacks were not the solution. We accomplished nothing. Nothing good."

Nguyen shook his head. "At least you were willing to take action. To *try*." He turned away. "I am leaving—"

"Our people have suffered much tonight, Colonel. There is work to do. I cannot do it alone."

Nguyen stopped walking.

"But," Pham added, "I believe that we can do it together." He held out his hand.

Nguyen clasped it and squeezed tightly. "Together."

Several moments later Colonel Nguyen bowed politely. "If you will excuse me, Mr. Kincaid. I need to have a . . . conversation with my wife."

Ben nodded. "There's still the matter of the woman who was murdered," he said to Mike.

"That's where you're wrong," Mike replied. "We found a handgun in the shack where her body was found. The bullets match. She wasn't shot during the ASP attack. She killed herself."

"Suicide?"

"Yeah. I think she'd been there for some time before she was found. Here, I took a picture."

Ben took the Polaroid. He recognized her immediately. It was the young woman he had rescued from the first fire. The one who disappeared.

Mike pulled a sheet of paper out of his coat pocket. "While I was still in town I got a copy of the corpse's prints from Deputy Gustafson and faxed them to the FBI database in Washington. We got a response about an hour ago and someone relayed it to Collier over the radio. Take a look at this."

Ben took the paper and read. His jaw fell. He couldn't fathom it—

But of course. It was the final piece of the puzzle. Now it all made sense, everything he had seen and heard, everything Vick had told him. Everything.

"Mike," Ben said. "I think I'm going to have a chat. . . ."

"Want me to come with you?"

"No. Maybe I can get Colonel Nguyen—" He spotted the Colonel sitting in front of his home, locked in a tight embrace with his wife. "Never mind. You get Christina to a hospital." After making sure no one was listening, he whispered a few more words in Mike's ear.

"I'll take care of Christina," Mike said. "Are you sure you can do this?"

"I—" His voice cracked. He inhaled deeply; after a few moments, he was able to continue. "I'll be all right."

Mike nodded. "Good luck."

"Too late for that," Ben said. "Much too late for that now."

* 68 *

"Thanks for coming," Ben said, when Belinda entered what was left of Coi Than Tien's barn.

"I came as soon as Mike told me where you were." She ran up to Ben and clasped his hands. "Are you all right?"

"I'm fine."

"I heard you were trapped inside that church. My God—you might have been killed!" She reached up and brushed some of the black soot from his face. "I was so worried."

"Belinda—" He gently pushed her away.

"What's wrong? What's bothering you now?"

"Belinda—" Ben's eyes began to well up. He fought it back. "Belinda. I know."

"Know what? I don't understand."

Ben looked down at the dirt. He hurt so much he wasn't sure he could go on. "I know you killed Tommy Vuong."

"Me?" A horrified expression crossed her face. "Is this some sort of sick joke?"

"Of course not."

"What could ever make you think I killed him?"

Ben unfolded the paper in his pocket. "Cindy Jo Simpson. The last name threw me off at first, but then I remembered that you were married previously. Your husband's name was Hamilton, and you didn't retake your maiden name when you were divorced. I had Mike check it out. You were born Belinda Todd Simpson." He crumpled the paper in his hand. "Cindy Jo Simpson was your younger sister."

Belinda fell back against several bales of hay stacked against the wall.

"I remember Mary Sue described the woman who visited Vick as resembling you, only younger," Ben said. "And when I first saw her in the smoke of the Truong home, I thought she was you. Small wonder there was a resemblance."

All at once tears tumbled from Belinda's eyes. "How much do you know?"

"I think I've figured out most of it, but I'd rather hear it from you. Revenge, right?"

Belinda brushed the tears from her cheeks. "I told you my sister was always in trouble. And it was always my job to get her out of it. To set the world right again."

"I know Vuong was accused of rape about a year ago. Your sister was his victim, wasn't she?"

Belinda nodded. "It was a date rape. She had been hanging around him and some of the others since she met them in Porto Cristo. She followed them up here. I think she had a crush on Tommy, but at first he wouldn't give her the time of day. Finally he asked her out. She was thrilled. So excited. So . . . vulnerable. On the way home he threw her down in the forest and started beating her. He was beyond mean—psychotic. She had bruises on her face and breasts that lasted for weeks." Belinda paused, trying to steady her voice. "And then he raped her."

"Didn't she report it to the police?"

"Yes, but she had no proof other than her own testimony. Tommy had a squeaky-clean reputation, and everyone knew she liked him and that she wanted to go out with him. They assumed it was consensual intercourse. He winked and jabbed and told them she liked it rough. And they believed him."

"Surely you could've taken the case to higher authorities."

"*I* probably could've, but unfortunately I didn't know about this at the time, and Cindy Jo didn't have the slightest idea what to do. It was only several months later that she called me. You see, there was another complication. Cindy was pregnant."

"By Vuong?"

"Right. She ran away from Coi Than Tien, from everyone she knew. She was so despondent, so ashamed. When the baby was almost due, she called me, desperate. She had no money, she knew nothing about babies, she didn't know what to do. She was distraught, practically irrational. The last nine months of isolation, guilt, and trauma had destroyed her. She was a different person. Very sick, getting sicker by the day."

"That was the reason you decided to personally head up the Hatewatch operation in Silver Springs," Ben said.

"True. But when I got here, I couldn't find her. Not a trace." She paused, drew in her breath. "But I sure as hell could find Tommy Vuong."

"So you decided to kill him."

"It wasn't like that. I told you I was in that bar when Vick and Vuong fought. The idea came to me in a flash. I could accomplish two great goods with a single stroke. I could take care of the bastard who raped my sister, and at the same time I could strike a blow against ASP, the men who have brought so much misery to so many people. The men who tied me to their cross and beat me like I was an animal.

"When Vick's head crashed down on my table, he left a smear of blood and a few hairs behind. I waited until John went to the bathroom, then carefully scraped the hair and blood into one of those plastic bags I always carry in my purse."

"You stole the crossbow and bolts from the ASP stockpile," Ben said.

"It was risky, but it was critical if I was going to implicate Vick and the rest of ASP. Frank had been watching the ASP camp for weeks. He knew when I should go and how to get in without being caught. He also told me Vick had picked up those crossbow bolts the day before. So naturally that's what I used."

"And then you planted the blood and hair on the crossbow, erected a burning cross—the ASP emblem—and waited for Vuong to fall into your trap."

"That's right. You know, even then I wasn't sure I would be able to do it. I wasn't sure I'd be able to fire the bow. I had to think about it for a long time. When he first saw me and our eyes met—" Her face was lost in shadow, and she whispered to Ben a few more details about what happened next. "But I did it."

"After you shot him, you left the crossbow where you knew it would be found."

"True. And I dumped a pile of ASP hate literature I had in my files near the cross."

"That was your first mistake," Ben explained. "The fine print on some of the brochures specified that they had been printed in Birmingham. Why would Dunagan and his gang import literature when they have a printing press at their camp right here? It was possible, but it struck me as unlikely. That's when I began to wonder if the brochures had been planted. I checked Jones's research on ASP's activities in Birmingham. Only three people were there who are also here. Grand Dragon Dunagan. Frank Carroll. And you."

"How stupid of me. I didn't even think."

"What happened to your sister?"

"Even after Vuong was dead, I still couldn't find Cindy Jo. I don't know where she had the baby. I know she didn't know what to do with her. She had no home, no help, no money. In her state of mind, she was utterly unable to deal with a newborn. But I still don't know why she left her in the Truongs' home."

"I think I do," Ben said. "She had been with the Coi Than Tien people for some time, so she must've known a good deal about them. Including the fact that Maria Truong desperately wanted a baby."

"I guess that's it." Ben could see tears once more beginning to form. "Cindy Jo had no idea the Truongs' home would be torched before anyone woke up and found the child. But when she learned what happened— when she learned what happened to her little baby—" Her voice was cut off in a choke.

"She did her best to save her," Ben said. "She was desperate to get inside that burning house."

Belinda held her face in her hands. "The trauma of losing her baby in that hideous way must've been more than enough to push her over the edge."

"So she killed herself."

Belinda nodded bitterly. "Mike told me. My poor poor Cindy Jo. She asked me to help. But I couldn't. I couldn't help her at all."

Ben put his arm around her.

"I don't know what happened to me," Belinda said, sobbing in great heaving bursts. "I've never done anything so . . . violent in my entire life. I just couldn't stop thinking about what that monster did to Cindy Jo."

Ben hugged her tighter. Deputy Gustafson's words echoed in his memory. *When something horrible like that happens to your own sister, it just does something to you. Tears you apart. Makes you go a little crazy. Makes you want to kill the man responsible.*

Ben held her in silence for a long time. Finally she brushed the streaks of tears from her face.

"Can you ever forgive me?" she asked, her eyes wide and pleading.

"I can forgive a woman who made a mistake because she loved her sister." He looked down at the ground. "What I have a hard time forgiving is a woman who was willing to let another man die for her crime."

"You mean Donald Vick? Ben—he's ASP. He's scum."

"You're wrong. He's not a bad kid at all—just one who made some stupid mistakes when he was young. Like everyone does. His family pressured him into ASP. He never liked it. He never participated in any of their destructive activities."

"I don't believe it."

"It's true. He didn't agree with the terrorist tactics ASP was using against Coi Than Tien—in fact, he tried to stop them. Remember Mary Sue mentioning that Vick had a Vietnamese visitor two days before the murder?"

Belinda nodded.

"That was Dan Pham. See, Vick was feeding Pham inside information about ASP's plans. That's how Pham stayed so well informed. Dunagan knew there was a leak, but he didn't know who it was. After he heard Mary Sue's testimony at trial, he realized it was Vick. That's why he decided to throw Vick to the wolves when he testified, and that's why ASP later branded him a traitor."

"But, Ben, that man came into the bar and started beating Vuong for no reason at all. I saw it!"

"You're wrong. I had a little heart-to-heart with my client. Now that the trial is over and the woman he was trying to protect is dead, he was willing to talk. You remember the testimony about a woman who came to visit Vick the night before the murder? That was your sister."

"Cindy Jo?"

"Yes. Apparently she and Vick had met in town a few days before and he offered to help her. Turns out Vick is basically a softhearted guy, even if he is an ASP member. She came to his boardinghouse and told him about Vuong, what he had done, how she was about to have this baby and didn't know what to do."

Belinda's eyes seemed to turn inside her. "That's why he sought out Vuong at the Bluebell."

"Right. She made him promise not to tell anyone, but he didn't promise not to do anything about it. In his naïveté, Vick tried to get Vuong to marry her, just so the baby wouldn't be illegitimate. When he refused, Vick told Vuong he should at least give her some money. When Vuong refused that suggestion and laughed in his face, Vick blew up. That's why he lashed into Vuong. That's why he called Vuong *perverted*. He was referring to the beating and rape. And that's why he got thrown out on his butt. He was looking after your sister." Ben paused. "Just like you."

The full horror of what he had said stabbed Belinda like a knife. She seemed frozen, transfixed.

"Even when he was on trial, Vick wouldn't tell Cindy Jo's secret, because he had promised not to, and because in his simple Southern way he thought an illegitimate pregnancy would ruin her reputation, if people found out. The fact is, the man you framed was the only man in this town who tried to help your sister."

"Oh, my God," Belinda said softly, over and over again. "I hated that man. I *hated* him."

Ben clenched his eyelids shut. "More hate. And with the same result."

Belinda looked up at him. "What are you going to do?"

Ben felt a clutching inside his chest. "You mean—about what I know? Belinda, I don't think I have any choice."

She took both of his hands and pressed her head against his chest. "Ben—if you talk, they'll try me for murder!"

"And if I don't, the jury that's deliberating will probably sentence Vick to death. For a crime you committed."

"Ben—" She threw her arms around him. "Please don't do this to me!"

Ben felt a hollow aching in his heart more painful than any of the physical beatings he had endured. He didn't answer her. He couldn't.

A rapid, chopping noise slowly filtered into the barn.

"That's Mike, isn't it?" Belinda asked. She looked at him accusingly. "You've been waiting for him to return. That's why you kept me here all this time. You've been waiting for him!"

"Belinda, I—"

She pushed herself away from him. "I can't believe you would do this to me!"

"Belinda—"

"Is he going to arrest me? Is that it?"

"I was hoping you would turn yourself in. It'll look better at trial."

Her astonished expression slowly became one of horror and loathing. "After what we've shared. After all we've— You're turning me in." She whirled away from him.

Ben reached out and grabbed her hand.

She slapped him away. "What do you want?" she said bitterly. "Did you think I was going to kiss you goodbye?" She glared at him, her eyes filled with contempt. "I thought you loved me." She turned suddenly and raced out of the barn.

Ben heard the helicopter land, and then, a few moments later, he heard Mike emerge and talk briefly with Belinda. Then they both climbed into the copter.

Ben remained in the barn, standing motionless in the dark, as the helicopter bearing the two of them disappeared into the night.

"I do," he whispered.

PART FOUR

*   *

The Reasons of the Heart

* 69 *

Swain was not happy about trying a second defendant for the same murder. It proved he had made a mistake the first time; he had tried to execute an innocent man. Rather than making him more forgiving, however, this knowledge made him defensive, inflexible, and dogmatic. He insisted that this time around there would be no mistakes, and that he would seek nothing less than the maximum sentence.

He would seek the death penalty. For Belinda Hamilton.

Ben had refused to cooperate, had refused even to talk to the prosecution. So Swain subpoenaed him. He was going to be compelled to testify, whether he liked it or not.

After Ben returned to Silver Springs, he tried repeatedly to visit Belinda, who was out on bail and staying at Mary Sue's under supervision.

She refused to see him.

Although the preliminary hearing went on for hours, Ben could only remember scattered incidents, fleeting images. A few high points. Far more low points.

He didn't want to be here. No one did. Even Judge Tyler looked uncomfortable. He had tried to convince Swain to reduce the charge from first-degree murder to a lesser offense. Swain wasn't listening. I'm the DA, he insisted, and the DA sets the charge. And so it went.

Ben had been trying to catch Belinda's eye since she came into the courtroom. She wouldn't even look at him.

The hearing began much like the trial Ben remembered so well. The coroner was called to establish that a death had occurred and that the death was caused by two crossbow bolts. After that, however, the shape of the trial began to change.

"The State calls John Pfeiffer to the stand."

John walked hesitantly to the witness box. It was clear he didn't want to testify.

After the preliminaries were completed and the foundations were laid, District Attorney Swain asked, "You and the defendant were at the Bluebell Bar when the fight between Donald Vick and Tommy Vuong occurred, correct?"

"That's right."

"Can you tell the court what you were discussing?"

John regretfully answered the question. "When Vuong came into the bar, she became enraged. She told me how upset she was about what Vuong had done to her sister. How he shouldn't be allowed to live."

"And later, during the fight, Vick's head smashed down on your table."

"That's correct."

"Were any traces of blood, or perhaps, hair, left behind?"

"I'm not sure. I think so."

Swain held a Ziploc bag in the air. "Have you ever seen a bag like this in the defendant's possession?"

"Yes. She carries them all the time."

"Did you ever leave her alone in the bar?"

"Yes, I believe I excused myself and went to the men's room at one point."

Swain smiled. "Thank you. No more questions."

Frank Carroll wanted to testify even less than Pfeiffer. Ben was afraid Frank might lose his temper and give Swain a sharp poke in the eye.

"Have you ever seen documents such as the ones marked State's Exhibit Six, which I just handed to you?"

"Sure. All the time."

"And what are they?"

"Hate propaganda. ASP prints this junk. They hand it out on street corners, post it on bulletin boards, stick it under people's windshield wipers."

"And where were these particular documents printed?"

Carroll checked the small print. "Birmingham."

"That's interesting. Who at Hatewatch was involved in activities against ASP in Birmingham?"

"Many people."

"Anyone who later came to Silver Springs?"

"Only myself. And Belinda."

"Mr. Carroll, we had our dust man go over each and every one of these documents very carefully. I think whoever left these documents at the crime scene was very careful. But not careful enough. Would you be surprised to learn that we found the defendant's thumbprint on one of the documents?"

"I wouldn't know."

"We'll bring that out later. Do you think the defendant might have had access to such documents?"

"I'm sure she did. We save it to use as evidence at future trials."

"Thank you. No more questions."

* * *

Slowly but surely Swain laid all the bricks into place.
The case he made against Belinda was strong and certain. Unquestionably she would be bound over for trial.

And then came the moment Ben had been dreading.

"The State calls Ben Kincaid."

Swain probably took Ben through all the proper preliminaries. He really didn't recall. His brain was working too
fast; it was too far ahead of the present.

"Would you say the defendant volunteered her
confession to you?"

"Well, no," Ben said. "I couldn't actually say she
volunteered."

"When she finally told you what she had done, would
you say she was filled with remorse? Regretted what
she had done?"

"No," Ben said sadly. "I couldn't agree with that either."

"She admitted that she planned to kill Tommy
Vuong?"

"Yes, she did." Again he tried to make eye contact
with Belinda, but she wouldn't look at him. Her head
was buried inside her arms.

"She stole the crossbow to implicate ASP, the organization that formerly had a camp just outside of town."

"True."

"And she smeared Donald Vick's blood and hair on
the bow to incriminate him."

"So she said."

"Then she hid in the trees outside Coi Than Tien and
waited for Tommy Vuong to come home."

"Yes."

"And when she saw Vuong approach, she killed
him."

"Not exactly," Ben said.

"What?"

Ben saw Belinda's head rise. "That's incorrect."

Swain was obviously surprised. "Why is that incorrect?"

"It's true Belinda was planning to kill Vuong, but when the time came and he was standing right in front of her, she found she couldn't do it. Just couldn't fire the bow."

Belinda lifted her head and peered across at the witness stand.

"You're saying she changed her mind?"

"Yes. Unfortunately Vuong saw her and decided to take advantage of the situation. He was a nasty brutal person, as I guess you know. He began shouting threats, saying that he was going to do worse to her than he had done to her sister. He started toward her." Ben turned to face Judge Tyler. "She panicked. And that's when she fired the bow."

Swain stared at his witness. "What are you saying— that she killed him accidentally? That she acted in self-defense?" Swain appeared incredulous. "She'd planned his murder in detail! Surely you're not suggesting she could fire that bow *twice* by accident! Or that two shots from a crossbow was a reasonable defensive use of force!"

"No," Ben said.

"Are you saying she went crazy? Trying to get her off on an insanity plea?"

"No. She's definitely not insane."

"Then I don't understand what you're—"

"She didn't have premeditated intent," Ben said firmly. "Not at the time she fired. She had recanted her previous plan. When she fired the crossbow, it was on impulse. In the heat of the moment."

Judge Tyler peered down at Swain. "You've charged

the defendant with first-degree murder, Mister Prosecutor."

"That's true," Swain said.

"That's an intent crime. Maybe you should try for manslaughter."

"Your honor, this is just the opinion of one witness—"

"He's *your* witness, Mr. Swain."

"He's obviously biased—"

"You took that risk when you subpoenaed him."

"Yes, but—"

"If you expect me to bind the defendant over for trial, you'd better have her charged with the right crime."

"Your honor, I—"

"I want all counsel in my chambers," Judge Tyler pronounced. "Now. Mr. Kincaid, you're excused."

"Thank you, your honor."

As Ben left the witness stand, for the first time, Belinda looked directly at him. Their eyes met.

And her expression changed—for the most fleeting of instants—to something that resembled a smile.

* 70 *

Ben sat by himself on the bank of the lake near his former campsite. The morning was still gray; the first rays of the sun were just beginning to peek out over the mountaintops.

He stared into the water and tried to clear his head of all the noise, all the confusion, all the regret.

All the sadness.

He heard a car chugging up the dirt road just outside the campground. A few minutes later Christina strolled up and sat beside him.

"What are you doing here?" he asked.

She shrugged nonchalantly. "Thought you might like some company."

"You were wrong." He turned away and stared across the lake. "But since you're here, how are you feeling?"

"Fine. Fit as a fiddle. Totally recovered." She cocked her head to one side. "How are you?"

He considered the possible answers. Fine? Fit as a fiddle? Somehow they didn't ring true. And he wondered if he would ever be totally recovered.

"Mind if I play some music?"

Ben saw her removing her harmonica from its velvet case. "Must you?"

"I'm in the mood." She began to play.

Ben did his best to ignore it. But the melody caught

his ear. It seemed very familiar. *When the shark bites . . .*

It was difficult not to grin. "Did you learn that just for me?"

"Nah. 'Mack the Knife' has always been in my repertoire."

"Yeah, right."

"Hey, you're smiling."

"Sorry. I won't do it again."

"Okay. Me neither." Her expression became preposterously grim. "Is this better?"

"Look," Ben said, "I know you're trying to cheer me up, but it's no use, okay?"

"Oh, well then. I won't waste my time trying."

"Good."

"I'll just sit here silently and not say a word." She made the motion of zipping up her lips.

"Much appreciated."

She remained quiet for about half a second.

"I just have one question," she said. "Your testimony about Belinda's hesitation, her change of heart. Was that true, or did you make it up to prevent her from getting the death penalty?"

"Christina, perjury is a criminal offense."

"You don't have to answer if you don't want to."

"Good. I won't."

Christina sighed. She pointed toward the horizon. "Look! It's the sunrise."

"Big deal."

"Au contraire, c'est . . ." The orange rays crept across the mountains and reflected off the clear blue water. *"C'est magnifique!"*

"Not interested," Ben said. "I've seen it before."

She took his hand and squeezed it tightly. "You have to see it like you're seeing it for the first time."

∗ Acknowledgments ∗

A book like this would not be possible without the expertise of others. I want to thank Kathy Humphries and Gail Benedict for their assistance with the manuscript and other clerical chores. Thanks also to Arlene Joplin for her criminal law expertise, and to Drew Graham for his editorial guidance. Thanks are due to Dr. Paul Tucker, longtime Arkansas resident, for his aid in making the town of Silver Springs come alive. Thanks also to Vien Van "Bob" and Cam-Huong Thi "Tina" Nguyen for their help in understanding the new Vietnamese immigrants and creating a Coi Than Tien that reflected reality. Belated and continuing thanks to Pat Cremin, whose unique insights into human nature are a character creator's dream, and to Kevin Hayes, for friendship and more favors than I could possibly list. Finally, my thanks and deepest admiration go to Morris Dees, for the inspiration found in his books and his life. Incidentally, every act taken, every word written, and every epithet spoken by ASP in this book is based on well-documented actions and statements by an American hate group—during the last fifteen years.

William Bernhardt

As Tulsa's first black mayor and a former college football hero, Wallace Barrett was a city treasure—until he became the prime suspect in the gruesome murder of his wife and two daughters. Seen splattered with blood and fleeing his house after the crime, the mayor needs a miracle. Enter Ben Kincaid.

WILLIAM BERNHARDT
NAKED JUSTICE

For a sneak preview, read on...

Ben Kincaid was late getting to his office the next morning, not that that was unusual. What was unusual was that his entire office staff—Christina, Jones, and Loving—were standing shoulder to shoulder just inside the front door waiting for him.

"Let me guess," Ben said. "You're on strike. Look, I don't blame you, but until some of our clients pay their bills—"

He stopped. The huge ear-to-ear grins on their faces told him that wasn't it. "Okay, what, then? Is today my birthday or something?"

"Where have you been?" Christina said, wrapping her arm around his shoulder and pulling him into the office.

"At Forestview. I had to take Joey to school, and then there was this big sign-up for the spring bake sale—"

"Never mind that." Christina pushed him into a chair while the other two huddled around. "We've been trying to get hold of you all morning."

"Why?"

Jones leaned forward. "I got a call the minute I came into the office, Boss."

"And?"

"The mayor wants you!"

Ben fell deep into thought. Was this about that incident with his daughter at Forestview last Friday? It was just a little bump. And she ran into him…

"Can you believe it, Skipper?" Loving grabbed him by the shoulders and shook him. "The mayor wants you!"

"That's nice…I guess."

Christina cut in. "Ben, do you even know what we're talking about?"

"Well, actually…no."

"The biggest cause célèbre to hit Tulsa in years, and you're totally clueless. What were you doing last night?"

"Well, let me see. I had soup for dinner, then I read *Goodnight Moon* to Joey about eight thousand times…"

She slapped her forehead. "I can't believe it. Everyone in the state watched the chase last night. Except, of course, you."

"Chase? What are you talking about?"

"Ben, the mayor has been charged with murder."

"Murder!" The light slowly dawned. "And he wants me to get him off?"

Christina and Jones and Loving all exchanged a glance. "Well," Christina said, "he wants you to represent him, anyway. *Entre nous*, I wouldn't get your hopes up too high on the outcome."

"What do you mean?"

Christina grabbed his arm. "I'll brief you while we drive to the jailhouse."

Because Mayor Barrett had specified that he wanted to see Ben alone, Christina (after considerable protest) agreed to cool her heels outside while Ben went into his cell to talk to him.

"Don't worry about me, Christina," he told her. "I'll be fine."

"I'm not worried about you. I'm worried about us."

"Come again?"

"I'm afraid you'll do something idiotic like not agree to represent him."

"In fact, I do have some reservations…"

"See! It's starting already. You're going to veer off on some wacky ethical tangent, and we're going to go hungry."

"Just let me talk to him. Then we'll see."

She grabbed him by the lapels. "Ben, promise me you'll take this case."

"We'll see."

"Ben!"

"We'll see."

Ben allowed the guard to lead him down the long metallic corridor. Mayor Barrett had the cell at the far end, a private suite, such as it was. A five-by-seven cell, with a bunk bed, a sink, and an open-faced toilet. Not exactly the mayor's mansion.

He was lying on the bottom bunk, his hands covering his face. When he moved them, Ben saw black and red lacerations on his face, and a bandage wrapped around his jaw and the back of his head.

The guard let Ben into the cell, locked the door behind him, then disappeared.

"How do you feel?" Ben asked.

"Better than I have a right to feel."

"My legal assistant told me you were in a traffic accident."

Barrett tried to smile, although between the bruises and the bandages, his face didn't have much give in it. "I crashed into a brick building with four cop cars, two television helicopters, and about half the world watching. Like I said, I'm better off than I have a right to be."

"Jeez. What were you doing?"

"Trying to kill myself," he said, with a matter-of-fact air that caught Ben unaware. "As it was, I didn't even break a bone. Goddamn air bags."

Ben paced nervously around the tiny cell. There was nowhere to sit, so he stood awkwardly by the cell door and contemplated the dominant question.

This was a part of criminal defense work that Ben particularly hated. Most criminal defense lawyers never asked the question. Since defending a client you knew was guilty raised a million ethical difficulties, most lawyers preferred not to inquire.

Ben, however, wanted to know the truth. He wanted to know where he stood. If he was going to put his name and reputation on the line, particularly in what was certain to be a high-profile case, he wanted to know he was doing the right thing. As his old mentor Jack Bullock used to say, he wanted to be on the side of the angels. But with such a horrible, heinous crime, how could he possibly ask?

Barrett sat up suddenly, hands on his knees. "Ben, I want you to know something up front. I didn't do it."

Ben gazed at him, his face, his eyes.

"I did not kill my wife. I did not kill my two precious daughters. How could I?" His eyes began to water, but he fought it back. "I couldn't do anything like that." He stared down at his hands. "I couldn't."

"I've read the preliminary police report. Neighbors say you and your wife had a disagreement yesterday afternoon."

Barrett nodded. "That's right. We did. I'm not going to pretend we didn't." He spread his arms wide. "It was that kind of marriage. We fought sometimes, like cats and dogs. But we still loved each other."

"What was the fight about?"

Barrett shrugged. "I hardly remember."

"The prosecutor will want to know."

"It was something about the kids. She thought I was spoiling them, giving them everything they wanted. Undermining her authority. And not paying enough attention to her. We'd had this argument before."

"How many times?"

He shrugged again. "I don't know. Many."

"Were these fights...violent?"

He twisted his head around. "Violent? You mean, did I hit her? Absolutely not."

"Well, I had to ask."

"Look, I don't know what people are saying about me now, but I would never hurt my wife. Or my girls. They're the most precious things in the world to me." His voice choked. "Were. I couldn't hurt them. Don't you think that if the mayor of the city was a wife beater, it would've come out before now?"

"I suppose." Ben pulled a small notebook out of his jacket pocket and began taking notes. "So you had an argument. Then what?"

"I can barely remember. It's all such a blur. And smashing into a brick wall didn't help."

"Just tell me what you recall. We don't have to get everything today."

"Well, I got mad. That doesn't happen often; most times I can just laugh it off. But this time she really got my goat, suggesting that I was hurting the girls and all. So I stomped out of the house."

"You left?"

"Right. Got in my car and drove away."

"How long were you gone?"

"I don't know exactly. Not long. Maybe an hour. I got a Coke at a Sonic—you can check that if you want—and I started to feel bad. So what if we disagreed on a few minor points. I loved my wife, and I loved my family. I didn't have any business running out like that. A strong man stands up straight and faces the music. So I headed back home."

"What happened when you got there?"

"I was in such a hurry, I left my car on the street and ran into the house. And—"

"Yes?"

He hesitated. "And then...I found...them. What was left of them."

"They were already dead?"

"Oh, yeah." His eyes became wide and fixed. "My wife was spread out like…like some sick human sacrifice. And my little girls…" Tears rushed to his eyes. His hands covered his face.

"I'm sorry," Ben said quietly. "I know this is hard for you."

Barrett continued to cry. His whole upper body trembled.

Ben took a deep breath. He hated this. He felt like a vulture of the worst order, intruding on this man's grief with these incessant questions. Guilty or not, Barrett was clearly grief-stricken.

NAKED JUSTICE
by William Bernhardt

Published by The Ballantine Publishing Group.
Available in bookstores everywhere.

EXTREME JUSTICE

by
William Bernhardt

Disillusioned with the legal system, Ben Kincaid now spends all his free time playing piano at Uncle Earl's Jazz Emporium. But when a once-famous jazz singer is murdered, Ben finds himself drawn back into the law—to protect a friend, and to find the truth.

"Writers of popular fiction must have some gift of readability, but only a few have as unerring a narrative flair as Bernhardt. This is one of the best new series going."
—*Ellery Queen's Mystery Magazine*

Don't miss *any* of the novels of

WILLIAM BERNHARDT

PRIMARY JUSTICE

The First Ben Kincaid Novel

by
WILLIAM BERNHARDT

Ben Kincaid wants to be a lawyer because he wants to do the right thing.

But once he leaves the D.A.'s office for a hotshot spot in Tulsa's most prestigious law firm, Ben discovers that doing the right thing and representing his client's interests can be mutually exclusive.

BLIND JUSTICE

by
WILLIAM BERNHARDT

Out of corporate life and on his own, Ben Kincaid sees the seamy side of the law every day. There's no glamour and little reward in defending the lowlifes who beat down his door.

When a friend is set up for murder, Ben has no choice but to enter the world of hardball litigation—and face a judge who despises him in a trial he is guaranteed to lose.

DEADLY JUSTICE

by
WILLIAM BERNHARDT

Ben Kincaid is not one of the few Tulsa, Oklahoma, lawyers who win headlines and big bucks. So when the notorious Apollo Consortium offers him a job as their in-house counsel, he takes it—for the money.

But when Ben wins his first case, he unwittingly sets up a bitter rivalry with his colleagues—a rivalry that will culminate in a fellow lawyer's death and Ben charged with murder.

CRUEL JUSTICE

by
WILLIAM BERNHARDT

A black Tulsa teenager is accused of brutally murdering a young woman. And as Ben Kincaid struggles to put together a defense, a young boy vanishes without a trace.

Then a bone-chilling discovery compels Ben to forge a link between the missing boy and the seemingly hopeless case of his client—igniting the fuse for the most explosive courtroom case of Ben's career.

.

DOUBLE JEOPARDY

by
WILLIAM BERNHARDT

Travis Byrne—a smart Dallas cop turned lawyer—is appointed by a federal judge to speak for the defense. But just as the trial is getting started, the mobster escapes.

Suddenly the FBI is after Travis for a murder he didn't commit, and the mob wants to kill him for a secret hit list he doesn't have. It doesn't take long for Travis to realize that something much darker is going on. . . .

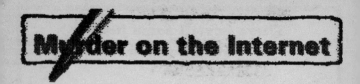